Afterglow and Nightfall

Afterglow and Nightfall is the fourth in the sequence of a quartet of novels planned to trace the destiny of the Brothers of Gwynedd in Wales in the thirteenth century. The first three volumes were *Sunrise in the West*, *The Dragon at Noonday* and *The Hounds of Sunset*.

Emeritus Professor E. G. Bowen, M.A., D.Litt., F.S.A., formerly Gregynog Professor of Geography and Anthropology, University College of Wales, Aberystwyth, writes of the quartet:

'Here in these four volumes we have the historical novel at its very best, from the hands of an experienced and extremely intelligent artist. They are first-rate! Quite apart from being so sound academically they offer magnificent reading. No one has yet put the situation in Gwynedd at this time so clearly. Historians who have given us the lead have left the job unfinished, and failed to create the atmosphere of the time. This is exactly what Miss Pargeter *has* done, by using the technique of the historical novel at its best.'

The first novel started with the words: *My name is Samson. I tell what I know, what I have seen with my own eyes and heard with my own ears.*

Samson's first allegiance, apart from his love of Cristin, his brother's wife, is to Prince Llewelyn, creator of a united and independent Wales. But *The Hounds of Sunset* tells how the principality had been truncated by the armies of Edward I, leaving Llewelyn to rule a much smaller state, in the heart of Gwynedd and Snowdonia, in the company of his beloved new wife, Eleanor, daughter of Earl Simon de Montfort.

The last act in the triumph and final tragedy of Prince Llewelyn ap Griffith begins with much legal bickering between Edward's henchmen and those who are loyal to, or depend on, Llewelyn. It appears that Edward, once again, is deliberately obscuring the law, procrastinating, encouraging his representatives and attorneys to seek more than is their right. Llewelyn is as ever patient, and rejoices in the renewed fealty of his younger brother David – the same David who had twice betrayed him.

But it is David who is once again the catalyst. Impetuous now in his loyalty to Llewelyn (as he had previously been in his treachery), it is his rash action that precipitates a new war against the might of England; and in effect forces on Llewelyn a moral dilemma from which there can be (for him) only one solution. The solution must, he knows, lead to his downfall and death.

The last part of this exciting novel, the culmination of the whole saga, devotes itself to the final campaign between Edward's armies and the light guerrilla forces of North Wales which are all Llewelyn can command.

Once again Edith Pargeter has brought scholarship, enthusiasm and compassion to her account of the final tragic days of the man who was the first true Prince of Wales.

By the same author

AFTERGLOW AND NIGHTFALL

BEING THE FOURTH AND LAST BOOK
IN A SEQUENCE ENTITLED
THE BROTHERS OF GWYNEDD

EDITH PARGETER

M

02901600

SBN: 0 333 21786 1 17717778

First published 1977 by
MACMILLAN LONDON LIMITED
London and Basingstoke
Associated companies in New York
Dublin Melbourne Johannesburg and Delhi

Printed in Great Britain by
THE ANCHOR PRESS LTD
Tiptree, Essex

Bound in Great Britain by
WM BRENDON & SON LTD
Tiptree, Essex

CONTENTS

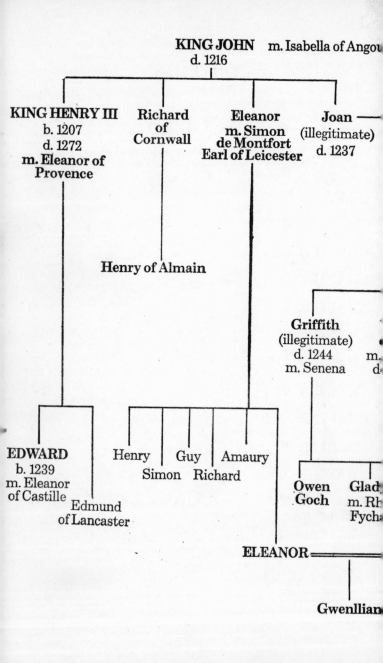

KING JOHN m. Isabella of Angou
d. 1216

KING HENRY III
b. 1207
d. 1272
m. Eleanor of
Provence

Richard
of
Cornwall

Eleanor
m. Simon
de Montfort
Earl of Leicester

Joan
(illegitimate)
d. 1237

Henry of Almain

Griffith
(illegitimate)
d. 1244
m. Senena

m.
d

EDWARD
b. 1239
m. Eleanor
of Castille

Edmund
of Lancaster

Henry

Simon

Guy

Amaury

Richard

Owen
Goch

Glad
m. Rh
Fych

ELEANOR

Gwenllian

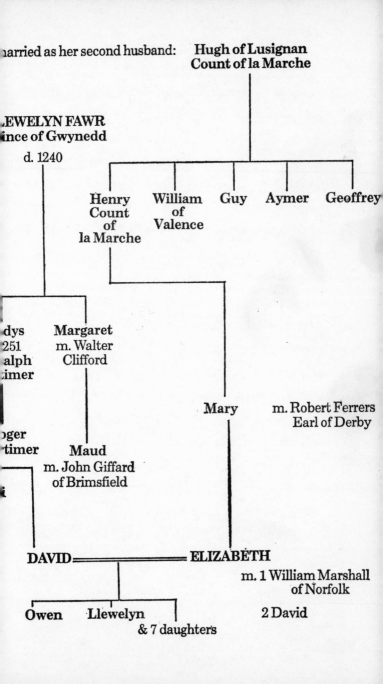

married as her second husband: **Hugh of Lusignan Count of la Marche**

LEWELYN FAWR ince of Gwynedd
d. 1240

Henry Count of la Marche   **William of Valence**   **Guy**   **Aymer**   **Geoffrey**

dys
251
alph
timer

Margaret m. Walter Clifford

Mary   m. Robert Ferrers Earl of Derby

oger
timer

Maud m. John Giffard of Brimsfield

DAVID ══════ **ELIZABETH**

m. 1 William Marshall of Norfolk

2 David

Owen   **Llewelyn**   & 7 daughters

The chronicle of the Lord Llewelyn, son of Griffith, son of Llewelyn, son of Iorwerth, lord of Gwynedd, the eagle of Snowdon, the shield of Eryri, first and only true Prince of Wales.

CHAPTER I

I, Samson, clerk, servant and friend life-long to Prince Llewelyn, born under the same roof and in the same night as my lord, have told how he laboured steadfastly to make of Wales a noble sovereign state, peer to England and in peace with her, how for a few years that aim was achieved, when after the treaty of Montgomery he lived side by side in amity with King Henry the Third until that monarch's death, and how thereafter, with the succession of King Edward, all things changed, and England and Wales were again driven to war.

Of that year of struggle I have told, when the lesser Welsh princes, not yet ready for the vision of nationhood and clutching each at his own local right, fell away before the king's lance, and a hard-fought war ended perforce in a hard-fought peace. By that treaty, drawn at Aberconway, my lord was forced to relinquish half his realm, won with his own hand, in order to keep inviolate his hereditary stronghold of Gwynedd-west-of-Conway, the mountain fastness of Snowdon. And having accepted with fortitude this grievous diminution, he did homage and swore fealty to Edward, accepting also the bond of his pledged word.

Yet in this great loss there was also great gain, for in sacrificing the labour of many years he achieved also the desire of many years, his promised wife, Eleanor de Montfort, the great earl's daughter and the king's own cousin, whom Edward had not scrupled to seize by piracy at sea and hold prisoner as his cruellest weapon of war, but whom now, appeased by victory, he brought forth to her bridal.

And one more thing, to him of great value, my lord regained on his wedding eve, the love and allegiance of his youngest, best-loved and most perilous brother, David, three times traitor and three times forgiven.

I tell now of what befell after the peace was a year old, of how that marriage and that reconciliation fared, and how the war continued by other means, with words for swords, and courts of justice for battle-fields.

From the marriage at Worcester we rode home to Gwynedd in the soft, moist October weather, all that great company of us, Llewelyn's household and David's together in amity, Llewelyn and David side by side, after so long of estrangement, and all the leisurely string of us, their retainers, drawn out after their heels like a bright ribbon trailed across the green fields of England, to the border at Oswestry.

Thus far, to mark his patronage and favour to the very rim of his English lands, King Edward paid the expenses of his cousin's travel and baggage, having already borne the cost of the wedding-banquet, and bestowed the bride on her bridegroom with his own hand. The same huge and heavy hand that had turned the key upon her to prevent that very marriage, until it could be celebrated on his terms and under his auspices. But Edward's shadow lengthened and dwindled behind us when we reached Welsh soil, and pressed the upland turf of our dismembered homeland above Glyn Ceiriog.

In vast content we rode, bringing Eleanor home at last to her own place. But ours was a contentment muted and still, no loud and easy happiness. We were like men spent after great endeavour, having both won and lost, and once having valued and acknowledged our losses, the more grateful for our gains and the more aware of them. With falconry and music we passed the gentle time on the journey, but our hawking was subdued and languid, and our music pensive and soft, like the autumn country through which we made our homeward way. At morning the sun was veiled and coloured like gold, and the dew feathered from our horses' hooves, and over the slopes of the hills the warm purple flush of heather burned slowly into the sombre fire of bracken. The skies over us were pale and lofty, and the birds flew high, and even their songs had a rueful sound, as though they, too, owned their losses while they hymned their gains. For it is great gain to be alive, and have heart to sing, but great loss, even in the beauty of autumn, to feel and dread that the golden summer is over.

Eleanor rode at her husband's side every mile of that journey. There was no need for any man to wonder what measure of happiness those two had in being matched at last, for though they spoke but little, and looked more often upon the fair, loved land than upon each other, feeling no need to gaze or to touch, they so shone that their radiance kindled the very air into gold about them, no midday dazzle, but the mellow and tender gold of the sun drifting towards its bed, after the long climb to the zenith.

They were autumn thoughts I had, those days, and there is no autumn without regret, however kindly the air, and bright the leaves, and rich the harvest. And I could not choose but remember that I, like my lord and friend, was forty-nine years old, drawing close to fifty when the year turned, and he had waited thirteen years for his love before he won her, and I longer still for mine, and fruitlessly still. Yet whenever I rode beside the horse-litters in which David's wife and children were carried, my heart was comforted, beholding Cristin among the cushions with Elizabeth's youngest girl in her lap, and the two elder sisters nestled one on either side of her, as confidingly as if she had been their mother instead of their nurse, and a happy and prolific wife instead of a misused and barren one. And then, as surely as the love and worship rose in me cool and fresh as spring water filling a dried well,

3

Cristin would raise her head and turn her iris-grey eyes to meet mine, and there I saw another manner of radiance, not fecund and joyous like Elizabeth's, not fulfilled and crowned like Eleanor's, yet radiance for all that, and knew that it belonged to me, and to no other man in all this dear world. For there are many kinds of harvest, and the bevy of vigorous, blossoming children that surrounded David and Elizabeth furnished but one make of precious fruit. There are others, invisible, unweighed, uncounted, not to be assessed by the world's values, vouchsafed sometimes even to those who find their loves too late.

But this was the bride's festival, and the bride's triumph. She looked about her at a fair, wild, melancholy world that changed with every mile, and up into a sky alive with birds and feathered with sailing clouds, and was filled with wonder and delight.

'No, this is not England! It is another earth,' she said, 'and another air.'

At David's entreaty we halted for one week of November at his castle of Denbigh, though Llewelyn would rather have gone home at once to Gwynedd-beyond-Conway, which was now his whole principality. But the reunion of those two brothers required a visible sacrament, therefore he accepted with good will the invitation extended, and while Tudor ap Ednyfed, the high steward of Wales, went ahead into Gwynedd with all but the prince's immediate household, we who were closest lingered and hunted in Denbigh, and were entertained lavishly until it was time to move on to Aber and prepare for the Christmas feast.

That stay at Denbigh came strangely to me and to many. David had held his two inland cantrefs of the Middle Country but a year, having been granted them by King Edward after the war that snatched them out of Llewelyn's hands. David was Edward's vassal now, like any baron of England, and owed no fealty to his brother, whose undoing he had surely been, second only to Edward. Yet

4

here, so soon afterwards, he was playing host to the brother and lord he had deserted and betrayed. It was not easy for good Welshmen to stomach, and there was no man knew it better than David. On the night before we left, at the high table in hall, he chose to get the matter into the open.

'I take it as a great grace,' he said in a clear voice, looking Llewelyn in the face, 'that you have consented to break bread and be a guest in my house, and a royal favour that your lady honours my hall with her presence. Since it's known to all men how we have been estranged, so I would have all men know that we are reunited. Concerning desert or blame we two have said no word. For my part, I'm content to be thankful for peace between us, and to pledge my good faith to keep it.'

Llewelyn understood his need, and readily went to meet him. 'There's no profit,' he said heartily, 'in looking back. We begin from where we stand, and no complaints. A few weeks, and we go together into a new year, and what we had or had not, and did or did not do, three years ago is no help and no harm to us now. Let's live with what is.' And seeing that they had at that moment, as David had intended, the silent attention of all that teeming household in hall, he added: 'And since we're at peace, and travelling is safe and easy again, I pray you'll come as before, and share Christmas with us at Aber, with your lady and the children.'

David grew pale at that, remembering the Christmas feast at Aber four years earlier, when he had plotted against the life of this brother who now publicly opened that life to him again. Out of that treachery arose all Llewelyn's losses, and all the grief and damage of the war, and the restrictions of the hard peace. But they eyed each other steadily and were content.

'With all my heart,' said David.

So they made plain to all men that whatever had happened between them, and however they were now divided

5

by fortune, Llewelyn prince of a shrunken Wales, but its prince still, David a baron holding from King Edward and owing feudal allegiance only to him, they were by their own deliberate choice brothers once again.

Certainly there must have been many who still doubted. Three times treacherous, who was David to pledge his good faith now and be trusted? Three times magnanimous and each time the loser by it, was not Llewelyn incurably his own enemy and his brother's dupe? Even Cristin, when I spoke out this misgiving to her, said only: 'God knows! But as they could never live together, so they cannot live separated. The prince is right, they must manage with what they have, and handle it as best they can.' Even as we, though that she did not say.

While we remained in Denbigh I had at least the opportunity of speaking with her now and then as we went about our work. Every word and look of hers was bread and life to me, I was rich while we were within the same walls, and for that reason the accord between Llewelyn and David was all the more precious to me.

'Elizabeth is satisfied,' said Cristin. 'She would be friends with everyone, and have contentment all about her. Where David goes, she will go, and whatever David undertakes, she will plunge her hands into it with him, to the shoulder, to the heart. But she was not happy when he left Llewelyn. She felt him broken in two, and is certain now that he is healed. Should we question her knowledge, because it is a child's knowledge? Children are guided by God. I am willing to trust where she trusts.'

And I where Cristin trusted, though I did not say that, either. So I went from her comforted, since I loved both Llewelyn and David, the one with every reason, the other against almost all reason. Are we not all in some measure children? And should we question what we know as children know?

Godred ap Ivor was in the stables when we went to

6

saddle up for departure. I had seen little of him while we were in Denbigh, which suited me well, and yet to some degree made me uneasy, so far was it from his old usage of me. True, his pursuit of me had passed through many changes, from his youthful calculation that my privilege with Llewelyn might be made to advance his career, and his shameless dangling of Cristin before me as bait to that end, through his malice and offence at finding us able and resolute to love in abstinence where he found it easy to gorge without love, to his realisation that he had a better and sharper weapon, and his persecution of her, so long a wife neglected and misprized, with an unsparing lust now loathsome to her, until he got her with child not for love, but in my despite. But it was common to all these phases that where I was, there he would follow me if he could, with his fondling fingers and insinuating voice, dropping poisoned honey. Now, unless chance threw us in each other's way, he let me alone, only watching narrowly from a distance. Since his wife miscarried and his son was born dead, the small pinpricks of his venom, though he used them still, afforded him no relief. His long hatred had corroded his being so deep there was no fit expression for it within his scope, and he was waiting for his hour of tremendous revenge.

But if he did not haunt me now, neither did he avoid me. He turned from the pony he was saddling, and his flaxen hair against the dappled shoulder showed in ashen pallor, more grey than fair. I could never look him in the face without being reminded how like we were in our different-ness, though he was taller, and still comely, and had been bright and debonair in his youth, and I was swart and dark and plain. As two carvers may copy the same model, and produce two alien stone images, yet each true to the original, so we both mirrored the father we shared, of whom he was the true mintage, and I the bastard.

'You're away then,' he said, and showed his even teeth in a narrow smile. 'There'll be changed times about the

7

court from now on, now he's got his princess at last. Your nose will be out of joint.' And when I made him only a brief greeting in reply, he watched me over the pony's neck with light, malignant eyes, and grinned without mirth. 'After so many years so close in his confidence and favour, you'll feel the cold. He's got himself a closer confidante now, and has better than music in his bed-chamber.'

There was never any profit in answering him, he kept his tongue always just short of public offence, though always insinuating foulness. So I merely said something empty about having no fears for my employment as long as the promising spate of lawsuits cast up by the war continued, and went about my own saddling.

'But I'm forgetting,' he said softly at my back, 'you're in favour with the princess, too. A double assurance is good! I tell you, Samson, my friend, they've set you an example. Have I not been holding up marriage to you for years as the only estate for a sensible man? If my wedded happiness could not convince you,' he said, grinning like a famished wolf, 'the prince's should win you over. Find yourself a wife, Samson – a beautiful, gentle wife like my Cristin. Only not barren,' he said, suddenly in a breathy whisper from a shut throat. 'Get one able to carry your son full-time, and bring him into the world alive. . . .' He strangled on the end, and turning, flung away silently among the bustle in the stable-yard, and left me stricken to stone.

I could not go from Denbigh and leave things so. I sought out Cristin, where she was busy with the little girls, dressing the younger ones for the day, and braiding Margaret's long hair.

'You need not fret,' said Cristin calmly, when she understood what was on my mind. 'Godred is not mad, he intends me no harm. If you have no other warranty of that, you have his own self-interest. He has a good office and some influence here in David's service, and I am the

8

privileged companion of David's wife. How long would he keep his place and his easy living if he did me any hurt? Or his life and liberty, for that matter?'

'With such a load of hatred in him,' I said, 'he may some day forget even his own interests for the pleasure of sating it, and you here within his reach, and I far away.'

'No,' she said with certainty, 'not Godred! Never! That is one thing he never forgets. Hatred can wait its turn, if it threatens his comfortable bed and fat table, and the money in his pouch. Besides, it is not me he hates the worst. He has ceased even to use his tongue on me. I do not matter enough to him now to be persecuted. Godred has done with me, except as his body-servant, the mender of his clothes and fetcher and carrier of his wants. I wish I could be as sure he will never attempt anything against *you*! *You* matter to him altogether too much. You are the shadow on his self-esteem, the spot on his skin that he scrubs and gouges at, and cannot scrub away. Guard yourself, Samson, wherever he is. No, I know you are not afraid of him, but I am in earnest. Do not be with him but among people. Never alone!'

'He never seeks me out now,' I said, 'as he used to. Perhaps I am making too much of a moment of spleen.'

'He has had little chance lately,' said Cristin. 'In England it was my one consolation that you were out of his reach. And even after the peace was made, there was no visiting between the prince's household and ours. But now they're reconciled there'll be the old easy in-and-out between them, David's people and Llewelyn's rubbing shoulders freely every few weeks. Within a month we're to come to the prince at Aber.'

She was gazing at me very earnestly as she said it, frowning at the risk she saw in this free mingling, but then she drew breath softly, and so did I, seeing the sweet reverse of that danger. She said again: 'You need not fret. My bed is with the children, close to Elizabeth's chamber. There he never has any call to come. With five of them to care for, I'm seldom anywhere else, and even if Nest takes my place, and I sleep in my own chamber, he never troubles me. He has plenty of other beds, as he always had, mine only chills him to the bone. You need not fear for me. You can go in peace.'

'Before the new year,' I said, 'you will come after us to Aber. It is only a very short while. God be praised!' I said, very low, and 'God be praised!' said Cristin in her turn almost silently, and smiled.

We came over the high, rolling hills of Rhos towards evening, but before the sun was low, and so to the crossing on the Conway at Caerhun. A mellow afternoon it was, the westward sky all soft and misty gold, and the colours of the forests like fading flames, as we emerged upon a grassy crest, and saw the silver coil of the river below us, coming from the south and widening before our eyes into tidal water. Thus, from above, we could see the pale tints of the sand under the silver, and the deep blue-green of the channels where the salt sea mingled, and beyond the valley the high mountains soared, fold upon fold and peak behind peak, all gilded with that molten western light that dropped out of the sky like tears from the eye of a veiled but splendid sun. They were like a great army drawn up in battle array, with no break in the wall of their lances, or like a giant castle of bronze and steel, impregnable, without gates. To us they were home. We knew the ways in, where no way showed, and had the password that opened the invisible portals. To her, born in Kenilworth in the rich lowlands of England, raised in the cloister of Montargis in the green, civilised pastures of France, God knows what they were, but it was wonderful. She was the first to rein in, and sit and gaze, and all we drew aside and left those two together, waiting, as he waited, and with the same agony and rapture, for her to speak.

She looked down at the serpent of river that marked the

10

harsh limit of the lands left to her lord, and her face was bright and still and aware, and her eyes, wide-set under a lofty ivory brow, immense and attentive, golden-hazel, green-flecked, the colours of a radiant autumn in her early summer face. Eleanor's eyes were always mirrors through which God gazed. Those who looked into them saw themselves there, and all but the best turned their own eyes away, and dissembled. They mirrored and matched what she saw. The mountains of Wales did not bow their heads nor quench their golden light before her, and neither did Eleanor lower her eyes. Once she had lifted her head to behold their summits, there she was held. I saw the reflected gold colour her cheeks, and the parting of her lips widen into the promise of a smile.

When she had looked her fill, she turned her head the little way she needed to look into Llewelyn's eyes, and he was gazing at her with a face withdrawn and almost grim, but as for her, she never ceased to reflect unshadowed splendour. Once she glanced down again at the spilt ribbon of the Conway, before she spoke.

'All that lies beyond,' she said, 'is yours?'

'And that is all,' he said, 'that is mine. It is not what I had thought to bring you, when I plighted my troth to you. Nor am I the man I meant to offer you.'

His voice was low and equable, for he had been resolute from the first in accepting his diminished state and making the best of it, as he had made the best of his remaining bargaining power to exact from Edward better terms of peace than many had thought possible. But the grief of loss, and especially the thwarting of his lifelong ambition for Wales, was none the less bitter for that, and all the more desolating now that he had brought his wife at last to behold for herself, on this journey through the ravished Middle Country, the magnitude of his deprivation, which was also hers. And for all he would not suffer his pain to appear in his face or shake the firmness of his voice, he could not be so wrung and she not know.

11

A moment she was silent, her eyes still upon the distant peaks, and the flush of the west reflected in her face. Then she said: 'As to the lands, they may be narrower than once they were, but they are loftier than anything my cousin has in his realm, and there is room enough there for me. As to the man,' she said, and turned and looked at him with burning certainty, 'he has never been greater than he is now. My heart could hold no more.'

'God willing,' he said very quietly, 'there shall be more, some day, when the time favours us and we have paid all our dues. If not for us, for those who come after. I will never cease from hoping to give back to you in honour all that I have failed to keep safe for you now. And there will be room in your heart for all.'

'I need nothing more,' said Eleanor. 'I want for nothing. I have what I wanted.'

Such a way she had with words, enlarging and glorifying them so that the briefest and simplest utterance spoke more than gilded phrases. A moment they sat eye to eye, caught away from us and we forgotten. Then he reached a hand to her bridle, and they led the way down together out of the hills to the Conway shore opposite Caerhun, and there we crossed the silver barrier into Gwynedd, and Eleanor had come home.

That evening we rode only as far as Aberconway, along the river-bank, and there at the abbey we spent the night, and the following day took the coastal road to Aber. The weather was changing then, there was a wintry wind, and the touch of frost before the dawn. There was beauty still in the colours melting and changing over Lavan sands, under the vast steel-blue shoulder of Penmaenmawr, and mystery in the distant grey thread that was the coastline of Anglesey drawn along the horizon. Eleanor looked about her with wide, grave eyes of joy, at the sword-edges of the cliffs on her left hand, at the white curl of foam hissing along the sand on her right, at the far-off point of Ynys Lanog of the saints across the grey waters, at the tumbled, screaming flight of gulls all about the clouded sky. The grandeur of our land did not daunt her, rather it fulfilled her own greatness of heart and mind. She had said well, there was room enough for her in the mountains of Gwynedd. She was not made for the cloistered life, nor for a small, confined sphere of action, she with Earl Simon's blood in her veins.

Thus we brought her in great but sober happiness to Aber, and there made ready for the Christmas feast. And whatever loss Llewelyn still suffered, in her he knew nothing but gain.

David brought his family and a princely retinue to share the festival with us, as he had promised, and things were almost as in the old days. But he brought with him also a fine, Davidish fury over his usage at the hands of the justiciar of Chester, and would hold council with his brother and demand his sympathy. And that, too, was like old times, and did them both good rather than harm. David without a passion to occupy him had always been David looking for mischief, and if he could not have battle in the field, he would as soon have it in the justiciar's court as anywhere.

'You have already had sour experience of law under the treaty,' he said. 'What do you say to this? There's a claim out against me for lands I've held barely a year and a half, and had openly from the king's own hand. William Venables has taken out a writ of entry against me for possession of Hope and Estyn!'

It came as a true astonishment to Llewelyn, as his startled face bore witness. For whatever the prince's tangles at law might be, David had come out of the recent treaty as an ally of the king, and a favourite into the bargain, set up in life with two of the four cantrefs of the Middle Country, and granted the lands of Hope and Estyn, on the borders, to provide him with a second castle in addition to Denbigh. For any man to come forward and lay claim to those lands, in the teeth of that grant, was surely an instance of the litigious madness that was driving so many lords and tenants into follies that would prove both ineffective and costly. There were enough recent and genuine grievances to be set right, after a year of turmoil during which lands had changed hands three or four times, and the treaty of peace made provision for any man who felt himself to have legitimate claims to put them forward in whatever court was appropriate. But others had caught the acquisitive fever, and were digging up tenuous claims traced back to a grandsire who had once held a manor under very different circumstances, or an ancestor who had married a minor heiress and never succeeded in getting hold of her dower lands. The whole country on both sides the march seethed with lawsuits. But it was something new for one of the king's recent gifts to be challenged.

'Venables?' said Llewelyn, frowning. 'On what grounds can he possibly put forward any such claim?' The Venables family was old and of importance in Cheshire, and as Mold had bounced in and out of Montalt hands a dozen times within a century, so at some distant point a Venables might have had a precarious hold on Hope.

'Do I know,' said David impatiently, 'until he opens his plea? Whatever his line may be, I'm ready to answer it. How can there be a better claim than mine? That is not the issue! Venables has sworn out his writ in the justiciar's shire-court at Chester, and the justiciar has accepted it and summoned me there to answer it. Into England! Into Chester! He cannot do it, and he knows it. It's plainly stated in the treaty that causes concerning land shall be tried according to the custom of those parts where the land lies, whether it be Wales or march land. Chester is an English shire-court, and Hope and Estyn are in Wales, and I will not appear to any plea concerning them in the justiciar's court. I blame Venables for the attempt, but Badlesmere more for abetting it.'

'You and I, it seems,' said Llewelyn with a wry smile,

14

are contending against the same monster. My case was exactly as yours when I opened my claim to Arwystli. Like you I was cited to Montgomery, a royal town, when the impleaded land is wholly Welsh.'

'And you accepted it!' said David, between reproach and sympathy. 'It was your mistake. You put yourself in their hands once you acknowledged such a court.'

'I made a proxy appearance to present my writ, and that was all. And I wrote at the same time to the king, and made the very point you are making, that I should not have been cited there, and did not accept that it was proper procedure. You'll find, as I found, that he has a legal answer to that. He'll tell you, if you challenge him, what he told me. He'll agree with you as to the clause in the treaty, but point out that in cases between two barons or magnates holding in chief of the crown it has always been customary, even where Welsh law is concerned, to hear them at fixed dates and places, appointed by the justices. He'll tell you you must not resent falling in with this procedure – just as he told me.'

'I've not forgotten!' said David, glowering. 'He himself appointed you a day at Oswestry, and you conceded the place but not the process of law. And little enough it got you! Only a reference back to the king himself, and a hearing before him at Rhuddlan.'

'Under Welsh law,' said Llewelyn.

'Granted! And he presided over a hearing by Welsh law, with the proper Welsh judges in court to hear the pleas, and by rights you should have got your verdict then and there. Edward had an answer even then! He adjourned the court, arbitrarily, on his own responsibility, without allowing the judges to pronounce a verdict. Did you not feel, then, that there would always be a legal answer, if your case showed signs of coming to a successful conclusion? Oh, I've followed the Arwystli case from the beginning,' he said, 'and learned by it. I can also devise answers – even to Edward's answers!'

15

'Granting they're in the wrong over this business of Hope,' said Llewelyn reasonably, 'you can hardly blame the king for that before you've informed him of it. You may well be wasting all this rage, he may take his officer's action as ill as you do. He gave you the lands, he'll surely do you justice if you do but apply to him.'

'That I shall do, and profit by your example. But I'll deal with Badlesmere, too,' he promised, gnawing his lip vengefully. For this Guncelin de Badlesmere, then justiciar of Chester, was no friend of his, and they had had high words before over other matters, David's lands lying so closely neighbour to the county of Chester. 'I have not yet had any satisfaction out of him,' said David, brooding, 'for his thinning out my forests, as if they were on English land, and cutting great roads through them across the border. Half the cantref is up in arms about it. Those are our hunting coverts, and our pig-pastures, yes, and our protection, too. What right have they to destroy them?'

'You are not the only one,' said Llewelyn drily, 'to be breathing fire over that ordinance. The same thing is happening in our cousin Mortimer's lands in the middle march, and by the clamour he's making over it, it's no more pleasing to a marcher baron than it is to a Welsh prince. The king has a reasonable plea enough. You know yourself it's true that the forests are the best haunts of robbers and masterless men, and safe roads through will be to the benefit of trade on both sides.'

'Well for you!' said David fiercely. 'Your forests they cannot touch, yours is still a principality, and sovereign, if it is smaller than once. But even you would do well to keep a close watch on these new roads . . .' There he bit off whatever had been skipping so vehemently from his tongue, and prowled the room for some minutes in silence, to begin again abruptly upon another course. 'You have been given another day to proceed with your plea on Arwystli, have you not?'

'The fourteenth day of January,' said the prince, 'at Oswestry.'

'And will you go? And concede the place?'

'I shall send my attorneys,' said the prince, 'and bear with the king's ruling that causes in chief are heard where the justices appoint. I shall make no other concession. The plea must be heard by Welsh law, and no other.'

This matter of Arwystli was becoming increasingly important to him by reason of the delays and prevarications he felt he had encountered in pursuing it. Most of that cantref, which lies in the very heart of Wales, remained in the hands of his arch-enemy and traitor, Griffith ap Gwenwynwyn of Powys, who had plotted against the prince's life in peace and taken the opposing side against him in war, and like most gross offenders, could never forgive the man against whom he had offended, but now from the safety of King Edward's overlordship and favour pursued every possible means of pestering and wounding him. Arwystli had had a troubled history, sometimes held by Gwynedd, sometimes by Powys, but in ancient times it had been considered unquestionably as belonging to Gwynedd, and Llewelyn grudged it bitterly to a renegade Welsh lord who now aped and flattered the English and did all possible offence to his own Welsh neighbours, besides his spite against the prince himself. So there was far more at stake in this matter than the worth of the land in question.

'And you?' said Llewelyn, watching his brother with wary affection. 'What will you do? There's this to be thought of, neither you nor I can wish to seem obdurate against the authority of the king, and even when his officials are at fault, the summons comes in his name. To enter a formal protest is fair, even necessary. To make an equally formal appearance in answer to the summons, while rejecting the *court's* authority, might be wise.'

'I had thought of it,' said David. 'That I might even enjoy,' he said, with a dark and mischievous smile.

'By your attorneys, I would advise,' said Llewelyn hastily, foreseeing David's enjoyment dropping into the smooth surface of Badlesmere's shire-court like a stone into still waters. But he smiled.

'In person,' said David, 'or where's the sport? Oh, never fear, I can be discreet where my own good's involved. But I'll make Badlesmere sweat!'

'Whatever the case,' said Llewelyn mildly, 'you need not fear the result. What plea can Venables possibly put up, to compare with your right, when the king himself gave you the lands, and so recently? The man's a fool to waste his time in the attempt.'

At that David looked at him long, and seemed to debate within himself whether to say what was on his mind, or leave well alone. In the end he did not speak, but shrugged off the matter for the time being, and returned to his wine and his Elizabeth, who was as fierce in the cause of Hope and Estyn as he was, and eternally confident of his wisdom and rightness in all he did. As for Eleanor, she listened with a thoughtful face but a silent tongue, and left them to dispose of their legal problems as they saw fit. Out of deference for her, I think, David had somewhat curbed what otherwise he might have said outright against Edward, for not only he, but half the lords and chief tenants of the Middle Country were seething with resentment at the arbitrary ways of the king's bailiffs, and their encroachments on ancient Welsh rights which had never before been threatened. In a single year the administration had made malcontents of those who had gladly sheltered under its shadow when war loomed, and enemies of those who had fallen away from Llewelyn to serve the king and save themselves. There was a kind of rough justice in it, that they had rushed to embrace English protection, leaving Wales to its fate, only to find out, and so soon, that they did not all like the governance they had invoked, and were already looking round for someone to rescue them from it. In vain, if they looked to Llewelyn. He had set his seal to a treaty, and his word was his bond. The men of the Middle Country lay in beds they themselves had made, and found them beds of thorns.

I met David again later that evening in the inner ward of the maenol, taking a breath of the night air before he went to his rest. He was standing under the stars, gazing up with a still face at the guardwalk above the postern gate, where once he had kept vigil by night, waiting for the men of Powys to ride in silently to the work of murder, and set him up as prince in his brother's place. As soon as he was aware of me, I knew he was remembering that time, and he knew as much of me. I never had asked him, I never was to ask him, anything concerning that night. When Llewelyn called him back to him, asking nothing, and he came in desperate and rebellious love, making no confession and expressing no penitence, all question was for ever put out of my power. But when David was alone, he remembered, and so did I.

I would have passed by and let him be, but he spoke me softly and calmly: 'Samson!' and I stayed. 'Samson,' he said, laying his arm in the old way about my shoulders, 'after that hearing at Rhuddlan, when Edward adjourned my brother's plea so strangely, that same month he set up a commission to enquire into how barons of Wales had been accustomed to plead in land disputes. I remember they sat at Oswestry towards the end of the month. Reginald de Grey had the commission, and one of the king's clerks with him – Hamilton, that's the man. William Hamilton. Edward claimed it was set up to make doubly sure of proceeding justly. But I have it in mind, Samson, that it was for exactly the opposite reason. Tell me this, since the commission sat two full months ago, and reported its findings immediately, can you think of a reason why those findings have never been made known? Did anything ever come of them? Nothing! Yet the record of that inquisition is lying somewhere in the king's treasury, very quietly. It is on my mind, Samson, that it will never be

19

heard of again, at least, never in Wales. For good reason! It must have found absolutely for Llewelyn's claim, that Welsh land is ruled by Welsh law, and no other.'

I said, and meant it, that while I did not cherish any blind confidence in the king's disinterestedness, neither did I think this judgment on him as yet in any way justified, and we should await the outcome of the January hearing at Oswestry. It was common knowledge that English law was always tedious in its delays and prevarications by comparison with the clear simplicity and promptness of our own laws of Howel the Good, and further, that Edward was so in love with its complexities as to be a little mad on the subject.

'Edward's madness,' said David with a hollow laugh, 'like Edward's generosity, exists only in the service of Edward's interests. I advise you, for my brother's sake, keep a careful watch on everything the king says or does, and in particular everything he writes. When he becomes most voluble and obscure, then watch him most carefully. And if the Oswestry session proves me wrong, I'll do penance gladly, and you, my beloved confessor, shall set it for me, as sharply as you will.'

I said that the prince's men of law were inevitably in expectation of trickery to begin with, that being the nature of law-men everywhere. And then I said, to lighten his sombre mood, that in any event his own case was different, since he held what he held by the king's own wish.

'We shall see!' said David. 'You heard Llewelyn say that Venables is a fool to challenge the king's grant? To the best of my knowledge, Venables is no fool at all, but very shrewd, and with an eye to his own good. Who's to say that someone – oh, not Edward! – has not whispered in his ear where his best interests lie, and how far he may go with impunity? My demon prompts me that this is the king's way of recovering what he already regrets having given. And that, too, will be seen, all in good time.'

We walked back to the tower together, and he took his

arm from about me, and yawned, and turned towards the stairway. But there he paused and looked back, and in the dim light from a single torch I saw his face sharply and sombrely outlined.

'One more thing, Samson! Should you ever be in those parts where they are, look for yourself at Edward's new trade roads through the forests. Granted a clear way, where officers can patrol freely, may be good for trade. But ask yourself whether any merchant, with pack-horses and a few stout journeymen, needs that breadth of open land. Then remember how we moved up from Chester to Flint, from Flint to Rhuddlan, how many thousands strong, in that last war, with the foresters felling and the labourers carting ahead of us. Oh, speak out on me!' he said, seeing how I watched him without a word. 'Do you think I have forgotten on which side I fought then? Curse me, if you will. But after that, listen to me!'

'I shall never curse you,' I said, 'until he does. And he never will. And I am listening.'

'Samson, I cannot get it out of my head or my heart, or wherever it so lodges and oppresses me,' said David, 'that after all the arguments at law are exhausted, those roads are Edward's last argument.'

I was present in court when the bench of judges under Walter de Hopton sat at Oswestry, that Hilary session, to hear the prince's plea on Arwystli, for I went as a clerk to Llewelyn's attorneys. Therefore I know all that passed in that courtroom, and I set it down here that it may not be lost or forgotten. For this was the first time that ever the two opponents joined battle fully over this plea, almost a year having been drained away in delays and adjournments.

We were well primed before ever we left Gwynedd, and the prince's stand was unshakable. He acceded to the king's ruling that such important cases between lords must be heard at places and times fixed by the judges, surrendering

21

the exact position stated in the treaty, that a cause should be heard in the lands where it arose. But not one point more would he yield. Arwystli was Welsh, had always been Welsh, lay in the very heart of Welsh land, and could not be, and never had been, subject to English common law. On that we stood absolutely.

The hall where the bench sat was full, for the meeting of those two implacable enemies, even by proxy, drew men from all the country round to watch, and especially lawyers, eager to observe the conduct of such important pleas. Griffith ap Gwenwynwyn came in person, with a bevy of law-men about him, and kept close to their sleeves during the hearing, ready to pluck and whisper and prompt, for he was certainly as skilled in prevarication as any of his advisers, though he preferred to work through them. His big frame had run somewhat to fat since I had last seen him, his thick brown beard and hair were laced with grey, and his walk slower and more ponderous than of old. He was then in his middle sixties, strong as a bull, but growing clumsy, and his English finery of furred gown and ample surcoat made him look bulkier than he was. He settled himself solidly in his place behind the line of his lawyers, and swept the court with sharp, narrowed eyes, dwelling longest upon the prince's attorneys, seated opposite. Most of Arwystli was in his hands, he would not let it go without a long and bitter struggle.

We had three justices on the bench before us, two Welsh and one English, but there was not a man in court who did not know that the judgment rested with the presiding judge, and the others were there merely to supply a fair balance and a knowledge of Welsh customs and traditions. One of them was Goronwy ap Heilyn, a good friend to us and sometime among Llewelyn's own lawyers, who had accepted office under the king in this commission with the true intent to maintain and protect justice for his fellow-countrymen, for he was a man of Rhos, and knew and loved the north. The other was Howel ap Meurig, no friend to us, which at least made the bench appear impartial. He was an englishified Welshman who had abandoned his own country for royal service more than fifteen years earlier, and done very well out of it, with a knighthood and a coat of arms to show, but he was no more on an equal footing with Walter de Hopton than was Goronwy.

I had seen this Hopton before, but never so close. He came from a border family that held land both in Hereford and Salop, and he was in middle life, perhaps fifty then, but looked younger, being very neat and smooth, with well-shaven chin and pale, plump cheeks, and very quick, cool eyes that he kept half-hidden under large white eyelids. He was himself no mean litigant, as a great many men had already learned to their cost.

As soon as the judges were seated and the court in session, Hopton signified to the prince's chief attorney that he might proceed. Master William rose, and at once demanded that Griffith ap Gwenwynwyn, as the opposing party, should attach himself by producing hostages, according to Welsh law, after which formality the prince would willingly prosecute his right in the matter according to *cyfraith*, the Welsh code of Howel the Good. This on two grounds, that the land in question was wholly Welsh, lay within the borders of Wales, and both the parties claiming it were themselves of Welsh blood and estate; and further, that the treaty obtaining between England and Wales laid it down that claims of land within the boundaries of Wales should be conducted according to Welsh law. Both tradition and custom, and the letter of the treaty, demanded that the cause be tried by Welsh law and no other.

Griffith's lawyer got up to counter, prodded briskly by his lord.

'The Lord Griffith,' said the attorney, 'is a baron of the king's Grace, a marcher lord holding the land of Arwystli by barony of the king, as he does all his other lands. He is ready to proceed and defend his holding according to the common law, as is his right.'

'Though the Lord Griffith is a baron of the king, and a marcher,' said Master William, 'that cannot affect the land of Arwystli, which cannot possibly be called march land. March land is that which is close adjacent to Welsh land. This cannot be said of Arwystli. It lies in the central parts of Wales, and within the boundaries of the principality, and is purely Welsh. There is no way in which it can be considered as march land. Moreover, the Lord Griffith and all his forebears are of Welsh condition, as can well be proved according to Welsh law, if the bench require such proof. I ask again that this cause be conducted according to Welsh law.'

Hopton looked under his pale eyelids at Griffith and his covey of lawyers, but did not have to prompt them for an answer. The second in rank rose from his place, and leaned for a moment to his lord, who was whispering in his ear some last admonition.

'If it please the court,' said the man, smoothing his sleeves, 'there are any number of lords marchers who hold lands not merely adjacent to the border, but as deep into the heart of Wales as is Arwystli, but nevertheless hold them by barony from the king, as they do their other lands. I instance Maelienydd and Gwerthrynion, which are held by Roger Mortimer, but lie in the distant parts of Wales. A case was brought against him for possession of certain of these lands, and he was impleaded not by Welsh law, but *coram rege*, in the king's court at Windsor, and that case was concluded in Shrewsbury, under the king's justices. I can cite other such cases, all concerning lands deep in Wales, but pleaded by common law. Should the court require that these be proven here, I am willing to prove them. His Grace King Edward is in seisin of all pleas arising between his barons of the march and of Wales, to be heard before him in his court, according to common law. Should such a case be prosecuted otherwise,

24

the lord king's prerogative is prejudiced, and the crown deprived and affronted.'

There was heard the true voice of Griffith himself, who knew only too well how to turn what sounded like a plea at law into a sly reminder how vulnerable was the position of special commissioners appointed by the king. As they had been set up, so they could as quickly be put down. As a plea the peroration might sound strong, but was in fact very weak, for how could the king's prerogative be infringed by strict observance of the terms of a treaty the king himself had argued out, agreed to and sealed hardly more than a year previously? Not even precedent should be able to upset a clearly stated ruling so recently laid down. For quite apart from the general principle stated in the treaty of Aberconway, that cases should be tried in those parts where the disputed lands lay, and by the kind of law there applying, there was also a special clause particularly laying down this rule in cases brought by the prince of Wales. There it was set down in so many words that if Llewelyn wished to claim right in any lands taken and held by others than the crown – excepting only the Middle Country, which was ceded in full – the king would show him justice according to the laws and customs of those parts where the impleaded lands lay. I remember even now how the Latin ran – *secundum leges et consuetudines partium illarum in quibus terre ille consistunt*. There could not be a clearer undertaking. Nor was Griffith's parade of precedents much to the point, since it could not wipe out that clause, and further, the prince of Wales was not a baron either of Wales or of the march, but a sovereign prince, and again, could not be used as were those barons. The procedure in the treaty had been devised and agreed particularly to define his position and the treatment to which he was entitled.

Legally, then, this was pleading high in sound but low in relevance, and the real purport was at the end, in what was rather a warning, even a threat. 'Beware,' said Griffith's attorney, shrewdly eyeing Hopton in particular, but the two Welsh assessors also, 'how you take even the least risk of infringing the king's prerogative, whatever sanction of treaty and seal you may have for the act that incurs his displeasure. Wise men, if they are not sure of their ground, defer.'

I wondered then, and was ashamed of the thought and put it from me, whether King Edward's own men of law had not conferred with Griffith and put this pointed pleading into his mouth. But it seemed too base a procedure, and I told myself I was falling into David's too suspicious frame of mind before we had tested out the king's honesty and goodwill. Whereas from Griffith this was just what might have been expected. So I absolved the king from complicity. Since then I have wondered, many times.

'You wish to make a counter-plea to this?' asked Hopton, looking at Master William and keeping his bland face inexpressive.

'With the court's permission.' And the old man took up all those points which Griffith's plea had merely covered over without touching. That he had made no mention of the special provision made in the treaty for this very purpose, and approved, indeed laid down, by the king. That as tenure by marcher barony was not the same as tenure by English barony, so the status of the prince of Wales conformed to neither, for which reason the provision before-mentioned had been devised. So far merely in refutation, but then he went further.

'The lord king, as all men know, is lord of many lands and provinces, and each of these lands under his dominion has its own laws and customs according to the traditions and usages of that part where it lies. Gascony, Scotland, Ireland, England, each has its own ways and laws, and that greatly to the enlargement of the crown's privileges, and not at all to their derogation. The prince of Wales seeks only the same right for his person and his principality, that he should also have his own law, the law of Wales,

26

and proceed according to that law, and not otherwise. And especially he invokes those clauses in the treaty of peace between himself and the lord king, by which the king himself, of his own will, granted Welsh law to the prince and people of Wales. I say that this is his entitlement by common right, as those other nations gathered under the king's lordship have their laws and customs, and their language. But also by a particular right, laid down by the king in treaty, he seeks to enjoy the privilege so markedly granted him under the royal seal.'

Adam, his clerk, who sat beside me in court, was glowing and grinning by then, for the old man's blood was up, and he had never spoken to better purpose. I had thought Griffith might attempt no further in that line, having to all appearances the worst of the argument, but he did pluck at his man's sleeves and send him into the lists again, somewhat less confidently but volubly still.

'With the court's leave, it must be observed that all those several nations, however they may do in other causes, in the king's court are governed by a single common law, and not by varying and opposing laws in one and the same court. The king's Grace is in seisin of pleas in his court between his barons, whether Welsh or marcher, and therefore in that court and by common law this plea should proceed. According to that law the Lord Griffith is ready and willing to answer all claims, but not by the *cyfraith* of Howel Dda.'

'And my prince,' said Master William, 'lays claim to the Welsh law expressly granted to him by the king in the treaty, and is ready to pursue his right to judgment, and to answer any and all claims, by that law and no other. For if he abandoned that right, it would be a concession without precedent, and greatly to his diminution.'

On these opposing declarations the parties stood, and neither would give way. It was open to the bench to weigh and decide between the two claims, indeed that was held to be the reason why this commission had been set

27

up, and not at all to adjourn and defer and commit all perilous decisions to another court, but I knew then that that was what they would do. Not only because Goronwy, and I believe rightly, would come down on the side of the treaty and of Welsh law, while Howel ap Meurig as surely would incline to Griffith's side and find plausible reasons for it, which would leave Hopton in the position of having to cast the final vote himself. That would in any case have been reason enough, for he was too cautious ever to let himself be placed in so vulnerable a position. But I believe he had another and more absolute reason for avoiding. Those reasons he gave were sound enough, but I do not believe he ever had to do more than seem to consider. It was never intended that the prince's claim should come to any conclusion that day. Apart from the record, all those pleadings and counter-pleadings had been breath wasted.

'You are absolute in maintaining these positions?' said Hopton mildly, turning his half-hidden eyes from one attorney to the other. They said firmly that they were, and neither could nor would move from them.

'This matter is of such importance,' he said then, 'the parties provided on both sides with such weighty arguments, that it seems rather to have been lifted out of our competence. Both make direct appeal to royal privilege and claim royal sanction, the one by treaty, the other by baronage, and there is substance in both, and both touch the crown prerogative closely. I must confer with my colleagues.' And he did so, with great earnestness and in low voices, while his clerks wrote away busily for some ten minutes, but we knew what the end of it would be. I could not blame the bench too much for taking the easy way out of their trap.

The clerk rapped for silence at length, and Hopton delivered his judgment. 'We are agreed that we cannot of our own power interpret the clauses of a treaty drawn by the king, except in his presence and with his guidance. Nor

28

could we take any decision affecting the prerogative of the crown without the sanction of the crown. We are therefore agreed that this case must be adjourned *coram rege*, and we appoint both parties a day for that hearing in the king's court, one month after Easter, on the last day of April, so that his Grace can decide the questions of law here involved, and make his will known.'

And on that the bench rose, and Griffith ap Gwenwyn-wyn rose after, with a swirl of his furred gown, and stamped gleefully out of court with his rookery of lawyers on his heels. And we went away irritated and disappointed, but not really astonished. It was ill news to take back to Llewelyn, though I did not think it would come as any great surprise to him, either, however arduously he had reserved his judgment. One thing I was sure of, and that was that he would not attend on the day appointed in April, for there was no course open to him but to stand on his Welsh right. If he once surrendered it, they had a precedent for ever after, and to use against other men. Or if he did send proxies, it would be only to state his position and stand immovably upon it, as he had done in Oswestry.

Llewelyn and Eleanor were in Ardudwy at that time, and there we returned and reported what had passed. But we found David there before us, without his family on this occasion, for he had ridden west in haste and excitement, in the fresh flush of battle, to compare his own fortunes in litigation with his brother's and was half furious, half perversely gratified, to find his worst prophecies confirmed. I heard his voice uplifted in the high chamber before I entered the hall, and his law clerk, Alan of Denbigh, met me in the stables and gave me the whole story.

'Oh, he made his appearance there in Badlesmere's court, as summoned, to the day and the hour, but not by his attorneys. He went in person, and took no one with him but me, and that only to have a witness both while he stayed and after he left, for he never had any idea of acknowledging the competence of the court, and he had

29

no trust in them for what they might get up to behind his back. And right he was! He waited until the case was called and Venables put in his writ, and then he stalked out into the centre of the room alone, where no one could fail to see and hear him. You know him! He made a figure, there's none can do it better!' And he grinned, remembering, and so did I, imagining David bestriding the floor in his arrogance of beauty and disdain, to the eclipse of Badlesmere and all his assessors.

'He said that he was there only out of reverence for the king's Grace, and to make plain that he did not own the competence of the court and was not bound to answer for his lands there, for they were a part of the true soil of Wales, and belonged in no way to Cheshire, where alone Badlesmere's writ runs. And then he pronounced his summoning there as illegal, and cried aloud like a trumpet that he committed the lands in question to the peace of God and the king. And stalked out, and left a dead silence behind him for a long while, till they got their breath back, and what was left of their legal dignity. Man, it was a massacre! But they'll make him pay for it! No royal officer likes to be outshone and outfaced in his own court, and if Badlesmere is no strong man, there's one strong enough and to spare behind him.'

'And after he left?' I asked.

'It was pitiful law, they were hardly themselves, but it was very pointed spite. They let Venables proceed with his plea, as though nothing had happened, and brought in that David had refused to plead, though he'd made no formal appearance at all, only repudiated the competence of the court. It made him angrier than ever when I followed him with the news. Lucky I was there to see! There was only one assessor there who had the honesty to speak out against the judgment and refuse his agreement, and that was the earl of Lincoln's steward. He opposed them from beginning to end, and has had his opposition enrolled. That's one good man we can call to witness for us.'

We had fared no better, and so I told him. It behoved the princes to work together in these matters, and see that their efforts fortified each other.

'They'll have their heads together now,' said Alan. 'The lord prince may allow himself a few days for thought, but my lord will certainly be drafting his letter to the king in his mind this minute, and it will be a strong one.'

Over the wording of that letter David haled me, too, into service. It was written that same evening after supper, in Llewelyn's high chamber, the prince sitting quietly by and forbearing from urging prudence or changing the fiery words David dictated.

The facts of the hearing at Chester David recounted to the king briefly and truly, and with the same force demanded, rather than requested, a just remedy. It was a prince's letter, courteous enough but worded to an equal, who owed him fair treatment and could be called to account if he did less than justice.

'Write,' said David, staring before him across the glow of the brazier to where Alan sat at the table with his parchment and his pens, 'write that in view of the illegality of the process, I beg his Grace to have the plea, the judgment and the persons of the doomsmen who gave that judgment, brought to his own presence. Further, I request that the pursuit of this plea in the shire-court of Chester be suspended.'

'You are taking a high line,' said Llewelyn, but without disapproval.

'If I fail in that now, how can I begin after? Wait still, Alan, I have more to say. If this matter is to move at all, and not be deferred and delayed and lost by creeping inch upon inch, I must find the answer to what Edward's answer will be, and spare at least one letter. Write this, Alan! "Since your Grace, by the ordinance of God, is king of many countries, speaking varying tongues and administered according to varying laws, which your Grace has seen no cause to change, let the laws of Wales, also, if it please

31

your Grace, remain unchanged and respected as are those of the other nations under your crown." '

I saw Llewelyn's eyes open wide and dark under his deep brow, and a faint and private smile touch his lips and vanish again. For David had wrested out of his own heart the very principle, almost the very words, Master William had advanced in court, and yet no one had recounted to David in detail, at that time, what had passed in Oswestry. The outcome he knew, but certainly not all the arguments. He had come to the same lofty place of his own passion, and seen the same vision, he who had exchanged his rights in Gwynedd for lands of the king's gift, and fought for the king against his own people. True, this high flight was in defence of his own possessions, yet the cry he uttered was not only for himself.

And he had said more even than he knew. It was Llewelyn who had heard and marked the true meaning. In a moment naked and unguarded David, three times renegade, had cried out for the rights of Wales, and cried from the heart, with all the patriot authority of the prince his brother.

CHAPTER II

———

Now as to the progress of these two lawsuits, so fatal in themselves, and so ominous as they represented hundreds of others, that plagued and maddened lesser men throughout all those lands no longer in Llewelyn's principality, what happened to both during the remainder of that year can be easily told, for though many letters passed, and many men sat and deliberated, or seemed to deliberate, the sum total of what befell is, nothing!

David sent his letter, and I will not claim that nothing at all came of that, for King Edward instructed the justiciar of Chester to hold an inquisition among the men of the lands neighbour to Hope and Estyn, to determine whether those impleaded manors were in Wales or England. That inquisition was duly taken, and the men of the neighbouring parts confirmed with one voice that the lands were Welsh, and no law but Welsh had ever applied to them. But David's vengeful joy was curbed by sour disbelief, and wisely so, for in spite of this judgment, taken at the king's wish and published openly, Venables continued his plea in the Chester court as though nothing had changed, and was allowed to do so. Soon David was writing another peremptory letter to Edward calling attention to the anomaly, and demanding a remedy. Thus he persisted in his part as a spokesman for Welsh rights, and saw no illogic in it, and no bad faith, as indeed there was none. He had a party at his back by then, all those in the Middle Country who smarted under the same whip, and saw in him the champion who burned all their inarticulate complaints into one fiery utterance, loud enough to be heard even in Westminster.

As for the prince, he proceeded with less noise, and more forbearance, feeling himself tied as David was not. He did not wait for the date Hopton had appointed *coram rege*, but wrote well in advance to Edward, setting out his own view of the process to date, and why he would not and could not, pending a decision about the process of law to be followed, obey the summons to appear on the last day of April. He asked the king to receive an envoy to explain personally all that was involved. Edward replied courteously and willingly, inviting the approach. And the prince sent Brother William de Merton, the warden of the Franciscan friary at Llanfaes, to be his advocate at court.

Friar William was elderly and austere, well versed in law and of honest and forthright mind, though he knew how to furnish his severities with a courtly dress. He was also devoted to the prince and his house, and undertook the office with goodwill. But when he reached London, in the first days of April, it was to find the king making ready in haste to go to France, where he had business with King Philip, and also other matters concerning his many and quarrelsome relatives in those parts, and all Friar William was able to bring back with him was the king's verbal acknowledgement that he had done his errand well and prudently, that the matter was understood, but was too complex to be dealt with summarily, and must await his return, when he would give it his full attention. So when the day appointed by the Hopton bench came, the suit was not pursued, and the prince sent no attorneys, though Griffith ap Gwenwynwyn, as I heard, did put in a formal appearance to keep the issue alive, and the official record favourable to him.

'No help for it,' said Llewelyn, sighing. 'Not even King Edward can be everywhere and deal with everything at the same time.'

Friar William had brought personal letters for Eleanor

34

with all the news from court. The queen's mother was recently dead, and the county of Ponthieu, in the north of France, which she had held, now came to her daughter. 'Which is to say, to Edward,' said Eleanor, 'and though he has indeed business with King Philip, trying to keep the peace between him and King Alfonso of Castille, yet I think my cousin will be spending half the time of his visit making sure of his hold on Ponthieu.'

'Compared with which,' Llewelyn owned honestly, 'Arwystli may seem a very small manor, and my claim of little consequence. But justice is not a small thing, nor of little consequence.'

'And we are not the only people suffering from his passion for order in all things,' said Eleanor, still pondering the news from London. 'It seems he has set in motion a great inquest into the tenements and liberties of all his shires, and drafted panels of commissioners to do the probing. There'll be indignation enough in England, without looking westward into Wales. Every man who holds land to the value of twenty pounds a year is to be distrained by the sheriffs to accept knighthood, whether he wants the honour or not. That will set them by the ears! It's more burden than honour, these days. A strange man,' she said, frowning, 'my cousin Edward!'

'I do believe,' said Llewelyn, 'that you feel some affection for him, even after all that has happened.'

'I *know*,' she said, smiling, 'that *you* do! Of myself I'm never quite so sure. I am not as crystal-clear as you, and not as generous. I do not forget, because he showed us such marked honour and such lavish entertainment at Worcester, that we both suffered for it over and over beforehand, against all right, and that paying a blood-debt, though it goes some way to repair a wrong, does not bring back to life what was killed. Three years of my life with you Edward stole from me, and from you those three years and more. It is over now,' she said, 'and I am too happy by far to bear any grudges or want any revenges, but I remember, and I have learned. I can look at Edward as he is, and find much to like, and still keep my distance and stay on my guard.'

I was there in the high chamber with them, that summer night at Llanfaes, at a desk in the corner of the room, copying music for Eleanor, for she not only played two or three stringed instruments herself, but also took a great interest in the music of the prince's chapel, and eagerly sent for new compositions when chance offered.

'Samson knows,' she said, appealing to me, 'for he was with me then, how Edward first came to me in Windsor, when I was his prisoner. No way ashamed, and yet he was not easy. I had not seen him since I was a small child, and beneath his notice.'

She had not been beneath his notice in Windsor, but every way a match for him and more, for she had nothing to be ashamed of, and much to accuse him of, had she so chosen.

'Well, it is past,' she said. 'I could get nothing from him, but neither could he from me. Once we had made certain of that, and set our jaws to face it out, we got on very well together. Like two enemies who respect each other, brought together in the prison of a common enemy, and making truce between them in order to make life more possible. I got to know him very well, my cousin Edward, the best of him and the worst. The strength and the weakness. He is very strong. And very weak,' she said.

'There are not many would say that of him,' said Llewelyn, amused, 'who have fought against him, as I have. Or watched, even from a distance, his handling of men and events. Whatever else he may be, I see him as a giant.'

'You have not done the fighting over a chess-board, brow to brow,' said Eleanor, 'as I have. At such close quarters you hear the hard breathing, not the fanfares, and see the sweat and not the banners.'

'And were you victorious?' he asked, laughing, but marking her words very attentively for all that.

36

'I wish I could say so! I would have given every mark I had to be able to beat him,' she owned, reflecting his laughter, 'but I am not good enough. But once I came very near it, and brought him up short in stalemate at the end. For half an hour he dreaded I might defeat him. If you had seen him then, stiff to the finger-ends, and his jaw set like a man-trap, you would know Edward as I know him. If he could laugh at himself or bear that others should, if he saw any other human creature as having quite the same rights as he has, if he could take a fair fall and give fair credit ungrudging, then he would be great indeed. But he cannot and he does not. A giant he is, his ability is towering. But inside the giant there's a dwarf, fearful of being uncovered, and if ever his armour is pierced, to him hatred would come easy. I do not fear the giant,' said Eleanor, suddenly grave and vehement, 'but of the dwarf I could be very much afraid.'

The king remained in France until the middle of June, making himself known to the officials of Ponthieu, and staying some time in his fine new city of Abbeville, but two weeks after his return home he wrote to the prince concerning the discussions he had had with Friar William de Merton, regretting, very graciously, that the exigencies of his business in France had kept him from dealing with the matters discussed at once. But he promised that he would do so in his Michaelmas parliament, and assigned a date for the hearing, the thirteenth day of October, which he said he had also appointed to Griffith ap Gwenwynwyn, in order that the business in hand might be settled in his own court. To that end, he desired Llewelyn to send to Westminster some of his trusted and discreet men, informed about the case in hand and versed in the law of Howel the Good, and in the customs pertaining to the lands concerned. Then the king would hear the case and do such justice that the prince should be well satisfied.

Llewelyn heaved great vindicated breaths at this reason-

37

able response to his approaches. 'I felt in my bones,' he said, cheered and glad, 'that it was the old trouble – so many officials and bailliffs between us, we cannot get to grips, and as soon as I am face to face with Edward the fog clears. Could he have spoken more directly than this? I am to send attorneys skilled in Welsh law – you see, he grants me my Welsh law! – and the rest lies with him. Even the day is a good omen,' he said. For the thirteenth of October was the first anniversary of his wedding day, the day of St Edward the Confessor, so sacred to King Edward and to his father before him.

I remember still every word of that letter, and I tell you, it could not in any interpretation be made to mean anything but what it clearly said, and had Llewelyn been far readier to detect trickery than ever he was, he must have come to the same conclusion, that no man could commit himself so fully, and then draw back or move aside.

So that summer passed in good hope, and in caring for a principality still prosperous in its ancient customs, and still growing in markets and towns, so far as its mountainous lands permitted. For the prince never lost sight of his aim, even now that he was curbed into half his former territory. There was still much to be done by good husbandry, and even within the limits of Snowdonia growth was possible. He had, moreover, the delight of taking his wife with him about this lovely, stony, glittering land of his, and watching his own love reflected in her face. There was in her a splendour that had waited, unaware of its hunger, for this wild, forbidding land, and found in it nothing daunting, but only liberty. She had a bardic strain in her, she brought the trouvère music of northern France to our western wilds, and found meaning echoes in our songs, and after a while she began to make her own songs, marrying those two in melodies to melt the heart.

When we both had leisure from other matters, she would have me teach her something of the Welsh language, and studied earnestly and quickly, asking me at every lesson

38

for ingenious words of endearment and love in her new tongue, to be used, surely, for Llewelyn's ears only, when they lay in each other's arms. In all things, great or small, she found by grace fresh means of giving him astonishment and delight.

When the autumn drew on, and the appointed time for parliament was nearing, the prince wrote from Aberyddon to the king, repeating as a reminder almost the very terms Edward had used in bidding his envoys to the session, 'in order,' he said pointedly, 'to pursue my claim to Arwystli in your Grace's presence, according to the law of Howel the Good, which is Welsh law.' And he went on to beg the king to do justice without further delay, since the prince had already brought up the matter before both the king and the king's justices, and it had cost him high to send so many envoys all over England, and so far quite vainly. He did not know, he said, at whose instigation his cause at law had been thus obstructed.

'You are severe with him,' said Eleanor, cautiously approving.

'That was not my intent. I put the case plainly, so that there can be no misunderstanding. I have quoted him his own bidding word for word, so that *he* shall know he has not been misunderstood. Or if he claims he has, and his instructions do not mean what I have read them as meaning, he has time to say so before the case is heard.'

So this letter was sent ahead of the envoys, and brought no protestations in answer, which was reassuring. Llewelyn began to be confident of the result, for it seemed certain at last that his claim to have Welsh law over Welsh land was conceded without further argument. The prince therefore sent another letter over another matter, punctiliously thanking the king for declining to entertain in his court a plea that manifestly belonged in the prince's jurisdiction. This was but one among hundreds of cases then embittering the whole air of the borders. The widowed lady of Bromfield had for some time been suing her brother-in-law of Ial for certain lands which he held of the prince, but being a troublesome and mischievous woman she had sued first in the Welsh courts, then in the English, putting the unlucky lord of Ial in danger of offending both overlords, since if he answered in the king's court for lands he held of the prince, that would be insult to the prince, but if he failed to answer a summons to the royal court, that would certainly blacken his face with the king. Both he and Llewelyn had appealed for a ruling, and Edward firmly remitted the case to the prince's court, and that with very pleasing promptitude. Possibly he found the lady of Bromfield more trouble than she was worth, and was not sorry to get rid of her.

'Well, let's at least give thanks where they're due,' said Llewelyn, and wrote a warm acknowledgement. And this case also we took as encouragement, and began to believe that all was going smoothly at last.

Llewelyn felt a particular responsibility in his dealings with this Margaret of Bromfield and her family, for her husband had been his ally and friend until the pressures of war broke him, for his lands were very exposed to English attack. He had left two young sons, still children, for whom Llewelyn felt a guardian's concern, and he took care to watch how their lands were administered during their infancy, and to intervene when he thought they were being abused. These lands were no longer a part of his principality, but fell under the king, and the prince could exercise only a friendly influence, but the king had been gracious and accommodating in the matter, and Llewelyn did not fail to send thanks for his consideration.

'Everything I have incurred,' he said, 'I will discharge, whether it be the payment of the money due, the deference owing from vassal to overlord, or the simple acknowledgement of favour or kindness. If his pride is to exact all, mine is to render all. As I stand on my own rights, so I'll do full justice to his.'

This he said, and made good, and his annual payments

of the money due under treaty were indeed made regularly, promptly and in full, and often allocated by Edward to this need or that in his kingdom, or to discharge one of his debts, long before they were due, so certain was he of getting them to the last penny.

By the same messenger who carried Llewelyn's letters, Eleanor also wrote to the king, in response to some point he had raised concerning her mother's will. Scarcely a letter went from her without some courteous but insistent reminder about her brother Amaury, who was still a prisoner in Corfe castle at the king's pleasure, but all her pleas had so far failed to move Edward. Some of the servants of her former household were likewise prisoners, for no crime but that of accompanying their mistress when she sailed from France to join Llewelyn, already her husband by proxy, in Wales. Popes and bishops had interceded for Amaury, for he was a papal chaplain, but King Edward, for all his piety, was proof against popes, and ceded no grain of his rights to archbishops, and turned a deaf ear to all. It was the one sorrow Eleanor had, that all her efforts could not deliver her own men from their chains.

But at that time, in the bright autumn at Aberyddon, we had high hopes that things were moving in a better direction, and soon we might be able to secure justice at law, and clemency for the captives.

About the twentieth day of October David came riding in, in better spirits than we had seen him lately, for the rubbing of the royal officials in the Middle Country increasingly chafed him, but now he was glittering and full of news.

'I'm tossed out of Hope to go and amuse myself elsewhere,' he said. 'Cristin tells me to get from under her feet, for the love of God, for she has her hands full without me.' He flung an arm about my shoulders at the mention of her, for he had always known how things were with us, 'She's very well, and very happy, with a child in either arm, and Elizabeth purring like a cat. Not one daughter this time, but two! And pretty as flowers, and loud as black-birds!'

'So they always are,' said Llewelyn, hugging him heartily. 'There's not one of yours but comes dancing into the world. I give you joy! And Elizabeth? All's well with them all three?'

'Would I stir,' said David, 'until I was sure of it? Twin girls, and made in her image! There cannot be too many Elizabeths in the world. I speak who know best. Five daughters she's given me, and think of all those happy husbands, when the years have rolled round!'

I do, I think of them now, remembering that prophecy. All those little girls of his, so vastly and indiscriminately loved, for David was gifted for fatherhood, go dancing before my eyes to their fate, and all the husbands who might well have exulted in them, as he did in their mother, are pale and void as mist, sucked empty of promised joy. But that belongs not here. Doubtless God has the whole account recorded.

'One babe, and the women are still just sufferable,' said David. 'Two, and there's no holding them. I am not even allowed to choose names, they're already chosen – Eleanor and Elizabeth.' He looked at the princess and smiled. 'What else?'

'I am proud!' said Eleanor, and leaned and kissed his cheek. It was the first time she had so touched him, for truly she did not commit herself easily, as Llewelyn was prone to do, though never did she shut out any who approached her with entreaty. And it seemed to me that by that salute David had gained a kind of credit, considered and bestowed with open eyes, as when a seal is appended to a document until then invalid. He had, I believe, had some doubts of his standing with her, not without reason. She was not bound to him by blood, as Llewelyn was, in the inescapable tie that fetters love hand and foot. And she was wise from the heart and mind together, the best wisdom in this world. I think David had

42

feared her. Her eyes were mirrors of truth, and he knew what his truth was, and leaned aside and avoided. But where she sealed with her own ungrudging seal, I trusted, and was glad.

David had then almost forgotten his grievance over Hope and Estyn in his family joy. Also his second protest to the king had secured, if not a suspension of the Venables plea in the Chester shire-court, at least an indefinite delay, for the case had been adjourned *sine die*, pending a decision by Edward, as to the findings of his own commission. So when we showed David the king's letter, clearly asking for envoys versed in Welsh law, even he, after reading and re-reading the lines with close care, could find no flaw, no way by which any man of honour, much less a king, could extricate himself from what was there set down.

It turned out very differently when Master William and his companions came back from Westminster in the last days of October, and made their way to Aberyddon. As soon as they rode into the bailey, wearied and dusty from the journey, our thumbs pricked, and when they came in to Llewelyn all of us present there knew from their faces and the discouraged sag of their shoulders that they had nothing good to tell.

'So we have not sped!' said Llewelyn heavily. 'Well, speak freely, it's best to know how we stand, and there's no man doubts you have done your part well and ably.'

'My lord,' said the old man, 'I had rather you learned the king's mind from the king's own mouth than from mine. Here is his letter. What words he has used to you I do not know. All too many he has used to me, and with all possible patience and consideration, but I am as far off from knowing his intent as I was before. I can guess at it many ways, and fear it one way in particular, but determine and be sure of it I cannot.'

'Yes, this is familiar!' said David bitterly. 'This is Edward! Yet how *could* he get out of what he wrote to

43

you? – even he? Or was it some unpractised clerk who wrote that last letter, and forgot to leave the boltholes open? He said it in so many words – "the law of Howel the Good" – no "buts", no "ors", no "unless". . . . Some honest fellow in the chancellery will be in trouble for that.'

'Do you tell me,' said Llewelyn, breaking the seal of the scroll with a sharp pluck, 'that Edward does not read over and ponder before he sends? I think not!' And he unrolled the parchment and read, with set face and darkening brows, but without outcry, once in silence, then aloud to us all.

' "We have listened attentively in our present parliament to all that the lord prince's attorneys have put forward on his behalf in the cause between him and Griffith ap Gwenwynwyn, concerning Arwystli and certain other lands. We find that the lord prince's attorneys had not been given full powers to act for him in the case, and though we might, therefore, have ruled this as a default and proceeded to judgment in our court, and indeed perhaps ought to have done so, we have instead adjourned the case to our next parliament at Westminster, to a date three weeks after next Easter. Since the peace between us declares that disputes in the march must be decided according to march law, and such as arise in Wales according to the laws and customs of Wales, we order the prince of Wales to appear before us, either in person or by his lawyers, fully empowered by him and well versed in that law which the prince desires, or in the law which the aforementioned Griffith prefers, that justice may be done as God and right decree, and our council approve, and there may be no further delays.

' "Dated at Westminster, the twenty-fifth day of October, in the seventh year of our reign." '

He looked up over the scroll. 'Not given full powers! How can he say it? He knows you were fully empowered, and fulfilled every condition he laid down. Now he demands you shall come with authority to deal in *either* law, where before he spoke only of Welsh law. "That law

44

which the prince desires, *or* in the law which Griffith prefers . . ." He is not asking simply for men *versed* in both laws, and able to dispute over which applies – no, he is saying I am to authorise you to go to him prepared to plead by whichever law *he* claims applies! To submit in advance to having my case tried however *he* decrees, when he knows and I know that Arwystli is Welsh to the bedrock, and never has been subject to any law but Welsh.'

'It is a means of delaying for another half-year,' said David, smouldering, 'and after that he'll find yet another means, and always paying lip-service to justice and law. Still professing he wants no more delays, as if you were the one to blame, and still luring you on to hope, with his virtuous testimony that march law applies to the marches and Welsh law to Wales, as though he were not standing in the way of that very principle. No fox could twist and turn better. Whatever words he uses will always serve his purpose, for he will always reserve to himself the sole right to expound what they mean, in the teeth of language, in the face of truth.'

Llewelyn looked at Master William, whose weary old face was as grim as his own. 'Did you gather anything, from all he had to say in court, to give us a better opinion of what he is about? I myself could put a dozen different interpretations upon this letter, and doubtless I have put the worst. Let me know your mind.'

'In my view,' said the old man, 'his Grace uses words not to expound, but to conceal his meaning. The conclusion I could draw from one sentence he refutes in the next. But one thing was clear. His Grace did not intend to permit the case to begin at this session, whatever pretext might be needed to halt it. No, still one more thing is certain – Griffith ap Gwenwynwyn was in no fear or concern at all, from the first.'

'No, for he had his assurance in advance,' said David sourly. 'He was contending in a match he knows he will not be allowed to lose.'

'Yet he himself has pleaded Welsh law when it suited him,' said Master William. 'Last year the men of Montgomery brought suit against him that his fair and market at Pool were to the damage and loss of the king's market at Montgomery, and he retorted with a plea that he need not answer for anything concerning Pool in the king's court, for the town lay in Wales, and every lord having a town in Wales could hold market and fair in his own lands without hindrance. It's true he lost his case then, for it was the king's profit at stake, but nonetheless he stood fast on his Welsh status, not a word then of pleading as a baron holding from the king. This case I cited before his Grace, but I was silenced by the ruling that I was not properly empowered. I was not allowed to proceed.'

'You could not have done more,' said Llewelyn consolingly. 'Where ears are shut, your eloquence and knowledge are wasted. Never fret for that, it's no fault of yours. So have others pleaded Welsh law,' he said, laying the letter by, 'and been allowed it. My cousin, Mortimer, for one. It seems the same privilege is not to be allowed to me, unless I fight hard for it. As I will!'

'What do you mean to do?' asked David, quivering. 'Fight, you say! With what weapons?'

'Law,' said Llewelyn emphatically, divining his flight and plucking him to earth. 'However it may be loaded against me, I have no other permissible weapon, and I shall use none. But whatever the unbalance, I'll contend as long as I have breath, in whatever court Edward may sanction, and by one law and one law only, and we shall see who has the longer endurance. I'll wait his half-year, and send my envoys, empowered to argue to the death in both laws, but not to proceed with my plea in any law but Welsh. And whatever the next shift may be to silence me and sicken me into withdrawal, I will never withdraw. There's more at stake than Arwystli, and for more Welshmen than Llewelyn.'

46

It was from that day that the prince's faith in King Edward's honesty was first shaken. If he fought on, as he was determined to do, in the name of Welsh rights rather than for any gain he could expect in the matter of Arwystli, it was in the conviction that the scales were weighted against him. But in a sense this was still a legal game, which might be won even against unfair odds. It was not a life and death matter.

It became so, I believe, that same December, just after we kept St Nicholas' day. There was a session of the Hopton commission held at Montgomery on the ninth, and Master William's clerk Adam attended, in the case of a Welsh tenant of Mortimer who had a grievance there. He came back in great excitement and indignation, and would see Llewelyn at once.

'My lord,' he said, 'I was in court when Griffith ap Gwenwynwyn brought in a plea against the crown for certain lands that were taken from him when he was your vassal, and after the war held by the king. Griffith claimed hereditary right to them, and Mortimer and the bailiff of Montgomery appeared against him for the king, and pleaded Welsh law.'

'So may every man, Welsh, marcher or English, it seems, even the king,' said Llewelyn with a wry smile. 'Every man but me. And what had they to urge by Welsh law?'

'Why, my lord, that a man who claims hereditary right to any land, and fails to prosecute his right for a year and a day, he has forfeited his right. And then Griffith ap Gwenwynwyn rose up in person, and said outright that Welsh law, this so-called law of Howel the Good, ought not to have any force against him, for the king's Grace had it in mind to annul it wholly.'

Llewelyn was still as stone for a moment. Then he said, and his voice was quiet and mild: 'Did he indeed say so? Loud as ever?'

'Loud, my lord, and certain, and without shame. As one having official knowledge. Wherever the king's writ now runs, he said, law is to be the king's law. And then the justices were horribly disturbed and out of countenance and Hopton spoke up in a great hurry, and said they did not believe, for their part, that the king wished to annul the law *in toto*, but only to correct certain parts of it which were not wholly in accordance with right, and to remove some which were no way acceptable, and manifestly ought to be removed.'

'Yes,' said Llewelyn, with the dry rustle of a laugh, 'doubtless Griffith has spoken too soon. It is his way.' He was silent for a moment, deep in black and brooding thought, and then he roused himself to thank Adam and dismiss him. 'You have done me good service,' he said, 'and it shall not be forgotten. Let Master William know what you have heard.'

When we were alone he said ruefully: 'Out of the mouths of infants and fools truth drops at the wrong moment. I should be grateful to Griffith for letting me know the worst.'

I said, though without certainty, that I would not take Griffith's word, thus used in court argument concerning his own interests, for what was in King Edward's mind.

'Neither would I,' said Llewelyn, 'if Hopton had not rushed so hastily to put a better gloss on it. He tried to sweeten it liberally, but note, he did not deny it. There must be truth in it! He means to bring all Wales, all that he holds, all that is not my principality and safe from him, into the jurisdiction of English law, as well as into his shire order and under his bailiffs. And yet he promised to all Welshmen, as he promised to me, our own law unviolated. It is written into the treaty, and it should bind him, as God knows it does bind me. And I still cannot believe,' he said, fretting at old memories and doubts, 'that all the time that treaty was making, clause by clause, he was in deliberate bad faith. I cannot believe it! It never showed in him or in his envoys. There was hard bargaining to hold what we held, and when it was ceded, I believe that was done as honestly as it was grudgingly. Had it been light to give, he would have given it lightly.'

And I, too, remembered every day of that month-long negotiation, and it was fought fiercely, but I believe cleanly. But my mind misgave me that we were dealing with one who entered into undertakings in good faith enough, and yet when they began to irk him could find the most just and virtuous reasons for qualifying or discarding them, who could re-examine his own given word, and convince himself that it meant something quite other than it said, and that he would be false and recreant if he did not follow the newly-discovered spirit and repudiate the letter. Studied from under that drooping eyelid of his, that alone marred his grandeur as it had marred his father's grace, doubtless words slid obliquely from their original sense to spell out what Edward desired them to mean.

'His own law naturally seems to him the best, for us as for the English,' said Llewelyn, 'that I can understand. And ours, being alien, may seem to him distasteful and disordered. But he has promised to observe it faithfully, and let him twist and recant as he will, and with all the power in his hands, if I must fight him to the end of my life to pin him to his word, I will do it. If he prevails against me, what hope will any other Welshman have of justice? I am bound by the treaty, there is no weapon allowed me but law, and even that, it seems, even that I must wield with my hands manacled.'

This matter of the Arwystli suit, which had now become a touchstone to determine the king's sincerity or duplicity, and affected every man of Welsh blood who had a grievance at law and hoped to right it by the code he knew and trusted, was not the only cause of vexation to the prince at this time, though it was the gravest. There were many other suits entangling him, some of them malicious and brought only to plague him, some collusive, to afford Griffith ap Gwenwynwyn legal cover, and assist him to manipulate the irritating delays in which he took such pleasure.

There was also another matter which had dragged on for some years, and was causing great annoyance and loss. Before the recent war a certain merchant ship had come to wreck in rough weather off our coast, and the men of Gwynedd had fished ashore such of the crew as survived, and salvaged all the goods the ship was carrying, which then legally belonged to the prince, who held right of wreck in all his lands. But after the peace was made, and the rush to law began, the owner of the vessel, one Robert of Leicester and a rich man, went to the king with the tale that his ship had not been lost by wreck, and the prince had no right to the goods she carried, and so he had obtained royal letters enabling him to bring suit for recovery of his merchandise or its value in the Chester shire-court, where naturally he had no difficulty in getting judgment in his favour.

Now this was in any case wrong in law, for the suit, if he wished to press his claim, should have been brought in the land where the loss complained of occurred, that is, in Llewelyn's own court in Wales, and therefore its process in Chester was an affront and infringement of the prince's sovereign right. In addition to this, the justice of Chester from then on proceeded to distrain on whatever property of Llewelyn fell into his hands, and as we relied on Chester for much of our buying of necessities, we suddenly found it unsafe to send there to buy in supplies, for as fast as they were paid for they were seized for their value against the sum claimed by Robert of Leicester. The prince suffered diminution of his right by the slight of his court, a challenge to his right of wreck which could never have arisen by Welsh law, and the repeated loss of his purchases, together with danger to his messengers if they attempted to keep them, for the justiciar's men were not gentle.

There were also, of course, those clashes along the border which wise chiefs discouraged, but also took for granted, and paid out the compensation due when just complaints were made against their men. This had always been done on an even footing, each side in conference with the other either admitting or disputing the charges made, until sensible agreement was reached, and each paid its score fairly. But at this time such encroachments were greatly aggravated along the marches of Salop, led by Griffith ap Gwenwynwyn and his sons, and willingly aided by many of the local men, and when Tudor went to the border to meet the sheriff of Salop and make mutual amends for all trespasses then charged, notwithstanding that most of the Welsh offences had already been paid for and the steward was willing to amend those remaining, the sheriff refused to make any such amends on his part unless he should receive direct orders from the king to do so. This again was not only an unjust imbalance, but a breach of treaty, though Llewelyn did not therefore charge it against Edward himself, for we knew only too well that the king's officials were arrogant and exacting beyond their master, and he could not know everything that was going on in all parts of his kingdom.

Thus all these vexed matters stood in the early spring of that year twelve hundred and eighty. In February the prince wrote to the king informing him of the distraints at Chester and the dispute on the Salop border, mindful that after Easter parliament would again assemble at Westminster, and determined to ensure that all his complaints were documented before his envoys must again appear in Edward's court. The king replied in the matter of the goods from the wreck, disclaiming all previous knowledge of the affair, which we could hardly accept, seeing Robert of Leicester had taken out royal letters before ever he could bring suit at Chester. At the coming parliament, said Edward, the prince's attorneys should be able and ready to inform him fully about the case, and he would do right, as was always his will and intent.

'Very heartily,' said Llewelyn, 'we'll do our part, if he'll do his. He shall not be able to say he was not fully informed.' And once again he asked Brother William de

51

Merton to be his special envoy and take all these affairs in his care when parliament met, and armed him with his best legal advisers, and with all manner of attestations from the clergy and friars of Gwynedd to show that the prince's right to have Welsh law in the Arwystli case was irrefutable.

Now it chanced that at this time John Peckham, the new archbishop of Canterbury, who had held office just a year and was full of zeal for the wellbeing of his whole flock, in Wales as in England, was in correspondence with Llewelyn concerning a long-standing dispute between the prince and the bishop of Bangor, which Archbishop Peckham greatly desired to bring to a happier composition. This again was but one of the fruits of the recent war, like so many of our vexations, for by and large the prince had always a warm and affectionate relationship with this Bishop Einion. But the lot of such a bishop, subject to his prince and greatly dependent on his goodwill and protection, but equally subject to Canterbury and the papacy, and through his archbishop very much exposed to the grace or enmity of the king of England, too, was not easy in time of war, and kindly and pious though Einion was, I would not say he was cast in any heroic mould. When he received his archbishop's letters ordering him to promulgate the excommunication of Llewelyn as a rebel against Edward, he had small choice, short of heroism, but to obey and pronounce, and so he did, and thereafter was so uneasy for his safety, I think needlessly, for the prince gave very little thought to him then, that he fled into England until the peace was made. Afterwards he came back to his see, but we found him more than usually prickly and difficult, and doubtless there was some stiffness also on the prince's side, after all that had passed. But I think it was the soreness of his conscience that kept the bishop so long estranged, and made him pick upon every real or imagined slight, or trespass upon the Church's rights, to prop up his self-esteem. Certainly Archbishop

Peckham understood the tribulations and abrasions of trying to balance the privileges of prince and primate, and was well qualified to make peace between the two in Wales, and being an ardent, busy person, was pressing his services upon Llewelyn to that end.

'And indeed I should be glad to be friends with my bishop again,' said Llewelyn. 'He was never so thorny until now, and he has been a good friend in the past. Since the archbishop is well-disposed, why should we not make use of his good offices? I'll write and bid him here into Wales. Who knows but he may help us more ways than one!'

'Don't embroil him in law,' said Eleanor. 'Poor John Peckham has had enough of meddling with my cousin's prerogative there.'

The new primate had indeed suffered a sharp lesson at Edward's hands, for he had come into his high post bursting with reforming zeal as a champion of the Church's pure rights and privileges, and felt strongly that the king was all too rapidly consolidating the crown's hold in fields formerly held to belong to the clergy. In particular, with his frenzy for law, he was infringing, or so Peckham felt, the jurisdiction of the clerical courts. The new archbishop set out to issue a stern warning, with a number of sweeping sentences of excommunication against certain kinds of people who seemed to him to be offending not against morality, but against the supreme rights of the Church. As, for instance, all those who procured letters from lay courts to impede trials he held to belong to courts ecclesiastical, or any officer who flouted the writ requiring him to arrest an excommunicated person. The king had a quick eye for such impertinence, and within two weeks the archbishop was summoned to appear before king and council in parliament, and made to withdraw three of these general sentences on sharp legal grounds, a humiliation he was not likely to forget easily.

'Oh, I'll not drag him into my lawsuits,' the prince

promised, laughing. 'But he's been taking a friendly
interest in Amaury's case, as well he may, being the Holy
Father's deputy in England. If we can get him here in
person, then we can solicit his help for your brother
without fear of being misinterpreted.'

She embraced the idea with delight, for Amaury was the
one cloud upon her happiness. 'Yes, oh, yes, for Amaury
we can entreat his help without trespassing, he is very
much the archbishop's business. If he can win what I've
begged for so often without grace,' she said with ardour,
'I won't grudge it to him that I've been so long denied.
Even if he could prevail on Edward to allow a visitor, that
would be something!'

'That we may ask for at once, and of the king himself,'
said Llewelyn. 'At the worst he can but refuse, and if he
is surprised into giving his consent, so much the better.
And the archbishop we'll reserve until you can work on
him yourself, for if he can refuse you, love, then no other
need try. When Brother William de Merton goes with
my lawyers to attend this Easter parliament, Samson shall
go with them and carry my invitation to the archbishop,
and ask permission of the king to visit Amaury in Corfe.
If the request is made publicly and without warning, it
may be harder to refuse it. And if it is refused, then we'll
enlist the archbishop's help and try yet again.'

So Eleanor joyfully put together a few books which she
thought might be approved without suspicion, and certain
personal gifts for her brother, and also a purse of money
for his use, for Edward was not celebrated for making
generous living allowances to his prisoners, or paying
for much in the way of service for them. And I learned many
messages from her and from Llewelyn, some concerned
with Amaury's own properties and business abroad, more
with her affection and anxiety for him, and the efforts she
had made and would continue to make on his behalf.
And when Master William and his companions set out for
London, I rode with them.

Further south than Westminster I had never been but once, and that was with Earl Simon's army in the days of his glory, when he won his battle at Lewes and gathered England into his hands. Now I rode to his youngest son, four years a prisoner for no crime but being a de Montfort, and drawing to himself, as the only man of his house within reach, all the hatred Edward felt for that whole detested race, all the more black and bitter because once he had worshipped the great earl, more truly than ever in his life he had worshipped any other but himself, or ever in his life was to worship any thereafter.

We arrived in Westminster more than a week before parliament was due to meet, and went in a body to an audience of the king, to present our credentials, and there before a large company of his officers and counsellors I made my request on the prince's behalf. It sounded mild and innocent enough, and came unexpectedly, and I had thought that Edward might give his consent as a matter of policy, since there were several of his lords spiritual present, who knew very well that the pope had expressed impatience and displeasure at Amaury's long detention. But Edward was never to be trapped into making a hasty answer that he might soon regret. He sat erect in his great chair, dark-gowned and sombre and huge, and looked at me impassively across the table, his face austere and still his left eyelid markedly drooping over the large brown eye.

'We take due note of the lord prince's petition,' he said in the most deliberate and reasonable of voices, 'but it should not be addressed to us, and we must be held excused if we cannot answer it. The Lord Amaury de Montfort is not in our keeping, but in that of the lord archbishop of Canterbury.'

And that was all! So simple it was to deny without denying. We were dismissed graciously, and he had done us and our lord no wrong. Yet in some degree, I considered when I thought it over in quietness, he had committed himself to a statement, and before witnesses enough, and

could not withdraw it. He had not said such a visit could
not take place nor that such a request should not have
been made, but only that it should not have been made to
him, for he was the wrong authority. Well, if I was turned
away from one court of appeal, I could spare the time
and the effort to seek out another. I went straightway, and
made enquiry for Archbishop Peckham, but here I met
with another check, for they told me that he was not in
London at that time, but on a tour of the middle shires
making his pastoral visitations, and had last written from
Trentham, in Staffordshire, a week ago.

I was crossing by the infirmary gardens to the stables,
determined not to give up so easily, when I saw among the
people emerging from the gateway of the farmery a large,
bulky, comfortable figure in a black, clerkly gown, pacing
with an easy gait I thought I should know. Indeed, he was
sure of me before I could be sure of him, and came up to
me bountifully and broadly smiling.

'Well, well! Samson it is! I thought I should know that
thrusting walk. What brings you to Westminster again?
It's long since we saw you here.'

'The prince's business, as always,' I said, 'and as always,
you may be very useful to me in carrying it out.'

'I'll walk with you,' said Cynan, 'wherever you're bound,
for it seems you're in more haste than I am.' But he shook
his head when he saw I was leading him towards the
stables. 'Not leaving us again so soon, and I've but just
found you?'

He was not greatly changed in the last few years, except
that he had put on yet more flesh, and his forehead had
grown taller as his black hair receded. Always he was neat
and well-brushed, never a speck of dust on his gown, and
his smooth, pale hands ringed and placidly folded. Cynan
was accomplished and discreet, and had been many years
about the court, but he had never forgotten his Welsh
blood. He was comfortable where he was, and little tempted to throw away his comforts, and after his own fashion

56

he had played fair with his English masters and given them zealous service while they played fair with Wales. But where he considered they were breaking faith and dealing unfairly, he had felt himself free to inform the prince accordingly, whether in peace or war. Many times his own head might have paid for its dual loyalties if luck, as well as skill, had not been on his side.

I told him what my business was in Westminster, and how it was thwarted, and what I had learned concerning the movements of the archbishop. At Peckham's name Cynan grinned hugely at some private glee.

'About his pastoral visitations!' he said fatly. 'So he is, the good, stubborn man. And so he did write a letter to the king just eight days ago, and I saw the look on the royal face after he had read it, and kept well out of his way the rest of the day. Those two are like oil and water, my friend! Peckham writes lovely letters – I know more of them than I should, but I'm in the chancellery now, and moderately close to Burnell's confidence, and there's no great love lost there, either. This is the way of it! The king had forbidden Peckham to include in his visitations the royal free chapels, and Peckham is absolute for his right to visit, and doling out excommunications freely if any try to prevent. Except his Grace, of course! This last letter was a fair example of their exchange. Peckham deprecates his own unworthiness, but insists on the church's rights, and *will* visit, with God as his warrant. They've put every obstacle in his way, even armed men, but go he will. In the last line but one he tells his Grace that God will take vengeance for the wrong done against the Church by his Grace's order. In the last, he prays the blessing of God on his Grace and all those who loyally love him.'

'Do you tell me this,' I asked curiously, 'to warn me off from pursuing this obstinate archbishop into the midlands?'

'Far be it from me!' said Cynan devoutly. 'Rather to assure you of an interested listener, and one with a strong motive for sanctioning what you ask. Did not his Grace

57

himself say it rested with Peckham? So be it, and his Grace must stand by his word. At least try it. And, I tell you what, put it into his mind that should there be any question of your integrity, it may be guaranteed by having a trusted chancellery clerk travel with you. I spoil for exercise here, I grow fat. A few days of country air would do me good.'

So he was always, with his smooth, innocent hand turning men the way he would have them go, and usually laughing, though often behind a demure, unlaughing face.

'After Trentham,' he said, considering, 'he was heading for Lichfield and Stafford. Somewhere there you will find him. Go safely! If I cannot be sowing the seed until your return, at least I'll be cultivating the ground.'

And with that he left me, ambling away in his bland, benevolent fashion through the stable-yard and the gardens towards the southern reach of the Long Ditch, and the outflow into the Thames. And I went to claim my horse, rested and fed and ready for the road, and set out northwards for those midland shires where the archbishop doggedly pursued his right even against arms. And I tell you, my regard for him and my hopes of him were rising together.

I made for Stafford, as Cynan had advised, and was much interested along the road, for I had never seen so much of England alone. At Stafford they directed me on to Eccleshall, where the bishop of Lichfield had a castle, and there at last I found Archbishop Peckham in residence, on Palm Sunday. Between the services of the church I asked for an audience, by no means the only one thus asking, and late in the afternoon I was admitted to his presence.

He was sitting in a round-backed chair at a table in a small, dim room, a man barely of the middle height, and round of body, though not fat. They said he practised great austerity, and recommended it to others, though he did not impose it, and therefore his rotundity must have been by nature, and not at all the fruit of indulgence. I never doubted that if he bore the reputation of abstinence, it was deserved. That man's sins were not of hypocrisy. His face, too, was round and ruddy and candid, shaven very smooth, with an effect of great friendliness and infinite curiosity towards all men, though then he looked tired and vexed and discouraged, as well he might. He measured me, and pondered. His eyes were kindly but harried.

I made my reverence, and first presented him the prince's letter of invitation, telling him how I had enquired for him in London in vain, and therefore made bold to follow him to this place. He thanked me for my errand, and did not then immediately unseal the letter, having other unfinished business, but said that if I would wait he would send for me again in the evening. And at that I begged his indulgence a few minutes longer, and made my prayer for Amaury, telling him as in innocence what the king's answer had been.

'You speak,' he said, 'as one not altogether unmoved by the thought of this prisoner. Perhaps not simply a messenger?'

Feeling myself safest as well as happiest in speaking full truth to this man, I said: 'I have known the prisoner from a boy. I care for him, having so known him, and for the princess, his sister, more, knowing her as a loyal servant may. There is here no design but to comfort all those who grieve apart. Your lordship knows better than I what such severance can mean.'

'I commend your loyalty,' he said. His voice was warm and brisk and very firm, the voice of a kindly, choleric man. 'His Grace did not forbid,' he said thoughtfully.

'No, my lord,' I said. 'He said only that the Lord Amaury is in your charge, not in his, and therefore he could not presume to give or to deny.'

'And you are willing to submit all that you carry to scrutiny by the king's castellan at Corfe?'

'Most willing,' I said. 'And further, my lord, if it be thought wise, I would welcome a witness to the interview, who could report all I may have to say or to hear when I speak with the Lord Amaury. It may be that the chancellery would wish to have such a report, for the sake of us all.'

I saw his eyes gleam at that, and knew that he had taken the point at vantage, for such a presence would not only protect him from possible blame, but involve the chancellor Burnell in the decision, Edward's most trusted officer. According to Cynan, who missed nothing that went on about the court and its offices, the relations between Peckham and Burnell were civil, but watchful and armed, and I think not as a matter of jealousy – for Burnell had been Edward's candidate for the vacant primacy, and warmly urged, and Peckham appointed by the pope in the king's despite – but because those two were of such opposed natures that they could not get on together. Indeed, as it proved later, a great many men, saints among them, found it very hard to live in amity with Peckham, even though the man at his best could get halfway to being a saint himself.

'You deserve,' said the archbishop, 'that your prayer should prosper. You carry no letter of authorisation from your prince?'

I had no such letter of credence, for we had not thought it necessary, but I had my own seal which carried the prince's sanction, and I said that the princess's gifts to her brother were open to inspection if he should require. He said, very kindly, that he himself was perfectly satisfied, but that for the sake of complete openness my suggestion that a clerk should accompany me might be a good one. Then he asked me to wait upon him again in two hours, when he would give me a letter to carry to Corfe, and also whatever was needed in reply to the prince's message. And so I left him.

When he sent for me again it was to present me not one letter but three. He was as instant in appreciation and acknowledgement as he was in complaint and reproof where he thought it due, and it was plain that the prince's

60

invitation, indicating his desire to be reconciled with his bishop, had given the primate pleasure.

'This,' he said, 'I can despatch directly to the lord prince, if you are likely to be absent from him for long. Though I dare say there is no great haste, for the visit cannot take place for a few weeks.'

I said that I would gladly be the bearer, and intended a return to the Welsh court as soon as my errand to Corfe was done.

'Very well,' he said, 'I entrust my answer to you. This second letter you will take to the chancellery on your way through London, and wait to know if the chancellor wishes to send a witness with you, as I have suggested to him. And this third you will deliver to John de Somerset, who keeps Corfe castle for his Grace. I have recommended the bearer to him, and myself given approval to the visit, but he is still the person responsible for the prisoner's safe-keeping, and you will observe any conditions he imposes, and accept his veto should he feel unable to admit you.' But his manner said that, however his recommendation was worded, it would hardly be for the castellan of Corfe to overturn the arrangements Archbishop Peckham had approved. And very devoutly I thanked him, made all my precious missives secure in my saddle-bags, and set off on the long ride south again to Westminster.

I presented my letter at the chancellery as soon as I arrived, and was not surprised at being told to come back next day. No doubt the matter would have to be referred to Burnell himself, but I did not see him on this occasion. He was a busy man at all times, and the preparations for parliament kept him occupied. When I returned to the same small, dark office next day, the official who had my business in hand was writing busily, and gave me but the edge of his attention.

'Ah, yes!' he said. 'You are the envoy who wishes to speak with the Lord Amaury. The chancellor has agreed to the provisions suggested by the archbishop, and you already have his letter to de Somerset.' He rang the hand-bell he had on his table, and in a few minutes Cynan came in, large and dignified and demure, and stood eyeing me steadily while he waited for his orders, like one measuring a new acquaintance with whom he is to spend a few days of his time. 'Master Cynan will accompany you,' said the officer, returning to his writing. 'I see you understand English well enough, but should you need it, he speaks Welsh. If your errand is honest, he'll be of assistance to you.'

'Unquestionably he will,' said Cynan, as we went together out of the chancellery. 'No need to look over your shoulder on this journey, no one will be following or watching you, that is my business. No need even to guard your tongue. I've had long experience in rendering reports acceptable from very unpromising first drafts.'

I asked how he had contrived the matter as he wanted it, and how, indeed, he came to be advanced so far into Burnell's confidence as to be in a position to know of all that went on.

'Oh, it's policy to select Welshmen for advancement now,' he said, 'wherever it can be done with safety. See how many of us the king is employing about his private business, and into Welsh lands especially. The best of his advisers have told him plainly that it takes a Welshman to rule Welshmen, and if suitable Welshmen run short, a seasoned, hard-headed marcher is to be preferred to some imported baron from Essex or Kent. There's good sense in that, if his Welsh bailiffs were not compelled to enforce English law, and answerable to English masters. Oh, Edward means to hold on to what he has gained, and tie it down by every manner of chain he can devise, but he would like to keep a measure of goodwill where he can.'

I said that from what I could hear he was having very little success, for the Middle Country was seething with complaints against his officers and their arbitrary ways.

62

In choosing his Welshmen he was all too given to preferring renegades to the honest men.

'True,' said Cynan, 'and doubly foolish, for the honest men resent them for turning their coats, and the renegades set out to be doubly zealous, to prove their new loyalty to the king, and make themselves even worse hated. I will say for the chancellor that he knows how to pick his men – and I should know, being one of them. But kings are expected to reward service, and the renegades look to be paid their price. How did I get my way? It was no great trick. I took care to put myself markedly into Burnell's notice yesterday, when you brought the archbishop's letter, and hinted that knowledge of Welsh might be an asset, from every view. I think he would be glad to have de Montfort freed and sent back to Rome, for his part. The young man is a stumbling-block to bishops.'

The next day we rode together from London, with a pale, bright sun rising, and had very pleasant travel on our way south to Guildford and Winchester, and so southward and westward still into the high heath of the Purbeck hills, where in a cleft of the downs Corfe castle rises on its high mound, a very formidable stronghold. We had much to talk about on the way, for he would know how his young nephew Morgan did, who had come to lend one more right arm when we were at war, forsaking his service under the crown, and was now well established in Llewelyn's body-guard. And I was greedy for all he could tell me of those manipulations of law which plagued us, and how far they were honest, if infuriating to us, and how far calculated to serve some darker purpose. Cynan owned he was himself in doubt. Of the king's zeal for codifying and reforming there could be no question, but where a passion for order ended and a lively and unscrupulous self-interest began was a matter hard to determine.

'His father,' said Cynan thoughtfully, 'had a gift for turning everything to his own account in conscious virtue, and convincing himself into the bargain, and there's more of his father in Edward than most men think for. I would not say but his law may prove every bit as pliable as his use of words.' And he stroked his full, smooth chops, and pondered. 'I tell you this,' he said, 'the more it may seem to your prince that his Grace is pushing him to the limit of his endurance, the more stubbornly he should endure. For whether it has yet entered Edward's head to *drive* him to revolt or not, very surely it would occur to him to make the utmost use of the first act of rebellion. I will not say he wants it, seeing he's hard to read, but I will say if it came he would welcome it. It's all he needs by way of excuse and opportunity, to finish what he could but half-do last time.'

I said he need have no fear where Llewelyn was concerned for he was well aware of the danger of allowing himself to be provoked, and was resolved to fight only with the legitimate weapons of law, which were not forbidden to him. This in addition to what bound him more than caution, his seal upon the treaty of Conway.

'I know, I know,' said Cynan, sighing. 'God knows no man has the right to question the prince's patience. But every man has his breaking-point. Bear it in mind, at least. Bear it in mind!'

At Corfe we wound our way up to the castle gatehouse, and I presented my letter for John de Somerset. The castellan kept us waiting some while for his decision, but the archbishop's consent and the chancellor's vicarious presence, to say nothing of Cynan's impressive person in itself, made up his mind for him at last. Once admittance was gained, Cynan improved the occasion and his own image by laying claim to more than the hour's visit at first ordained, and hinting plainly that no other attendance was required, since he alone bore the chancellor's charge to hear what passed and render account of it. So after some delay we were brought into the tower room where Amaury spent his solitary days, and there shut in with him.

A very lofty room it was, far too high for hope of escape, even if ropes would have brought the captive down to better ground than the inmost ward, with many more walls between him and freedom. He was immured here almost within sight of the sea, with the soaring air of the Purbeck hills, open and heather-tinted, and cloud-shadowed, for ever outspread to view from his narrow window, and for ever out of reach. That added a dimension to his grievance, as though hell had been lifted and propped on high above paradise, to refine the torments of the damned with the constant vision of bliss. But for the rest, once the eyes could leave that outer radiance and look round within, he was lodged in decent comfort, and with many refinements, though of little worth to him, no doubt, after four years.

It was a square stone room, not great, but with hangings on the walls and rugs on the floor, and a small brazier burning red in the centre over a great flat stone. There was a round table and two cushioned chairs, and a high-built bed against one wall, and a chest for his linen and gowns, better provision than many had in Edward's hold, but no fair price for the wrong done him. And as soon as he rose from his chair and dropped his quill beside his half-written parchment, turning to face us, I saw that he had not changed at all, nor ceased to keep due account of all his wrongs, and his father's wrongs, and the wrongs of his brothers dead and his one brother living, and the wrongs of his sister, whom he loved, alone of all human creatures, almost as well as he loved Amaury de Montfort.

This youngest son of Earl Simon was not greatly like his brothers, had not their broad, brown nobility, the eyes wide-open and wide-set, the large, candid gaze. The great forehead, that he had, and the mind within was a match for any, but he was made in a leaner, hungrier mould, and darker-coloured, his face gaunt, his eyes deep-set, black and brilliant, quick to anger and to scorn. Unjust confinement had made him burn still blacker and more bitterly, but taught him to contain his rage and wait for the hour when it could be loosed to better effect. He looked at us without welcome, as though we had interrupted him in the composition of important work. Then he knew me, and for an instant bright golden sparks flared in his eyes. I saw him cast one glance at Cynan, and douse the betraying flames. Cynan saw it, too, and smiled.

'They told me,' said Amaury, 'that I had a permitted visit. I appreciate the courtesy to a prisoner, but you must forgive me if I am slow to understand. They told me nothing more.'

'Be easy,' said Cynan comfortably, 'for Samson knows me as well as you know him, and there's no need here for discretion. Keep your voices low, if you will, though I think there's nothing to be feared.' His own voice was soft but serene. He plucked up the stool that stood by the bed, and set it down against the door, and there he took his seat, his ear inclined to the latch. 'What enters my left ear, within here, goes out at my right,' he said, 'but never a word unchecked from my mouth, I promise you. And whatever my right ear picks up from without, you shall hear of.'

'You are Peckham's man?' said Amaury curiously, for he had expected no such usage. 'You are not likely to hear me slander him, he has been kind after his fashion. And I have learned to save my curses, they are wasted in this solitude.'

'Burnell owns my time and labour,' said Cynan, hoisting the collar of his gown against the draught from the door, 'but he has not bought my blood, nor tried to, to do him justice. You may forget I am here, unless some overzealous warder creeps about the passage outside.' He closed his eyes. 'Use your time,' he said.

So Amaury and I sat down together, he still silent and wary for a while, but coming gradually to life, and finding the tongue that had been stilled for want of company through most of his days and all his nights. 'Samson!' he said, tasting a known name, and drew long breaths. 'This is better than I looked for. Afterwards I shall miss it more. For God's sake, talk to me of my sister. I am starved of news and of voices. You may croak, and you will still be music to me.'

I delivered him the gown and the gifts she had sent him, and the purse, the books being detained for examination before he could be allowed them, and he took and handled all slowly and long, for pleasure that they came from her. 'I have little need of this,' he said fingering the purse, 'for I am not stinted, at least, nor cold, nor threadbare as yet, but I take it gladly for her sake, and will use it when I may. Has my cousin relented towards me so far? It has taken long enough. It must be at her entreaty. I could loathe him less if I could believe he has a real kindness for her.'

I told him we had to thank Archbishop Peckham, though Eleanor had asked and asked times without number, and still continued her entreaties whenever she could get a hearing. And I told him how the archbishop was to visit Wales after the present parliament, and there was hope, at least, of persuading him to use his influence still further, for which reason this visit must pass without arousing the least regret or suspicion in the king's mind.

'Oh, report me tamed, submissive and resigned!' said Amaury, with a short, hard laugh that proved him none of these things, but was nevertheless live laughter, however sour its note. There was colour burning his lean cheek-bones, and a spark in his eyes. I doubted I had sounded too hopeful, and led him to a peak from which he must fall with some pain, and yet he was not the man to believe easily in any good fortune, after all this while. 'Say I pray constantly for Edward's Grace – so I do, that he may meet his favourite, Justice, brow to brow, and get his deserts in full. Your witness beholds me, meek as a lamb and obedient to the king's will. It will give him pleasure to believe that even a de Montfort may be chastened.'

There was so much bitterness in him that it filled the

67

veins of his spirit like blood. But at least prison had not dulled his brain, nor rotted his body, nor in any way unfitted him to bear a masterly part among other men, if ever he could get free. His person was princely rather than clerical, and he was but thirty-two years old, with a life before him. Only Edward stood in his way. And what could I promise him, but that Eleanor and the prince would never cease their efforts for him until he was set at liberty?

'That I never doubted,' he said, 'of her at least. She was always loyal, and never could rest while any of her acquaintances were abused or cheated. I doubt if I deserved her fondness, but that I came from the same sire. He had but one daughter after his five sons, but she is his best imprint and his nearest match.'

Whatever else this difficult man failed and fell short in, for his sister he had a deep and constant reverence and affection, and for that alone, even if I had not felt and sometime shared his manifest wrongs, I keep for him a kindness owing nothing to his merit or mine.

So I spoke of her, seeing it was the best gift I could give him, who could not give him any assurance of liberty. I told him how she lived among us prized and worshipped, what delight she took in her new country, and how it fitted with her spirit and welcomed her into its heart, and how his injuries were the only thing that marred her immense happiness. For in Gwynedd nothing fell short of her hopes, but rather exceeded them, and her married joy was excelling.

'She will bear him princes,' said Amaury, and in his tone I read all his thirsty hopes that her sons would take back from Edward all that Edward had taken from their father, all that Edward had taken from their grandfather, who had been Edward's paragon and then Edward's antichrist. I said that was also Llewelyn's hope, for which he would die gladly if he could not achieve it living, and that both Eleanor and Llewelyn waited without impatience upon God's will and God's time to grant them children.

'You comfort me!' said Amaury, and I knew he was foreseeing, whether he fully believed in it or not, rather Edward's loss and chagrin than Llewelyn's triumph. For he had never met this brother on whom so much depended for his fitting vengeance. But Edward he knew, and with all his being hated. 'I would I could have met him face to face, my Welsh kinsman,' he said, and when I would have protested that so he surely would, he met my eyes and laughed and I was mute. 'Oh, no,' said Amaury, 'if ever Edward finds it expedient to let me out of his cage, it will be to hurry me overseas, not to turn me loose to roam in Wales. He will never feel safe while there's a male of my race at liberty in his realm.'

It was no more than truth, however hard to believe that a monarch so unshakably fixed on his throne should still fear the very name of de Montfort, fifteen years after the threat of its power had passed from England, and even in the person of a young cleric who had been only a child when the old conflict ended.

'Though I grant him his grudge against Guy,' said Amaury ruefully, and asked after news of his one remaining elder brother, that unfortunate and misguided Guy de Montfort who had murdered the king's cousin, Henry of Almain, at Viterbo, and kindled again a hatred that might have died naturally but for his act. He had paid heavily for a deed done in bitter passion, being shut up in an Italian prison, excommunicate, deprived of all lands and offices and even the common human rights other men enjoyed, for many years, notwithstanding there were many influential men about Europe, kinsmen and friends, who felt sympathy for him, and from time to time tried to procure some relief for him. At this time he was already absolved from excommunication, but landless and rightless still, but there were rumours in Paris, so we had heard, that he had escaped from his prison in Lecco and was in hiding somewhere, probably under the unacknowledged

69

protection of his former lord, the king of Sicily, who had every reason to hope that a most able general and governor might some day be reinstated in the Church's grace, and could be used again in office. The French de Montforts, for all their high favour with King Philip and the pope, had pleaded in vain for his restoration.

'Who knows?' said Amaury with a sour smile. 'Guy may be a free man again before I am, and I have slaughtered nobody. Though I will not say I have never thought of it, nor that it might not have been a satisfaction.' And he plied me with many more questions about his family, and charged me with many commissions to Eleanor, who was concerned about his lands and affairs while he was captive, and had supplied me with a list of matters on which she wished to know his will. His replies I committed to memory. It seemed that the very act of recalling his lands and offices and asserting his will concerning them was refreshment to him, as exercise is to the body. So in the end we left him cheered and revived when our time ran out.

Cynan signed to us when he heard footsteps in the stone passage, and the heavy jangle of keys at the lock. He rose and put the stool back in its place, and was standing at my elbow when the king's castellan came in to tell us that the visit must end. Before these witnesses Amaury arose with me, darkly composed and again bitterly grave, and took leave of me with his thanks, and his loving greetings to those who had sent me.

The last thing he said to me, as we left him, was: 'Say to my little sister that my prayers and my blessings are always with her. For I do not think I shall see her again in this world.'

And though I knew that he meant only, as he had before said, that Edward would never release him but to hustle him out of Britain, yet the words stayed with me long after the door had closed between us, and hung heavy on my heart all the way back to London, as though he had prophesied a death.

CHAPTER III

By the time we came back to Westminster I had somewhat put by the chill of Amaury's farewell, and on the
whole was fairly content with my own errand, for the
prisoner surely could not be held for ever, when pope after
pope had complained of his detention, and many friends
whose loyalty Edward could not doubt had advised and
urged his release. When we reached London I was anxious,
rather, to hear how the delegation to parliament had fared,
and made haste, as soon as I had parted from Cynan, who
had his own report to render to the chancellor, to hunt
out Master William's clerk, Adam, and hear what he
had to say.

'Whatever else it may be,' he said, 'it is certainly delay,
and no period put to it this time. There was a very full
session yesterday, after Brother William de Merton had
had several interviews with the king in council, and all the
attestations we brought with us had been studied, or at
least handled and looked at, for hang me if I know whether
any man paid attention to them, or whether the answer
we got was already determined on long since. All the
written word we have to take back with us is a brief letter
to the effect that his Grace has presided in parliament to
consider the Welsh articles, that a decision was reached
with general agreement, and we are to report it fully to
the prince by word of mouth. Not a word more, except,
no doubt, a pious ending about his Grace's tireless endeavours to do the prince all possible justice! And the
devil of it is, it may still be true! A more earnest and

benevolent face you never saw. But his eyelid was more than usually heavy, over the eye he sometimes chooses to blindfold from spying on his own proceedings.'

'But what was it he had to say?' I asked, for Adam was apt to run on when he was aggrieved, and there was enough of the lawyer in him to come to the point only after many circlings. 'What is this decision reached with general agreement?'

'Why, the king began with an avowal that his intent is to observe the treaty in all points – as far as the royal majesty and duty allow. Mark that, it's the text and no mere rider. For he went on to say that not by that nor by any other treaty could he, even if he wished, surrender any prerogative or liberty handed down to him by his forebear kings of England as free custom in time of peace. So his treaty clause becomes: "according to the laws and customs of those parts in which the disputed lands lie, *and according to the manner of procedure observed by his forebear kings in similar case*". It says but the half of that, but according to the king it means the whole. Oh, he quite accepts, he says, that the Welsh should have their own laws – such as are just and reasonable and don't infringe the rights of the crown. Such he'll keep faithfully. But he has no right and no power to do anything that derogates the rights of the crown or the kingdom of England, for these belong not merely to him, but to the kings who'll come after him. A sacred trust! So if any Welsh laws and customs seem to him unjust or bad or senseless, then his regal dignity will not allow him to countenance them, for he took a solemn coronation oath to root out all such from his kingdom, and no later oath or agreement can possibly relieve him of that sacred vow. But all our Welsh ways that don't offend, those he'll keep faithfully – so far as they're in harmony with justice. Make what you can of so many words, what I make of them is that he alone is to be the judge of what is good and what is bad, and can bless or discard Welsh law exactly as it suits him, without appeal.

And holding up his coronation vow as a shield! The words of the treaty are all subject to an unwritten saving clause – "saving always my royal interests".'

It might have been David speaking, but that David would have been in a piercing, princely rage, and Adam worded with the sour humour lawyers acquire from long experience of justice and injustice dressed alike and indistinguishable.

'At the end of it all,' I said, 'he must have declared *some* intent. What follows now?'

'Why, he intends to send a commission into the Welsh lands and the marches, to enquire into exactly what are the laws and customs of those regions, by taking evidence on the spot. And also to cause the rolls of his own reign and the reigns of his predecessors to be searched for precedents that may be applied to this case. Though God knows they'll find none, for there are none. And when he has all the evidence from both enquiries before him, then he'll accept their findings and do justice!'

'And when,' I said, 'is this commission to begin its work?' Though I knew already that this detail had been omitted. For I was becoming by degrees as black a cynic as Adam or David.

'Ah, that is not yet stated! From parliament to parliament can be half a year. From the announcement of intent to the sittings of this enquiry can be stretched as far as Edward pleases!' said Adam. 'And that is all we have to take back with us to the prince. But I tell you this,' said Adam, suddenly both graver and brighter than throughout this exposition, 'if he has not yet found a legal way of flatly refusing us Welsh law, but only delaying it, in my eyes that's a sign that in the end he has no way out but delay, for he knows he cannot, without showing as rogue and contemptible, declare Arwystli to be English or march land. If he could find against us he would have done it long ago. All he can do, with any appearance of decency, is fend us off with pious pretexts. And all we have to do,

73

to win in the end or force his hand to plain roguery, i
outlast him in patience.'

It was a good, sound legal thought, and went with m
gratefully all that day. But also it put it into my mind tha
there had already been one such enquiry, taken in the yea
of Llewelyn's marriage, that inquisition of which Davic
had spoken, held by Reginald de Grey and the king'
clerk, William Hamilton. Its findings had never been mad
public. Because, said David, they must have proved simply
that to Welsh lands Welsh law applied, and no other dic
or ever had.

So I sought out Cynan again before we rode, the next
morning, and asked him, if he might without risk tc
himself, to probe into the treasury records and discover
what Grey's commission had reported, and send me word
in simple code whether the verdict they gave was white,
that being Welsh, or black, or some shade of grey between.
It could neither hasten nor influence this new inquisition,
but it could provide us with good armaments, if David's
suspicion proved true, against any slanted verdict Edward
might produce from his latest device.

'Grey is a solid English baron, and true to Edward as
any man in England,' said Cynan, 'but an honest man for
all that, no liar. Hamilton – well, he's a crown clerk, a
king's man. But if this enquiry was taken when you say,
then he had no cause to believe his brief was other than
it seemed. The treaty was new, the sides had not hardened,
the arguments were legal, not partisan. None of the
manipulators had yet got his bearings. I suspect people
told truth, and truth was written down. Yes, I will get you
these findings, these crossbow quarrels, if I can. But be
careful,' said Cynan, 'how you shoot them! There may be
fat, comfortable, cowardly men like me between you and
your target!'

I had hoped that we might return to Wales by way of
Denbigh, but it did not happen so, for Llewelyn had sent

74

word that we should join him in Carnarvon, and thither we rode by the nearest and most convenient way, and for that while I had neither sight of Cristin nor speech with David, to tell him what I had asked of Cynan.

Brother William de Merton reported to the prince all that had been said and done in Westminster, and more sourly, what had been said over and over while nothing was done. And I, more happily, gave him the archbishop's letter, heartily accepting his invitation and promising to come to Wales in June, and went on to render a full account of the conditions under which Amaury was held at Corfe, and all the messages he had sent by me, and the wishes he had expressed with regard to his lands and benefices, and his cousins in France.

Eleanor took great comfort from all I had to tell, and found pleasure in writing his greetings and his commissions to John de Montfort in Montfort l'Amaury, happy to have something positive to do for her brother, and encouraged to believe that with Archbishop Peckham's help more might yet be achieved.

I told them, also, of the undertaking Cynan had given me, to try to discover what report had been lodged and carefully forgotten in the treasury, after Grey's commission of two years earlier.

'That was well thought of,' said Llewelyn. 'Provided he does not expose himself to suspicion with his probing! Even to have those parchments in my hands, I would not put Cynan's life in danger.'

He had swallowed Brother William's faithful recital of Edward's declaration in parliament with a wry face and a burst of exasperated anger, but certainly without much surprise.

'He'll run out of the means of delay in the end,' he said, grimly recovering himself, 'and however he may wish to keep me penned into my present bounds, and have Arwystli held by a time-server deep in his debt, I fail to see how he can possibly deny me Welsh law in the end. He winds about the clear words of the treaty with so many more, and so obscure and devious, as to hide their meaning utterly, but he cannot change what he agreed, and I still do not believe he is prepared to go so far as to break his oath and dishonour his seal, when all his subterfuges are exhausted. I have only to counter every move he tries, and wait out every delay. I am skilled at waiting. I have studied the art for years.'

Sometimes the princess came to my little copying-room to try over music with me, for that was one of the ways she had of making unexpected gifts to Llewelyn, all the more if he was weary, or vexed. And then she would talk freely, as once when I was in her captive household at Windsor, and the only servant she had there who knew the land to which her heart inclined, and the lord she longed to reach. So I had entered once and for all into her confidence, and that lady was gifted for friendship as she was for love.

Thus she came to me on a June night, shortly before Archbishop Peckham was expected among us, and after we had tried over the song she was perfecting, she with voice and lute, I with the crwth, she sat considering our performance and nursing her instrument like a loved child, and then she smiled, and said: 'I have become a maker of love-songs. That is his doing.' A moment she was silent, then she said: 'Samson, if my cousin held an enquiry only two years ago into the manner of pleading for barons of Wales in Welsh and marcher-land cases, why does he need to set up another one now?'

I said honestly: 'Not for anything it can uncover, only for the time it will take enquiring.'

'So I thought you would say,' said Eleanor, and smiled. 'And so says Llewelyn, and can even laugh, and own that sometimes he has not been above prevarication himself, when an immediate reply was inconvenient. But whether it is that I have an uncommonly black view of humankind, or whether I know my cousin too well for comfort, I see

76

more in this new move than a simple means to delay. I think he needs a new commission because the first one did not provide him the answers he wanted, and this time he must and will take all the necessary steps to ensure that this one shall. There'll be a carefully selected bench, well-chosen witnesses, sessions will be held in the places most likely to be favourable to the king's wants, and the questions asked will be drafted to draw the right responses. I think, Samson, we should be well advised to be thinking out, and drawing up, a schedule of questions of our own, to supplement Edward's. Will his judges, for instance, ask whether there are in Arwystli duly appointed Welsh judges, properly authorised to administer Welsh law there, and exercising those duties regularly? I doubt it! But there are, and if Welsh law did not apply there, those judges would never have been placed in office, they would not be needed, and they would have no authority. I think,' she said, stroking the strings of her lute with a small, wry smile, 'we could be of the greatest assistance to his Grace in the matter of drafting apt and useful interrogatories. We might put them in as a petition from the prince, out of pure good-will to be helpful.'

Enlightened and astonished, I said that she was like to prove the best lawyer we had among us, and that it should be done – out of pure goodwill!

'In the meantime,' she said ruefully, 'we have not even a date for the commencement, and be sure he will give his men as long as possible before they must report their findings. Let's use the time to enlist Archbishop Peckham's good offices. We'll both urge his help for Amaury, and if Llewelyn is too proud to plead his own cause, well, I am too proud not to.'

So quietly we made ready those pertinent matters that could with best effect be forced upon the commission's notice, and waited for the archbishop to come. It was the second week in June when he rode into Carnarvon, sparsely attended, and for such a prelate with very moderate ceremony, so that at first we thought him personally modest and austere, while in fact he was neither, except in his appetites. Pride he had, and proper respect he would exact to the last grain, but it was not expressed in haughtiness on his part, or demanded as servility from others.

Friendly and inquisitive I had thought him, and so he was, and well-intentioned towards everyone, but for all that his kindly, sharp eyes could be steely and censorious if any resisted or differed from him, and his smiling, benevolent mouth was tight and obstinate in repose. The most diverse opinions were held of him. Some said he was a true saint, doing his best to follow his Saviour's commandments and tireless in his efforts for those who appealed to him in distress. Others that he would give and serve lavishly such as flattered and grovelled to him, and as readily out with bell, book and candle against all who dared to contradict him. Some revered him as a strong and able administrator and defender of clerical rights, others called him a meddlesome busybody who could not keep his fingers out of anyone's business. Some averred his compassion and sympathy were wide enough to encompass all who came, others said he was prone to favourites, and so narrow that his maledictions were more frequent than his blessings. Some thought he had a gift of delicate understanding which the ungodly could not appreciate, others said wrathfully that the man trampled in heavy-footed where angels themselves would have walked softly. And it can be said of Archbishop Peckham that almost everything ever said of him was true.

He was of limitless energy, quick and agile in movement, and blew through the corridors of Carnarvon like a brisk wind. In the saddle he looked like a sack of Aberconway wool, but he rode fast and daringly for all that, enjoyed hunting, when he had leisure for it, and here he was removed from his pastoral cares for a while, and Llewelyn saw to it that he had good sport. At the high table in hall he was inclined to turn the talk into one long, benevolent homily, but benevolent it was, and we took it as it was meant. Indeed he made a very good impression, and if his well-meant interference in all manner of things not directly his province was sometimes maladroit, yet everyone accepted it with good humour for its evident kindliness. I have heard that others found him harder to bear, and he was always shocked and hurt at the resentment he could arouse at his worst, hurt as children are hurt when they have made an innocent advance and been rebuffed. We took care not to ruffle him, and not all because we had hopes of his aid. Both prince and princess liked him well.

In his handling of Bishop Einion he must have been more adroit than usual, and doubtless it was flattering to have the archbishop of Canterbury busily trotting back and forth with soothing words. Also I think Einion in his heart wanted to be reconciled, and was glad to have the excuse of his clear pastoral duty to heed his primate's counsel. For though it took several visits to bring him to terms, he did gradually yield to persuasion, and agreed to compromise on some of the thorny issues that most vexed him, where the rights of church and crown clashed. Llewelyn in turn took conciliatory steps to meet him, and the archbishop, delighted with his success, brought them to sit down together in peace before he left us, and gave his blessing to the accommodation he had helped them to reach.

He was much interested, while he stayed with us, in Llewelyn's hounds, a strain which the prince himself bred and trained, and as Llewelyn then had a litter of three couple almost ready for the chase, he promised to send them as a gift to the archbishop as soon as their training should be complete. And in the most friendly fashion the primate parted from us, and was escorted by most of the court for the first few miles of his journey home.

'He has promised to continue his efforts for Amaury,' said Eleanor, after he was gone, 'and I am sure he will not fail of his promise, for he says the case is to come up in the October parliament. I shall write to Edward and add my own plea. And he seems truly to have some feeling for Llewelyn's cause, and some understanding of his complaints. *My* complaints,' she said, and smiled, 'for the prince made none to his guest, but I was not so delicate. The archbishop says he will speak up for us with Edward, and I believe him.'

So, too, did I believe him. For with all the things that were said and were all of them true concerning Archbishop Peckham, one thing I never heard any man say of him. Obstinate, bigoted, crass, often misguided he might be, but he did not lie, and he was never false.

Llewelyn had not, until then, made any reply to Edward's declaration in parliament. Now he did so, with biting gentleness setting down his pleasure that king and council in assembly had emphasised their wish to keep the treaty of Aberconway in every particular, and to do him right. Then drily he had me list all the particulars in which they did him wrong.

'Surely three years,' he wrote, 'should be long enough to settle one simple article, which the very wording of the treaty shows can and should be settled without delay or difficulty, given the will. Unless, by any chance, I have enemies whose interest and design it is to prevent such a consummation?'

The affair of Robert of Leicester he also appended, for though the king had assured Brother William de Merton that he would order the justiciar of Chester to cease all distraints on Robert's behalf against the prince's goods, nevertheless a further seizure had been made. At which the prince professed a surprise he hardly felt, though he avowed his inability to believe that the current distraint was made with the king's knowledge, and prayed him to reinforce his order to let be.

'I grow as fluent a liar as Edward,' he said, grimacing at the end of this letter. 'We are so far apart,' he said, suddenly grieving, 'and I have a principality to guard and cherish as well as he, and how can I go hunting after him where he goes, to pluck him by the arm and make him face me man to man? When I was in his company, for all his hardness I understood him, and for all his might, I was his peer and we spoke as peers. Now at this distance I have lost him, and I feel that loss.'

The letters flew back and forth that summer, for Llewelyn had many things to complain of, and Edward seemed to feel some guilty need to justify himself. But the first letter that came, soon after the foregoing was despatched to London, was from Archbishop Peckham, sending hearty thanks for his hounds, and for his entertainment in Wales, and that was cheering and helped to balance Edward's long and verbose epistle from Langley, which arrived a week later, again earnestly avowing his good intent to keep the terms of the treaty, but insisting that those terms were not completely clear, and that he must preserve his royal prerogative and do, in this matter, whatever had been customary in similar case in the days of his predecessors. Together with much piety concerning his duty to consult the prelates and magnates of his realm, a course to which Llewelyn should not take exception, since no one could suppose such grave and wise men would give their lord bad advice.

'Since he will have given them the advice first,' said Llewelyn, between amusement and despair, 'from his point of view that may very well be true.'

In other matters the king was more accommodating, and said that he had ordered the justiciar of Chester to restore the goods recently seized, and to instruct Robert of Leicester to take his case, if he wished to pursue it, to the prince's court, where it belonged, and not to trouble the royal courts again unless he alleged he was denied justice at the prince's.

'I am heartily tired of law,' said Llewelyn in a great sigh. 'I was not cut out for a litigant.'

And still the king had not so much as appointed the members of his commission. Llewelyn could not even hasten to discharge the labours that disgusted him, and be rid of them. Still he must wait, and even the stoutest heart can be eaten hollow by too much waiting.

In middle August came another letter from the archbishop, long and circumstantial. The prince opened it with curiosity, for he had expected none just then, but read it with disbelief and consternation. Then he called in Master William to view its terms with him, for every sentence rang like an echo of Edward's utterance in parliament. But here that pious apologia was underlined and reinforced by even stronger reservations. In one respect only it showed finer than its example, it spoke in far plainer terms.

Almost word for word the archbishop repeated that the phrase in the treaty to which we attached so much importance, 'according to the laws and customs of those parts where the lands lie', could not be understood otherwise than as meaning the laws and customs by which kings of England had been used to rule those parts in the past, and determine causes arising there. Its sanction could apply only to such laws and customs as were just and reasonable, since the king by his coronation oath was bound to banish from his realm all that were unjust and unreasonable. And here the archbishop went even further than Edward had gone, for he launched out into a long denunciation of certain of our Welsh laws as being against right and against religion. Cases of homicide, which we distinguished from murder, were dealt with in Wales by enforced arbitration to bring the parties to peace, and make reparation for the wrong done, instead of proceeding to summary judgment. God knows we thought this better and more Christian than ploughing ahead to still more killing, but plainly Peckham felt otherwise. However, his main theme was that the king's coronation oath was inviolable, and no subsequent oath such as the sealing of a treaty could

82

make it void. And he made a great virtue of having interceded for us as he had promised, and procured for him
the concession – compromise, I believe, was the word
used – that such Welsh laws as were just and reasonable
should be maintained, to which plea the king had graciously assented. Thus the archbishop laboured to obtain
justice for us!

'This,' said Llewelyn, stunned, 'this we must look upon
as a concession? Do words no longer mean anything but
what Edward decrees they shall mean? And am I to believe
that this man shut his eyes and ears while he was here with
us, and understood nothing? Or has Edward so worked
on him since, that he is no more than an echo of his master?
No, for he goes beyond Edward! He is prompting Edward
to tighten the noose! If it rests with him the laws of Howel
the Good will be wiped out wherever the royal writ runs.
Thank God it does not yet run in Gwynedd!'

Both Master William and Tudor spoke out in even
stronger terms about this juggling with words, which was
as little convincing when it came from Peckham by letter
as when Edward pronounced it solemnly in parliament.
Either the words 'according to the laws and customs of
those parts where the lands lie' meant what they said, or
no words could be held, with any certainty, to mean anything at all, for all were subject to manipulation at the
king's will. Nor did the portion of law to which they
applied come within any possible body of jurisprudence
offensive to even the most censorious mind. Peckham
might object to certain points in our criminal procedure
as much as he would, but this was a straightforward
matter of rival claims to land, and of the formula by which
those claims should be judged. At best the archbishop's
partisan declaration was irrelevant. At worst it must be
dishonest.

'No!' said Eleanor. 'I cannot think he ever set out to
deceive. Even if he did not truly abhor falsity, as I believe
he does, he is too sure of his own rightness, too confident

83

all men must agree with him, to be able to dissemble. Too vain, if you will! No, he meant what he said here among us, he has tried to speak up for our case, and believes he has done us service. And he means what he has written now. He has gone back full of zeal to study this law of Wales, and found too many points where it offends his religious rigour.'

'Helped, no doubt, by Edward and all his men of law,' said Llewelyn grimly. 'I remember very well the terms in which the king spoke at his Easter parliament, as Brother William reported them. You hear the echoes here! Word for word the same, until he goes beyond even Edward.'

'Yes,' she said, 'I don't deny it. But nowhere has he said that the Welsh way offends where land is disputed. No, truly I believe this is an honest man. He may set his face against Welsh law on certain points, but he will not stand by and see you wronged and deprived where he finds no fault with Welsh law. Even if we must feel that we have an enemy in him, I believe it will be an honourable enemy.'

'I should find it easier to think so,' said the prince, 'if he had not taken up so wholeheartedly the most specious plea of all – that these few words to which Edward voluntarily set his seal may not mean what they plainly say, because Edward's coronation oath *may* not be compatible with them. Had he quite forgotten the words of his coronation oath when he set his seal to the treaty? Should it not have been clear to him then whether there might ever be conflict? Whether he ought not to put in some saving clause to cover his duty to his realm? Can you believe that Edward ever worded anything without weighing every letter before he passed and sealed it?'

'I did not say,' she said ruefully, 'that Edward need always be an honourable enemy. I spoke only of the archbishop.'

'I am not sure, love,' said Llewelyn, reluctantly laughing, 'that you are paying Archbishop Peckham much of a compliment. If he is no rogue, then he has swallowed the ing's twisted arguments whole, and taken them for honest, and I doubt that makes him a fool. I am not sure which I would rather deal with. Certainly if this is an earnest of his friendship, as he preens himself, it might be better to have him for an enemy.'

'All we can do,' she said stoutly, 'is to go on putting him to the test. Judge him by his fruits!'

'So we will,' said Llewelyn, and smiled at her. 'So we must.'

And at that it stayed, though even she was more saddened than ever she owned. But she would not either lose faith and let hope go by default, nor condemn a man before his deceit was proved beyond doubt.

It was not until the fourth day of December of that year, when we were once again preparing for the Christmas feast, that Edward at last appointed his three commissioners, the bishop of St David's, who was keeper of the king's wardrobe, Reginald de Grey, and Walter de Hopton, safe king's men every one, though that was not to say they might not also be just men, however little likely to command much trust within Wales. Their business was to inquire and report, so said the commission itself, by what laws and customs the king's forebears had been wont to rule and judge a prince of Wales or a Welsh baron of Wales in any disputes arising. For this task they were allowed half a year, for their report was not required to be delivered until the fourth day of May of the year following. The places where they were to enquire were appointed in advance, and by whom but Edward? And even had their fourteen questions been drawn up by an unbiased arbitrator – which I doubt – the juries before which they would be used, the witnesses to be called, depended absolutely on the will of the commissioners.

David did not bring his household to spend Christmas with us that year, for once again Elizabeth was within a month of her time. He came instead for a brief visit in the new year, alone and in no festive mood, for his own affairs proceeded no more favourably than his brother's. He came to me in my copying-room, the evening before he left again for home, and leaned at my shoulder over the parchment I was working on, as many years ago he had leaned, with his blue-black head against my cheek.

'We all of us posture and dance to Edward's tune like slaves,' he said morosely. 'Wales is become a prison, where lords and commons alike struggle to maintain their rights against a load of chains. Venables still pursues his case against me for Hope, and in spite of all Edward's pieties, in spite of all the declarations that Hope is Welsh, he's still allowed to pursue it in the Chester shire-court. Llewelyn is still denied Welsh justice over Arwystli, on one pretext after another. In the west de Knoville refuses to meet on the border for mutual reparations, as was always done, but summons Llewelyn's bailiffs to him wherever he chooses, out of their own land.'

'Howbeit,' I said, 'they do not go!'

'Not yet, but how long before Edward's nagging wears my brother down? He cannot bear this constant haggling and meanness, it is not in his nature. Either he will break, and give in, send his men like servants wherever the king's seneschal calls them – oh, not out of fear or weakness, unless disgust is weakness! – or else he must burst out in revolt, and drive the royal bailiffs out of Wales.'

'He will do neither the one nor the other,' I said. 'He has only one course open to him, and that is to outlast the king at every turn, in patience, in stubbornness, to hold fast what he has, and go on contending to his life's end for what more he ought to have, and for every point of his right and prerogative. But not in arms.'

'You think not?' said David, and eyed me consideringly along his shoulder. 'Not if all the chiefs of Wales outside his own principality, all those who suffer now worse than he does, our nephews in the south, the princes of Maelor and Cardigan – not if all these banded together to complain to him of their wrongs, and begged him to deliver
86

them again, as he did once before? Would he not move even then?'

'He would not,' I said, 'even if he were free to do it. He would not, because it would be playing into Edward's hands. But it does not arise. He is not free. He set his seal to a treaty, he swore fealty to the king, saving his sovereign right in his own land. Whether Edward has broken treaty by his curious games with words, is for Edward's conscience to answer. But nothing that has happened yet serves to set Llewelyn free from his oath and the sanctity of his seal. Why ask me foolish questions? You know him as well as I do.'

'Yes,' he owned with a sigh, 'I know him.' And he was silent for a long time, darkly regarding his own linked hands. Then he said softly and mildly: 'Yet time may force his hand. What we do cannot always depend only on our own will. We find ourselves doing things we never meant to do, in spite of all our struggles, in spite of our own natures. I never thought I should return to my brother's grace, even if he opened his arms to me a third time, but when the hour came he called me, and I had no choice. No choice at all! And you – do you remember once, Samson, how I raged at you for bringing Cristin's husband back to her, when she could as well have gone on believing him dead, and been happy with you? Could you not, I said, have slipped your dagger into his ribs then, when you alone knew he lived, and left him unmourned in the south? And if you were too nice to do your own rough work, I said, there were those could do it for you. But you would neither go that way yourself nor let me. How long ago can it be? Dear God, it must be more than twenty years! Have you forgotten?'

I had not forgotten then, I have not forgotten now. I said: 'Cristin has been your friend as well as mine, you know her as I know her. Do you think I could ever have approached her over her husband's body?'

He lifted his head and looked at me steadily, with his

eyes the soft blue of summer distances, Snowdon's colour in clear, settled weather. 'No,' he said, 'on the face of it, impossible. Impossible, since she is the woman she is, and you the man you are. No, I saw you would not thank me for it if I set you free, much less put your hand to the work yourself. Not for your life! And poor wretch, is it Godred's fault he stands in the way? He's been no bad servant to me. And yet,' he said, 'I foresee even your hand may be forced, some day. In the end you may have to kill him. And when you come red-handed from the deed, I think she may very well be waiting for you, and not turn away.'

But I would not answer him a word, for that way I refused to look, and in this mood I found in him nothing but dismay. And after a while he went away to drink himself below the level of remembrance, and I was left to my disordered thoughts.

So passed that Christmas.

The king's commission began their sessions at Chester early in the new year, and then their procedures became plain to see, and though we let them alone there, where they could manage things much as they liked, we had our own questions ready to present as a petition at their next sitting, which was at Rhuddlan. I think Master William's appearance there, as soon as the bench sat, came as a shock to the commissioners, but before a full hall and assembled witnesses they could not decline to receive the prince's petition and enroll its contents before any evidence was taken, and so they did. Master William took care to pronounce in court what was there set down: that the prince requested that his own interrogatories should be added to those drawn up by the royal officials, since the purpose of the enquiry was to determine the truth. In particular he asked the commission to enquire of witnesses whether in those disputed lands there were duly accredited Welsh judges, whose duty it was to administer Welsh law there, for clearly if Welsh law did not apply there would be no need for such judges to be appointed and sworn to serve. And in case any difficulty was experienced in getting answers to this question from other witnesses, the prince here provided the information himself. The sons of Kenyr ap Cadogan were duly appointed judges of Welsh law in Arwystli, and Iorwerth Fychan held the same office in the lands between Dovey and Dulas.

Having ensured that this testimony was enrolled, the old man withdrew and left them to hear their witnesses, and then we had certainty that, whatever happened, the existence and the names of those judges could not be omitted from the rolls.

It was not long after this small victory for Eleanor's scepticism was recorded, that her determined faith also had its reward. For though parliament's discussion of Amaury's case had concluded without any apparent change or decision, nonetheless the princess's appeal and the archbishop's intercessions must have had their effect, for early in that year twelve hundred and eighty-one the king suddenly released Amaury, not from all restrictions upon his liberty, but from close confinement, and removed him from his tower in Corfe castle to the safe-keeping of Archbishop Peckham, who lodged him comfortably at Sherbourne and greatly eased his conditions. That was blessing and relief enough, more than he had yet expected, and greatly enhanced by Peckham's personal kindness to him, in which we found it easy to believe. For nothing would so dispose that good prelate to further benevolence, as the sense of benefits already conferred, and the conscious glow of good deeds done.

We began to credit that a better understanding all round was not an impossibility. To believe in it was to labour for it, and to look for every happening or utterance that could be regarded as evidence for its approach.

In the January of this year Griffith ap Gwenwynwyn took up again that case of the thirteen vils in Cydewain which he had formerly claimed against the king, but this time he

took out his writ for them against Roger Mortimer, t
whom the king had granted that cantref, and therefor
the disputed vils among the rest.

'Roger claimed Welsh law last time, when he appeare
on Edward's behalf,' said Llewelyn, interested. 'Now let'
see how he will proceed on his own. We have need of goo
precedents.' And he sent a clerk to observe how the plead
ing went at Montgomery when the case came up. Griffit
pleaded that Mortimer had formerly defaulted of puttin
in an appearance and claimed judgment against him, bu
Roger by his attorneys at once replied that by his atten
dance he had now amended any default, for by Welsh law
which applied to the disputed land, a defendant could mak
up to three defaults, but could not therefore have judg
ment pronounced against him and lose his seisin of th
land unless he defaulted a fourth time. Naturally Griffit
hotly contested Mortimer's right to demand Wels
law, upon the old plea that both were barons of the kin
and ought to plead by common law, while Mortime
stood firm on the fact that Cydewain was Welsh, and onl
Welsh law could apply to it.

It was so like his own first encounter with Griffith tha
Llewelyn could not but hang eagerly on the outcome, fc
the sake of the unsettled fate of Arwystli. The justices, a
before, considered the two pleas so strong and so contra
dictory that they needed further guidance to decid
between them, and postponed the case until April, an
then once more into June. This brought us to the time whe
Edward's inquisition must already have made its repor
due in May, and we were all waiting in anxious expecta
tion for the king to make public what it had to say.

Llewelyn was then in frequent correspondence with h
cousin Mortimer, chiefly by reason of their shared resen
ment against Griffith, for Mortimer was as enraged by th
legal war waged against him as was the prince, and bor
it with much less patience, being a hot-blooded and forth
right man. He had strong feelings about the folly of forcin

90

English law upon Welshmen, and was uneasy about what he could not but hold to be infringements of the treaty. His loyalty to the king was far past question, but he was wise in the special marcher wisdom, and knew how to deal sensibly with Welsh tenants no less than with English, and certainly was not without sympathy for them. He, too, had been forced to gouge out new roads through his forests, which displeased him as if he had been wholly Welsh himself, instead of but the half. Those two cousins, though they had often fought on opposing sides, and even in peace had contended many a time over other issues, never in life bore any malice or dislike each to the other, but always a hearty respect, and a degree of wary affection, and now, stung over and over by the same gadfly, they exchanged rueful and angry sympathy, and ended closer than for many years.

It so happened that at the end of May one of the brothers of Llanfaes, who had been to London on Brother William de Merton's business to the Franciscans there, came back bearing a message which he said was for me. In his dealings with a small matter involving the chancellery he had encountered Robert Burnell's clerk, Cynan, and had been charged to give me word, he said, of the colour of a certain healing herb, shy of growth and hard to find out, of which that same Cynan had spoken with me when last I was in Westminster. I knew then what this embassage meant, and my heart leaped, and I waited for Cynan's verdict with held breath.

'He bade me tell you,' said the friar, 'that this rare herb bears a flower as white as snow.' And he folded his hands and smiled, incurious about what this mystery could mean, but aware that it filled me with joy, and therefore himself pleased.

I took the word to Llewelyn at once, and he seized on it as gladly as I. 'Well, now we know, and the knowing is all. Grey and Hamilton got true answers, and reported that Welsh land is, always has been, and always ought to be, subject only to Welsh law. We can never say that we already know what they found, for Cynan's sake. But if it come to the worst we can recall that this inquisition was held, and ask to know its findings. Now let's wait for what Grey and his fellows will answer this time. Edward must declare himself soon.'

And some days into the month of June, so he did, in what he wrote to the prince could be called a declaration, for it was as mysterious as Cynan's white-blossomed herb, and even harder to interpret. The tone of his letter was serene, friendly and gracious, all encouragement, but its meaning was as cloudy as the summit of Snowdon in rainy weather. Somewhat thus it went:

The king desired to inform the prince of Wales that he now had before him the findings of the inquisition on the laws and customs which had been followed in Wales and the marches of Wales in the time of the king's father and his predecessors, and also the result of the search into the official rolls, and that the findings in both cases agreed. The king had therefore caused it to be proclaimed that those same approved laws and customs should be observed now as before, and by this letter he signified to the prince that he might proceed with his cause, for the king had instructed his justices of the courts concerned to respect and observe the findings of inquisition and inspection, and to show Llewelyn speedy justice in accordance with them.

'So much talk of findings,' said Llewelyn in blazing exasperation, 'and not a word of what those findings are. All I am told is that I may proceed, and I shall have justice – speedy! he dare use the word, after four years – in accordance with what he has discovered. But what that is I am not to know. Only one thing is made *almost* clear, that if I pursue my claim it must be before the king's justices, in the place they choose. Well, I conceded so much before, I may do so again. It is the only thing I will concede.' And he delivered me the parchment, and asked me

92

'What do you make of it? See if you can read between the lines better than I. Need he be so guarded if he had found, or bought, or made evidence for denying me Welsh law?'

I read it over, recalling how absolute had been the result of the first such enquiry, and it did seem to me that the king was taking care to sound reasonable and conciliatory, as though making ready to yield a step or two with the appearance of grace. Just so he would certainly have written if, in spite of all his precautions, the evidence ran all against him, too clearly for him to manipulate it further, and he found himself faced with the necessity for allowing the case to proceed by Welsh law, and still keeping his own countenance. His way, when he could no longer resist an event, was to take it over and direct it, as though it had been his own conception from the beginning. Not that I did not realise that he might have many other delays to deploy, but it did seem to me that he was on the point of surrendering this one.

So I said, and Llewelyn considered it with me, and felt as I did. However cautiously, we should accept this proffer, and bring the claim for Arwystli once again before the Hopton bench.

'And now I remember,' he said, burning up eagerly, 'that Roger has the fifteenth of this month appointed him to answer Griffith ap Gwenwynwyn over the vils in Cydewain. We shall see what comes of that. Arwystli is as Welsh as Cydewain, the situation is exactly the same. If Roger wins his plea for Welsh law, the message becomes clear.'

He therefore sent me to Montgomery to watch the process of his cousin's case, a pleasant enough jaunt in the June weather, with long days and fair skies, and a kind of hope in our hearts that all might yet be well, that Edward, when his stratagems were done, would not thwart justice to the end, that misunderstandings could be eased away from between two princes who still had, in spite of all, a high respect and regard for each other.

I sat well back in the court at Montgomery, and watched

Griffith, fierce and gaudy and loud as a turkey-cock among his rookery of black-gowned lawyers, come sweeping into the room armed for battle, and take his place centrally behind his spokesmen, ready to prod and prompt as always. The court was full, but Mortimer himself did not attend, being by no means so in love with litigation as his opponent.

It was not a long hearing, since the bench sat mainly to deliver judgment held over from two previous sessions. But Griffith's lawyers stated in formal terms his claim to the lands, and to have them by common law, both parties being the king's barons. Roger's attorneys replied with his claim that the lands were undeniably Welsh, and entitled him to Welsh law, and by Welsh law he was not in default, as Griffith had previously claimed. Then it was for the bench to give judgment.

There was no reluctance in the presiding judge this time to weigh claims equally and deliver a verdict he had withheld from Llewelyn. His face was placid and assured as he spoke out the considered view of his bench, undoubtedly approved in advance in higher quarters, or why those two adjournments? He found that the land claimed was Welsh, and should be impleaded by Welsh law, by which three defaults could be made without loss of seisin, therefore Mortimer was not in default, and Griffith's writ by common law brought him nothing. Mortimer was left without day, in possession of his lands, and Griffith was subjected to a fine and lost his claim.

And this despite the undoubted fact that here was a plea between two parties both marcher barons of the crown. Welsh law was upheld, and judgment given by it. And past question, if Cydewain was Welsh, so was Arwystli, and so must be impleaded and judged. It was in all points the complete justification of the stand Llewelyn had taken from the beginning, and I was so elated, I hardly had time to enjoy the spectacle of Griffith ap Gwenwynwyn glooming and storming out of court with lowered head and baleful brow, like an angry bull, all his train of lawyers scurrying after him with gowns flying, a thunder-cloud about a lightning-flash. Once, at least, that master-litigant met his match, though he did not therefore give up all hope, but clung by the edges of his claim, hungrily and vengefully, waiting for a new hold on his lost vils, such as might arise, for instance, if Roger, the immediate incumbent, died. Into the interstice between the lord's death and the heir's grant of seisin Griffith was willing and eager to crawl, like the worm that is drawn to the dead.

But I rode home happier than I had been for many a day, because I could again believe there was justice to be found somewhere entangled in Edward's network of law. And I told my lord and my lady, we three privately together, all that had passed.

'God be thanked!' said Llewelyn, heaving a great breath that eased him of a year of struggle and despondency. 'At last we have Edward's cypher put into plain speech. Welsh land may have Welsh law, even where the dispute is between two barons of the king. Edward can hardly reverse his own decision now this is made public. The cases are exactly similar, and no less is due to a prince of Wales than to a baron of the king. Now I can go forward with my suit with a good heart. The way is open at last!'

He resolved to prosecute his case at Montgomery in the October session of the Hopton bench, and at once wrote to Roger Mortimer and gave him joy of his victory, all the more heartily, as he freely owned, because it afforded the perfect precedent for what we hoped would soon be ours. Mortimer replied with a cordial invitation to the prince to visit him at Radnor while the lawyers argued the case at Montgomery. Thus he might be close at hand to watch events, and also Mortimer had certain matters to put to him that might be to the advantage of both cousins.

That was a happy and hopeful time with us, a family alliance shaping with the strongest baron in the middle march, and every prospect of winning Arwystli, and with

95

it a better promise of a just relationship with England
The treaty, our one protection, began to appear safer than
for some years.

Late in September we set out for the marches, and
Llewelyn had but one disappointment, that Eleanor
thought best not to come with us. 'You will be altogether
occupied,' she said, 'with men's business, both at Radnor
and Montgomery, and though I should be very glad to
meet with your cousin Mortimer, for this time I think I
would rather not ride so far. You will not be long away,
I'll come slowly south as far as Bala, and wait for you
there.'

He was concerned at once, for she had always been so
constant at his side. And though she smiled at him with
clear eyes and open face, he held her by the hands and
looked at her earnestly, and was uneasy.

'You are paler than usual. It is not like you to sit at
home. You are not ill, love?'

'No,' she said, and laughed, and I thought her glow
was even brighter than of old, pale though indeed she
was. 'No, I am very well. All is as it should be with me.
But this once I will to stay behind, and when you come
back as far as Bala you shall find me there to greet you.'

So he let her have her way, though not quite easy about
her. But she shone so bright in those last days before we
left that he was cheered and reassured. Whatever she
wanted he would do, even if it severed him from her for as
long as ten or fifteen days. As for me, I wondered, for it
needed a powerful motive to cause her to leave his side,
however little he, in his humility, questioned her ability
to live without him so long. And perhaps I watched her
even more devoutly than usual in those days, and noted
that she kept her own apartment until well into the morning, upon various pretexts. But on the morning that we
rode for Radnor she came down early to speed us on our
way, and I saw her at the turn of the stairway pause and
hold by the wall a moment, and marvelled at her look, for

her cheeks were pale and her eyes heavy, and yet her lips so smiling, and her eyes so glad and hopeful when she believed no man was watching her.

And as I gazed, she laid her hand upon her body under the heart, and that was so tender and protective a caress that my heart opened and swelled with knowledge, and I stood so lost in enlightenment that I forgot to take myself out of her sight, but was still standing like a man in a dream when she came on down the stair.

Seeing me, she checked only for an instant, startled, and then smiled in content, and came on more slowly. And as she came she opened her eyes wide and wonderfully to let me into her mind, and laid a finger to her lips. So I understood what she felt no need to say, that she was not yet sure, that by the time he returned to her in Bala she would be sure, and then her news would crown his joy if he came triumphant, and be the blessed consolation for all losses if fate and Edward still denied him justice.

Thus she passed by me silently, and went out into the inner ward to kiss Llewelyn and speed him on his way. And I, as she had entreated me, held my peace and followed after like a biddable child.

At Radnor we had a hospitable welcome from Roger Mortimer and his lady, who was a de Breos, marcher through and through, like her husband. This cousin of my lord's, his elder by some years, was a gaunt, dark, fiery person, loud-voiced and impetuous, but large of mind, too, with true feeling for his lands and his people, who lay between Wales and England, torn both ways when there was dispute, and never utterly at home in either camp. There were two sons of the house, Edmund the heir, and Roger the younger, able, unchancy young men, like so many marcher sons not yet possessed of their own lands, and therefore full of all the enterprise and daring necessary to their kind, without the responsibility their father carried. They featured rather their mother, being fairer in colouring and slighter in build, while the lord of Wigmore and Radnor himself showed a strong resemblance to his Welsh grandsire, Llewelyn Fawr, in the shaping of his bold, thrusting bones and the taut flesh that covered them, in his hawk-nose, and the deep, bright caverns of his eyes. He was the blacker of the two, and the leaner, but when he sat beside Llewelyn at the high table the mark of their great forebear was clear in them both, and they might almost have been brothers.

What the lord of Radnor had to propose to his cousin we did not at first learn, though clearly he was blazingly scornful and bitterly resentful of Griffith ap Gwenwynwyn's overweening presumption, and the liberties that highly successful renegade took even with chancellor and king. But Roger's approaches were held in check until we who were bound to appear at Montgomery on the sixth of October had set out for that royal town. We went in high hopes, not because we were too easily elated and too trusting of Edward's honesty, but because we had that invaluable precedent of Mortimer's successful defence by Welsh law to prop us, and were willing to whip it out and flourish it before Hopton or any other royal justice if he barred our way. It was so recent that it could hardly be outweighed by any other precedent. We felt we had a shield that could not be penetrated even by Edward's arrows.

In this high mood we rode, I but a private observer for my lord, up the winding hill through the town of Montgomery, and out on to the high rock where the castle stands, and into the wards, and thence, having committed our mounts to the grooms, into the great hall.

There was no knowing from Hopton's bland face whether he had his orders in advance, as we thought probable, or even if he had, what they were, and we held our breath when Master William got up to make his formal claim on Llewelyn's behalf to the whole land of Arwystli, and the land between the Dovey and the Dulas, and that by Welsh law, as was implied from the opening of the cause, now nearly four years past.

When he sat down, that was the moment for Griffith to make his protest and claim the common law, so setting the old cycle revolving helplessly once again for four years more, or for the bench to demur that the rival claims of the two systems had never yet been settled. We waited, and Hopton sat mute, courteously waiting for the defendant to reply, either in person or by his attorney. The pause was long, I think now intentionally long, and we drew cautious breath and knew that one peril had passed. The Mortimer precedent was too recent and too famous to be denied, every man in the court knew of it. We felt safe then. No one was going to deny us Welsh law, and invite the obvious rejoinder. Yet I wondered, even before a word was said, why Griffith, hunched and hugging himself behind his sombre troop, had a small tight grin on his face, as though he enjoyed a joke very private and sharply sweet of taste.

For my part, I was shaken when he got up himself to make his counter-plea, instead of leaving it to his attorney. He hitched his furred gown about him at leisure, and ran a sharp glance along the line of us where we sat, and I dreaded then that after all he had something still hidden in that wide sleeve of his, but could not guess what it would be.

'If it please the court,' he said, all reason and sweetness, 'I am willing and ready to answer to the plea, in the proper form, and will not dispute the manner of procedure but in one point. Since the prince of Wales and I myself are both barons of the king, I ought not to answer unless the lord prince brings a writ to court.'

We did not at first understand why he should be in such secret glee at having this defence in hand, for it sounded feeble enough and Master William rose to answer it, I think, in as great innocence as we.

'The prince's writ,' he said, 'was duly taken out and

delivered into this court when this plea was begun. The date was the seventeenth day of February of the king's sixth regal year. I myself delivered it.'

Hopton pondered the date, or affected to, and said: 'That was not, I think, before the present bench? I was not then in office.'

'It was before Master Ralph de Fremingham,' said the old man, still confident. That was the first presiding justice of this commission for east Wales, who held office but a few months, and was removed in somewhat dubious circumstances.

'We have no record of this writ,' said Hopton smoothly, 'and since the defendant pleads that as a baron he should not answer without a writ, it seems that we cannot proceed at this sitting, but must make enquiry further to try and recover it.'

Now the pattern of deceit began to appear all too clearly, for courts surely keep records, and those records should be complete, and even if the clerking of the Hopton commission proved inefficient, the writ must have been listed in the chancery rolls. It should have been a simple matter enough to refer to chancery and prove the issue, though it was a reflection upon Hopton himself that such a reference should have been necessary. But he made no mention of chancery, and no apology for his inability to prove the writ by the archives of his own court.

'My colleagues,' said Master William, 'will bear witness that I brought and handed over the prince's writ at the first hearing. It must be in existence, and it should not be impossible to find it. I must protest against any further delay.'

'It is regrettable,' said Hopton magisterially, as though it reflected not at all upon him, 'but since we have not the writ, and cannot proceed without it, there is no other course open to the bench but to adjourn until it can be recovered.' And he ordered that word should be sent to Ralph de Fremingham, to enquire if he held the writ and the opening of the process, and bid him send them into court the eighth day of December, by which date he trusted to be able to proceed with the case. And on that, with Griffith grinning like a gargoyle on a tower, Hopton adjourned the plea until December.

As for us, we went out dashed into a new kind of despair, not because the pretext in this case was itself so grave a matter, for writs can be taken out a second time if need arise, but because it came as a plain indication that however many obstacles we overcame in this cause, there would always be others raised to baulk us. The plain truth was, that Edward had served notice upon the prince that whatever happened, he should never have Arwystli.

'In the name of God,' said Adam, as we went dispiritedly to the stables for our horses, 'why should Fremingham have that or any other writ, or any part of the records? Is that how they run their courts, and Edward so proud of his gift for law? In Wales we should be ashamed of such wretched clerking.'

'He will not and cannot have it,' said Master William bleakly. 'He may very well recollect that it was brought, and say so, but of course he'll say he has kept none of the records in his hands, and why should he? And he at least will be telling the truth. The prince's original writ will never be seen again. Nor, I warrant, will the entry of that first hearing survive long in the roll of the court after this, even if it has not already been removed. No, it is not a mere delay of two months they've secured by this stratagem, it is the time it takes to swear out a new writ from chancery and begin the process at law all over again. If,' he said heavily, 'the prince's heart can stand so grievous a mockery and humiliation. He has been bled slowly of his heart's-blood for years. Somewhere there is an end to what even the saints themselves can bear.'

CHAPTER IV

That lamentable news we took back to Llewelyn at Radnor with very heavy hearts. He knew from our faces not only that his just hopes were dashed yet again, but that they would always be dashed, for the hands that held supreme power had themselves set up an impassable barrier against them, in Edward's interest and Edward's will.

He heard us in silence to the end, and then with an equable voice and a face chilled and stony said some words of reassurance and comfort to the old man, whose voice trembled in the telling, and who ended nearly in tears. Then he commended him for his courage and pertinacity in a very unrewarding cause, and dismissed him gently, and his colleagues with him. But he asked me to stay. We had found him closeted with Mortimer when we came, and there was then no other left in the room but we three and Roger's chaplain and secretary. The silence hung heavy upon us all for a while, and Mortimer leaned his elbows upon the table and watched his cousin's face doubtfully, as Llewelyn sat straight and still in his chair, following with fixed eyes the departure of an old regard.

Remembering, I find it astonishing how often his respect and liking for Edward received wounds that might well have been mortal, and yet revived to live again. Even after this, I know he had some illusions left, and still believed there were things to which Edward would not stoop. It took another and a stranger stroke, perhaps the only one Edward ever struck at him in innocence, to give his lingering liking the *coup de grâce*.

When the prince had thus sat still and alone among us some while, Mortimer reached out a lean hand and grasped him by the shoulder. 'You are used very shabbily,' he said bluntly, 'and I am sorry for it. I tell you openly, if you had beaten Griffith at his own game, and whipped Arwystli from under his nose, I should have been as happy about it even as you. The man is insufferable to me and to many.'

Llewelyn stirred into life again, the dark colour flooding back into his face. 'Unhappily not so to the king,' he said harshly.

'He has been useful,' said Mortimer, and shrugged.

'In helping to contain and discipline me,' said Llewelyn remorselessly, 'and is still being used to the same end.'

'His plea will stand,' warned Mortimer with compunction. 'The law will uphold him, he has a right to demur at answering without a writ. I don't presume to guess who was obliging enough to make away with it for him, since he could hardly get at it himself. As to the king's Grace, he is my liege, and I'll say no word of him. But what will you do now? Will you send your men to court in December?'

'To be subjected again to what they have suffered so often on my behalf? No! I'll rather write yet again to the king, and deal directly with him, though in my heart I know it will be fruitless. At least he shall know that if I am cheated, I know it, and despise the act and the cheat.'

Mortimer got up abruptly and began to pace the room, making two or three rapid prowls about the table, until he halted as suddenly behind Llewelyn's chair, and dropped both hands upon his shoulders. 'I take it,' said he, 'that we are in confidence here?'

'You may trust Samson as you trust me,' said Llewelyn.

'And that I do,' he said heartily, 'for though we've fought often enough and hard enough, I should be a fool indeed if I thought you could ever fight unfairly, with eyes in your head like yours. I am more likely to do a little conniving and insinuating myself, and I'm no great hand at it, either. I've been long in coming at what I had to say to you, chiefly by reason of this cause of yours. I waited to see what tricks Griffith would shake out of his sleeve this time, and whether you and I were as close in enmity to him as I thought. It seems you have even better reason than I to man your defences against him. But make no mistake, he has not done with me, either, he is only waiting for another chance. There's no end to his effrontery, and none to his greed. I am in fealty to the king, and I am his man, and there's an end of it, whether all his acts seem good to me or whether they do not. But as to Griffith ap Gwenwynwyn, he is a very different matter. You and I have a common enemy, and a common use for reliable allies. Why should not we two enter into a treaty of alliance? To support and aid each other in all matters whatsoever, saving only our fealty to Edward? Old foes or not, we've dealt honestly with each other, and we come of the same blood, and I'm no happier when you fall victim to an overweening trickster than when the same snake comes striking at my heels. What do you say?'

'I say,' said Llewelyn, flushed with surprise, for he had not guessed at this, and it had a warmth and candour about it that came very gratefully to him then, 'that there's never an Englishman with whom I would rather be on good terms, and never one I'd rather have to keep my back against a false world. I have an oath of fealty to keep, like you, but you of all men are never likely to lead me into imperilling that. Yes! I say yes, such a pact I'll gladly make with you. As solemnly as you will.'

'I mean it solemnly,' said Mortimer. 'I have a soul to stake, and I'm willing to take that load upon me, if you are.'

'In time of peace?' said Llewelyn. 'On what terms?'

'Peace and war and all,' said Mortimer hardly. 'Why not? Saving our vows to Edward, that goes without saying.'

Llewelyn considered, and saw in his mind an embattled neighbour to Arwystli, and neighbour to him if ever he won Arwystli, a strong line of defence deep into mid-Wales, a way into the south. All the prohibitions against enlargement he knew, and all the dangers barring his way, and yet the offer was honest and greatly to be desired, and the ally, impetuous and ungovernable as he was, honest to the backbone. And that was pure delight to him, after so much dishonesty. He said: 'Saving our vows, yours and mine both, yes! I am your man, if you are mine!'

It was but three days later that they drew up between them, and sealed with the most solemn sanctions, their treaty of mutual assistance and perpetual peace and accord against all enemies, saving only their obligations to King Edward, and in Roger's case also to the Lord Edmund, the king's brother, under pain of excommunication if they failed of their promises. The bishops of Hereford and St Asaph took cognisance of their vows, which bound them, as in peace, so in war, the one to the other.

Thus those cousins, one half-English, half-Welsh, the other wholly Welsh, were brought together by their mutual hostility to Griffith ap Gwenwynwyn, and their common detestation of greed, malice and falsity. And fortified with this pledge, and embittered and stiffened by the duplicity of Edward's court at Montgomery, we turned homeward in mid-October, to meet with Eleanor at Bala.

She came out to the gate of the maenol to meet us when we rode in, having caused the watch on the wall to notify her as soon as the prince's banners were seen in the distance. She was bravely adorned, and so beautiful with joy that the heart ached, beholding her. She walked like a queen, erect and ceremonious, her head raised and her gaze high and bright, as though she had been a crystal cup full to the brim of magical wine, and must not shake one drop from the rim.

When he set eyes on her he trembled and checked hi
horse, knowing that something miraculous had befalle
her, but not knowing what it could be, and so dazzle
that he had no heart to question or wonder. I was clos
at his side, and I saw the severity and sadness and dou
resolution cast out of him in a moment, as though a fres
wind had blown drifts of cobweb and mist away, and lef
him, too, bright as the sun with the reflection of he
certainty.

He lighted down to her like a man in a dream, and too
her face between his hands and held her so, gazing at he
face for a long time before he kissed. And she wound he
arms about his body and strongly embraced him, an
neither of them had a word to say, not then nor all th
while they walked together, hand in hand, back into th
maenol. On that occasion she did not welcome him home
in words, for there was no need when her every look an
movement and every thread of her vestments was a prince'
welcome. Nor did he feel any wish to ask how she did
and how she had done those days without him, for that
too, was in her face. And if she had seen in his distan
countenance, before he was transfigured, how his affair
had sped at Montgomery, she spared to ask and remind
him, for she had other plans.

Afterwards, in hall among the whole household, everything went as it always went, yet with a kind of secre
and ceremonious wonder, as if we played a pageant of ou
own daily life, with redder torches, richer laughter, sweete
music and stronger wine than ever graced meal in hall on
working days. Until the prince and princess, surely at he
instance, withdrew early to their own chamber. And there,
I think, in his bed, in his arms, on his heart, there she told
him.

It was he himself who told me, and never knew that I
needed no telling. I think he was in great need to open hi
heart to someone, for he was so full of joy that he could
not contain it alone, and as in older days the stars of ou

106

shared birth drew him to me. I had still a small room close
to theirs, and I lay long awake, for their sake exultant and
fearful and grateful, taking to myself a morsel of his
burden and his blessing even before he offered it. And I
was in no way astonished when my door opened, and in
the light of my tiny lamp I saw him come silently within,
and shut out the world behind him. He had a woollen
gown wrapped about his nakedness, and above its high
collar his face looked strangely young and in great awe.
Fine, abrupt bones he had, that took the light and caused
him to shine in outlines of gold, and the close-clipped traces
of beard he wore only drew those lines in softer, broader
strokes and mellowed their sharpness. His eyes, which
were always the soul of his face, shone huge and dark,
with a profound brilliance under their brown depths. He
was fifty-two years old, and I had good reason to know it,
being day for day the same age, and I would have sworn
this man was new to the burning maturity of thirty years,
and the blessed burdens of marriage and fatherhood. Such
illusions the night commands, and the little lamps of night
light up for us.

'Are you waking, like me?' he said in a whisper, and
came to my bedside, as I rose among the covers, and stood
looking down at me with that rapt smile I saw on his lips
once before, on his marriage-day. 'I am too full to lie
still. I have left her sleeping,' he said, seeing how I gazed
at him. 'She will not miss me. She has company, the nearest
and dearest wife could have or desire. Our child sleeps with
her. Oh, Samson, Eleanor is with child!'

With all my heart I gave him joy, and made room for him
on the edge of the brychan beside me. He had little need
of words from me, so many welled up from within him to
his wonder and her praise.

'All that beauty and bravery and generosity,' he said,
'will be repeated to the world's gain. Oh, Samson, I feel
myself enhanced and diminished both, diminished and
comforted. Why should I dare hope to do all things, alone,

107

to make a nation in one lifetime? I am only man, and fallible, it is time I admitted it, and now I may, for there will be a future, and it belongs to another generation, and will be shaped by other hands. It does not matter if my hands grow feeble. I will cede my rights and my burdens into my son's hands without reluctance, and never grudge him his battles and his triumphs. What I have failed of achieving, he will achieve, or his son after him.'

I said, and truly, that now he was more than ever justified in standing by the treaty that was the best protection Wales had, and all his arduous patience and faithfulness under provocation was vindicated.

'I know it,' he said. 'There was never any other way possible, and not only for my sworn word and honour, but for the preservation of what is left to us. I am bound, but God grant that before my boy is grown, he need not be bound. He has pledged no fealty, sealed no treaty. He will take his own way, and in as far as I can prepare the ground for him, I will do it. I will serve as long and as humbly as I must, and stand down when I should, ungrudging, if I can see a better man to come. The great-grandson of Llewelyn ap Iorwerth, the grandson of Earl Simon de Montfort, Eleanor's son – how can he be less than glorious?'

Had it been any other man who so left himself out of the reckoning, I tell you, I would have been certain he did so only in the assurance that another would reprove and repair the omission. But with him that was not so, for he had always this rare humility that had no falsity in it, but was experienced from the heart. And I felt no need to say to him what my own heart knew, that the son of Llewelyn ap Griffith would have the seeds of splendour in him even had his mother been much less than the jewel she was.

'You may yet find yourself nursing a daughter,' I said, to draw him a little nearer to the earth. But he only laughed silently.

'And I should be sorry for that? Then she will make some
108

discerning king a most imperial queen. And she will have brothers to follow her.'

'One brother,' I said, thinking of those four of whom he was the second, and the great trouble and loss the other three had caused him between them. 'One will be enough, so he come lusty and strong into the world.' But at that, too, he only smiled.

'Ah, but her sons will be true brothers, and stand by the heir as extra arms for sword and shield. How could she bear small and envious children? Oh, Samson,' he said, 'we have waited three years for this sign from God, and neither of us ever said word about the waiting, never until now. And truth to tell, I have been so glad of her, and so greedy, I seldom thought of children, and might have felt some jealousy if I had, yet now that I know – something I never thought possible, and how to contain it I have still to learn! – now that I know, she is twice as dear even as before.'

It was wonderful how this promise of an heir put new life and heart into us all, from the highest to the lowest, how it made endurance seem easy, and the pinpricks of provocation light to bear. But Llewelyn did not let pass any occasion for just complaint, all the same, for now it was his future heir's prerogative that was slighted, and not merely his own. He wrote to Edward plainly concerning the frustration he had suffered at Montgomery, and the scandal of the loss of his writ, making it clear that he had no intention of countenancing an appearance in December, nor any faith in Master Ralph de Fremingham's ability to produce the writ, since there was no conceivable legal reason why it should be in his possession. He required, instead, that proper enquiry should be made for it, or for the record of its issue, where such records should be expected to be, in the royal chancery.

Early in November Edward replied at length to this letter, in a strain which was becoming familiar to us, so

109

civil and anxious to please – though of course unable! – that I could see between the lines not only the droop of his left eyelid, but also the small, ironic curl of his lips that never quite became a smile. He opened as he always opened, by vowing fervently that he had faithfully considered the matters put to him, and would most happily do what Llewelyn asked of him, if he could do so without wronging anyone else, that he felt for the prince, and that his intent was, as it always had been, to observe the treaty of Aberconway faithfully, so far as he was able. But he could not, on that account, do less than justice to his barons and magnates, who also had rights.

'More, it seems,' said Llewelyn, 'than I have.' But he said it now with an even voice and an unfurrowed brow, even with disdain.

He had talked these matters over earnestly, said Edward, with his justices and council. Greatly as he longed to accede to the prince's wishes, he was advised that Griffith ap Gwenwynwyn had been perfectly correct in saying that as a baron of the king he was not obliged to answer without a writ. Another search of the rolls only confirmed this, and there was no way round it. For though they had hunted assiduously through all the records of writs issued, the original writ said to have been sworn out by the prince could not be found. And as the case could not proceed at all without the issue of a writ, without gross injustice to Griffith, there was nothing to be done but swear out a new writ and begin again. The prince, he said, with sad sympathy and mild reproach, must not resent the necessity.

To my way of thinking it was a cruel and insolent letter, meant to sting, but its point was blunted by Llewelyn's calming happiness, which strengthened his purpose and resolution rather than weakening them, but armoured him against humiliation and insult.

'He may bait me as he will,' he said, 'but he shall not gain anything by it, neither a step in retreat nor a spark to amuse him.' And for the Christmas season he let this matter lie, and we went with high hearts to Aber to keep the feast, and sent messengers to bid David and Elizabeth join us there.

They came riding in from Denbigh some days before the Nativity, having heard Eleanor's news, and Elizabeth flew to embrace the princess and give her joy, and thereafter hardly left her, being so full of good advice and sisterly confidences concerning childbirth and children that the days were not long enough to accommodate all she had to say. She was by five years the younger of the two, and yet had eight children of her own, and what she did not know of bearing and raising them was not worth knowing, but all was offered with such glowing and child-like goodwill and such visible reassurance and vigour and joy that Eleanor loved and bore with her, smiling. She was in serene health, the sickness she had suffered and hidden in the first days was gone, and her beauty was radiant, assured and glorious during all the time that she carried her child.

Elizabeth had brought with her only her youngest daughter, eleven months old, leaving the rest of that lovely tribe with their covey of nurses at Denbigh. It went against the grain with her to go anywhere without them, but in a hard winter it was something of an undertaking to transport so many little ones about the country. Therefore the only attendant she had with her was Cristin, and to complete my joy, Cristin without Godred. David had brought but a small company, and left all his knights at home. For this brief while I could brush sleeves with my love about the maenol as we went about our duties, and feel no need to look round for Godred's lurking, peering face. No need, either, to keep from looking round, for loathing of the bitter spark I should see flare in his eyes when they met mine. It was a good Christmas.

I said to her when we met in hall that first day that David, for all he had given his brother joy most affectionately,

111

and kissed Eleanor's hand and cheek with reverent tenderness, was somewhat quiet and grave, liable to fall into deep thought, and thought that darkened his countenance.

'We've seen him moody before this,' said Cristin. 'He may well be weary, he's been in the saddle more than at home these last weeks, up and down into the south and the west, visiting his nephews in Iscennen, and Meredith ap Owen's sons in Cardigan, and I know not what others besides.'

'For what purpose?' I questioned, astonished, for though doubtless he felt some family affection for those young men in the south, his dead sister's sons, yet it was David's way to expect them to come to him, rather than go running after them.

'To compare his grievances with theirs, I suspect,' said Cristin with a shadowed smile, 'though I doubt if he'll get much comfort that way, or they, either. There isn't a chief in the Welsh lands who is not burning with his wrongs, and when they lay two fires together, who knows how far the blaze may spread? The sixteenth of this month he should have made an appearance in the Chester shire-court, where Venables is still encouraged to sue against him for Hope. Grey is justiciar there again, and all the Middle Country is taking that as a sign the noose will tighten from now on.'

'And he defaulted?' I said.

'He paid no heed whatever. He was somewhere in the west then, he got back only in time to ride with Elizabeth on this visit. And half of him he has left somewhere far distant, occupied with other matters than celebrating Christmas,' she said, and shook her head anxiously. 'And yet so quiet and so contained! We have not seen him in a fury but once in the past six weeks. Time was, he would rage over his mangled forests, and the many exactions he considered illegal, and being cited into Chester for this due and that, and a hundred things besides. Not all for

112

himself!' she said, and her smile was wry and sweet, for she suffered, as I did, from an old and incurable affection for him. 'Lately I've heard him cry out but once. I think you will hear of it. I am sure Llewelyn will.'

I asked her: 'What was it happened?' And I chilled as I listened for her answer, for when had David been tolerant and patient, and withheld instant and fiery outcry when his prerogative was infringed by so much as the touch of a finger? And I saw him for myself sombre, withdrawn and mute.

'They have killed two of his men,' she said. 'A party went into Chester market for salt and honey, and to sell wool. There was some quarrelling there between them and some of the justiciar's people, but they kept their tempers and set out for home, and were over the border by Hope when the English waylaid and set on them. There was an English man-at-arms killed in the squabble. David's men drew off, but there were more of the English, and they cut out two of the Welsh and had them away into the shire, prisoners. Murder, they made it in the shire-court. They hanged them. By Welsh law it would not have been murder but homicide, and a blood-price would have salved it. But David's men are dead. And they were men he valued. And their widows cry to him.'

I was sick, for however the Welsh fall apart into warring clans, however they fail of comprehending anything larger than their kinship and their tribe, within those bounds they cleave by their own, and every death cuts into the flesh of all. And David, as in my heart I knew, was Welsh in the old way, for all his English upbringing, and the many ways he had been tugged by his many affections.

'And he so still!' I said, seeing him even then at the high table, inclining to right and to left and making civil reply, with the sweet veiled smile upon his face.

'They are not the first,' she said, 'to be slain for offences we would have compounded rather to heal. And not all in his cantrefs. There are many with the same burning

113

grievance. And he, I doubt he has them all by heart.'
She watched him as I was watching him, with her great,
iris-grey eyes that darkened so when most she was wrung.
'Samson, he may speak out to you, who does so now to
none of us. If you can bring him to confession, do it for
his sake. Not that he needs absolution, God knows he's
been out of all nature virtuous and forbearing. But he does
greatly need to shed whatever this load is upon his heart.'

'Does he not confide in his wife?' I asked. And Cristin
smiled her pardonable scorn for such a question.

'He takes nothing to her but what is sweet, open and
gay. He'd no more cast a shadow willingly upon her than
he would upon his children. He may drag them all into
the blackness of the pit with him yet, and they'd go, and
never think twice. But that's another matter.'

I said that if he offered me any chance I would do what I
could with him, but if he had it in mind to unburden
himself to the prince, Llewelyn might well do more and
better than I.

Howbeit, David kept his counsel and his ominous calm
all through the Christmas feast, awaiting his best occasion,
for he did not speak until the day, well into January, when
Llewelyn got word from Reginald de Grey in Chester of a
sudden and fresh distraint upon his property, in satisfaction of Robert of Leicester's long-discredited claim for his
goods lost by wreck. If Llewelyn blazed up at this letter,
he did so but briefly and hotly, and then recorded the new
offence grimly among those matters he had still to take
up, not with Grey, but with Grey's master. David, instead,
burned into a fierce and corrosive silence, and made occasion, after we left the hall that night, to shut himself in
with Llewelyn and me in the prince's private audience
chamber. He had found the moment he sought, I knew then
that he had come to speak, not to keep silence.

'This matter of your goods taken in Chester,' said
David, standing tall and stiff over the glowing brazier,
and himself burning almost as fiercely, 'is only the latest

outrage of many, you know it as well as I. And do you believe Grey ever took up this persecution afresh, without direct orders fom Edward? He would not dare, after such clear orders went to Chester earlier, to cease distraints and refer Robert to the Welsh courts, where they admitted the case belonged. No, Edward has held this goad in abeyance for a while, until it suited him to use it again, and it is *his* hand that has acted against you now. And what will you do? How long will you go on enduring wrong after wrong? And watching us endure worse? You at least, within your own principality, are master of your own house, and cannot be arraigned or challenged, cannot see your rights and your lands taken from you, and your tenants robbed and ousted. They are not so lucky in the Middle Country. They have no such immunity in the south and in the west. We are worse treated than you, and we do nothing. Nothing!'

'If what I enjoy is immunity,' said Llewelyn drily, 'it is the strangest immunity ever I heard of. True, no one has yet crossed my borders to meddle within, but enough mischief can be done from without. Still, I grant you I can no longer do anything to help those cantrefs that have passed out of my hands. They are no longer my men in the Middle Country, nor in the south, nor in Cardigan, and I am no longer their lord.' He did not say that David, also, was no vassal of his, but David could not help but be reminded whose fault that was. 'If you think I do not feel for those who used to be mine,' said Llewelyn with warmth, 'you are foolish and mistaken. But I have no right now to speak for them or act in their name. Those grievances you have you must take to your own liege lord. I cannot help you.'

'You could,' said David, 'if you would. Where else can they look for help? Where else can we, all of us, look for leadership, if not to you? I tell you, there is not a chieftain in the whole of Wales outside your realm who is not groaning and raging under his wrongs, and burning to rise and avenge them. They come to me now with their complaints, as I am coming to you. Day after day new outrages, new exactions, new offences against the law and custom and order of our lives. And the treaty promised us we should enjoy our own manner of life unmolested. Now it has gone beyond oppression. Men of mine, men I valued, have been done to death, who by Welsh law would have been alive this day.'

That story he told, and after it, his tongue loosed and his thoughts racing, many another such story from many another cantref. 'I have been busy these last weeks,' said David passionately, 'putting together the grievances of all my own tenants and chiefs, yes, and all the men of Rhos and Tegaingl, too, who have no Welsh lord to whom they can go for help. And I've ridden the length and breadth of Wales and talked with the princes of Maelor and Cardigan, and our nephews in Iscennen. Do you want to hear what your sometime vassals cry against England?'

'Go on,' said Llewelyn. 'I am listening.'

David drew breath and began. It was a long recital, man by man, lawsuit by lawsuit, distraint by distraint, delay upon delay, offence piled on offence against the laws and customs of Wales that had been guaranteed to us by treaty, and were safe now only within Llewelyn's domain. Old allies of his brother now spoke through David's mouth, their young nephews cried out in David's voice, while that voice grew steadily larger and calmer and more princely in authority. And Llewelyn watched and listened with a still face and patient eyes as David spoke for the nation of Wales, he who had been a dangerous obstacle to achieving that nationhood. For it was a national cause he argued, and he knew it, and knew the irony of his pleading, before the brother whose life-work he had helped to frustrate. His face burned to the brow, as if he heard within his own mind all those words Llewelyn forbore from uttering. But he would not turn back.

'And your wrongs,' he said at the end, and his voice

look for a moment. 'Those, too, I know. Do you need be reminded?'

'No,' said Llewelyn, 'I need no reminders.'

'It is not only Arwystli. It is not only these robberies in Chester, nor the crude devices to delay justice, nor the border raids that are still countenanced, when you have paid the money due from you promptly every year, to the last mark. No, it is the manner and insolence of Edward's usage in all things. He has his officers order your men to appear before them wherever they choose, instead of meeting on the borders as was always done aforetime. He makes use of the most detestable of his Welsh renegades to visit your court and conduct his minor matters of business with you. Oh, saving the arch-renegade of all,' said David, turning crimson but with unflinching eyes, 'David ap Griffith – who is no longer available. . . .'

'Hush!' said Llewelyn, stung and reproachful. 'This I will not hear!'

'No, I pray you pardon me, I had no right. Such things I should say only to myself, never to you who never have said them to me, and never will say them. But I do not forget, and I can feel the keenest pain when such a man as Rhys ap Griffith is sent into your court at Aberffraw with the king's authority, and feels free to insult you in your own house – '

'He paid for it,' said Llewelyn equably. For that bout of insolence had cost Rhys a hundred pounds sterling to quit him of the prince's prison.

'*He* paid,' said David. 'Edward has yet to pay. What manner of man would be so blockish and unfeeling as to send him to you? This is how he approaches us all. He tramples on every soreness and every bruise.' He drew breath, wearied and drained, and flung himself down in his chair. 'Well, I have done, I have told you.'

'And what,' said Llewelyn, 'do you want from me?'

'You are the prince of Wales. Where else should we go with our wrongs? Knowing that you also have yours? I

117

want you to tell us, all of us, what we are to do, and what you mean to do.'

'I mean,' said Llewelyn, 'to go on pressing every issue with the king, resisting every encroachment at law as best I can, and bearing what I have no choice but to bear. There are realities by which you are bound, as well as I. There is not one of us but must sleep in the bed he made. I am the prince of what is left of Wales. I was the prince of greater Wales, but when the testing came I had not done my work well enough. I failed Wales, and Wales failed me. These men who come to you now with their complaints and bid you carry them to me for remedy, how many of them fell away from me then, to keep their own little plot of land safe? How many were willing to sue for Edward's peace rather than lose their small inheritance to preserve Wales? How many betrayed Wales? Now, because they do not like the rule they were glad to accept then, they send you to urge on me an action that could only be a second and final ruin. What they want now is what they wanted then, to preserve their own small rights. David, never think this is a sudden, miraculous, united Wales you are offering me, the nation I wanted then and long for yet. These are still only a thousand little divided souls clinging desperately to their own privileges and their own lands, and seeing nothing beyond. As they turned from me to Edward, when he seemed best to promise them security, so now they will turn from Edward to me, now they are looking for another saviour. Oh, I do not hold them so much to blame. They are not yet ready to be a nation. But they are the reality with which we have to reckon. There is no salvation there. Not yet!'

'Nor ever,' said David, stiffening again in desperation, 'unless we deserve and fight for it.'

'Not yet, believe me, however well we deserve, however valiantly we fight. We have seen what Edward can do even if he beggars himself in doing it. The same he could do again, and more. Never think Edward does not learn

118

from experience. If Welshmen took arms now, Wales would be lost for ever. He would not halt for awe of a winter campaign, next time, nor waste six months on calling out his feudal muster. He would hire and buy, and bring ships and men from France, and take in archers and lancers at his wages. Welsh archers among them,' said Llewelyn, with sharp and sorrowful bitterness, and smiled ruefully at his brother, but David was mute. 'What I want for Wales,' said the prince, 'goes far beyond anything that could be gained now. That was my failure, that I tried to go too fast. The time for my vision is not now – not yet.'

He waited, and David had nothing to say, but sat steadily gazing at his brother, and his face as withdrawn and resigned as his brother's.

'But you are right,' said Llewelyn, answering what had not been said, 'that is not my reason for enduring still, and urging endurance upon you. All I have said is true, but as at this moment it is of small consequence. For the truth is, David, that this Wales that I long to see will never be won by my hand, unless time and God loose my hand. I am bound in honour and fealty to Edward, and to the terms of the treaty I made with him.'

'Which he has broken,' blazed David, 'by small means, like a mouse gnawing, a hundred times over, and laughs at you for keeping it.'

'No,' said Llewelyn immovably, 'for however I may overrate Edward, Edward knows and does not underrate me. If in the end I must despise him, as I pray God I never need, he will never be able to despise me. No, Edward may take every advantage, wring out every delay, he may well desire to laugh as he does it, smoothly parrying every letter I write to him, but he will not be able to enjoy his gains. He may discard his honour, if he so pleases. He will not be able to sever me from mine.'

'In the name of God!' said David, pale with passion but very still. 'Knowing Edward as you now know him, this giant of meanness, this great prince utterly without greatness, this monster who knows only one loyalty, to Edward, and acknowledges only one treason, against Edward – dear God, have I not reason to know it, who took my treason into his arms twice, and found a welcome for it there? – knowing all this, you hold fast to your oath and seal for *his* sake?'

'No,' said Llewelyn gently and patiently. 'No way for his sake. All for mine.'

I went out with David when he left his brother that night, so softly, with such a chastened face and quiet voice, after such submissive avowals of his own dues owed to Edward, and such resigned acceptance at last of the rightness of Llewelyn's stand. I followed at his shoulder by night along the corridors of Aber, and waited for him to speak. And he had nothing to say. He was out of words, having spent so many. Also he was very weary, much of his own strength also spent in the struggle he had lost. Since he did not at once go in towards his own apartment, but turned along the stone passage and went out into the darkness of the inner ward, I went with him, and he did not send me away, but slowed to bring me abreast of him, and laid his arm about my shoulders as we came out under the stars. A night of clear frost it was, we could see the glitter of rime along the crest of the wall, and hear the steely ring of the watchman's heels on the guardwalk above the postern gate. The sound drew David's gaze, and in the faint starlight I saw his face again sharp with remembrance.

'I see he keeps it guarded now, as well as barred,' he said, deliberately probing his old wounds and mine. 'God put a moat about it, that night. As well to be sure. There will never again be anything to fear from me, but who knows, there may be other Davids at large.' He turned his head suddenly, and stared into my face. 'You are still unsure of me, Samson, own it! You may, without penalty. I have not been notable for constancy. If you think I may

120

still play him false or work to his harm, say it openly.'

Truth to tell, many a time I had asked myself that same question, and found no certain answer. Yet when it was he who asked, I found myself clear in mind, with no need to hesitate.

'No,' I said, 'I do not believe you will ever forsake him again. For better or worse, you said, he had won you. I never knew you to mean anything as solemnly as you meant that. But time and chance and a single moment of anger or folly may still work to his harm, even against your will.'

'And you do not trust my temper or my wisdom,' said David, without resentment. 'I think you trouble needlessly, seeing I am no vassal of his now, and nothing I do reflects on him – even though *you* may know, as I know, that at heart I am more his vassal now than ever in life I was before. My formal fealty is to Edward, and with Edward I have to deal, whether I keep it or break it. But if you need reassurance, I swear to you, Samson, I will not take one step before me, write one word, or so much as open my mouth, without weighing the consequences to Llewelyn and to Wales. Tongue and temper I'll watch, if you'll credit me I can, and for his sake above all. There, are you content?'

No question but he was in grave earnest, and I could not doubt him. On that note we parted and went to our beds. And from that night he made no more mention of the discontent that boiled through Wales, but came out of his abstraction and was very good company, merry without fever, even-tempered, resolute and amenable, as though he had put off a shadow. And when they left us to return to Denbigh, he kissed his brother and made his goodbyes with a bright, quiet, cloudless face, and a particular and solemn affection.

Cristin, carrying Elizabeth's youngest girl, warmly wrapped in woollen shawls, gave me her hand through the curtains of the litter, and drew eased and thankful breath as she watched him mount.

'He speaks now of taking up his men's case at law, since they were seized in land which is Welsh, even if it is not part of the principality of Wales. Not that a blood-price will bring them back, but at least it will provide for their families, and go some little way to vindicate and avenge them. And who knows, perhaps help to protect others who may get embroiled in the same way at Chester market. He may even consider appearing the next time he's called to the shire-court, if only to claim Welsh law and fling out again, as he did once before. By Welsh law he is not yet in default. And yet,' she said, drawing her slender black brows together in frowning wonder, 'does this sound like David to you?'

'He has promised,' I said, 'to do nothing without considering its prudence, for the prince's sake.'

'As a judge of what's prudent,' said Cristin, reluctantly smiling, 'David is likely to prove the most perilous justice on any bench. Yet it's something if he'll make the attempt.'

He was away out of the gates then, Elizabeth riding with him for the first few miles, and after them went the litter with its nest of furs, and the little rosy girl half-asleep in Cristin's lap. I watched until a hand waved from between the curtains at the gate, and then they were out of sight, and we were left to turn our attention once again to the long struggle, courtly in more senses than one, that showed now so urgent a face.

I think I had not fully realised how urgent, until I was at Llanfaes on Llewelyn's business, towards the end of January of that year twelve hundred and eighty-two, and Brother William de Merton spoke to me of his great disquiet at the way the prince was being treated, and told me, in confidence, that he had ventured to write directly to the king a strong protest and a stronger warning, urging the damage that must be done to relations between Wales and England if the injustices continued. For the prince, he said, had faithfully kept his side of the treaty, and had great occasion for complaint at the delays and obstacles

122

npeding his lawsuit over Arwystli, since these clearly
onstituted a breach of the terms of the peace, just as the
istraints made on behalf of Robert of Leicester infringed
ie prince's sovereignty in his own lands, the merchant
ever having brought suit in Wales, as he should have done.
s Archbishop Peckham had brought his weight to the
ing's support, so Brother William came sturdily to the
efence of Llewelyn's right, and that unasked, out of his
oncern for the peace, in part, but most of all for
istice.

Llewelyn and Eleanor were at Nevin, in Lleyn, at that
ime, and thence the prince also sent a long, considered
etter to Edward, protesting at the Chester distraint, and
equesting the release of the detained goods. Then he came
o the matter of Arwystli, strongly contesting the latest
levice for delay, and demanding a just remedy.

'For your Grace may be assured,' said Llewelyn in
onclusion, 'that in this matter we are far more concerned
t the humiliation to ourselves than about any profit that
an possibly accrue to us from the impleaded land.'

For all its force it was not a letter composed in anger
or despair, but in stern dignity, and for all its admission
hat he recognised and resented the humiliation put upon
im, it was a proud and princely letter, a reproof from one
nonarch who kept treaty strictly, to another who misused
t. We did not then know it, but it was the last letter the
rince of Wales ever wrote to the king of England. He
hought of it then rather as a new beginning, setting out
he ground on which he was prepared to fight with fresh
eart for his son's inheritance, but certainly not to imperil
t.

By the same courier Eleanor also wrote to her cousin. It
vas the second day of February, and she was in the fifth
month of her pregnancy. But she still had time and thought
'or those unfortunates of her former household who
emained prisoners after so long. One John Becard,
is she had recently heard, had been pardoned and released

123

at the entreaty of one of the king's magnates, and though
she was glad he should have his freedom, it hurt her that
her own frequent pleas for him should have been passed
over, and his liberty restored only at someone else's instance. And so she told the king roundly. It was to me she
dictated that letter, and though I do not recollect it word
for word, after all this time, I have the gist of it by heart
for ever. Somewhat thus it went:

'I should be glad to have some word from your Grace
and beg you to send me news of how you do. I have been
surprised and grieved that your Grace allows my husband,
the prince, to be annoyed by this merchant who still
persecutes him, for as the prince is ready to show justice
to every comer, according to the laws and customs of his
land, I find it strange that credence should be given to such
a complainant, before ever he has brought suit in the
prince's own court, where this case by right belongs. I beg
your Grace to give us a just remedy in this affair. I have
also heard that certain of my men, captured with me, have
been restored to your peace through the pleas of others,
when I myself have often petitioned your Grace on their
account, and have not been heard. I had not thought I
was so estranged from you that you would turn a deaf
ear to my prayers, and rather restore these men to your
peace for the sake of others. Howbeit, by this writing I
once again pray your Grace to receive to your peace Hugh
de Pomfret, Hugh Cook, and Philip Taylor, for since these
are poor men, and English, it will be easier for them to make
a living here in England than elsewhere, and it would
be cruel to send them into exile from their own land.

'Dated at Nevin, on the feast of the Purification of the
Blessed Virgin.'

'Now take heart,' said Eleanor, when these letters had
been despatched, 'for if Edward opens his prison at my
urging, we may receive it as an omen of good. His grip is
tight indeed, but one by one we have won my men out of
his hold, and if he lets these go, then I'll press again for

maury. They have suffered long enough, all of them, for the crime of escorting me to my marriage.'

It was in this spirit that they waited, so immovable in their resolve to hold station, and neither give way a step nor encroach a step, that I had to recall the grave and ominous face of Brother William de Merton before I could truly assess that point to which we were come. And within two weeks, as though heaven itself could not deny Eleanor her will, we received word that the three men she had prayed for had been granted their pardon and set free, at the instance of the princess of Wales.

'Now I believe,' said Llewelyn, clasping her gold head joyfully between his hands, 'that we shall make him into a feeling human creature yet, between us. Still a cheat and a manipulator at law, I don't doubt, but I can excuse a man for holding on tightly to what he hates to lose, provided there's a limit somewhere to the means he'll employ. And I mean to outstay every pretext he can raise against me. He shall wear out before I will.'

But still I could not forget Brother William, whose solemn view it was that Edward's means had already gone beyond all fair limits, and would not scruple to go further yet. So it came to this, that we might well lose Arwystli to Griffith, the arch-traitor, in defiance of all legal process whatsoever, the issue being decided in advance of law and outside law, in the king's mind and will. And though Gwynedd could stand without Arwystli, yet the omen was very evil even for all that remained. For where would legal contrivance end, if it succeeded here? So I was less happy than they, even in this one earnest of Edward's grudging goodwill, though grateful even for that.

Thus we came back in March to Aber, to prepare for Easter. Some days before Palm Sunday we rode in, and it was early spring, very moist and mild and sparkling, and in such days, bright with the palest green of young leaves and the first butter-gold of flowers, there was no man living could resist the burgeoning hope that things must yet go well, that wrongs would be righted and enmities turned to friendships, and men and nations find a way of living in peace.

Tudor ap Ednyfed, the high steward of Wales, had a manor in Tegaingl. And that being one of the cantref of the Middle Country retained by King Edward in his own hands, Tudor now held his lands there of the king and had all the vexations common to all those in that situation, wholly loyal to the prince but owing formal fealty also to Edward for one manor. Such were the complications that he was forced to pay frequent visit to his tenants there, and at this time he rode thence to join us for Easter.

He was not expected until the eve of Good Friday, but instead he rode into the maenol in the afternoon of Palm Sunday, and in great haste, flung his reins to a groom and came striding into the high chamber where Llewelyn was.

'My lord,' he said, hoarse with long riding and the dust of spring, 'I pray your pardon, but this cannot wait. The word that came into my hall this morning I've ridden to bring you as fast as I could. There's battle and slaughter broke loose at Hawarden! In the night a Welsh force has stormed and sacked the castle. Clifford is prisoner, and all his garrison killed or captive.'

Llewelyn was on his feet by then, with a cry rather of impatience and exasperation than dismay. 'They are mad!' he said, and wrung his hands over such suicidal folly, seeing in this no more than a sudden ill-judged blaze of anger among the local tenants, unable any longer to endure submissively the exactions of Edward's bailiffs. 'The poor fools will pay for it heavily. What can they hope to do, a handful of half-armed men, without leaders and without plans?' He clenched his fists and shook them in despair at his own helplessness. 'And I can do nothing for them, to make their peace again after such a madness!'

'No,' said Tudor, 'it is not as you suppose! These are not half-armed farmers breaking out in rage, they are not without leaders, they have not struck without planning in advance. This has been very well planned, and very well done, but that it should not have been done at all. Hawarden fell like a felled tree, and they are marching on Flint, the town of Flint is rising to join them, the town of Rhuddlan is massing men to encircle the castle. I tell you, my lord, the whole of the Middle Country has risen in the night, at a planned hour, with a planned purpose. Villagers, tenants, lords, all are up together. My own people were left out of the secret to keep it from reaching my ears and yours too soon, but no question they're out with the rest by now. This is no border raid. It is war.'

Llewelyn stood braced and still, and looked upon him for a long moment without words. When he spoke again his face was set like stone, and his voice low, level and chill, for though he questioned, he already knew the answer. And so did I. 'Who made the plan?' he said. 'Who raised the cry that brought them out in arms, to their destruction and mine? Name him!'

'Who else,' said Tudor, 'but your brother, the Lord David?'

CHAPTER V

William thin the hour I was in the saddle, with the prince's
writ to commission fresh horses wherever I needed, and his
orders to bring David to him as fast as we could ride. I
rode alone. Tudor wondered at that, I think. If Llewelyn
was to have his brother brought into his presence, it
would have seemed to Tudor more reasonable to send a
strong party and bring him by force. Llewelyn thought
otherwise. The night of reconciliation at Worcester he
remembered, and every word of his last interview with his
brother here in Aber, in January, only two months past,
and there was a manner of doomed, disastrous sense in all.

'He has set himself up to speak for Wales,' he said, 'and
now he has dared to strike for Wales. Very well, let him
answer to Wales. I have no authority at law to drag him
here in chains, he is no longer my man according to any
known code, feudal or Welsh. But he has put his hand to a
plough that is mine, and I will hold him answerable in
the only manner he will acknowledge. Go and find him,
at Flint or wherever he is, and bid him here to me on his
fealty, not to me, but to Wales, unless his vaunted indignation for this land is a shabby lie like all the rest.'

Tudor said warily, for we trod through a legal marsh
that sucked dangerously at our feet: 'There is no man has
drawn sword yet within your principality. The Middle
Country is no longer a part of Wales by law, whatever it
may be by right.'

'And I can therefore abandon it?' said Llewelyn, with a
brief and bitter smile. 'My brother by his act has declared

128

that it is. He will stand by what he has done. And I cannot evade it.'

'And if he will not come?' said Tudor.

'He will come,' said Llewelyn with certainty.

I had no means of knowing, until I crossed the Conway, where I should find David, or how general was this call to arms. But as soon as I was out of the principality I saw for myself that not only David's two cantrefs, but also the two seaward ones which were retained in the king's own hands, had risen to the call, every hamlet was mustering men and weapons, and moving to encircle those points from which the royal bailiffs operated. And there was such exultation and such hope blazing across that countryside that I felt my own heart uplifted, against all reason, for dimly I knew, even as I rode, that by this headstrong and passionate act David had endangered and perhaps destroyed everything to which Llewelyn had devoted his life. Still, they cried greetings to me, and sped me on my way with directions and blessings, and the heat and ache of it got into my blood, and I exulted with them. How could I not, being Welsh?

David, they said, up to the last word they had of him, was at Flint, and the town there was his, and the English, such as were in the town and not the castle, dead or captive. But the castle, being so placed on that great plain of rock jutting out into the estuary, was strongly held, and could be supplied by sea from Chester, and they doubted if any attempt would be made to take it, for since it could be isolated and passed by at will it was not worth the men it would cost in the assault, or, above all, the time, where time was more precious than gold. For in the surprise of this rising lay its best strength. So it was possible, they said, that David had left force enough to hold down Flint from the landward side, and himself rushed on to Rhuddlan, where the Welsh of the surrounding trefs were penning the garrison into the castle, and picking off such of the defenders as they might, leaving the sea-way open, for

129

they had no force as yet sufficient to block it. For Rhuddlan, then, I rode.

Other news I gleaned as I went, and could not choose but marvel how well he had done his work. It was no botched and misshapen rebellion he had offered Llewelyn at that last meeting, but the entire fruit of his able and fiery mind, and all those journeys of his had been threads in the web he had woven, and all held firm when the moment came. Not only here, they told me, but in the west, in Cardigan, in the vale of Towey, everywhere Wales was in arms. The men of Maelor were raiding Oswestry, in the west the Welsh of Llanbadarn had attacked the castle, and in the south David's nephews had raised their standards in Iscennen. And it was terribly sweet to me as I galloped to behold this red blaze sweeping across the whole face of my country, lighting up what had never been offered to Llewelyn before, a Wales entirely and passionately at one. And terribly bitter that it came at the wrong hour, called forth by the wrong man for the wrong reasons, and to what consummation I dared not guess. One half of me boiled like fevered blood, exulting in David's prowess, and one half raged and mourned that when Llewelyn, the true creator of this shadowy nation, cried out to it for fealty and heroism, then it fell short and played him false. For he asked that men should see beyond their own small boundaries, and they could not. And David cried out to them now that within those narrow fences their rights and interests were affronted, and they rose to him as one man to fight for them.

He had not lied to me, when he promised he would do nothing, utter nothing, write nothing, without due consideration of the consequences for Llewelyn and for Wales. He had considered, he had calculated, he had made his own judgment, and acted accordingly. Moreover, his tactics were right, for by striking the first blow at Hawarden, as close as possible to the borders and Chester, he ensured that no royal troops from Cheshire should be able to move west and interfere with whatever was toward in the rest of Wales. With Flint and Rhuddlan besieged, it would be all they could do to cling to the sea-ways and keep the garrisons fed, while David and his allies secured as much as possible of west Wales and the south, and – for I foresaw that this had all along been included in David's plans – gained time to raise also the levies of Gwynedd, which alone had been kept in the dark until the hour struck. After Christmas he had sounded out the prince's mind, and found it absolute against action, and therefore he had shut us out of the secret, and acted alone. Allies, yes, he had allies, enough, but there was but one mind and one will directing that insurrection, and one soul that must answer for it in the judgment.

I had thought to ride well into the night, take but a brief rest, and come to Rhuddlan in the dawn, for the soft days were lengthening, and the frosts were gone. But it was no more than deep of dusk, and I was still far from the valley of the Clwyd, when I saw a small knot of horsemen galloping towards me in purposeful haste, and made out one who led, and three who followed. It was then twilight, but with that gleam about it that draws light from every outline, so that flowers shine like faint lamps, and faces have the pure pallor of saints, and though the foremost rider showed under his blown cap of black hair only such an oval of light for a countenance, yet by his seat in the saddle, and the set of his shoulders and head, I knew him for David, and drew rein and waited in the middle of the way, for the man to whom I had been sent was coming to me of his own will.

I watched him come, and it was as if some years of happy and tamed living, wife and children and all, had been blown away by a wind out of time, and left him the David of my old remembrances, as bright and deadly as a lance, and miraculously young. The horse under him went as eagerly as if the two had been charmed into a centaur, and shared the same burning blood. He had been

131

happy with his Elizabeth and her darling brood, but this was a different happiness that drove him at a gallop towards his judgment. I think he was never quite complete when he had not a battle on his hands, and the life he valued and delighted in was not at risk.

Even from the distance he knew me. I recognised it not by any change in him, but by the very omen that there was no change, that he drove on at the same speed, without even a tightening of his hand on the rein, until he was within twenty paces of where I sat in his path, and then checked his tall roan horse smoothly with hand and knee, and brought him to a stand almost within touch of me, so that we two sat side by side. He was light-armed, in a short tunic of mail, and his head bare, and the speed of his ride and the sharp evening wind had drawn back the blue-black locks from brow and cheek, and tangled them high on his crown. His face had a blazing, blanched brightness, half happiness, half desperation. He could have been angel or devil, but either of terrible beauty.

He smiled at me, distantly, as though I had come between him and a dream, and myself showed but like a shadow, and he said: 'Samson, here? Are you sent to me?'

'I am sent,' I said, 'to bid you come to the prince at Aber, upon your professed fealty not to him, for you owe him none and are no man of his, but to Wales. If your new-found devotion to Wales be not a lie like all the rest.'

'Then you call me where I am already bound,' said David, unmoved by any word or tone of mine, 'and never think but I've left all my fires well-fed behind me. And you'll need to ride hard to keep pace with me into Aber.'

I wheeled my horse and spurred after him, for he waited no longer, but galloped on. I fell into line beside him, and those three knights of his escort, mute and watchful, kept their station behind us as we rode.

Never a word more did we have to say to each other while that journey lasted, until we crossed again into Gwynedd, left the Conway behind, and changed horses on my authority in the dawn. For while the night lasted he set such a hazardous pace that we had no thought or care to spare for anything but the way. When we reached the first vil where Llewelyn's men kept guard I offered the prince's writ, and David was prompt to take advantage of it, as though he accepted, along with the fresh horses, the entire terms on which he was summoned. Then for the first time, as he tightened the girth and tried the length of the stirrup, he looked me in the eyes and said: 'Well, have you nothing to ask me? Nothing to say in praise or blame?'

I said there would be a time for that when we came to Aber, my part was simply to summon him, and that was done.

'As well!' said David. 'I will not make my defence twice over, I have urgent business waiting. Once must do both for you and for him.' And he was in the saddle again lightly, and away for Aber, with his back turned to the pale eastern sky where the sun just showed a golden rim. And as I rode after him I knew, from those few words, that he expected to have to defend what he had done, though he felt no guilt concerning it, and no doubt of its blazing rightness and wisdom. But I felt doubt, and could not get the weight of it off my heart. For this was the first time that David, three times false to Llewelyn and three times restored to grace, had turned traitor instead to Edward, who never forgot an injury, and never forgave, and who recognised, as David himself had said, only one loyalty, to Edward, and only one treason, against Edward. The king had twice embraced and sheltered Llewelyn's renegade, and seen no treason in him. He would not be so complacent now the same treachery had been used against his own head. For David, though not a principal party to the treaty of Aberconway, had sworn fealty and done homage to the king as Llewelyn had, and the breaking of that oath was unforgivable sin.

We eased our steaming horses as we approached Aber,

and slowed to a walk when the outer wall of the maenol came in sight. It was a clear morning, not even cold, and the gulls were wheeling and spinning high over Lavan sands. So calm it was, the light breeze setting from the north-west, that I fancied I could hear all the little bells in the hermitage of Ynys Lanog chiming softly in the distance, across the strait. I remember no more peaceful morning than that, when all Wales outside Gwynedd was already at war.

'I hope to God,' I said, suddenly chilled, 'that you know what you are doing, and what you have done.'

'I do know,' said David. 'No man living, not even my brother, understands so well what I have done. I have burned down behind me all the bridges, holed all the boats, pitted all the fords, stopped every way and filled up every bolthole. I have made it certain that I can never go back. Now there is only one way to go, and that's forward. Now let's see if Llewelyn has learned as much.'

He had risen from his bed as soon as we were sighted in the distance, leaving the princess sleeping. When we had handed over our horses to the drowsy grooms and passed in through the hall, where the household was as yet but half-awake, he was waiting for us in the high chamber, alone. He rose from his great chair as we came in, but did not move to meet his brother, and at sight of his face David also stood, and fronted him from a clear space below the dais, offering neither his knee nor his kiss until they had spoken out what they had to say. He never took his eyes from Llewelyn's countenance, but when I would have withdrawn, seeing my errand was done, he reached out a hand to my arm and held me, and Llewelyn saw that gesture, and said:

'Yes, stay with us. There is no other witness either of us could bear, and who knows but we may need one faithful chronicler?' And then he said, staring upon David: 'I accuse you! I say to your face, David ap Griffith, that you are traitor and forsworn, and your hands are not worth

134

any prince's enclosing within his own, and your oath not worth recording, and your seal not worth the wax it impresses. What you have owed in your time to King Edward you know better than any, and what you have pledged to him you know, and now you have broken fealty and shamed your homage. That is your own damnation. But you have also damned me! Everything I preserved, against you, *you*, Edward's ally, Edward's creature, at Aberconway, you have ruined for ever, and ruined me with it. No matter what I do now, my honour is lost.'

'No!' said David in a low, fierce cry, though until then he had moved no finger and made no sound. 'That is not true!'

'It is true. I am pledged to keep the treaty and the peace with England, and both lie in broken shards about my feet. But worse than what you have done to me is what you have done to Wales. This is too soon, and dishonourable, and disastrous, and it is you, *you* who have dashed Wales out of my hands and out of my son's hands. Do you not realise even now what it is you have done?'

'I know what I have done,' said David, his voice labouring in his throat, 'and you do not. I have done it with open eyes, and alone. I have listened to the wrongs and complaints of Welshmen all through the Middle Country, and borne them, as they have, until I cannot bear them any longer. Not only my own people, but the men of Rhos and Tegaingl have come running to me with their injuries. Where else could they go? To Badlesmere and Grey in Chester? As well to the devil himself! And to you, almost secure here in Gwynedd? What I have done is to travel this burdened land and seek out all the princes of like mind, and find bitter discontent and bitter wrong everywhere, justice delayed or denied, English law thrusting out Welsh law, and English custom Welsh custom. Until I was clear in heart and mind that Edward had broken treaty time after time after time, and there was no breach of treaty to be made now that had not already been made,

135

except the last, the resort to arms. So then I had to weigh every care, every end that might arise from what I began. And that I have done, and I found no other way but this.'

'Having first,' said Llewelyn, with deep bitterness, 'sounded me out and found me determined to keep faith. And gone away from me like a secret thief, with a smooth, compliant face and a submissive voice, pretending honest patience, and carrying my honour away in your hands. You have lost me my honour, and you have lost me Wales!'

'No!' cried David, quivering. 'I have asked nothing of you! You have pledged nothing to me! I left you clear of what I did for this very reason, that you might not be touched. There is not a shadow or a stain upon your honour, all you have pledged you have kept, and so you may still. Am I asking you to break treaty? *I* have acted, and I shall continue to act, and on my head be it! You remain aloof and immune. What have you done? Nothing! You are innocent. *Mine* is the guilt! Hold your principality still, and leave me to end what I have begun. Whatever we can add to your realm we will add, and if we lose it will be our loss.'

There was a silence between them then, that came down upon all our hearts like the weight of a kingdom or a world, and I stood trembling where all my life I had stood, between those two and torn towards both. For though that love was not even, yet on both sides it went very deep, into my blood and my memory and my bowels, rending me. And for awe of the drawn-out anguish that bound and severed them, I could say no word. But at last Llewelyn stirred a little out of his stony stillness, and took up the struggle again, so low and gently that his voice was like the voice of prophecy that troubles the sleep of sinners and saints, but leaves common mankind alone.

'Fool!' he said, without heat. 'Do you think fate allows any neutrality to me? I have sworn fealty to Edward. My choice now is not between insurrection with you on the one hand, and cold neutrality on the other, hedging about what I have. Have you not understood what homage and

oath mean? Or do they never mean anything to you?'
Even this he said gently, as one explaining fidelity to some
untutored alien soul unacquainted with the codes by which
noble spirits live. 'My choice,' he said, 'is between insurrection with you, and taking arms to suppress your
insurrection in the king's name. There is a vow binding us,
and I owe him service. If he call me, what am I to answer?
That is all my choice! And either way is dishonour! A
manner of death! *This* is what you have done to me.'

I looked at David, and his face, all soiled and weary
from the night ride, was drawn so pale and bright that
the bones stood out like knives, and his eyes burned bluer
than periwinkles in the sun at the edge of forests. He stood
straight and held up his head, but all within he was wrung
like a twisted clout. Still he put up his planned and fore-
shadowed fight, and never took his eyes from the ending
he desired.

'If you come with us,' he said, hoarse with passion, 'you
will have wronged no man. The treaty has been breached
time and again, twisting words, loading legal scales,
backing away from solemn oaths – Edward has trampled
it underfoot long since, and you know it. You are absolved
from it ten times over. If I have forced your hand, as you
say I have, it was done because there is no other way open
to us all, everyone who calls himself Welsh. Oh, cry out
on me, as you have every right, that I of all men should
be silent and bow my head when the cause of Wales is
cried aloud, and the standard of Wales is raised, yet still
God help me, I *am* Welsh, birth and blood urge me, the
very air I breathe wrings my vitals, and tells me *I am
Welsh*! I cannot get away! We can look for no justice now
from Edward. We cannot hope to preserve, under him,
our own laws, our own manner of life, our own ancient
customs, not by patience and reason, not by law. *Edward
is the law!* He moulds it in his hands, he interprets it at
will. You know it, as well as I. He has practised it upon
you as he has upon me. There is no way now but war, and
every Welshman in the Middle Country, in the south, in

137

the west – everywhere – cries out for justice and freedom
by the only means that is left. Look!' he said in a hoarse
cry, and flung himself forward on his knees under the
dais where Llewelyn stood, and wreathed his hands about
his brother's ankles. 'This is your call to arms, above all!
Edward has given you what you have worked and prayed
for, a Wales united at last! If you do not seize that weapon
and strike with it now – *now*, when it is offered! – you will
never have another chance. This – *this* is what I have done
for you!'

He was so shaken that his fine, long hands were clasped
close on the prince's feet, and even in the low candle-light
his knuckles stood out white as frost. His face was uplifted,
the tangle of black hair still erected by his ride strained
back from his temples as though he had flown down to his
abasement out of the skies. And still Llewelyn stood
unmoving, if not unmoved, and looked down at him eye
to eye, without remorse or compunction, but without
anger, either, as though his eyes saw clean through flesh
and bone and into his brother's mind, as it may well be
they did at last.

'So you did know,' he said, 'what you were doing to me.
And now you come with this talk of my standing apart
in my innocence, knowing as well as I know that it is
impossible. You are not even honest!'

'You would not listen,' cried David, his voice thick and
laboured in his throat, 'you would not act! I saw the
Wales of your vision offered to you at last, I, who had
never before been able to see and desire it with a whole
heart, far less believe in it! I heard it crying out to you.
And all you would say was that you were bound! I could
not bear it! I have cut your bonds. Now for God's sake
rise up, take arms, be a prince again! It is too late to undo
what I have done. By this Llanbadarn is in flames, like
Flint, our nephews are out in the vale of Towey, the Middle
Country is roused from Dee to Conway. If you choose
to go with Edward, and keep the bondage of your seal,
you could hold and kill me now, and doubtless Edward

would bless you for it, but that would not put out the fire I have started.'

His voice by the end of this was loud and defiant and glad, that had begun choked and wild. He had no doubts and no regrets, and he was never going back, that he knew. But still he clung with wide, blazing blue eyes to Llewelyn's face, and could not look away, and even so fiercely his brother looked down upon him. Neither of them saw or heard anything outside their two selves. But I, for the sheer pain of watching them, turned my head aside to fix upon the dark, worn figures in the tapestry hangings behind the dais, the carving of the arm of the prince's chair, the blackened candle-sconce in the wall. And there, mute and still at the back of the room, where she had entered from the narrow door that led to their sleeping-chamber, Eleanor was standing.

I do not know how long she had been there, for the curtains cut off any draught from the door when it opened, and always she moved very surely and softly. Certainly she was incapable of stealth, and had entered in innocence, and the sight of those two locked in their death and life contention had halted her as soon as she came in, and held her unwilling to break the spell that bound them. She had come but two or three paces into the room, and the curtains still shadowed her, but silently and carefully she had closed the door behind her, that no one else might hear what passed between the brothers. And then she stood and waited, for had she tried to withdraw, that would have been as shattering a disturbance as if she had advanced to walk between them.

She was entering the seventh month of her pregnancy, and her body rounding, so that she stood with her hands lightly braced along her high girdle, and leaned a little backwards, and being so beautiful, she had that strange and royal grace that the Mother of God has in paintings and statues that show her in the time of the visitation. Her face was grave, considering and aware, and her eyes were on Llewelyn's face, and never left it but to look once full into mine, and though she gave me then no smile and made no sign, her glance acknowledged and was glad of me as one always and wholly, like her, a true lover of her lord. We stood apart, but we waited together, for those two to resolve the battle between them.

'There is no need to remind me,' said Llewelyn, staring down upon his brother with a darkened and shuttered face, 'that you have left me no choice but between two dishonours.' And he made one strong step back, and tore himself out of David's clasping hands. 'Now get out of my sight,' he said with terrible gentleness and more terrible despair, 'while I make that choice.'

David got up from his knees slowly, like a wounded man, and turned and went out from him reeling a little as though exhausted, but still his face was bright and resolute as he passed me. When he was gone, Llewelyn sat down slowly in the great chair, and then Eleanor moved from her place and came to him out of the shadows. Released from his bitter concentration upon David's presence, he felt hers, and turned to her as plants turn to the sun knowing who came before ever she stepped into the light.

Confronting this cataclysm that threatened her fortune, her peace and everything she loved, she looked as I saw her look once when she stood between the knights of her household and Edward's Bristol pirates, and addressed the chief of her captors with the fearless courtesy of queens, and the large, involuntary contempt of the noble for the base. Never did she protest at what was done and could not be undone, never turn her back on what must be faced and dealt with, never repine over what was past remedy. She looked the hour in the face, whether it smiled or frowned, and chose her course with a single-hearted gallantry, seldom in doubt, never in fear.

He watched her draw near, and when she was close he reached out and took her hand, and drew it into his breast. Always her approach reflected light over his face, but then it was a still and solemn light. He asked gently: 'How much have you heard?'

'Enough,' she said.

'I am glad. I would have told you, but now there is no need.'

'None,' she said. 'It is no choice at all. Between betraying Edward and betraying Wales there can be no choice.'

He drew breath long and deeply, eased of uttering what was inevitable, and had been from the moment David struck at Hawarden. 'They are two ways of dying,' he said, 'and both with dishonour. But he says truly, nothing now do can undo what he has done. With me or without me, Wales is at war. Of all the things I cannot do, the furthest out of my scope is to take the field for Edward against my own people. And after that, hardly less impossible, to let them fall helpless into Edward's hands, and never draw sword to aid them.'

'There is no need to tell me so,' she said with resolute serenity. 'There is but one way to go, for you and for me. We go with Wales. Nor can we launch into this war with half our hearts and half our forces. Since we must go, let's go with our might, and triumph if we can.'

'Since I am throwing my honour into the scale,' he said with bitter resolve, 'I may well throw everything else in after it. The lot was cast for me without my will, but what I make of it now is on my own conscience. I had not thought, my heart,' he said, laying his cheek against the hand he held, 'to have dragged you into such a wilderness for love of me.'

'Never say so!' she said, and her green-gold eyes flared, and her long fingers curled and closed over his mouth, caressing him with passion. 'There is more in it than that! I go with you not only because I would go with you to the ends of the world, no matter how barren, and find there all the roses I want or need, and beyond that into hell, and think it a cool and pleasant place with you beside me – though so I would! No, this is my war no less than yours. I have a mind and a will, and honour to be staked and lost, like you, and in this matter I judge as you do. If you are Edward's liege-man, so am I his liege-woman. If you must

141

bear the burden of a guilt you have not earned, then half that load is mine, and I claim it. Everything that is yours, whether it be glory or shame, is also mine. But your son whom I carry is guiltless. If you and I by staking our two souls can win for him a free Wales to be his inheritance, then I say let us submit our own dishonour gladly to the judgment of God, and pay whatever penalty is exacted with a high heart. So we sin together,' she said, 'and atone together! We can neither avert nor avoid this war. It only remains to fight it.'

'Fight it and win it!' he said, shaken half into laughter and half beyond into astonished grief, for there was never any of Earl Simon's sons, not even the eldest and best, looked and sounded so like his sire as did then this only daughter, this ivory dove among the eagles, with her world in peril, and the seed of kings and heroes quickening in her womb. He opened his arms and drew her down into his heart, circling all his dreams and labours and hopes within the compass of her rounding waist.

And I, who had held still for fear of troubling their immense solitude, slipped away out of the room unnoticed while they clung together in that three-fold embrace, and waited without, not far, until he should call me. For those two, having no comfort but in each other, and having accepted a war they had not sought and did not want, would not now be long inactive about it, even for love's sake. They would pursue it, rather, with all their gallantry and force, most of all for love's sake.

Nevertheless, for all the deeds he did thereafter, and all the pride and sovereignty of his leadership in the cause of Wales, I testify that a part of him died that day, when he tore himself free perforce from his plighted fealty and troth, and followed his brother and ill-demon into the last of his wars against England.

It was not ten minutes before he opened the door. And she was gone, and he was calm and hard as stone, and his

142

eyes had deep fires burning in them, no passing sparkle, but the slow, enduring heart-red that burns through days and nights without failing or changing. His voice was low, brisk and mild. He said: 'Samson, call David back to me, and wait until he leaves. I need you here.'

So I called David, who was sitting with his head in his arms, asleep upon a trestle table in a corner of the hall, with the common bustle of life passing him by this way and that. At my touch on his shoulder he awoke and fell into a brief, strong shuddering, and started upright with a hand to his hilt and a wrung smile on his mouth, but his eyes still innocent and dazed and blue, a waking child's eyes. Then he knew me, and the frost of awareness clenched the blue into spearhead sharpness, and the lines of his face into sword-edges, and he was wide awake with a leap, as was usual with him, and laughed, for laughter was his armour.

'I thought you were Edward,' he said, 'and here's not my judge, but my confessor. Well, have I sped? God knows I left nothing to chance that I could ensure, to nail him to what he finds a cross. Oh, Samson, the first true gift ever I tried to bring him, and I throw that and myself at his feet, and look up at him, and his face, oh, God, is the face of a murdered man before he dies. Oh, Samson, must I be fatal still?' And by that he had left laughing, and his eyes were huge and veiled. But the next moment he laughed anew, for he, who derided most things, derided most of all himself. 'I should have stayed in Denbigh getting handsome daughters,' he said. 'It is what I am best at. At least a whole company of young men will have reason to praise me.'

I could not choose but note how he named Edward, and yet thereafter, meaning his brother, found no need to say other than 'he', for there was but one he who so occupied the whole ground of his heart and mind. So I said only: 'He bids you to him.' And he looked with unwonted earnestness in my face, to find what I had seen in his brother's face, and he came with me.

143

When we entered the high chamber Tudor was there before us, and the captain of the prince's household guard with him, and two clerks sat at a table below the dais. Llewelyn turned from them to meet us. I saw David's eyes noting these presences, and the parchments already strewn on the board among them, and the single brief glance they gave to him, such of them as looked up at all. He knew then that his cause had taken a great leap forward while he snatched his few minutes of exhausted sleep, and things were now gone far past any further argument or reproach. Never again would there be mention of what he had done. The blame for disaster would never be shaken off on to his shoulders, if the end was disaster, nor could he ever lay claim to the whole glory if the venture ended in glory. I think he knew with what deep anguish and shame Llewelyn accepted the destiny forced upon him, I do believe that in his rebellious and audacious heart he felt it almost as deeply that he was the cause, but his eyes were fixed upon the end he had set before him, and by comparison with that, no pain of his or his brother's was of any consequence.

'My writs go out within the hour,' said Llewelyn. 'I require from you an account of all your planned moves as they stand now, and the disposition of what forces you count on. But briefly!'

David dictated, and one of the clerks took down the list of those actions planned in secret, in various parts of Wales, to take place all in the same day, the eve of Palm Sunday. All these, he said, should now be under way. Also he told which princes and chiefs had committed their armies to the enterprise, and what numbers they represented.

'You did your work thoroughly,' said Llewelyn, without any word of blame but without any warmth, either. 'Very well!' he said. 'In two days my first levies shall be with your men at Rhuddlan. In three I myself shall join you. If you move your main base within that time, send me word where

I shall find you. One of us may need to go south. Also there should now be consultation. Only a national council can speak for a nation.'

Thus he made it plain that the whole nobility of Wales ought at this crisis to stand as one, and utter with one authoritative voice its declaration of injury and its resort to the remedy of war. And David said at once, and submissively: 'If it please you to call your magnates to a parliament, and if it can be done quickly enough, I offer Denbigh. If they come there they will see for themselves what is in train already, and that we are at one in setting about it. There can be no factions.'

'As good a place as any,' said Llewelyn. 'They shall be called there. Six days from now? As much as possible must be done before Edward ever gets word of the rising.'

'He cannot have heard yet,' said David. 'We should have two or three days of grace, but we cannot hope for more.'

'Then you had best take what rest you need, and go back to your siege,' said Llewelyn, and would have turned from him without a word more, to get straight to the business of sending out his writs, at which the clerks were penning away busily. But David, with a face suddenly blanched beneath its dust, started forward so sharply as to halt the movement, and clashed to his knees again before his brother.

'As the lord prince orders,' he said, and lifted up his joined hands, palm to palm, towards Llewelyn, and so kept, unfaltering and unrelenting, though for what seemed a great while there was no move made to acknowledge or respond to his challenge. Deliberately he did it, before witnesses, remembering and reminding us how not an hour previously Llewelyn had told him that his hands were not worth any prince's while to enclose within his own, nor his oath of fealty worth recording. With those words still in his ears, and his sworn fealty to Edward but one day dead, nevertheless he kneeled and demanded, so motionless that it seemed he would grow into a praying stone monument there if he was refused.

145

There was a stillness and silence in the room, even the pens unmoving, while those two eyed each other long and hard, probing after a surer ground and a clearer understanding. So long it continued, and so remote and chill was the prince's face, that I thought he would end by turning away and leaving the petitioner to stay or go, live or die, as he saw fit. But the uplifted hands never quivered nor sank, but continued their silent clamour for admission to grace and subjection, and the fixed, passionate face implored and confided, and presently Llewelyn advanced his own hands slowly, and took his brother's between them, and held them hard. And David opened grey lips into which the red flowed back impetuously with the returning blood, and drew breath and began in a high, clear voice, like a priest exalted and translated by his office:

'I become your man from this time forth, and to you do homage, and shall be faithful and true during my life. . . .'

Once before, very long ago after his first defection, he had offered this, and been plucked rashly from his knees and embraced with the words unspoken. This time he went on steadily to the end, and without pause or tremor passed over those phrases excepting the duty he owed and had promised to the king, for now at last he had but one sovereign lord, as the prince had none, but only God as overlord. And Llewelyn held him steadfastly to the end.

Thus David, who had pledged many fealties up to this time, and kept none, entered of his own will and at his own insistence into the last homage of his life, and having so entered, rose instantly from his knees and went out, taking no leave and no rest, chose himself a fresh horse from the stables, and rode out of Aber with a lighter heart than when he entered it, and went to begin the long labour of making good what he had sworn.

The prince's writs went out throughout the land that same day. With far happier hearts than their prince the men of Gwynedd rose. Only when the north was already

146

blaze, and all men could cry out their grievances and atreds aloud, did I fully understand how bitterly deep vent their sense of fellowship with their own kinsmen utside the principality, where no Llewelyn stood between Velshmen and their English bailiffs.

'There's nothing for bringing quarrelsome kin together,' aid Eleanor ruefully to me, the day before we rode from Aber, 'like a common enemy whose arrows strike at them all. But it does not always last even through the battle. The longer I live, the more I see, Samson, that many men may have heroism in them, but few have constancy, and very few have it so at heart that when they feel it defaced, they may die of it. And for those very few, I think, this world has little use.'

It was not like her to sound disheartened or despairing, nor did she then, she was but measuring the possibilities of the future, and finding them bleak, and assessing also her own endurance, which did not fall short.

'I do not know,' she said, 'but David may be justified, and Edward has breached the treaty time and time again. But even if we are forsworn and recreant, as *he* believes, and our cause dishonoured, still the cause of Wales is not, and if a man can die for that and be proud, perhaps he can also offer up for it what is dearer than life, and not be ashamed. If we venture it, he and I, we shall discover how God looks upon it, shall we not? If he knows Llewelyn as I know him, he will not undervalue the sacrifice.'

In those days of preparation she took a full and active part. And when all was done that could be done before action, and we mustered to ride for Rhuddlan, she came out confident and serene, with her ladies at her back, and kissed her husband as if he were leaving for a day's hunting, and waved us away as long as we were in sight, in case he should look back at the last moment.

After we were gone, it may be she wept. I doubt it, but I do not know, I never saw her weep. If ever she did, it was in solitude.

147

CHAPTER VI

We joined forces with David south of Rhuddlan where he was encamped to wait for us, having ringed the castle from every landward approach, secured the town and done what damage he could to the Clwyd frontage and the little port where sea vessels put in. Time was then the most precious and effective ally we had, to waste it on winning such a castle as Rhuddlan would have lost us weeks, if not months, that we could not afford. There were other strongholds more vulnerable, and of greater use to us, and Llewelyn had already marked them down.

'Ruthin is not so firmly held, and they never look to see us there, the coast roads being their best approach and our greatest weakness. Now the men of Maelor are up, we have allies there to help us. We should do well to move up the Clwyd, and send ahead to them to meet us, you at Ruthin, me at Dinas Bran. If we move fast enough we may get both, and have a line of castles down the march.'

'Lestrange has newly garrisoned Dinas Bran,' said David.

'So much the better, he'll be over-confident.'

It proved as he said. The forces of both brothers, with the best-mounted levies of the Middle Country, swept south-east up the line of the Clwyd, and while David surrounded Ruthin, the prince rushed onward to Dinas Bran, overhanging the valley of the Dee. A wild and rainy ride we had of it over the hills, with a gale blowing, but in such weather, even if he had yet heard of the rising and considered his own situation, doubtless Lestrange thought us still far away, and unlikely to trouble him, so

148

r south. We had scouts ahead, despatched before we set
ut, who brought us back word that the Welsh of Maelor
ɔ the east of us, and Edeyrnion and Cynllaith to the
ɔuth, had risen joyfully to the prince's call, turning their
acks even on the plunder of Oswestry, twice raided, to
ɔin in the assault, for Lestrange, who held the castle for
ɲe crown, was kin by marriage to Griffith ap Gwenwyn-
ɩyn, and very well hated.

We closed in from three sides upon Dinas Bran, high
n its great grassy ridge above the river valley. We from
ɲe north, approaching over the hills, had the best ground
ɔr attack, and came as the greatest shock to a garrison
ɲat thought us still busy with Rhuddlan and Flint.
ɻoreover, I would not say the watch they kept was very
ɔmpetent, or we should not have got within striking
istance of the main gatehouse before they gave the alarm.
ɩpeed, which had been our greatest asset in reaching them
ɔ soon, was also our strongest weapon in attack. They
ɩever had time to get the bars into their sockets before we
ɩove in the doors, and were among them, and put our
ɩrst parties up on to the walls to dispose of their archers,
ɩot only to have a commanding ring round the mêlée in the
astle ward, but also to prevent them from shooting down
ɩpon our friends from Cynllaith as they stormed up the
ɩill to join us. After that it was no great feat of arms, and
ost us but a few men wounded, to get possession of the
ʋhole castle with most of the garrison, though Lestrange
ɩimself with a small, well-mounted party got out by a
ɩostern gate when he saw the castle was lost, and made
ʎlean away before we knew he was loose. But Dinas Bran
ʋas ours to garrison afresh for Wales, and the Welsh
ɔf those parts were eager and ready to man it in the
ɩrince's name.

Thus we held, within a few days, a strong line of castles
ɩunning south-east from the sea almost to Oswestry, and
ɩuarding the whole of the northern march fronting Chester:
ɩom the north Denbigh, Ruthin and Dinas Bran, with

Rhuddlan itself still in English hands but isolated at th
northern extreme of the line, and Hope a somewhat vul
nerable but as yet useful outpost, much nearer to Chester

'They've tried hard enough to wrest it from me by law,
said David grimly, when we conferred with him again i
captured Ruthin. 'Now let them come and try what the
can do in arms.' He foresaw already that the time migh
come when he would be forced to abandon a position s
exposed to the danger of being outflanked from Chester
'As yet it's safe enough,' he said, eyeing the chances th
future held, 'it takes time for Edward to get his lumberin
muster into motion. But once he's launched, I may wel
have to relinquish Hope.' He grimaced at the double soun
of that, and laughed. 'But it shall cost them dear and d
them little service if I must abandon it.'

'This time,' warned Llewelyn, 'we should be fools t
think Edward will hold his hand until the feudal host i
ready. He knows as well as we how cumbersome the ol
way can be. He prefers paid men.'

At that time we had not and could not yet hope for an
news from the court, and did not even know where Edwar
was at that moment, and whether he had yet heard of th
sudden blaze of rebellion that was flaring through the west
For it was still no more than five days since David ha
stormed Hawarden, when we returned to Denbigh t
prepare for the coming of the princes and the holding o
the solemn parliament of Wales.

Denbigh was teeming with activity, armourers an
fletchers hard at work, the first visitors riding in, and thei
grooms and men-at-arms loud and busy about stables an
hall. The prince's couriers had reached every part of Wale
that was open to us, and all the chiefs of the north cam
in person to the gathering, that it might have all possibl
authority. This time there was no question of dissent
There was barely a man who was not heart and sou
committed to the struggle, for there was none whose ow
rights were not threatened.

150

From Cardigan, Griffith and Cynan, the sons and heirs of Meredith ap Owen, who had been a loyal ally of the prince lifelong, sent their seneschal, for they were still busy about securing the town of Llanbadarn and the country round, though their attempt upon the castle had been only partially and briefly successful. They could, nonetheless, prevent it from being relieved or receiving fresh supplies except by sea, and to send ships round to that western coast was by no means so quick and simple as to despatch food from Chester to Flint or Rhuddlan. Given a few weeks, they could starve out the royal garrison without cost to themselves.

From the vale of Towey came Griffith, the second of the prince's three nephews, together with envoys from his two brothers, to report that the combined forces of all three had risen in an onslaught on the castles of Llandovery and Carreg Cennen, both of which had formerly belonged to their house, and had been retained by the crown after the last war. With an old and strong royal enclave at Carmarthen, and Pembroke almost more English than Welsh, Edward had hopes of extending his hold by founding such another centre of administration at Dynevor and had also garrisoned the other castles along the Towey by way of outposts of this new royal region. Now, said Griffith, he stood to lose them, for though Carreg Cennen had not yet fallen, its fall was as good as certain, and Llandovery was already breached, and John Giffard, who held it from the king, had been forced to abandon it and withdraw into England.

Strange indeed were the shifting alliances and enmities of the border families of England and Wales, after so long of inter-marrying for land and policy. This same John Giffard, once an ardent follower of Earl Simon de Montfort, and later one of those young men who turned most violently against him, was married to Maud Clifford as her second husband, and that lady was cousin to Llewelyn and David, her mother being Margaret, daughter of

Llewelyn Fawr. Giffard had been installed by Edward in Llandovery to the deprivation of his wife's young kinsmen, and now they in their turn had driven him out and regained their own by force of arms.

One more piece of news we gained at that conclave, and that was brought by the lord of Ial. 'Did you know, my lord,' he said, 'that your brother, the Lord Owen, came to spend Easter on the lands King Edward gave him, near the Cheshire borders? We made no approaches to his tenants, for fear it should get to his ears, and be betrayed.' Llewelyn looked at David, then, for that must have been by his orders. 'But when we rose, and they heard of it, they were up after us in a moment, and had hoped to carry him with them. It was a vain hope. Last night they brought word he's fled into Chester, to join de Grey.'

'It's no surprise,' said David indifferently, 'and he can do us no harm there now, Grey already knows only too well what we're up to, and by this time either he from Chester or Gilbert de Clare from Gloucester will surely have got word to Edward, wherever he may be. All Owen can offer them is his own single sword, and we have nothing to fear from that.'

It was a true but a cruel word, from the youngest to the eldest of those four brothers. For Owen Goch, who for some years in their youth had shared the rule in Gwynedd equally with Llewelyn, until he made war against him in the hope of gaining all, and so lost all, was certainly of little consequence by that time in the affairs of either England or Wales. Edward had made his freedom and establishment in lands a condition of the treaty of Aberconway, and Llewelyn had given him the peninsula of Lleyn, and Edward added to his portion some manors bordering Cheshire; but I doubt if either of them had given a thought to him since that time, and all Owen had wanted, after so long of confinement, was to live comfortably and quietly on his own lands, and trouble no one. Now he was again cast, much against his will, into the turmoil of war, and found himself again landless, his eastern tenants having declared for Wales, and his western lands being just as surely lost to him, now that he had chosen to take refuge with his English protectors in Chester.

'I must send to his bailiff in Lleyn. At least his going solves one problem for us,' said the prince with compunction. 'I am glad he's safe out of our hands, for he never would have come in with us against the king, and as you say, he is no threat. He has taken no forces with him, and he can tell them nothing more than they already know.'

There was never to be a time when all those four brothers of Gwynedd stood side by side as one. Their fragmented fortunes contained within them all the history of Wales. But for the rest, there was no one missing from the muster but Rhys ap Meredith of Dryslwyn, always enemy to Llewelyn like his father before him, and the renegades of Pool, when the prince rose and put to the assembled parliament of Wales the issue that had brought them together, and with one voice, and a loud and passionate voice at that, they declared that the treaty of Aberconway had been breached time after time by England, until it had no further validity, but was null and void, and left to Wales no remedy but in arms. And formally they denounced the treaty, and gave their assent to the solemn acceptance of war.

Then it remained only to plan the next moves. And young Griffith begged, and the envoys from Cardigan supported his plea, that either Llewelyn or David would come south with them, and use his authority to direct their campaigns there.

'I will go,' said David, 'if the prince wills it.'

'It would be best,' said Llewelyn. 'While I complete the raising of Gwynedd. Take with you whatever part of your own forces you need, and I'll supply their place here as my levies come in.'

A hundred lances David took south with him, and a score of mounted archers, and among the lances was

Godred. I was in the bailey that morning to watch them go, along with all the rest of the household, maidservants, menservants, grooms, falconers, pages, shepherds, armourers, cooks and scullions, every soul who could drop his burden and down his tools for a few minutes to see a gallant show and wish a great venture well. And I saw then, and heard, and felt, in all the tremor of movement and quiver of voices about me, how we had not so much taken a brave leap forward into an enlarged future, but harked back into a noble, turbulent, fruitless past, the heroic past of a Wales torn and self-tearing. It was like the old days, they said! But I would have had it like new days, days never before known, the beginning of an unbreakable unity and a new grandeur. And how many of us were ready for it, even then? Yet there was ardour enough in the courtyards of Denbigh to make a nation, had a few more of us had any clear vision what a nation was.

Against my judgment I had hopes then. The trembling of the air with so many farewells and godspeeds set my heart shaking with it, and caused me to catch my breath like the rest. Both hope and despair were so native to Wales, they grew like weeds, and died like flowers in frost. And who could be sure that David had not judged his moment rightly, after all, and dealt his strokes wisely, and won a kingdom for us? It could have been so!

The troops massed and mounted, and I saw Godred among them, but if he saw me he said no word and made no sign. By his face I think he was glad to be turning his back upon Denbigh and his barren wife, and his face towards the loose skirmishes and casual plunder of war, in which he moved like a houseless vagabond, free of kin and kind, his bed and his food where he found it, and no questions asked. When I first met him, before ever I knew he was my father's son and my love's lost husband, in this fashion he was living, travelling light through a world in which there always had been and always would be room for him somewhere, a bed, a woman, food and a fire, and

154

lord to hire his agile body and ready sword. He owned nothing but the clothes he stood in, and his arms, and a horse, and to say truth even the horse was stolen from the earl of Gloucester's stables at Llangynwyd when it became clear that the castle must fall, and Godred deemed it wise to remove himself elsewhere. Other assets he had then, a comely face, a light, winning voice, and a heart livable and reclaimable as gaily as tossing a ball. All soiled and faded now, but still living, and keeping yet their colour and sap, like flowers pinched but not killed by frost. And often I thought that if I had not found him then, and restored him to princely service in Wales, and to the wife he had thought dead, and perhaps even mourned for a day or two with the surface of his shallow and sunlit mind, all we three might have gone through the world happy.

David came out from the great doorway of the hall with his wife on his arm, and Cristin walking behind with his two sons, one by either hand. David kissed them, kissed Elizabeth, and mounted, and wheeled away at the head of his column without a glance behind. There was no time for long farewells when he was already in arms, even his face bright and tempered for battle.

Elizabeth watched the cavalcade form and follow, until the gates closed after them, and the echo of their hooves had died away down the long, steep slope into the town. The little boys were bounding and shouting beside her, but she was still, narrowing her brown eyes to watch until the last glimpse of David's erect head was lost to her. He did not turn, and she had known he would not.

She had watched him go from her thus once before, after he had bestowed her and his children safely in England, and set his household troopers to prowl the middle march and harry the border cantrefs from Shrewsbury. But then it had been with all the might of England on his side, and now he rode against the same power, and his act was bitter and particular offence to the king who had maintained

and protected him then. And she was born English
daughter to the earl of Derby and kinswoman to Edward
himself through her mother, and though she would have
followed David without question wherever he chose to lead
her, yet all her mind and heart stood in solemn awe of the
terrible undertaking in which he now dared to engage, and
it was with open eyes and conscious daring that she took
her stand beside him, and blessed what he did. Married
to him at eleven years old, she had borne her first child at
fourteen, and motherhood had not put an end to her own
childhood, but only prolonged and glorified it, so that she
seemed but the gayest and most loving of older sisters to
her own brood. But when David rode from Denbigh that
morning to unite the Welsh of the south, in defiance of
King Edward and all the power of England, I watched
her face, the merry, good-natured face ever ready to kindle
into laughter, and now so grave and so aware, and I saw
her grow up before my eyes.

Denbigh being the best base from which to control and
guard all that long eastern march, Llewelyn made it his
headquarters until David's party should again come north,
and though we were often out patrolling the line of fortresses, and sometimes withdrew to Conway and Aber
and the western cantrefs to deploy the incoming levies
as they mustered, it was always to Denbigh we returned.
Such fighting as we had was limited to testing raids along
the border. It seemed that all the barons of the march
were putting their followings on a fighting footing, but
not yet making any move to attack, rather merely holding
their defences. We heard, but not with certainty, that a
royal muster was expected in May at Worcester, but had
heard no word of the usual summons going out for the
assembly of the feudal host.

'He would rather by far raise his armies at his own
wages,' said Llewelyn. 'I expected it. I wish we could get
some word from Cynan. Wherever Edward is, there Burnell

will be, and his clerks with him. Give him time, and he'll
find a messenger.'

A week after he had left us, David sent word from the
south that all was going well, the capture and partial
dismantling of Llandovery and Carreg Cennen completed,
and having left his nephews to keep a tight hold upon the
vale of Towey, he himself was rushing with his own company to Llanbadarn, to help the sons of Meredith ap
Owen finish what they had begun there. In mid-April a
second courier brought news that the castle of Llanbadarn
was taken and slighted, and all the English forces in the
south and west had withdrawn into their strongholds
of Cardigan and Dynevor, and were pinned down there
so securely that they dared hardly venture out even on
foraging raids. A week or two more to make certain of his
dispositions, said David, and he would be able to bring
his own force back to the Middle Country and stand
shoulder to shoulder with his brother, to withstand the
inevitable main thrust of Edward's revenge.

It was not until May, when the king's first army assembled at Worcester, that we got reliable news of Edward's
counter-measures, for there Cynan found a trustworthy
Welsh Franciscan on his way home to Bangor by way of
Cwm Hir abbey, and confided to him a long letter for the
prince. The friar delivered the letter faithfully to David,
who sent it on to Llewelyn in advance of his own return.
About the twentieth of May it reached us at Denbigh.

'Your thunderbolt,' wrote Cynan, 'struck us at Devizes
some three days after it was launched, and shattered the
Easter mood with a vengeance. No question but it was a
thunderbolt. If any tells you the king had planned to
provoke the storm, don't heed him. But he'll make use of
it to the last drop of blood now it has fallen on him. If he
had anything of the kind in mind, it was not expected to
catch fire this year. Probably gradual encroachment was
intended, as costing less in money, though more in patience.
Take warning! One of his first measures, when he was able

to speak and breathe for rage, has been to open negotiations with his Italian bankers, for loans so huge that he must intend to buy enough mercenaries to settle with Wales once for all. Put no faith this time in winter. His hate is such that neither frost nor snow will stop him, and the opportunity he has been offered he has already recognised, and will not lightly relinquish.

'I write in comparative safety at this time, and therefore at length, for God knows when I may next find the means To present you all I know: At Devizes he enacted a number of furious orders and writs, giving instant command to his justiciars, but Gloucester has now been appointed to take command in the south. His Grace has not so far called out the feudal host. He sent instead to six earls and a number of crown tenants to raise their forces and meet him here at Worcester in the middle of May, as now they have done. These to be paid at his wages, mark. But the earl of Hereford is up in arms already, claiming his feudal right as constable, and I foresee the king will be forced to raise the host according to custom, much as he chafes at its carthorse paces. Further: he is calling out the whole fleet of the Cinque Ports at once to provision and fit out for sea, and he has sent out for supplies, horses and arms to Ireland, Gascony and Ponthieu, which province he now holds in right of the queen, as you know. He is asking in particular for Gascon crossbowmen. Every omen shows that he will spare nothing, drive every man but himself to death, and if need be himself after, to take his revenge. and in particular on the Lord David, the serpent he warmed in his bosom.

'That he has prevailed on his archbishop to send out letters ordering the excommunication of all the rebels, notably the lord prince and the Lord David, will be no surprise to you. Thus far I hear that our Welsh bishops have been in no haste to promulgate these letters. I pray their dullness of hearing may long continue, but they are also men, and subject to Canterbury and Rome.

'The best I have kept for last, that some good may show out of this much ill. Archbishop Peckham has urged the necessity for showing a front of justice and reason before the Holy Father, if his goodwill is to be invoked in this conflict, and has preached once again on his old text, that the detention of the Lord Amaury de Montfort is an offence and a scandal against the papacy, hardly likely to incline his Holiness to look with favour upon his captor, or any enterprise of his captor. And the king has at last agreed – it was like drawing a tooth! – that Amaury shall be free to sail from England when he will, and return to Rome, or to any place he pleases out of these islands. He is already loosed, and by the time this reaches you he may well be at sea, or even landed in France. Peckham has stood by him manfully.

'The king will certainly come himself to Chester, to confront the only enemies worthy of him. I may well be among those who follow him north, but in the expectation that I must be silent a while, until time again serve your ends and mine, I wish you a fair deliverance, and pledge you my service to the death.'

'I hope he may never have to make that good!' said Llewelyn when he had read this most helpful despatch. 'Well, thank God there is at least one good thing come out of it all. I have not thrown away my oath quite for nothing. Now Eleanor may take some comfort from her brother's release, if we have nothing more to offer her. And we know what we have to face. Edward will not wait for the feudal muster, even if he must call it now. He'll have them follow him north, and come north himself at once with what he already has.'

'He is quick enough to call for excommunication,' said Tudor bitterly, 'for treason to his own head, did ever you hear him even censure treason against you?'

But that was possibly the sanction Llewelyn, within his own country, had least reason to fear, and in balance against his Christian efforts for Amaury he held it against

159

the archbishop not at all. The good news he sent at once to Eleanor at Aber. He could not then go himself, for we had much to do before David returned and Edward set out on his march to Chester, where by our reckoning Grey was already in command of some hundred and fifty lances, possibly more, and a great number of foot, of whom all too many were archers.

'He is arming half his footmen with bows—longbows or crossbows,' said Llewelyn, gnawing his lip as we made up the tale of our enemies. 'And according to the rumours from the south, they're bringing up crossbow quarrels by the thousand from Bristol. There's no relying on Edward to make war twice alike.'

'There are things that will not change,' said Tudor soberly. 'His best way in at us is still by the coast, and there he has his new roads, and so he has at a dozen places where he has hacked a way through the forests down the march. And he will still have an eye on the harvest in Anglesey, if he can come at it by any means, and we can neither hurry that forward and garner it now, nor bid it hold back until the winter. And he has the ships.'

'It is true,' said Llewelyn. 'I have been remiss in not providing more and better ships of our own. All those years of peace I could have done more, and saw no need.' And that was true, for those small craft that we used for shorewise traffic and for fishing were ample to our normal needs, and though he had been provident enough in the old days of constant vigilance and uncertainty, and done more to provide Gwynedd a navy than any prince before him, yet after the peace of Montgomery, during the years when he lived in amity with King Henry, he had not continued his precautions at sea, or more accurately, he had not extended them as he might have done. He had not planned for war then, nor foreseen what manner of war it would be when it came, never having faced Edward in the field until then. And after the harsh peace of Aberconway he had intended long endurance, endless patience, and honest labour to husband the peaceful resources of Wales, putting war far out of his mind. It was not a mistake Edward ever made. I could not choose but remember David's warning, how those forest roads would be Edward's last argument, after all his legal pleas were exhausted.

'At least,' said Llewelyn, 'we'll make the best use possible of what ships we have.' And he compiled a list of what was in service, and we made a rapid dash across into Lleyn and Anglesey, to set a coastal watch and commission our sea-captains, though we did not expect the Cinque Ports ships for some weeks yet, for they had to fit and provision, and had a long voyage to reach the Dee. And on our way back to Denbigh we stayed one night at Aber.

Once more those two lay the night through together, and when she came out on his arm in the dawn, to see us away again, she was as she always was, calm, resolute and kind, though pacing heavily now by reason of the child so near its entry into this turbulent but beautiful world. Never did Eleanor live upon the heart and courage of any other, or take from any other one particle of his strength, but always she gave, always she added, and her bounty was never exhausted. She was happy then because of her brother's restoration to liberty, seeing it was for her sake he had fallen into the king's hands, to be the scapegoat for all his hated race, six years a prisoner for no offence. 'You see, Amaury is already on his way to Rome,' she said, 'and only a month ago I would have said we might have to wait a decade yet to prise him out of our cousin's clutches. So may other matters resolve themselves before we look for the resolution, and more happily than we dare believe. It is not Edward alone who orders the future. Archbishop Peckham has played his part once, and may again.'

Llewelyn was troubled for her, and marked with anxious eyes every movement she made, her slower gait and careful balance, and he would have had her remove to Llanfaes,

161

which was certainly not threatened for some time to come, and would have been quieter for her. But she laughed at him and shook her head.

'I will not go one step further from you than here,' she said. 'I would rather come nearer, but that would only divide your mind when most it needs to be single, and you see there is no need, I am marvellously well. Go with a light heart, and never doubt me.' And she linked her hands behind his head and drew him down to her, and kissed him on the mouth. 'Nothing you do can wrong me,' she said. 'Nothing you do can be done without my hand joining its will and its weight to yours. For twenty years of peace I would not give up one day of my sharing with you, come war, or danger, or hardship, or whatever God send.'

He was never so ready with words as she, but he had his own eloquence. Silently he embraced her and kissed, and I think she had her reward in full, though she was never so concerned with getting as with giving.

Then we mounted and rode, and she stood to watch us go, with her women protectively about her on either side. Those two who came with her from France were always closest, feeling her belong to them in a particular way because they had been prisoners with her in Windsor. They were Englishwomen both, in her mother's service from the time when Eleanor was a child at Kenilworth, and exiled with her to the retirement of Montargis. Close at her shoulders they stood as she waved us away to the war. He looked back at the last, and so did I, and she shone erect and bright in her yellow gown, the colour of marsh marigolds, with one hand cradling the leaping child, and one raised high in salute to us, and the gay colours of her women like an embroidered hanging framing her. That is how I remember her best.

When we reached Denbigh David was there before us, the wards full of his troopers, and the children running hither and thither in excitement among them, tugging at the trophies they brought back with them, and demanding stories of their battles. Those were the late days of May, and quick with beauty to break the heart. From the walls of Denbigh on its lofty rock all that green countryside below looked new out of paradise, so fresh and vivid was the budding of the trees and the springing of the grasses, and the meadows so gold and purple with flowers and woollen white with lambs, and on the distant mountains the last fragile veils of snow against a sky blue as periwinkles.

David came striding out to kiss his brother, with that blinding brightness about him that came to its fullness only in stress and danger and the challenge of combat. He made report of his doings in the south with the ardour of success, but also as dutifully as ever did newly-fledged knight to his lord, such care he had to maintain before all men the vassalage he had wrested from Llewelyn almost against his will.

'I have left everything there in good order,' he said, 'but they will certainly be drafting in men as fast as they can, and the royal enclaves being sited as they are, with access from the south, they can reinforce Carmarthen without hindrance, and Cardigan they can provision from the sea. But Rhys Wyndod may be able to keep Dynevor isolated. He has it well surrounded, but they would have only a short way to cut a corridor if they get men enough. We shall be sent for if they need us there. And I got word as I came,' he said, 'of the feudal muster. It's called for Rhuddlan, in the first days of August. They say Edward has twenty-eight ships already in commission. But if the winds play our game, it may take them five or six weeks to make the circuit into the Dee. We have a little time yet.'

They rode the length of the front-line defences together. Llewelyn had his men strung in compact parties, each including some bowmen, along the edge of the forests, from close by Rhuddlan, overlooking the king's new

163

coastal road, to Hawarden opposite Chester, thence southward by Hope and round the hills above the Dee to Dinas Bran, a line just within what we claimed as the border of Welsh land, but withdrawn only to the point where every company had safe cover at its back, either difficult hill country or deep forest, or indeed both together. South of the upper Dee our command passed to the men of Maelor and Cynllaith, and south again to the rebellious tenants of Griffith ap Gwenwynwyn in Powys.

In all this planned line, the only salient was the castle of Hope, jutting well out into the lands securely held by English lords.

'We'll hold on to it as long as we may,' said David, who had fought so furiously for it at law, 'and make it cost them as high as we can, but it is not worth keeping it when it begins to cost us as dear. They'll not attack it on their march to Chester, but wait until they have all their army massed, and their communications secured. He'll want to come at you, brother, by Flint and Rhuddlan, as he did before, there's no other way. But I fancy he'll want to clip my wings here in Tegaingl before he dare turn his back on me. With me here he'll not find it so easy to guard his flank as last time.'

Never did he scruple to speak of that last time, or show any sign of shame in harking back to it, or, indeed, try to dissemble or forget that he had then fought on the side of the invaders. And never by word or look did Llewelyn remind him.

'The king is on the move by now,' said Llewelyn. 'The earliest we can hope to hinder him is after he's passed Oswestry. From Dinas Bran something might be done.' And for the first few days of June he took a small company of us south with him to that castle, and thence we pushed raiding parties as far to the east as we dared, and waited for King Edward's army on its way to Chester. In a high summer once I watched Prince Edward's army closing in upon Evesham, where Earl Simon in the sprung

164

trap, waited with dignity for his death. Now in the early summer, from a hill-top above the winding Dee, I watched King Edward's army advancing upon my country with the same cold, confident discipline, learned from Earl Simon and turned against him then, bearing down now upon my lord. A strange, unearthly sight it was. We in our forests made our sudden assaults and rapid marches unseen and unheard, so quickly that we were come and gone before there was orderly sight of us or distinguishable sound. Edward with far greater numbers, too many for speed or stealth, made his slow, methodical way by full daylight and in the open, plodding inexorably like a great armoured beast, and surrounding his main body with a cloud of probing outriders, in restless, darting flight like the clouds of flies that accompany a drove of cattle. For miles before we had sight of man or horse we could detect their progress, for there hung over them in the air a faint, floating veil of bluish vapour and dust, hardly thick enough to be called a mist, for the season was not arid, but moist and mild. This serpent of vapour moved towards us over the green, rolling land, weaving as it came, and presently, before there was any colour or detail, came the sound of them, distant, rhythmic and continuous, a strange, murmuring, throbbing jingle, compounded of all manner of small sounds, but chiefly the tread of innumerable feet of men and horses drumming the earth. The light jangling of harness was there, too, the faint creak of the wheels of baggage carts, the chink of mail and clash of plate, the squeak of leather rubbing against leather, and the murmur of voices. Then, some time after this human river-music had reached us, came the first colours and lights, points of brightness scintillating through the cloud, lance-tips and pennants and the flashes of the sun fingering steel, then the whole dancing crest of the column in gleaming reds and blues and golds of flags and banneroles, the mane of the dragon, and at last the serried shapes of men and horses, the flesh and blood of the fabulous beast.

165

We kept pace with them northwards along the march, they below and we in the hills, and the rest of that journey we did them what damage we could, picking off any outrider who ventured too far west and let himself be encircled, in places favourable to us darting down upon their fringes in sudden raids, killing and looting, especially cutting out, where we could, one of the wagons, stripping its goods, and disabling it if we could not get it clean away. By night we tested the watch kept on their camp, and found it all too good, but made our way past it once or twice, and did them some hurt before we drew off again. There was not much we could do to so orderly and drilled an army, but every man and bow and horse, every morsel of food we could strip from them, counted as something gained. But never once did they break formation to follow us into the hills, where we should have had them at disadvantage. Edward's will ruled them all, and Edward was not to be trapped into any rash act, his plans were made and he adhered to them.

Thus we accompanied the royal army almost to Chester, where they arrived about the tenth day of June, and then we drew off and left them, rejoining David in Hope. He had had fighting, too, in advance of the king's coming, for Reginald de Grey had sent out a strong company under one of his bannerets to probe up the valley of the Dee and establish a forward post some miles south of the city, and though the Welsh had contested the attempt and cost them heavy losses, Grey had reinforced the camp, and David had not been able to dislodge him.

'He is already thinking he can cut me off here,' he said, 'and so he might, if I had any intention of staying here to fall into his hands. Hope has served its purpose. In a few days I think we must give it to him – what's left of it!'

Three days we spent dismantling the defences, breaching the walls, undermining the towers, and the broken masonry and rubble we emptied into the two castle wells until they were filled up and useless. What David did to

166

his well-loved fortress cost the English two months' delay, and a great sum to repair. When it was done, and the whole site desolate, we drew off into the hills to westward. We were there keeping guard when Grey himself rode into the shattered shell, and appointed a constable with a strong garrison under him. By our count he left there more than thirty horse, and about the same number of cross-bowmen, with a great number, we guessed at more than a thousand, longbowmen. We saw the reason for such immense numbers when they began to bring in scores of labourers, carpenters and foresters, and set to work frantically on trying to clear the first well, and fetch down a tower that had been left perilously leaning. The archers were deployed all round the site to protect the workmen.

'A pity,' said Llewelyn, 'if they should be disappointed since it seems they expect to be attacked. And a pity if they should begin to feel safe, and remove all those good bowmen to be used elsewhere.'

'Archers are useless by night,' said David, 'and there'll be no moon. And I have men here who know every way into Hope, and every way out, dark or light.'

Then some of his following proposed to test the new garrison that very night, and Llewelyn approved, for clearly if so many archers could be pinned down in this first capture, and prevent a further advance, or delay it for some weeks, it would be of the greatest service to us. There was ample cover in the hills around, small companies left to fend for themselves here and harry the repair work could easily lose any pursuit, even supposing the constable would countenance so rash a move, and could as easily be provisioned from the west, and rested at need. But he did not realise, until we missed David and looked for him in vain about the camp, that he had himself slipped away with his men to lead the foray.

He came back to us three hours later, smelling of smoke and leaving an ominous red glow far behind him in the ruins of Hope. His teeth gleamed like ivory in a soiled face and there was blood on him, but not his own. Every one of his men came back with him, none bearing more than a scratch to show for the venture, and David was brought up sharply by Llewelyn's furious reproach.

'Had you leave for any such folly, you who undertook this war in the name of Wales? It's easy to be daring, any fool boy can risk his head, but you are carrying the heads of all those you've committed to a life and death fight, and you may not indulge your vanity. Guard the life of every man who follows you, yes, as far as care can be carried, but guard your own for the sake of those who depend on you.'

I looked for a hot reply, or a haughty, dutiful, formal submission such as David had flaunted like an arrogant banner aforetime. But after a moment's shocked silence he stooped his head and kissed his brother's hand, so candidly and lightly that it passed for graceful penitence generously given, rather than a vassal's acknowledgement of rebuke.

'That was just,' he said. 'Very well, agreed, an end to childish games. I promise you I'll leave this to others now. But it was well worth the testing. That fire you see down there in the shell is their store of grain, and all the cords and some of the timber they've brought in for the work. And if they stop up the hole by which we got in undetected this time, there are some of us know of others. So spare to rend me!'

And he set to work, unchastened, to select a company of good, sound men, familiar with all the country round Hope as well as the castle itself, to remain behind when we withdrew to Denbigh, and by whatever means they found, to delay the repair of the defences, and so pin down all those archers in a constant alert. And an excellent job they made of it. Though Grey brought up as many as seven hundred woodmen, more than three hundred carpenters and forty stone-masons to the work, and kept about a thousand bowmen throughout to protect them, it took them until the end of August to clear out the wells and restore the walls, to make Hope a habitable base for an army's next move.

The day following David's raid, the princes with their body-guards withdrew to Denbigh.

We had not been an hour inside the wards, barely time for David to kiss his wife and shed his mail, when there was a commotion of someone riding in at the gates in great haste, and clamouring for the prince of Wales. Llewelyn was just crossing the inner ward to the hall, and turned at the cry. A young page on a blown and trembling horse, and himself streaked with sweat and dust from a hard ride, fell rather than alighted from his saddle, and flung himself at the prince's feet.

'My lord, my lord, pardon the bringer of ill news! Pardon!' he said, panting, and began to sob, with the hem of the prince's tunic pressed to his face.

'Child!' said Llewelyn, startled and dismayed, and bent to take him by the arms and raise him, but the boy clung and wept. 'What is it?' demanded Llewelyn in quick alarm, and the mild wonder dashed from his face. 'Speak up! Tell truth, and you cannot be at fault. What has happened?'

'My lord, I'm sent from Aber to fetch you. Come, come as quickly as you can! The princess . . .' He choked and swallowed.

Llewelyn gripped and snatched him to his feet, and jerked up the boy's streaming face to stare into the drowned despair of his eyes. 'The princess! What has befallen her? Such grief threatened the worst of terrors. '*She is not dead?*' he cried.

'No, no, not dead, but very sick . . . and growing weak. Two days in labour, and still no birth! Oh, my lord,' he wailed, 'they are afraid for her, we are all afraid!'

Llewelyn took his hands from him so abruptly that the child almost fell, and whirled towards the stables, and David, who had come out from the hall at the sound of the messenger galloping in, met and caught his brother in his arm, aghast at the sight of his face. 'What is it? What ails you?'

'Eleanor!' said the prince. 'You must manage here alone. I must go to my wife. Two days in labour, and no child – a bad birth ... Let me go!'

'Oh, God!' said David, stricken, and followed him into the stables, and I went after. Even if my lord had bidden me to stay, I would not have let him ride alone. 'No, it cannot be so grave,' said David feverishly. 'She has been so well, she's so mistress of everything she touches, how can she fail even at this? It will be well, you'll see! It will end with a son in her arms, and she in yours. But take my Saracen, he's fresh and fast ...'

It was David who shook and stammered, Llewelyn was steady and silent. He put aside, not roughly, the groom who fumbled in his agitation, and himself saddled the horse, David's tall English horse that was Edward's gift, with sure, rapid hands. When I also saddled up beside him, he met my eyes briefly, not refusing me though he had no part of him left then to welcome me, he was so far flown already on the road to her. We led out the horses, and he kissed David, and said he would come back when he could. And when the boy who had brought the news came creeping, smudged with tears, to hold his stirrup, frantic for some look or touch of comfort, he looked down at him as though with astonished recognition, and then compunction, and laid his palm with brusque gentleness against the boy's cheek.

'Take your earned rest,' he said, 'and follow me home tomorrow. And leave grieving, rather pray.'

In this manner, in mourne silence and leaving mourne silence behind us, we galloped out of Denbigh to attend the birth of the prince's first and only child.

They were watching for us on both roads, by the coast and by the upland track over the hills from Caerhun, which is the shorter way. It was late afternoon when we left Denbigh, but barely dusk when we came over the last ridge by the old Roman road, and dropped into the head of the wooded valley that winds down to Aber. I doubt if that ten-league distance was ever covered faster. The watchman on the hills signalled our approach to the watchman on the wall below, there was sun enough yet to catch the red and white flutter of his pennant and the steel of his lance. When we passed at a gallop he saluted us and fell in at our heels, and thus heralded and escorted we came down to the long wall of the maenol and the village under it.

All that way he had not uttered one word to me, intent only on reaching her side as soon as he might. Nor had we any need of words, or, God knows, any matter for speech, being both in dread and doubt and hope so alike that I had nothing to offer him, and he nothing to ask of me. We rode towards her, and that was all we had mind or will for then. And prayed every mile of the way, as he had bidden the wretched boy to pray.

There was no comfort to be found in any face that met us, though in every one was a desperate, heartfelt welcome. The guards at the gates opened for us before we drew near, and their eyes strained for our approach and followed after our passing. The grooms in the outer ward ran to take our bridles, and they had the same look, fearful of a word, a sound, a breath, that might tip the balance between life and death. So we knew what awaited us, even before the castellan came running out of the hall to greet his lord, and Llewelyn cried out to him: 'The princess?' and all he could get out from a faltering throat was: 'Living!' There was nothing better than that to be said.

Llewelyn leaped from the saddle and went in through the hall, and I after him, and all the menservants and maid-servants of the household, creeping wretchedly about their business, stood stock-still before him, and made their reverences as he passed with the same dazed and unbe-lieving eyes, many of the women smudging away tears.

There had been little sound before we entered, only subdued voices and few words, but as we passed there was silence. Llewelyn clove through the midst as though he saw none of them, and had almost reached the door of the high chamber when it opened, and one of Eleanor's women came out. It was Alice, the older of those two who had been prisoners with the princess after their voyage from France, and felt her to be in a special way theirs. At sight of her Llewelyn halted abruptly at gaze, for she had a shawl-wrapped bundle in her arms.

'It is come, then?' he said in a whisper, drawing careful breath of hope.

Her face was white and tired, and her hair awry, as though she had not slept at all since her lady's labour began. She said tremulously: 'Four hours ago. The lord prince has a daughter. She is whole and fine.'

She leaned to hold out the child to him, and turn back the shawl from its face, but he never glanced down.

'Then the worst is past?' he said, hoping and dreading 'Eleanor?'

She turned her head aside, and the tears came slowly rolling from under her closed lids, and for the weight and burning of them she could not speak. But without words she turned and went before him to the tower stairway. By the time we had climbed to the level of the guard-walk on the wall she had her voice again, though it struggled through aching grief.

'We made the bed for her lying-in not in the great bedchamber, but in the room with a door on to the wall. It was so hot and dark and airless within, she was better there. She loves the sun.' Her tears fell on the child's shawl. 'Oh, my lord, it has been cruel! She is torn—she has lost so much blood.'

I think he knew then that Alice, at least, had no hope, that her tears were already tears of mourning. He put her aside gently at the door, and went in.

There were four of them about the bed, the prince's

172

physician, the chaplain, and two of her women, and all of them turned their eyes upon him as he entered. In every face there was the same helplessness and resignation. They drew back from the bed as he drew near, and left her to him.

She lay under only a light linen cover, for it was indeed the height of a very hot summer. Her hands were spread upon the linen at her sides, transparent, bluish white, like broken lilies. Her hair was unbraided, for a braid might have caused her discomfort; and for the sake of coolness they had drawn it up from under her neck, and spread it back in a great aureole over a wide pillow. The very perfection of the halo, strand drawn out evenly by strand, showed that for some long time she had not moved her head. All that lustrous dark gold, darker than usual with the sweat of her anguish but radiant and vivid still, sprang aloft from a broad brow and smooth temples no longer of ivory, but alabaster, so crystal-clear that what blood she still had in her gleamed through in the softest of blues, like the tracery of veins in the petals of an anemone. Her closed eyelids – I had never before seen her so – had the same delicate texture, large, domed eyelids to cover great, candid eyes. Her mouth was folded firmly, like a budding rose, but a white rose, even the shadows that shaped it rather blue than rosy. Her cheeks were fallen and silver-white, her body under the linen cover lay straight and slight and frail, and so still that she might have been the carven woman she seemed, but for the dew of exhaustion and pain on her lips and her forehead, and the faint, slow rise and fall of her breast. If this was life, she still lived, and they had told us truth. But it was such life that to touch or breathe upon it would destroy it. Everyone in that room moved with slow and careful stealth, avoiding sound, for fear she should be startled through the doorway in which she hovered.

Llewelyn went on his knees beside the brychan, and leaned and gazed at her in silence, hardly breathing. The old doctor came creeping to his shoulder and whispered brokenly in his ear, as if he fended off blame for her condition.

'A bad birth, a difficult birth. . . . The child lay awry. We have stopped the bleeding now, but it went on so long. . . .'

'And such pain!' whispered Alice, crouched on a stool with the child in her lap. 'Day and night such pain, and never any respite, and hardly a moan out of her . . . But now she's worn out, she has no strength left.'

The chaplain said, as was his duty: 'She has received her saviour. I thought it needful.'

Llewelyn was still, watching the shallow rise and fall of her breast over the most gallant and generous heart that ever beat in a woman's body, and he never turned his head, though I think he heard all. Presently he said in a low voice: 'Leave us alone with her. If I need you – if she needs you – Samson shall call you.' And then for a moment, as in a distant dream, he bethought him of the child, and asked: 'There is a nurse? The little one is provided for?'

Alice said yes, the tears still coursing slowly from under her eyelids.

'Then leave us. One of you may sleep in the next room, in case of need. I shall watch with her through the night.'

They went away softly and closed the door after them. I asked if I, too, should wait without. He put his hands over his face for a moment, pressing hard as if to quicken tissues grown old, weary and stiff. 'No,' he said, 'stay with me. Stay with *us*! You knew her before ever I did, you first showed her to my soul's eyes. To no other but you can I uncover my heart now, and no other can I bear to have by, if she leaves me in the night without word or look. You need say nothing, but be with us. If God wants her, God will take her, but I can fight for her still. There were some in the old times, I have heard, wrestled with angels.'

On a table by the wall they had left a pitcher of red wine, and a bowl of cool, scented water, and soft cloths, and a little oil-lamp with a floating wick, that gave a dim, mellow light. He rose, and opened wide the door that gave upon the guard-walk, for even the night was hot. The sky was full of waking stars, and the air smelled fresh and sharp, of the salt marshes, and the sea. Then he came back to the bed, and remained on his knees beside her, looking earnestly into her face.

The trance in which she lay was not quite sleep, and not quite unconsciousness. Sometimes her lashes trembled, and seemed about to rise from the sunken cheeks, and then were still again. Once her lips quivered and curved, as though to speak, or smile, or kiss. But so white, so white, no blood in her, a spirit, not a body.

He took one of her wasted hands between his own, and caressed it. He bathed the sweat of weakness and fever from her lip and her brow as it formed, and drew back every strand of hair that seamed the smoothness of her neck. And time and again he spoke to her, laying his cheek beside her on the pillow, on the spread riches of her hair, whispering the endearments he kept for their bed. All night long he called her back to him from the perilous place where she stood hesitating whether to go or stay. But doubtless there was another voice calling her away.

Whether it was his caresses that reached her, or whether the change in the light penetrated her dreamless withdrawal, in the dove-grey of dawn before the sun rose I saw her lips move and part, and her brows draw together, and then she drew deeper breath, and when he leaned over her and said her name she opened her eyes, but so slowly, as if the weight of the world hung on her lids. In the dimness of the room her eyes looked dark, but as they clung to the face that bent so close to hers, they summoned a gradual radiance from within, and the clear gold lights came back into them. She knew him. She had no strength to move or speak, but even in its pallor her face grew

175

marvellously bright, and when he stooped his head and kissed her with careful tenderness on the mouth, her lips answered him as best they could.

He bathed her face with the scented water, and with the tip of his finger moistened her lips with wine, but for wine she made no effort, all the life she had left she poured towards him with her eyes. And as he ministered he spoke to her, patient and soft, calling her by the secret names he had for her, telling her that her daughter was whole and perfect and well-cherished, and that she need trouble for nothing but to rest and grow strong, and think of nothing but that she was loved; and that while she needed him he would never again leave her. And all the ways in which he loved her, and all the beauties he loved in her, he told over one by one, he who was so inexpert with words. There was never any of his bards made so sweet and desperate a song as he did for her, to hold her spellbound from taking the last step away from him. But I think he knew then that she had only paused a moment for love of him, to listen from very far off, hanging back on the hand that led her.

Lying as it does in a cleft of the northern hills, with the great mountain mass of Penmaenmawr to the east, Moel Wnion to the west, and Foel-Fras to the south, the morning sun never enters Aber. But to look out at dawn to the north, over the narrow salt marshes to Lavan sands and the sea, that is wonderful. The deepening light, first tinted like the feathers of doves, then flushing into rose, then glowing like amber, comes sweeping westward from Conway over the sea, to strike in a glitter of foam and sand on the distant coast of Anglesey across the strait from us, as if a golden tide had surged across the sea-green tide, and flooded the visible world with light. That was such a morning. The only time that Eleanor's eyes left Llewelyn's face was to gaze at the morsel of sky seen through the open doorway, and he divined the last thirst that troubled her, she who loved the sun. If he could not take her where it would shine upon her, at least she might still look upon its beauty from the shadows.

He sat down beside her on the edge of the brychan, and lifted her against his shoulder, and carefully gathering the blankets of the bed about her, took her up in his arms. She made no sign or sound of pain, but only a soft sigh, and with his cheek pressed steadyingly against her hair he carried her out on to the guard-walk, and the few yards round the stony bulk of the tower to the northern parapet, and stood cradling her as the sun rose, their faces turned towards the sea.

There in the open the air was sweet and cool, and below us, beyond the shore road, the reeds and grasses of the marsh stood erect like small, bright lances, every one separate, going down in lush, tufted waves to where the sands began, with a great exultation of sea-birds filling the air above. The level sunrays made all the surface of the strait a dance of fireflies, but beneath the glitter the deeps shone green as emeralds, and darker blue in the centre, and the shallows where the sands showed through were the colour of ripening wheat. Along the horizon ran the purple line of the coast of Anglesey, and in the centre of that distant shore was the Franciscan friary of Llanfaes, the burying-place of the princesses of Gwynedd. In the morning light it appeared as the distant harbour of desire, absolute in beauty and peace.

She lay content in his arms and on his heart, her cheek against his cheek, and her eyes drew light from the picture on which she gazed, and grew so wide and wise in their hazel-gold that there was a moment when I believed he had won his battle. He knew better. Very still he stood, not to jar or hurt her, and softly still he spoke, of Wales, that she had taken to her heart and that loved her in return, and of a future when there would be no more need of war, when this land would be free and united and honourable among the countries of Christendom, and kings and princes would pledge peace and keep it, and

177

her child's children, the descendants of Earl Simon, would walk at large as heroes among their own people, and equals among the monarchs of the world.

Her lips moved, soundlessly, saying: 'Yes!' It was right that she should take her leave of the world, as she had greeted it in passing, with a cry of affirmation.

The sun was just clear of the horizon, and the sky to eastward the colour of primroses, and to westward of cornflowers, when the faintest of tremors passed through her body, and her head turned slightly upon his shoulder, her lips straining to his cheek. One word she said, and this time not silently shaping it, yet on so feeble a breath that neither he nor I could have caught it but for the great silence in which we stood. But hear it I did, and so did he. We never spoke of it, but I know.

'Cariad!' she said, and her breath caught and halted long, gently began again, and again sank into stillness.

He held her for a great while after that, but there was no more sound, and no more movement, and that was all her message to him. She did not leave him without saying farewell. Yes! Cariad!

When he was quite sure that it was a dead woman he held on his heart, he carried her in and laid her upon the bed, and with steady hands smoothed her hair again over the pillow, and crossed the frail hands on her breast. Gently he drew down the lace-veined eyelids over her eyes, and held them a while with reverent fingers. After he had kissed her brow, and signed her with a cross, he turned at last to me.

'Call the women,' he said. 'She has no more need of me.'

When he went out alone from the chamber where she lay, his face was a better likeness of death than hers.

CHAPTER VII

He made no outcry, abandoned no duty, himself directed all the sorrowful business of her funeral rites. He spoke with man and woman, high and low, as courteously and directly as always, was short with carelessness, patient with honest weakness, gentle with the timid. And all with that face of stone. He did not sleep until nightfall, but when he had done all that remained to do and fell to his lot, then he shut himself alone into the chapel, and there remained until darkness.

When he came forth, at least his face lived again, had eyes bruised and cavernous, but alive, and though he kept his grief withdrawn and apart, some portion of his senses and affections moved among us again, for he had accepted what could not be resisted. First he asked for the child, and Alice brought her and laid her beside him in her carved cradle, sleeping. A big infant she was, with long, fine bones, the crumpled face of all new human creatures, and a fuzz of russet-brown hair like her father's. But when Llewelyn edged a finger-tip into one tiny fist, and she gripped it firmly and opened her eyes, they were wide and hazel, flecked with green-gold, Eleanor's eyes. He looked upon her long and wonderingly, and could not love her yet, I think, not because he held her mother's death against her, but because so small and unfamiliar a being had no reality for him, and he had not David's easy gift of approaching even day-old infants with assurance. But he felt a heavy, protective tenderness at sight of such helplessness and smallness, and at the thought that she

179

had lost as heavily as he had, for her mother was dead
and she had none but him left, as he had none but her
But at least for her he could be at rest, she slept and fed
and thrived.

Having assured himself that all was well with the little
one, and given orders for the morrow, he slept at last
And in the morning he called me to him, and had me stay
at his side thereafter. I was with him when he went to
look his last upon Eleanor in her coffin, before they
covered her. With her hair braided and a golden gown
upon her, she was beautiful still, but far beyond our reach
He kissed her brow and her lips, and I kissed the cold
hands folded on her breast. There was none other with us
'Thirteen years I waited for her,' he said, looking down
upon her still face, 'and less than four years I have had
her, and I suppose that was reward beyond my deserts.
Now for me, as a man, there is nothing left to lose, what
is there Edward or any other man can do to me that I
cannot laugh to scorn? In the world's eyes my honour is
gone, and now my love is gone, and there is no reason I
should regard my life a day longer. That and all else I will
throw into this war I never wanted. For now I want it!
With all my soul and strength I will wage it to the end,
and the kingdom I could not lay at her feet I will build to
be her memorial, God willing. And if I fail, another will
succeed, building higher on what I have built. This child
may bear the sons my dear love was not permitted to bear.
Who am I to say when God's truth and justice will come
to fruit? With what is left of my life I will fight for it, and
leave the outcome to God.'

We buried Eleanor de Montfort, princess of Wales, in
the friary of Llanfaes, in the heart of June, when all things
were blossoming and ripening for fruit, and the days so
fair the heart ached for their beauty, and more for the
beauty that was rapt away in its Junetide. We carried her
in solemn procession from Aber across the salt marshes,

180

nd rowed her from Lavan sands over the strait, and laid
er beside Joan, lady of Wales aforetime, daughter to
 King John and wife to Llewelyn Fawr, my lord's grand-
ire. There her mortal part rests until the judgment, but
urely her soul is gone like the flight of a lark, singing into
he world of light. It is for ourselves we grieve.

At night in hall the bards made music in her honour,
amenting the rose of the world fallen untimely to a killing
rost, praising her as the noble daughter of a noble sire,
s indeed she was, and prophesying the gift of her beauty
nd goodness to her own child in the days to come. And
e sat erect and grave through all, and did all that was
equired of him that day, taking pains to make all necessary
lispositions for the care of his little daughter.

He named her Gwenllian, for it was a name in which
Eleanor had found a pleasing music.

The next day we rode for Denbigh to rejoin David.

I knew, yet could not feel until we turned our faces again
o the war, how changed was the world for Llewelyn and
or me. When we had put Aber behind us, with all its
lenizens going about their daily business, and very properly so, then I understood how light my lord's life was
now to him, and yet how precious it might be to the
ause he championed. It was the only passion left to him,
and since a live man must go on living for his honour's
sake, what could he do better than cast the whole weight
of his powers, his gallantry, his strength of will and quality
of mind, into the battle for his sole remaining love?

As for all that great household we left behind, for them
t was very different. Death comes and goes about the
world, and plucks full-blown blossom and withered stalk
and dewy bud indifferently, and those who remain mourn,
yet even in mourning must be about the business of burial
and worship and legal settlement, and by the time that is
done the great rent in their lives is already partially stitched
up, and soon quite healed, since the living have little choice

but to live. So those good women in Aber wept for Eleanor, whom they had deeply loved, and wept longer than most mourners do, but they had also work to do, and the child to tend, and other affections of their own to cherish, and the great void that lady had left in dying must heal gradually until it vanished quite, but for a kind of sweet sadness that would now and again set one or other of the women saying: 'Do you remember . . .' And remember they would, every one. But time goes on, and memories have to wait for the leisure moments.

But for him nothing would ever again be the same, though life claimed its due, and he did not merely continue living, but lived at a fiercer heat than before, spent himself more vehemently, ventured his weal more rashly. The wound he bore would never be healed in this world, and the void in his heart never filled, and even Wales was to him from that day a changed worship, less reasoned, more devouring, a fire lit in her honour. There was no other way left for him to exalt her name and celebrate her memory, but in the exaltation and celebration of Wales.

We made almost as good speed back to Denbigh as we had on the way from it, the urgency of action beckoning us before, and too bitter and grievous memory galloping hard on our heels. If the prince could overtake the one, perhaps he could also outrun the other. From the day that she was taken from him he drove thus without pause, his eyes fixed always upon the war.

When we cantered up through the town at Denbigh and walked our horses up the steep ascent to the castle gatehouse, word of our coming ran before us. By the time we entered the outer ward David was plunging out to meet us, with Tudor at his back, and a dozen more of his own captains and Llewelyn's hovering, and all with searching eyes and wary faces, peering for the omens in the prince's countenance. David waved the hurrying grooms aside, and himself held his brother's bridle and stirrup. With drawn brows he peered up into Llewelyn's face, and

182

aited for a voluntary word, but the prince lighted down
1 silence, and in silence kissed him. David held him by
he shoulder, searching close.

'Well? What news? How is it with your wife?' Surely by
hen he knew, but there was no keeping the silence for
ver. Elizabeth was out on the steps of the hall, anxiously
vatching them.

'She is dead,' said Llewelyn, 'and I have buried her.'

'Oh, God!' said David in a whisper, and clung hard
vhen his brother would have put him by and walked on.
The boy did warn us! But she was in such blossoming
iealth, I could not believe it would go badly. Oh, brother,
am sorry!'

What is there to be said? Every day there is someone,
.omewhere, to whom the same words have to be offered,
.nd I suppose they serve the same purpose as the words
)f the burial rites, a kind of incantation reconciling man
o man, and man to his fate. It is hard to find any other
'orm.

'She was beautiful and generous and brave!' said David
n sudden helpless rage. 'How can God justify it? Even
nen do not tear out flowers for sport! Oh, Llewelyn, I so
grieve for you!'

'I know,' said Llewelyn, bearing with him at some cost,
'or with him all the words were spent, and even the best
.t little value. 'I know, you need say nothing. I take your
grief as it is given, and am grateful. She is gone. It is over.'

Elizabeth was at his side then, the little thing so prolific
.nd so joyous, teeming like the earth and with as slight
:ffort. Great piteous eyes she fixed upon him, and said,
rue to her nature: 'And the child? The child lives, and is
hriving?'

At her he looked with seeing eyes, and even smiled, for
she had that singleness and innocence that spoke closely
to his heart. 'I have a fine daughter,' he said, 'with eyes
like her mother's eyes. Yes, she thrives, she will be beautiful.'

'Poor motherless babe!' said Elizabeth with starting tears. 'If ever it is needful, I would take her with mine, one more would be no burden, and here she has close and loving kin.'

He said that Gwenllian could have no better mother than the mother of all her cousins, wanting her own, but that he dared not for his life take her from Alice and Marion and their waiting-women, who had lost one princess and could not be robbed of a second. And Elizabeth wept, and embraced him, and said he was right to regard their grief, for it must be great indeed. And David looked upon her as she spoke, with eyes fixed and hungry, as though he had but now been taught that worshipped wives can die, and husbands can be left desolate.

Llewelyn, for his part, suffered them as then he suffered all, patient under sympathy which could change nothing, and indignation which could restore him nothing, but with his eyes for ever fixed upon the only passion he had left, and that consecrated to her memory. And as soon as he could he turned Elizabeth aside to her own cares, and shook all the womenfolk bustling in her train, and turned upon David and Tudor, and the captains and commanders who waited apart to know his will.

'I have been absent more than three days,' he said, 'and much may have happened without my knowledge. Call such of the council as we have at hand. I want full reports from every part. We have struck for a country, and we have a country to keep.'

Thus plainly but without emphasis he made clear to us all that he had returned to take upon himself the whole burden of his principality, that this war which had been forced upon him against his will was now irrevocably his war, a national war, and to him as the prince of this nation belonged the supreme command of it. And that 'we' he had uttered, though by it he meant to include his brother and all those like-minded in the fight, was nonetheless royal.

'At your orders, every man of us,' said David, and went with Tudor to do his bidding.

That afternoon he presided over the council, and David presented him the report of all that had happened in his absence.

'There is indeed news,' he said, 'of the greatest importance, brought in two days ago, and sent here to Denbigh, naturally, in the belief that it would find you here in person. If I was wrong in not sending it after you to Aber, pardon me the error. I knew it would keep, for it is good news, not bad. All through May and into this month, Gloucester has been building up his forces in the south, in Carmarthen and Dynevor, with orders to reconquer Llandovery and establish Giffard there again, and put the English settlers back into the country round Llanbadarn. They've had no success. A few raids, and some looting, but very little gained. Our people there have held off from pitched battle, rightly, and avoided losses, and struck back wherever they could, staying mainly in the hills and forests. So to the main matter. About the tenth of this month Gloucester sent out a large force from Dynevor to raid towards Carreg Cennen, which they did for some days, and took a great deal of plunder along the valley, but on the way back to Dynevor our nephews on the one side and their allies on the other fell upon them unexpectedly at Llandeilo, and broke them utterly. A great victory and a great slaughter, and all that booty regained. William of Valence has lost his son there, and a number of knights were killed with him. And if Gloucester has not lost his command, he has his reputation. We have good reason to be pleased, this clash has set him back two months or more.'

'How great,' asked Llewelyn, 'was this force?'

'Rhys Wyndod reckons at least fifteen hundred foot, and maybe a hundred horse, counting Gloucester's own retinue and that of Valence. They left a garrison of fifty or so and a gang of labourers in the shell of Carreg Cennen, as if they meant to repair it and occupy it as a fortress
185

again, but now they'll be hard put to it even to get thei
men out, much less reinforce them. Rhys can pick them
off at leisure.'

It was indeed a victory, and promised a respite of some
weeks at least. Llewelyn burned, hearing it. 'That can also
give us breathing space here. They'll not move a man from
the south to add to the Chester army, far more likely to
send some of the next levies into Ystrad Tywi, and try
and hold the position there. Good! Rhys Wyndod and
his brothers have done well by us. And what goes forward
at Hope?'

'Very little, and very slowly. The companies we left there
cannot delay the rebuilding indefinitely, but they are mak-
ing it slow and costly. I have an eye,' said David, 'to
Hawarden also, for I doubt if that can be held, once
Edward gets into motion, but I'll hold it as long as I may.
The king has made no move from Chester so far.'

'He will not move,' said the prince with certainty, 'until
he gets his ships round Wales and lying off-shore in the
Dee. In any case he needs the time. With the numbers he
has to feed, and the distance he hopes to take them, he
cannot yet have amassed half enough stores of food or
arms, or made sure of his lines of transport. He'll be
doubly careful of his organisation this time. There's no
word yet of the ships being sighted at sea?'

'We may not sight them until they near Lleyn,' said
Tudor, 'but there we shall certainly get news. I doubt if
his first fleet is out of the Channel yet.'

'Edward will follow his old way,' said Llewelyn, 'by the
new roads to Flint, and so to Rhuddlan. I doubt if we
should put ourselves in his way before Flint, but we'll
make him pay dear for the miles to Rhuddlan. But since
he has the sea, in the end we cannot halt his advance, we
can only pin him to the coast. How long have we? Five
weeks – six? – before there'll be any action here in the
north?'

David reasoned that it would take five weeks at least

186

efore the king was ready to attempt anything more than moving up to his two advanced bases, for it would take him all that time to ensure his commisariat and his supply lines, and have his ships at hand.

'And we have all our men in arms and ready,' said Llewelyn, 'and no prospect for that time of much work for them here. It is not good policy, once Welshmen are roused, to keep them waiting in idleness, their fires burn down if they are not fed. I think we may well make good use of those five or six weeks. If the south is in this disarray, Gloucester discredited, a new commander not yet appointed, and the troops disheartened after Llandeilo, we could do them further hurt while they're shaken, and make sure none of them can be spared to join Edward here. If we can force him to pour in more men in the south, so much the better. They cannot be in two places at once.'

'Would you have me go back there?' asked David readily.

'No, your men of the Middle Country know this region best, and can best hold it if the pressure does begin. Gwynedd beyond Conway he will not reach yet, and if he does – before he does – we can be back with you in three days whenever you call us. I am going myself,' said Llewelyn.

His dispositions were made the same day, and those levies of Gwynedd that he proposed to take with him detailed. He had with him then only his own household guard and a small company of horse, and with the rest we mustered two days later at Bala, on our way south.

Cristin came to me in the armoury, the evening before we marched, and wished me godspeed and a safe return. I had not realised until then, being too much concerned with Llewelyn's weal and woe, that I had not laid eyes on Godred since we returned to Denbigh. She moved and spoke and looked with that eased freedom she had when he was absent.

'He's gone with one of David's patrols to Dinas Bran
she said. 'They'll be prowling the borders and the De
valley, you may even run into them on your way south
they happen to be upstream just now. But they'll be bac
here in a week or two. Dinas Bran is well garrisoned, an
the local men are jealous of their privileges. David we
understands the border Welsh. He has made himself thei
pattern, his reputation stands high with them. But I wis
to God,' she said, suddenly vehement, 'he had been conten
to be a good husband and father, and let go even of Hop
in the shire-court if he had to. Oh, Samson, I dread th
ending! I've seen Edward, as you have, and watched ho
he works. When we were in England, under his protection
I got to know that monumental face. Where his sover
eignty is touched, his supremacy challenged, there is n
compassion there at all, no human kindness. Whoeve
presumes to have rights level with his, is traitor and
blasphemer. God knows he cannot help it, God made hin
so! But *why*?'

I said that doubtless God had his reasons, who balanced
all and apportioned all, but I saw by her face that she
questioned whether the balance was always just or the
apportioning equitable.

'He has his own land,' she said, 'why must he also grasp
at everything within his reach? Oh, he preferred law to
the sword, while he was allowed the choice, it costs him
less and is just as effective, if slower. But sooner or later
I tell you truly, he would have begun to devour us, by
one means or another. He is a gluttonous appetite, and
nothing enclosed in the same seas with him will be safe
from him in the end. So I am wrong to blame David for
striking first. It would have come, whether he had held
his hand or no. He may even have done Wales good
service by forcing the issue now, before Edward was quite
ready.'

I had been thinking much the same, and admitted it
And now there was nothing for us but to fight to the end
188

with everything we had, and deserve victory, and if we could, wrest it from Edward and from God himself at whatever cost in our lives and souls.

'Do you know, Samson,' said Cristin, drawing close to me and raising to my face great eyes purple almost to blackness in the dim light within the armoury, 'what I have been thinking? It may well be a cowardly thought that I should put away, but it will not leave my mind. It is there every time I look at Elizabeth, or watch the children playing. In the grief I feel for your princess it mingles always, like a voice overriding grief. If we fail, she at least is safe. There is nothing Edward can do now to hurt Eleanor. She is with God, and out of his reach.'

On the way south to Bala we made a single night camp after we had crossed the Dee, for the weather was still so hot and fine that it was pleasure to lie out in open woods, above the grassy bank of a tributary stream that offered cool bathing after the heat of the day. The water came down clear and fast from the Berwyns, and the bracken on the slopes above was full green and half-furled, and the gorse in the gullies deepest gold. In the dusk I went some way along the waterside to stretch my legs after riding, and left all the sounds of the camp behind me.

I was thinking, none too happily, of all that Cristin had said, for there was that about her at times that reminded me of my mother, who had strange insights, and knew things the rest of us were not permitted to know. And it was true, and in my heart I knew it, that Edward's power, once roused, was far greater than anything we could muster, at least in arms and men and ships and horses, and against these weapons truth and justice seemed to carry but little weight. And still I feared the ancient enemy, bred from old loyalties and old customs that took no count of the idea of a nation. For we knew only too well that Edward had already issued the usual orders to his bailiffs and officers everywhere, to receive such of the Welsh as would

come to the king's peace, and show them grace. When th
fight became bitter and the way hard, many might we
heed that offer. But this time there was a sinister chang
for the offer of clemency applied only to the commo
people. For their leaders there was to be no such merc
And to me it seemed that this was more than a mere matt
of policy, to sift the genuineness of those captains who sue
for grace, before granting it. No, it was the king's warnin
to us that this time he meant to sever the Welsh from thei
own princes and barons, and take them bodily into h
own administration.

And like Cristin, I could not but feel it as a kind c
victory that the princess, at least, was safe for ever, tha
Edward had not and never again would have any powe
to touch or trouble her. But never could I face that though
without feeling like a traitor to her, for when had she eve
turned her back upon any of the battles and agonies o
living, or thought it better to be in quietude and hide from
the storm? She would rather have been here at Llewelyn'
side if she could, and shared every danger that threatene
him. What right had I to be grateful for the safety sh
would have rejected with contempt? Yes, even knowin,
Edward as Cristin knew him, and having no illusion
concerning the malignant extremes of which he wa
capable?

Her death was back with me in all its bitterness as
stood by the little river, peering down into the eddies tha
span about its pebbly bed under the overhanging turf o
the bank. The drier grass on the uplands beyond wa
thick and spongy, and the little knot of riders that passe
along the ridge at some distance made no sound. It wa
not until one of them wheeled out of line and began t
wind his way down the slope, and the jingle of his harnes
reached me, that I looked up.

There were four of them, in David's livery, riding th
crest above the Dee on patrol from Dinas Bran. Thre
had kept their station on the ridge, and were walking thei

horses easily eastward towards the castle, and the fourth, leaning lightly back in the saddle, was turning his mount with casual pressure of his knees down the slope, towards the river-bank opposite where I stood. And the fourth was Godred.

It was so long since he had approached me of his own will that I was curious, and stood to watch his approach warily enough, but without animosity. Whether we would or not, we were comrades in arms. His eyes were on me, and he was grinning in that private way he had, as if only he knew and could savour the sour joke the world presented to view. The rein lay easy in his hand, only his knees guided his thickset pony down the rough descent. Godred rode well, and knew it.

'Well, well!' he said, checking the pony on the level turf across the water from me. 'It *is* you! I thought I should know that priestly tilt of the head. So those were the prince's turfed fires we saw downstream. They show, Samson, my friend, you'd be at an enemy's disposal with no better care than that.'

'With you between us and the border,' I said, 'what need have we to fear an enemy? Five leagues at least to Oswestry and the Berwyns in between, besides your good sword. No prince was ever safer.'

'Pleasant,' he said, idling along the edge of the water and eyeing me with that small curl of his mouth that was barely a smile, 'pleasant indeed to know you have such faith in me. And how did you leave Cristin, when you rode from Denbigh? In good spirits?'

'As good as the rest of us,' I said. 'We're none of us making merry.'

'Shame,' he said, 'that her best and truest friend should be forced to leave her, just when her husband's away. She'll be quiet and solitary without the both of us.' And his light, sweet voice turned sharp as gall, yet soft as silk, as it always did when he was casting for me as for a fish. And I marvelled, for this he had not ventured of late, I had

191

thought because his hatred had taken a more extreme turn that found no pleasure in baiting me, but perhaps, after all, rather because he had some qualms as to its safety. For now the river was between us, and he licked his lips, savouring the steps by which he tested how far he could go.

'Hardly quiet or solitary,' I said, 'with eight children round her skirts and another nurseling on the way.' For Elizabeth was also with child, her normal and happiest state. And the first and last fruit of love had been the death of Eleanor! I was thinking only of that sorrow, still so large and heavy on my heart, and did not consider how he might take what I said to himself, and count it as a stab in return for those he dealt out, seeing his own son had been still-born. It was perhaps the only grief he ever felt that was not all on his own account, and I had not meant to revive it.

'Some can breed, and some cannot,' he said, showing his even teeth in a snarling smile. 'Like the prince, poor soul! I hear he's lost his wife, and got him a daughter. Well, there's always a grain of good in every evil. Take heart, Samson, there's room again in his confidence for another favourite now, your nose may be back in joint soon enough. Even room in his bedchamber for a little sweet music at nights!' He laughed, seeing me stiffen, for though he never believed the foulness he invented, nor used it upon any but me, and therefore I could let it go by me with little feeling but contempt, yet there was a bound set to what my heart could endure at this time from him or from any.

'Keep your tongue within your teeth,' I said, 'and drink your own poison. I am not now in the mood to listen to frogs croaking.'

'Oh, you take me wrongly,' he protested, still grinning. 'Who is more concerned for my prince's consolation and my friend's than I? If I cannot rejoice in the advancement of one close to me as a brother, I am a poor-spirited creature.' And he made a smooth, round gesture with his bridle-hand, to let what light remained gleam for a moment on the silver ring by which I had first known him for my blood-kin. 'And what better promotion than to your old intimacy? A pity about the lady, but at least, if she could not give him a son, he has got a daughter. If indeed it was he who got her!' said Godred, and giggled, a bloodcurdling sound. 'After so many years of celibacy, I tell you, Samson, there were some of us had doubts of him, more ways than one! And she so loving and anxious to oblige him with an heir. Do you know of any who may have lent her a little help in the business? But there, they say *you* were the one closer in her secrets than any other.'

I heard him through a roaring in my ears, and saw him through a red blistering darkness, and went lunging towards him half-blind, through icy coldness. When my eyes cleared, he was away in a long traverse up the steep hillside, his malignant laughter drifting back to me like the clatter of small, cracked bells, and I was thigh-deep in the river with my dagger out, the deepest stony gully of the bed before me, and the sudden cold of mountain water gnawing my bones to the marrow, even in the summer night.

I watched him go, no help for it, he was away to his fellows, and among them no doubt circumspect and clean-mouthed. But if I could have got my hands on him then, I should have killed him.

I said no word to any other, then or ever, of what lay only between Godred and me, and to tell truth, I was half ashamed of having let him get under my guard, even with so gross and unexpected a profanation, for whatever weapon he clutched at, I was his mark and no other. If he spat his slime upon names dearer to me than my own, it was not because he believed one word of what he alleged, or had any malevolent intent against them, but only because he knew all too well where my armour was penetrable. And after we mustered at Bala the next day, and moved south at speed, I put him out of my mind and out of my hatred, for he was safely left behind in the Middle Country, and for many weeks I was to see no more of him.

It was the prince's intent to make rapid contact with his most effective allies rather than harry the marcher lands as we went, for once we were securely based in Ystrad Tywi, and knew what forces we had to contend with in the three royal bases ringing that region, then we could expand our action to strike outwards as chance offered. So we wasted no time in crossing eastward to the central march to probe Mortimer's defences on the upper Severn, or Lestrange's at Builth, but from Bala swept south-west through Merioneth, and crossed the Dovey to join hands with Griffith and Cynan ap Meredith in Llanbadarn.

Those two princes had had their hands full, until the battle of Llandeilo, in resisting constant English attacks, meant to re-establish the foreign settlers who had been ousted from the region, and by the detailed account they gave us of the large scale of this settlement it seemed clear that the king had intended to turn the castle of Llanbadarn into such another centre of royalist power as Carmarthen in the south. But since Llandeilo the attacks had ceased, and the remaining English troops been withdrawn into the castles, where they were safe, and there was hardly a skirmish to be hoped for on their side of the Teifi.

The same situation we found as we moved through the western lands. Everywhere the English were shut up within their castles, and came out only very cautiously and briefly to try how hot their reception still might be. But everywhere Llewelyn gave grim warning that this would not long continue, and meant nothing more than a temporary lull, which we would do well to use by strengthening our own resources of men and supplies, for it was only a matter of time before Edward's reserves came into play. The date fixed for the massing of the feudal host was still a month away, the second day of August, and once that was reached the king would have immensely greater numbers at his disposal for the statutory period of service, and would certainly retain most of them at his wages afterwards, besides what he might recruit at pay from the marches and from France. We were quick to muster and quick to move, and they were methodical, cumbersome and slow, but like a heavy-armoured horseman on a barded horse, once in motion they were desperately hard to halt or withstand. So the prince warned, and was hard upon all complacence.

From Llanbadarn, seeing they were alert and well-found there, we turned inland, still moving south, and crossed the watershed to reach Llandovery, where Rhys Wyndod, eldest of the prince's three nephews, was again installed since he had recovered it from Giffard. Rhys, like his uncles, had suffered the delays and humiliations of English law over this same Llandovery, to which Giffard laid claim through his wife, and that case, like the prince's, had dragged on through plea after plea for three years, and died at the outbreak of war, when the king handed over to Giffard the custody of the castle and the commote, though he did not hold it long. Rhys had fought as doughtily for Welsh law as had Llewelyn himself, and with the same lack of success. For him, at least, arms had proved more effective than words.

He was a man then thirty-three years old, fair and tall like his father before him, and a good fighter when he was roused, though in the previous war, hard-pressed and ill-prepared, he had surrendered to the English, while his younger brothers fled to the north and continued to fight for their uncle. This time, as Rhys himself bluntly said, he had not only seen sufficient cause to steel him to fight to the end, there being nothing to gain by compromise if the English were determined to put an end to Welsh law, but also he had burned his boats to settle the matter, and was committed for life and liberty and all. Of Edward's clemency to Welsh chiefs who had once resisted him he entertained no hope whatever.

From him we learned how those royal forces remaining in Ystrad Tywi were disposed.

'They are on the defensive now,' he said, 'and hardly stirring out, for they have enough supplies for the men they carry, and they are surely waiting for reinforcements, and expecting them soon. So far as we can determine, they have about seventy paid lances left, and have split them between Cardigan and Dynevor. Since Llandeilo we've seen nothing of the earl of Gloucester, but we heard that his own tenants in the march, all the Welsh among them, are up in revolt, and so are Hereford's, so he may well have been withdrawn and told to go and set his own house in order. The whisper is he's lost his command, but we've heard nothing of a successor yet. They're hanging on by their teeth and waiting. As soon as the feudal levies come in, they'll get the men they want. I doubt if the king will even wait for the day of his muster, but send them their orders in advance to report here in Carmarthen instead of Rhuddlan.'

'Then we'd better be about giving him even more reason to spread them over the whole country,' said Llewelyn briskly, 'and prevent him from getting the numbers he needs to break Gwynedd.'

And so we did, all through July and into August. We left the castle of Dryslwyn alone, with the traitor Rhys ap Meredith and his half-English garrison within it, for it was strong, and would have needed siege engines to break into it. But we left him little else. We kept a close watch on Dynevor and Carmarthen, on the alert for any sallies they might make to replenish supplies, and when they did venture out we did our best to lure them further from their bases by exposing some pitifully small party of our own, but they had their orders, and were seldom to be drawn. Very rarely did we get to grips with them, and then but briefly, for they stayed very close to home.

During this month of July we lived most of the time wild. We had Llandovery as a convenient rallying-point for the exchange of news and plans, and from there covered not only the vale of Towey, but also began to move out and rattle the teeth of Humphrey de Bohun, earl of Hereford and constable of England, at Brecon and the countryside round it, and to harass Lestrange at Builth, for there the Welsh of the region were always heartily glad to rise against their English masters. We kept in touch also with Griffith and Cynan ap Meredith, and sent a flying company to their aid whenever they required it. But for the most part we had little fighting. They dared not move from their castles, and we knew them too strongly positioned there to try storming them.

It was not long before we got word who was to replace Gloucester as commander in the south. Early in July Edward appointed his uncle, William of Valence, earl of Pembroke, the eldest of King Henry's Poitevin half-brothers, who had come over, years ago, to make their fortunes by marriages with English heiresses. I saw him once at Oxford, a lean, black-bearded, imperious person, hot-tempered and proud, bitter in his opposition to Earl Simon's Provisions, and unscrupulous in the means by which he fought them. But give him his due, he was not a bad soldier. With his own household guard Valence had sufficient troops to be able to move between Carmarthen and Cardigan, and once he took out a large force, some hundreds on foot besides lances to raid along the Cardigan coast against Griffith ap Meredith's lands, and tried to reach Llanbadarn, apparently with the hope of reoccupying the shell of the castle, but we closed in from the hills to eastward, and hunted them back towards Cardigan. He got them back in good disciplined order, or his losses would have been greater.

From the north David duly sent us word by courier when there was anything to report.

'The king has brought his army and headquarters to

197

Rhuddlan,' he wrote late in July, 'and has got his first ships in the estuary, twenty-eight of them began their fifteen days of duty service on the tenth of this month. Twelve more have joined them since, and two great galleys from the Cinque Ports, besides some coastal boats got locally. We have kept close watch on the dock at Rhuddlan, and seen boats taking off men and arms to the ships off-shore, and returning empty. I believe Edward is putting aboard large numbers of archers and crossbowmen to be used at sea, if needed, but certainly in some planned landing. No move as yet to show what his plans are. Nothing will happen until after his August muster. He is busy now making his supply lines safe. There's little more to tell, except that I have withdrawn from Hawarden, as I was bound to do once they moved from Chester. I left them the shell. Hope is still rebuilding, and the wells still unserviceable. When my position is threatened, you shall hear of it.'

With the beginning of August, and the mustering of the feudal host, things changed with our warfare in the south. English reinforcements began to arrive in great numbers, our scouts brought us word of detachments of men being fed in through Carmarthen, to which the English had easy access from the southern marcher lordships, and distributed also to Dynevor and Cardigan, so many of them that it seemed clear Edward had ordered all the tenants-in-chief of some large region of his realm to do their feudal service under Valence, instead of joining the royal army at Rhuddlan.

'It is a tribute,' said Llewelyn, 'after its fashion. David's load will be lighter at least by these.'

It was what we had expected and intended, but it meant that we were now facing great odds, and had to base our movements, after the old Welsh fashion, on the high hills which we knew better than did the enemy, and on the speed of our sudden raids into the valleys, and as sudden withdrawals. If they came out in strength, and used that strength intelligently, we had nothing to match it, and could not and should not meet them in pitched battle or attempt to prevent them from occupying land. But what we could do was take back what they had occupied, as soon as they reduced the forces that held it, as they must in order to use them elsewhere. And as long as we were able to continue this system of reclamation and cession, and keep our own numbers intact, we could and did prevent them from moving away a single company to add to the main army in the north. And so we contrived all through August.

There were among these levies of foot, especially those from the march of Gwent and other baronial lands, large numbers of what they called Welsh friendlies, soldiers who served for pay and took their living as it came. During that month of August we got more than one recruit from their ranks, and gained not merely an archer or a spear-man, but also some useful information about Valence's resources and plans. In the middle of the month a deserter from a raiding party out of Dynevor told us that the king himself had laid down the campaign Valence should undertake. He was to furnish an expedition to conquer all the lands of Meredith's sons in Cardigan, and hand them over to the traitor Rhys of Dryslwyn, who naturally was expected to supply part of the army to carry out the assignment.

So we were prepared for the expedition when it came, and knew that its first aim was to bring us to battle, on the way to invade the lands of Griffith and Cynan. We were equally determined to avoid such action, and when the force issued from Carmarthen we had scouts trailing them all the way, and kept our main forces to the hills and forests, never far from the enemy but never confronting him. The English moved in a body up the Towey valley as far as Llangadoc, where Rhys's division joined them, and thence Valence crossed over the uplands to the river Ystwyth, and marched his men down that valley to Llanbadarn.

We kept pace with him most of the way, but little enough did he see of us, only our traces where an outpost of his camp was found wiped out at dawn and stripped of its arms, or a group of stragglers cut off and killed. We struck often enough to let him know that we were still there, and he dared not allow his precautions to flag, or dispose of any of his men. But we never emerged from cover to stray within reach of his archers, and he was too cautious to come after us into the forests. We had sent on word to Griffith and Cynan, and they were prepared to use the like tactics, avoiding encounters, denying the enemy all possible supplies on the way, and waiting for his passing.

The shell of Llanbadarn was that and nothing more when Valence came to it. No defenders were there to be fought, the place was derelict, and having no workmen with them, and no prospect of bringing them in sufficient numbers until the whole cantref was pacified, they did not bother to occupy it, but marched by and left it as it was. So this great march ended none too gloriously down the coast, joining hands with Daubeny's garrison at Cardigan, by which time it was into the first days of September, and the forty days of feudal service was over. Most of the horse were certainly taken into pay and remained after that time, but some of the foot soldiers were discharged.

For that month's work they had gained little, though it is true that Rhys ap Meredith did get hold of a part of the lands belonging to his loyal kinsmen, and the English helped him to retain them. Still, Valence must have been cautious in his report to the king, for a very large and powerful garrison was still maintained at Dynevor. All the chief castles along the march were in similar case, Builth, Radnor, Montgomery, Oswestry, all anxious to secure a strong enough grip on their own region to spare lances and foot-men to send to the king at Rhuddlan, but all compelled to retain their garrisons undiminished. It was what we had set out to do, and for more than two months we had done it. But we knew, every man of us, hat we, for our part, had raised by now every man we could raise, and stood only to see our forces dwindle, if some hard-pressed vils and commotes lost heart and lent an ear to the royal offers of grace, while Edward's numbers had not yet reached their maximum, but could be expanded steadily as long as he had or could borrow the money to pay his mercenaries. In the matter of numbers and resources time was not on our side. As regards the weather, it well might be in the end, but we dared not rely on it. His hate is such, Cynan had said of Edward, that neither snow nor frost will stop him. Put no trust in winter!

When we got back to Llandovery, it was the youngest of the prince's nephews, his namesake, who came out to greet us, and kissed his uncle's hand.

'My brothers are out towards Dynevor,' he said, 'with a patrol. Giffard is back in Ystrad Tywi, so we've heard, and with a strong following. He has the king's leave to take back this castle, and all he can capture of Iscennen. He has not ours! We are planning a warm welcome for him.'

'You may find me some office in that welcome,' said the prince. 'We've had very little action in this circuit we've made with Valence.'

'Very gladly we would,' said the boy, 'but I think there may be graver calls upon you than ours, my lord. There's a courier here for you from David. Yesterday he rode in, but knowing you were on your way back I held him here rather than send out after you. I think, from what he says of movements in the north, you may be needed at home.'

Llewelyn went in with him from the bustle of the courtyard to the dimness of the hall, and there the messenger from Gwynedd came to salute him and present his letter. We knew him, he was a trooper of David's household at Hope, until that fortress was slighted and abandoned to Reginald de Grey. Llewelyn asked him, before ever he

201

broke the seal: 'What goes forward in the Middle Country?'

'My lord, the Lord David sent me out the same day our outposts down the valley sighted King Edward's army advancing up the Clwyd. I thought he would have moved by the coast towards Conway. So he did in the last war. I think he has grasped that he dare not move further west while the Lord David holds the Middle Country. I think he is moving to break that hold, so that he may not be taken on the flank, and cut off from Chester.'

'I judge as you do,' said Llewelyn. 'The king keeps a measure of respect for my brother's prowess, however well he hates him.' And he broke the seal of David's letter, and read the message, brief enough and eloquent in its brevity:

'Luke de Tany, under Edward's commission, has landed an army in Anglesey, with all the fleet, more than forty ships, to cover him. The harvest is burned, garnered or lost, God knows in what measure. The king is marching up the Clwyd. Grey is crossing westwards from Hope, it seems aiming at Ruthin. Suddenly everything is on the move. It is time. Come!'

We made for Denbigh the next day, setting out at dawn, and beyond Bala Llewelyn took fresh horses and rode ahead with a small company of lances, leaving his household troops and the foot soldiers under Tudor to follow at their best pace. The town, when we reached it, was full of soldiery, and their bustle had a dourness and purpose about it that spoke loud in our ears, besides the relative absence of women and children about the streets. David had pickets out on the edge of the town, and a double guard on the gatehouse, the guard-walk on the wall was manned at every turret and angle, and the armoury was ringing with activity. There were all the indications of a garrison braced to siege conditions. Llewelyn looked about him sharply at all his brother's provisions, but could not fault them.

David was up on the tower, and when the watch signalled our coming he would have started down to us, but Llewelyn waved him back, and we went up to join him. He was unarmed, there in his own castle, but the stripped and austere state he kept spoke of pressures that might have him in mail and on the move at any moment. He came to meet us on the guard-walk, his face intent and grave.

'I'm glad you're come,' he said when they had embraced, and stood together staring out to eastward. 'Our situation here is not yet bad, but it is bad enough, I own it. I will not pretend I have done all things well.'

From that vantage point there was no warfare to be seen, and no enemy, only in the distance to the east, in the riverside plain, a few threads of smoke from sources hidden from us by the undulations of the land between. Llewelyn saw the thin blue drifts rising and dissolving, and knew what they meant.

'Yes, they are there,' said David. 'They have not struck at us yet, they passed us by, keeping close to the river, in the low ground. He is not yet ready, and Denbigh will not be easy to storm. But Ruthin is lost. De Grey moved west from Hope, at the same time as Edward set off with his own army up the Clwyd towards us. I could not send help to Ruthin for fear of an attack here, but he did not attempt it. What he has done is string the whole valley with outposts, and pass us by to join Grey, cutting off all the allies we have east of Clwyd. Now Ruthin is gone, and this advanced line of ours is breached, and the rest may have to go after Ruthin.'

'I never supposed,' said Llewelyn without passion, 'that we could have held it for long. You have held it for three months, I cannot see how you could have done much more. What do you know of his forces now? And how disposed?'

'By our count, he can command as many as eight thousand foot, and above seven hundred and fifty mounted, now he has the feudal levies up. And besides the longbow-men and crossbowmen distributed among his flanking armies and his ships, there's a large body of archers encamped with his own command at Rhuddlan. And see, this is how he has parted his forces.' He drew in the stone of the parapet with the sheath of his dagger, the long north–south gash of the Clywd, and the level stroke of the coastline crossing its mouth. 'His own army, the main force, here at Rhuddlan, and now patrolling the river valley. Here to eastward, working from Hope and drawing his supplies from Chester, de Grey. He has Ruthin now, and Owen Goch is with him. And here, moving into the valley of the upper Dee from Oswestry, the earl of Surrey has yet a third army, and is aiming at Dinas Bran, and with Ruthin gone, even if I had men to spare here, I doubt if we could get them to Dinas safely. They feed one another with men,' said David, 'according to where the need is, for they can all join hands. Edward has three ways in to the west, none of them easy, and please God we'll make them hard for him indeed, but none impossible, given enough men and horses and arms. By the Dee, by Ruthin, and by the coast. But he has not moved a step further west than Rhuddlan yet. He's wary of extending his line while we are still here on his flank. He wants us rolled back into Eryri before he ventures.'

'Yes,' said Llewelyn, 'he has learned. And what of Anglesey. You say they're already established there. Oh, small blame to you, how could there be? *I* neglected the need for power by sea, not you. How did they mount their landing force, and how far has it gone?'

'Edward began loading great store of crossbow quarrels and arrows into ships before the end of July, and putting archers aboard, as many as thirty in some of the ships. No secret where they were bound, but there was nothing I could do to prevent. Forty ships in all he had, to carry and cover his landing force, and we dared not even get within range of their longbows. All I could do was make sure that coast was well manned, both the mainland and the island, they have not won it cheaply. And I sent orders as soon as we saw what was in the wind, that the islanders should reap whatever part of the grain was ripe enough, and get it ashore to us. The rest they were to let stand as long as possible, and reap it as it fell ready, and fire it if the enemy landed before it was all in. Or if they could garner any of it and hide it there for their own use, that they could do.'

'Did they get any part of it ashore in time?' asked the prince, mindful of all the soldiers he had to feed if this should continue into a winter war. 'After so hot a summer, it could be well forward.'

'Yes, a part they did get in, and have sent us some and hidden some, for they knew there'd be no escape for them once the English landed. But the greater part remained. No help for it! Edward can judge how far forward a western harvest will be in a good season,' said David bitterly, 'as well as we. Before the end of August he put Luke de Tany in command, he that was seneschal of Gascony, and sent them off from Rhuddlan. They had a hard fight of it to get ashore, and still have to beat off constant raids, but once they had a landing-place cleared they've been able to ferry more men in, until they have a considerable army there. They have a tight hold on the southern coast of the island now, and on two-thirds of our corn, though some our people did burn in time. My men saw fires there.'

'If he's poured so many men into Anglesey,' said Llewelyn frowning, 'it is not simply to hold down the islanders or take the harvest. That army he means to use again, to come at us from the west and north while he moves in from the east. What has Tany been up to this past month, besides reaping what's left of our grain?'

'There's more to tell,' David owned. 'Too much by far! Edward has the dock at Rhuddlan ringed with archers thicker than reeds, but we've raided there as chance offered, and slipped spies in once or twice by night, and we have some idea of what's happening there. Ever since de Tany got his force ashore the ships have been coming and going daily, not only with arrows and crossbow quarrels, but with stranger goods. Timber and iron and nails and cords, and small boats, and with them great numbers of men who carry no arms and are not soldiers, but carpenters and labourers. All this month past they've been building a bridge of boats across the narrows, between Porthaethwy on the island and Bangor on the main, with forty ships and any number of coastal boats to protect the work and bring the materials in, and archers enough to keep us at a distance. If they have not touched land yet, they will any day now, the thing is all but complete. Edward has even detached some of the Cinque Ports ships and sent them home. He cannot afford to turn the south coast traders against him by disrupting their traffic for too long, and he has plenty of ships left, with his small craft, and may get more yet from France. I have that coast manned as strongly as I can spare the men for it. Nothing has been attempted yet. But I see it as clearly as you, he is holding this fourth army in reserve until he feels the time ripe to draw a noose about Snowdon from both sides.'

He eyed his brother darkly and steadily, unafraid even of those memories that separated them. 'I have much to learn,' he said, 'but I, too, am learning. It was like this, the last time? It's fitting that I should be made to understand the realities of war with Edward. It is less just that you should be made to suffer it over again.'

'Justice has little to say in the matter,' said Llewelyn, with that distant, absent gentleness that marked his dealings with difficult men since Eleanor left him desolate. 'Little to do with Edward's law, and less with his warfare. I don't complain of him – we began it. But his warfare is the logical end of his law, an extension of the same discipline. And both are loaded upon one side.'

I marvelled to see David smiling at him. A tight and

rueful smile it was, but it had its own warmth, all one man could spare to give to another at that pass. 'If that "we" is a royal one,' he said, 'it is too generous, and I denounce it. And if it means we, you and I, it is still generous indeed, for *I* began it, I alone. And if I ever was in doubt of the gravity of what I did, I'm in no doubt now. We are stretched to the end of our reach, so far as men and weapons go. And he is only just beginning to get his armies into motion, and has fresh men still to come. Did you know he has got his first Gascons? No question, we have one of them prisoner, he lost his way in the marshes of the Elwy, and we picked him off for what he could tell. Not a great company, this first one, forty or so foot and sixteen mounted crossbowmen. But there'll be more. We have no such reserve to draw on.'

'We have ourselves,' said Llewelyn, 'and no one else can let us fall. But you are right to look the truth in the face, we can fight no other way but face-forward. I never thought you had gone into this war lightly. Do you think,' he said with the faintest of smiles, 'I did not notice the quietness in the wards below? You have already sent the children away, have you not?'

'The day I sent to you,' said David. 'This is no place for them now. And Elizabeth and the women, too, though it was no easy matter to get her to go.'

'Where have you put them?' asked the prince.

'In Dolwyddelan, but I've sent word since to move them on to Dolbadarn. I can think of no better and safer place. If ever Edward penetrates so far into the mountains we're all lost. When you came, I was weighing in my mind the chances of holding Denbigh, and to be honest, I don't rate them high. Now that Ruthin's gone, we're in danger of being outflanked, and I don't intend to be shut up here like a rat in a trap, to be starved out in the end. I cannot afford to lose my army here, when Snowdon itself may need every man of us before the end. If I must abandon Denbigh to Edward, I cannot even afford to leave my castellan a strong garrison. It's either withdraw all, and destroy the place after us, or else withdraw all but a few, a skeleton force, and let them stand out the siege as long as they can, to give us more time. A sorry choice! I do not like asking any man of mine to stay and fight to the death here while I escape to fight on elsewhere. And even if he has my leave to surrender and get what terms he can, without fighting to the end, can we rely on any generosity from Edward?'

'Towards others, perhaps,' said Llewelyn. His voice was low and equable, implying nothing more than he said, but David heard no less clearly all that had not been said, that though the common spear-men and bowmen of Wales might look for clemency, being of little importance to the king once their resistance ceased, there would never again be mercy for the princes of Gwynedd. David had made his throw to win or lose all, and though for himself I think he had not changed his mind, his heart was shaken and racked for Llewelyn.

'I did this to you,' he said, 'and was certain I did well. Now I am stricken with doubts. What right had I to force your hand?'

'None,' said Llewelyn simply, 'but it is done, and the next step must be taken from here where we stand.' And seeing his brother's face desperately sombre, the eyes clinging upon him in hunger and thirst after some re-assurance he could get from no other creature, the prince sighed, and did his best for him. 'Child,' he said patiently, as he might have reasoned with his youngest and most perilous brother long before, when he was indeed newly out of childhood and greedy for glory, 'you trouble needless. You did me no wrong. I am of your mind, it would have come to this, soon or late. I was for late, for making him show his hand, you saw it otherwise. But it's all one now, and your choice of time may well have been right, and mine wrong. I have no regrets, none. Nor need you have any. We are here together, and that is good. And what men can do, we shall do.'

CHAPTER VIII

What men could do, that they did. The prince held
council briefly that same day with those of his own captains and David's as were at hand. The necessary work
they parted among them, and agreed as to how much time
and effort could reasonably be expended on holding the
threatened eastern line, now that Ruthin was lost, and
Dinas Bran under attack.

'I should be happier,' said David, 'if he would turn some
of his forces on to me here, and ease the pressure on Dinas,
but I fear he can see plainly enough that direct asssault
on Denbigh could lose him many men for little gain, and
cost him weeks of work, no matter how many he threw
into the siege. His aim is to isolate the garrison here as we
used to do his garrisons at Degannwy and Diserth, in the
past, and leave Denbigh helpless and useless while the
war passes it by. But here we have no means of bringing
relief and supplies by sea, as he had at Degannwy. No, he'll
try to draw a noose about Denbigh while I'm still in it, and
I cannot let him succeed. But I'll go when I must, and not
before.'

Since Gray was in Ruthin, and the earl of Surrey closing
in on Dinas Bran and the valley of the Dee, while Edward's
base at Rhuddlan offered a northern approach, the move
to outflank Denbigh might come from either side, or from
both together, to join hands about him. Llewelyn warned
him to take no risks by clinging to his castle a day too long,
for he could not be spared, and the worst disaster that could
now overtake Wales would be the separation of its two

princes, one from the other. They were now not only the symbol, but the reality of the unity of Wales. At that David looked up quickly from the scrawled map he was drawing of the lines of Clwyd and Conway, and the highlands between, and withdrew his mind briefly from the consideration of Edward's next advance, to fix a glittering stare upon his brother's face. And in a moment he went back to his frowning study of his own imperilled position, and said, very low and deliberate of voice, that he would not make any mistake that might threaten that unity.

Very shortly after the council ended, Llewelyn took his own company and returned westward to meet his foot soldiers, leaving the defence of the Middle Country to his brother, while he deployed his own army along the northern coast from Conway to Carnarvon, keeping close contact along that line so that men could be moved quickly wherever need might arise. Another line he strung along the western bank of the Conway, in case the English made any attempt to penetrate by some inland route over the high watershed between the rivers, and left a number of outposts on the eastern side of Conway to keep touch with any moves David might make, and bring reinforcements to him quickly if he should be hard pressed.

This work we began, since the foot soldiers were more than a day behind us in their march from the south, at Ysbyty Ifan on the upper Conway, where they were appointed to meet with us. And as they were in need of rest, there we were all encamped overnight. It is no great way from there to the castle of Dolwyddelan, and in Dolwyddelan Elizabeth and all her children had now taken refuge, and with them was my Cristin. I was out on the first rise of the upland road in the early evening, looking towards the west and thinking of her, with the knot of longing drawn tight about my heart, when Llewelyn came quietly behind my shoulder and said: 'Will you ride there with me? We can be there by dark and leave with the dawn.

I have a duty to see to the well-being of my sister and her children.'

So, perhaps, he had, and his affection for Elizabeth, who in her innocence had wrought so strongly on his brother, and deserved so well of them both, was deep and warm, and yet I knew he had rather my needs in mind then. When he laid his hand upon my arm I felt the touch pass into my flesh and blood like the comfort of a fire at the onset of a cold night. He had spoken but seldom and briefly since Eleanor died, always calmly, always to the point, always with consideration towards poor human creatures caught in this world's snares as he was, yet all his utterance lacking some part of him that we needed and missed, we who had known him when he was man alive. He touched me then, there above the Conway, and his hand was quick and kind, and his voice speaking into my ear was close instead of distant, and sounded to me strangely young, the voice of my eighteen-year-old star-brother when first I entered his service at Aber, long years before. So strong was that illusion that I was reluctant to turn my head and look at him, for grief at his silvered temples and lined brow, and more than all of his widowed eyes, that looked upon me with the awful compassion of those who have nothing to lose but through another's loss, and nothing to hope for but through another's gain.

I said: 'You ask foolishly. I will ride with you wherever you care to call me, whether it is towards my own weal or my own woe. And no one knows it so well as you.'

'God knows,' said Llewelyn, 'towards which of the two I am calling you in the end. But at least the woe should not have reached Dolwyddelan yet. Let's take the good where we find it.'

So we took horse gladly and rode together over the upland track to Penmachno, across the little river, and through the forested hills until we could see in the dusk the great angular tower rising on its ridge above us, and began the winding climb to the narrow inner ward, walled round every way. They kept a good guard, we were challenged before ever we got near the foot of the rock, and twice again on the way aloft. One of the men ran ahead as soon as the prince was known, and they came with flares to light us in, for the nights were drawing in fast then, though so far the clear weather held, and prolonged the daylight somewhat. Within the week the sky was to change, and autumn threaten with cloud and gales, but that night it was still and calm. Half the household came pouring out to greet us, the castellan leading them, and Elizabeth met us in the hall. She was within a month of her time then with her ninth child, and the balanced gait and careful step could not but remind him. David's heir, Owen, turned eight years old, stood close at her side, and was already as tall as her shoulder. The two eldest girls also came out after their mother, dark, glowing and beautiful, foreshadowing glorious women. The prince saw before him the blossoming shoots of his brother's tree, so lavish and so fair, while he was left barren but for one solitary bud, and never would love woman or get child again. And as I watched them, for all I could not question the will of God, I found his dispositions hard to understand and harder to bear, and it was all the more strange to me that what I saw in Llewelyn's face was a brooding, regretful tenderness that had no envy in it at all, but came terribly close to pity. It was made clear to me then, very sharply, that the more richly gifted she and David were in these radiant children, the more they had to lose, and the more to be feared were the weapons sharpened against them. And though David had the fire and challenge of his warfare to beguile and compensate him, she had no such distraction, but lived every day with the plain possibility of disaster.

She did not look afraid. Her face had lost its childish roundness of cheek and chin, and gained a clean-drawn firmness of line in the change. But though fear may be put away for oneself, she was surrounded by others at least as dear to her as her own life, and fear for such is infinitely more terrible, and with that fear, I think, she lived in close companionship night and day. Not that she doubted David's gallantry and skill. But now that childhood delightfully prolonged was at last put behind her, she knew that the gallant and the skilled can also die, can also fail.

She asked warmly how Llewelyn did, and only afterwards asked after David, with no show of haste or anxiety, and no protest at being sent away from him. Llewelyn told her that we had left him well, and Denbigh not so far threatened, and that he had orders not to take any risk of being cut off there. And he asked if she and the children had everything they needed, and if they were well, and whether there was any wish he could fulfil for them now that he was here. Thus with mutual courtesy, each grieved for the other, they went in to the high chamber together, and took the children with them. And in a moment Cristin came out to me.

'I knew you were here,' she said, 'before ever I saw it was the prince she was going out to meet. I felt you in the air of the evening, when you were drawing near.' She gave me her hand, and we stood close, hungrily gazing. I had not tasted to the full, until then, the three-months' fast without sight or sound of her, all that golden summer a desert, nor been pierced with so sharp an understanding of his loss, who could never again recover the presence and the radiance of his beloved in this world, nor clasp the hand she held out to him.

She had on a plain blue gown, and her black, silken hair was braided and coiled on her neck. Not even that summer, day after hot day out of doors with the children, had been able to burn the pure whiteness of her skin, that mates so seldom but so perfectly with pure black hair.

'There was not a day I did not miss you,' she said.

'And never a day,' I said, 'when I have not thought of you.'

213

'Was there fighting?' she asked, and her fingers closed and held me fast for a moment.

'Nothing heroic,' I said truthfully. 'As little fighting as we could contrive with the most mischief possible. The real battle will be here in the north.'

We went out from the noise and warmth of the hall into the night, and climbed to the wall, and looked out together over the rolling waste of heath and hill and furze and dimpling bog, bleached into black and white of crests and hollows under a half moon. The sky was immense and full of stars.

'He sent us here to be safe,' said Cristin, leaning her chin in her cupped hands on the parapet of the wall. 'But where is safety to be found? Now I hear we are to move again, further into the mountains, to Dolbadarn. What is safety? In time of peace women die in childbirth, cruelly, like the princess, and men stray into quaking ground in these uplands, and go under by inches with their feet held fast, until their mouths fill with peat-water and slime. And in war many survive, even many who never looked for survival. I think there is nothing to be done but go forward through each day as it comes, as straightly and honourably as a man may, and take a reasonable man's care, and after that not trouble overmuch. I see a kind of safety in that, live or die, soon or late. That cannot be the difference, since it comes to all. What matters is something else. Perhaps to live whole, and die whole. Whole? – erect? – I do not know the perfect word.'

I said that she had found two that were good enough for me. She might have been pondering how to describe Llewelyn.

'Tell me truly what we have to face,' she said, 'in the north and in the south. We see too close here, and see out of shape.'

I told her all that we had done in the south, and how we had left matters there, frozen into a wary deadlock, though that could not hold for long when the reinforcements

214

came in sufficient numbers. And I told her how we had found things in the east, and what was to be expected there within the next one or two weeks, for I reckoned it could not be staved off much longer than that. She listened with grave attention. In the moonlight her tall, blanched forehead and huge dark lakes of eyes were more than half her face. And by that bone-white light, for all her forty-six years, there was never a line nor a furrow to mar her marble smoothness.

'In the end,' she said, 'it will be as it was the last time. I was not here then, but I do know. And if it all comes to grief, some of those who come after will blame him in their wisdom, and ask why he fell a second time into the same trap, hemmed about here in the mountains like a forsaken garrison in a castle without a moat. And he has no choice, no choice at all! He sees the danger as clearly as man may, and he cannot forestall it. In the end, Eryri is not large enough. God should have given us a coast three times as long, ripped apart with difficult inlets of the sea, wasting months either by water or land to reach us. Or blessed us with a harvest that ripens in May, and can be in the barns before Edward can get his muster into motion. One year is much like another in the same land, and what the king has learned in one he can use in any other, and there is nothing we can do to change it. Only ships, perhaps, as you say, ships might have altered the balance. But he thought himself at peace!'

I said: 'No neighbour of Edward's will ever be at peace.'

'No neighbour of Edward's,' she said, 'and no brother of David's.'

I said then what I strongly felt, and urgently desired to be true, and yet could not be quite sure I believed, that this time David would be true to his pledges, and stand by his brother to the end. And this was the one thing changed from the previous conflict, that those two were at one, and would remain one. That unity might well be worth an army to us.

'It is October already,' I said, 'the wind has changed and the weather will change, and still the king is held fast on the Clwyd, and dare not move on towards Degannwy. Even with Ruthin lost, even if David must let Denbigh go, still it will take some time to move on to the Conway. We may have cost him enough already to make him think hard about continuing into the winter, even with our corn to feed his thousands. It may be he'll think better of it, and be open to terms again.'

'But even so,' said Cristin shrewdly, 'will it not be all to do again very soon? I do not believe he can keep his hands and his hounds off Wales for long.'

I was of her mind, and could not but say so, for to offer her false comfort was impossible. So we knew and acknowledged together what it was we faced, and with us all those creatures we loved, and the land to which our blood belonged. We stood together on the wall under the moon as long as there was any stir about the wards, very loth to part. But at last she said that she must go, for there was only Nest with the younger children, and if any of them awoke it would be Cristin who was cried for. And since my lord and I were to leave at dawn to join the army on the Conway, I must also get my rest. So we said our goodnights, as always, without great to-do or many words, and yet, as she went from me towards the low, dark doorway in the tower wall, I felt the strings of my heart being drawn out to breaking with every step she took away from me.

She also felt it, for every step was slower than the last, and in the doorway she turned and came back no less slowly, and stood close, looking up into my face. Here were none but we, and tomorrow all the many hundreds of garrison and household would be seething about us.

'Kiss me!' she said. 'This once, kiss me. After the morning, who knows when I shall see you again?'

I took her by the shoulders, God knows as fearfully as if I had been handling windflowers that bruise and wither

216

at a touch, though they are brave enough and strong enough to thrust their way through the snow into blossom. She made no move to touch me with her hands, but only raised her face to mine, and under my mouth her lips were cold and fresh and smooth, stirring only for an instant into frantic life before she withdrew hurriedly and went from me without looking back. I said after her, softly: 'I love you!' and her step checked once, and she said: 'I love you!' like a distant echo, never turning her head, and then the darkness of the doorway swallowed her up, and she was gone.

Only then did I begin to shake like a fevered man, as though I had been racked with a great storm of weeping that left all my body one bitter ache. For that was the first time that ever I kissed my love on the lips, in all those years we had known and sustained each other, and I could not but know that it might well also be the last.

I saw her in the morning, when we left, for she came out into the ward with Elizabeth to see us mount. She had the youngest girl in her arms, and the twins clinging to her skirts, and she was smiling as resolutely as Elizabeth smiled, sending the menfolk off to their war with a cheerful face and a good heart. Thus Llewelyn and I rode from Dolwyddelan towards the Conway to rejoin the army.

All along the river the prince strung his guard-posts against any crossing, with outposts on the eastern side to give due warning. We visited Aberconway and saw it well-manned, and thence, instead of the coastal road, which was always guarded, took to the uplands, the great rock highlands inland of Penmaenmawr, from the seaward crest of which we could scan all the expanse of the bay of Conway, from the peninsula of Creuddyn to the east to the distant point of Ynys Lanog and the shore of Anglesey on the west. Stormy we saw it then, all the miles of watery floor bright in a lurid sunlight but swept by strong winds, and the sky above heavy and bloated with cloud that drove before north-easterly gales in the upper air, and piled like toppling rocks on the western horizon.

'Autumn has remembered us,' said Llewelyn, 'I hope in time.'

We rode the whole circuit of the northern hills, and everywhere made our defences secure, concentrating strong companies the length of the coast fronting Anglesey and especially above Bangor, where Edward's boat bridge was to touch land. We went down to the shore there close in cover, and saw the bridge itself, a long snake of boats braced together, riding the water easily, though there was a strong swell there as the wind drove into the narrows. They had not brought the serpent fully to land, but anchored a separate long-boat ready on the more sheltered side, with a raised portion like a draw-bridge, having the whole thus ready for use but out of reach of attack from the mainland. Two coastal ships, teeming with men, most of them apparently archers, lay off on either side, and others along the Anglesey shore, and a small wooden turret on the end of the bridge itself was likewise manned by archers.

'A man has only to leave the trees here, and he's within their range,' said Tudor, scanning the heaving serpent, with the commander of the local company close at his elbow. 'But by that token, so are they within our range.'

'But better covered,' said the man ruefully, 'and bring up fresh ships if we show our faces. Twice we tried a raid, but lost too many men, and boats they can hole and sink as we approach, lying higher than our craft. By night we got a boat in, muffled, and boarded them, and killed the watch on the bridge, but had to draw off when one of them escaped us and gave the alarm. They keep even tighter guard now. Some damage we've done them by night, too, with fire-arrows, and picked off some of their men by the flames while they lasted, being in darkness ourselves. But they have so many workmen, the damage is soon repaired.'

'When they try to land troops,' said Llewelyn, 'they'll be open to archery, for they'll have this last gangway of theirs to get into place, and the first to come ashore will be within bowshot even from cover. Then it may well be worth risking men. Not now! We could lose more than we gain.' And he left a part of his own forces to strengthen the defences of Bangor, and having made the best disposition he could of the men at his command, he returned towards Conway by way of Aber.

All along that familiar shore road, his eyes were more often turned towards the coast of Anglesey, across the widening strait, to the friary of Llanfaes where Eleanor slept, than towards the royal maenol where his daughter was. It was for the child's sake he went at this time to Aber, but he did so from a sense of duty, and not from any consuming affection. He had seen her but once, after the birth that bereaved him of the creature he loved best in the world, and the child was still scarcely real to him. Even had she been a son, I do not think it would have changed things at all.

But when he saw her again, when heavily and out of duty he asked Alice to bring the baby to him, and her cradle was placed beside him in the high chamber, then it was another story. She was no longer so perilously tiny and new and fragile, but four months old and sturdy. The russet-brown feathers of her hair were a little lighter, almost approaching the dusky gold that was her mother's colour, and she stared up at him with large, golden-hazel eyes fringed with dark lashes, eyes that could already fix upon him and wonder, curious and unafraid. Perceiving a face watching her, and having as yet no reason to find any face unfriendly, she gazed and vaguely smiled. He felt for the first time, I think, the astonishment of this new life, and its close bond with the lost life it had replaced, and though she could never mean the same to him, she had a meaning of her own, as new as her being.

He called her softly by her name: 'Gwenllian!' savouring

the sound that had given pleasure to Eleanor, and carefully
he lifted the little one from her cradle, wrapping the
blanket around her, and nursed her in his arms, and she
leaned her head against his heart as infants do, for such
heavy heads upon such tender necks will always nod to a
support. But she was not all helpless, already she could
reach out her hands to whatever took her attention and
made her wonder. When he leaned to gather her to him,
the medallion he wore round his neck, the enamelled
image of Eleanor at twelve years old, Earl Simon's gift
to him before Evesham, slipped from the open collar of
his shirt, and lay visible on his breast. Towards that small,
brightly-coloured picture Gwenllian reached her hands,
and held and drew it to her, opening it wide in wonder at
those green-golden eyes of his love.

He uttered a small, grievous sound, and with one hand
shaded his face from view. And the child, finding him
bent still nearer to her, held her toy with one hand, and
with the other reached up to pat curiously at his chin, and
his lips, and made her own contented, wordless song, as
if she knew that with her own weapons she had won
him.

'This one has kings, princes, dukes and saints in her
ancestry,' he said, and lightly kissed the tiny palm with
which she stroked him, 'and she has the noblest grandsire
any princess could ever claim, and as illustrious a great-
grandsire, and her mother was the loveliest and bravest
and truest of women. If God wills, she will yet come into
her rightful inheritance, and bear the princes who will
finish my work, if I must leave it unfinished. We cannot
say we have not a lady to fight for.'

From Aber we returned to the defence line of the Conway, and waited there for news from David, for we were
uneasy in case he had misjudged Edward's speed when he
moved, and perhaps been trapped into accepting battle,
or worse, penned fast in Denbigh before he could break

out of the threatening ring. But after three days more our outposts beyond the river reported the first companies of his army withdrawing in good order to Rhydcastell, and there the prince rode to see them safely into the grange the monks of Aberconway had there, where there was ample shelter and plentiful supplies. We did not expect David until all his men were safely withdrawn. In a few days more he came, riding in with the core of his body-guard, the last to draw back into Snowdonia. He came in armour, having had some mild brushes by the way, but he had brought off all his army intact.

'Surrey is in Dinas Bran,' he said, when he had shed his mail and broken his fast, and all his men were bestowed, and all his mounts watered and fed. 'The way I heard it, Edward has granted it to him, with Ial and other parts there, and Grey has been given Ruthin, with all my cantref of Duffryn Clwyd. Unworthily come and unworthily gone! Not county administrations, you'll mark, but marcher lordships these are to be. He must feel himself safer so. Better a marcher baron who has to mind his own, and can use his own brains to get the wheels turning, than chancery officials with parchments in one hand and pens in the other. He may very well be right, but he'll have a fight on his hands with his own marcher lords in the end, for it can't rest there.'

'Which of them moved?' asked Llewelyn, knee to knee with him by the fire.

'Edward and Grey both! But I think Grey's was a decoy, for he moved first, and not far. Clocaenog forest to his western front was full of Welsh, and he knew it, and so did I. I kept my best watch to the north, and was ready for Edward when he moved, too. Not along the coast, but inland from Rhuddlan, over the uplands, and in force. His ground was easier, and I had not such stout allies in his way, those parts were never mine.'

'How far has he come?' asked Llewelyn. 'He's still well north of you, it seems, you came out by the south.'

'He moved his headquarters as far as Llangernyw.' It was a vil due west of Denbigh, and dangerously far advanced. David saw the prince frown at the risk he seemed to have taken, and fended him off, smiling. 'I was out of Denbigh by then, and with my eye on every move he made. I knew I could outstrip him. We had much the same distance to cover to this place, but all that distance full of Welsh irregulars in arms. He has closed his ring round Denbigh, but I was out of the noose. I do not think he will even attempt to stay so far west, now I am clear of him. He'll creep in on Denbigh, and stay close to the Clwyd. It could still be dangerous in Llangernyw. The Middle Country will occupy him a week or two yet.'

'And what of Denbigh?' asked Llewelyn.

'I've left it intact,' said David, 'I could do no other. The garrison I've left there may hold it as long as they think advisable, and then let it go to him on the best terms they can get for themselves, now we've had time to draw clear. He will not know how few they are until they let him in, and the place will be little use to him but as a repository for stores or reserves of men, now that line's broken. But I was loth to leave it.'

As it turned out, David's castellan held out at Denbigh until past the middle of the month, giving us ample time to have our more westerly line well manned and guarded, with couriers keeping contact across the Conway with the free companies of Rhos and Rhufoniog. Then he surrendered, in time, as we hoped, to spare his garrison the worst extremes of the king's revenge.

Thus by mid-October Edward held all the line of castles which had formed our eastward defence, and could move freely along the Clwyd valley, though he still had not cleared all the land between the Clwyd and Conway, and seemed in no hurry to move against us until he had, for still de Tany waited in Anglesey and made no move, clearly having orders not to attempt the crossing until the king gave the word. The lull was hard on the nerves, but every day he delayed was a day nearer winter, and also encouraged us to believe it possible that he himself had similar thoughts.

From this time our headquarters was at Dolwyddelan, from which the women and children had already been withdrawn, but much of the time we were on the move, watching both the north coast and the strait, and also the Conway valley, for the attack, when it came, would come from both directions. From the south we had then little news. Certainly the Welsh in those parts were still in arms, but the weight of numbers had turned severely against them, all the castles of the crown were strongly garrisoned, and there were reserves to spare for penetrating again into Cardigan. The prince's nephews could not make headway against such forces, but they could and did prevent them from being depleted by sending further divisions to join the king.

So things stood on the twenty-third day of October, when two of our outposts at Rhydcastell rode into Dolwyddelan, bringing with them a Franciscan friar, a tall man of middle years and grave bearing, on a sturdy mountain pony. Their manner towards him was rather that of an honourable escort than of warders on a suspect interloper, and when they reached the gatehouse one of them spurred ahead to be his herald.

'This friar came alone into Rhydcastell, up the Dee valley from Dinas Bran, and asks for the lord prince. He says he bears letters from the archbishop of Canterbury, who is himself on his way to join the king at Rhuddlan, by way of Chester. His messenger speaks good Welsh, and is of our blood. They call him John of Wales.'

The friar followed him in impassively, and dismounted, shaking down the gown he had worn kilted to the knee. He had a calm, fierce face, like a vessel of passion perfectly controlled, and his form was muscular and lean. He would as well have made a soldier as a friar, but his name I knew, for he had a high reputation among scholars of

223

theology, and I had heard Brother William de Merton and others at Llanfaes speak of him, they being of the same order. A strange time it seemed for such a man to appear alone riding into Eryri, in the teeth of a roused and by then bitter war.

'I am come,' he said to the castellan, who hurried out to meet him, 'to present to the Lord Llewelyn, prince of Wales, the compliments of Archbishop Peckham, and my own credentials as his messenger. I have letters and articles for the lord prince. And the purpose of the archbishop's journey into Wales and my own is to try to put an end to this warfare, and bring about a just peace. If there is a welcome here for such an errand, I pray you bring me to Llewelyn.'

We brought him in with all ceremony, Tudor taking the guest in charge and offering him lodging and water and wine, after the old, honoured fashion, but he would take nothing until he had discharged his embassage to the prince. Llewelyn was in the armoury with his penteulu, seeing certain minor damages to mail and weapons made good, and thither I went to tell him what manner of visitor we had. He reared his head sharply at the news, and opened his eyes wide, willing to go to meet every overture of peace, but putting as yet no great trust in this or any.

'So he has not altogether forgotten or discarded us,' he said, marvelling, and he was glad, whether good came of it or no, for he kept still, in spite of the archbishop's querulous strictures on Welsh law, a degree of respect and affection for that good, difficult man. 'And he sent us a Welshman! Well done! I do believe he has a genuine care for his wild western flock, however they plague him with their adherence to the old ways. Let's go in, then, by all means, and see what Brother John Peckham sends us by Brother John of Wales.'

He went in as he was, dun and plain in leather, to the high chamber, and sent for the friar to be brought in. And

224

when he came, the prince rose and went to meet him, paying him the courtesy and reverence of one noble man saluting another. Brother John delivered the letters he carried, and their bulk caused a brief smile to pluck at Llewelyn's mouth. It was to be expected that the archbishop would use many and ardent words, for he was never one to go sparingly with his tongue or his pen, and it needed little wisdom to foresee that most of the words he had used in these scrolls would be of reproach, accusation and admonition. Yet if he had had nothing at all but these to offer he would not have sent his brother-Franciscan venturing into the mountains.

'You will understand,' said the prince, 'that we need time to weigh the archbishop's letters fairly, and also that I may consult my council, since I am acting not only for myself but for Wales. I trust you'll lodge with us and rest here in Dolwyddelan until we have our answer ready.'

'I am to wait for that answer,' said Brother John, 'as long as may be needful, though I urge haste. I am to carry your word on to meet the archbishop in the king's camp at Rhuddlan. And he prays you may be wisely guided, and provide him an answer that may end this warfare between kinsmen.'

'Justly,' said Llewelyn.

'Justly. So he has said, and so I say also.'

'Tell me,' said the prince, 'where is Archbishop Peckham now?'

'I left him the day before yesterday at Aldridge, on his way to Chester. By now he may have reached the city. I do not think he will yet have moved on.'

'Then what the archbishop has to propose to us in these letters is purely his own? The king does not know what he has written?'

'That is truth,' said Brother John. 'Indeed, he has taken this step very much against his Grace's will, and expects to incur his displeasure.'

'And if these letters provide a basis for further dealings,

in the hope of a settlement, can we rely on truce while the argument goes forward?'

'For that I shall be able to answer only when I reach Rhuddlan with your reply, which is the chief reason for haste. At present this is but a sounding. But you know my archbishop, and you know that if he is once satisfied you mean to deal, and are in earnest, as he is, he can and will insist on truce being observed, so long as you and he continue to talk to each other like reasonable men.'

It was much to claim for any man, that he could venture into a deadly struggle without Edward's sanction, frustrate Edward's immediate plans, and hold him and all his army still while we bargained for a peace Edward did not want. Yet Llewelyn accepted that word without demur. Even Peckham might attempt it and fail, for all his valour, but he would not stop short of the ultimate effort, and if the truce he made was broken, he would not let even the king go unrebuked, whatever the consequences to himself. There was not much more could be asked of any man.

'I do not believe,' said David bluntly, when Brother John had withdrawn, 'in this displeasure of the king's. This friar may be honest in swearing his archbishop comes against Edward's will, Peckham himself may believe it, but I do not. November's on the doorsill, for all his new castles his plans have not gone forward so well as he must have hoped. I think this is Edward's way of sounding out the ground with us, without himself appearing to be bending from his purpose.'

'The better reason for taking advantage of it,' said Llewelyn drily. 'We dare not over-value our situation or under-value his. We are back where we began, David, in Gwynedd west of Conway, but for those outposts that must draw back to us as soon as Edward moves. We are not broken, nor near it, we have no reason to despair, we are not suing for peace. But by God, we had better not refuse it if it is offered on any reasonable terms. I have watched Edward come to this station once before, and

226

judged him then, as you judge him now, to be weighing his chances and ready to welcome a move for peace. I know the peace I got was hard enough, but it was to my advantage and to his, rather than fight to the end, and we both knew it. This time he has proceeded differently, he is not beset as he was then. This time he began with a longer view than one summer. I do not think he means to stop short of victory. And since we will not tamely yield him everything he wants over a conference table, and I doubt he'll agree to any terms short of that, I advise you to be ready, as I am, to set your back against the rocks of Snowdon, and make him pay dearly for every stone.'

We called to Dolwyddelan for that council all the princes and captains and chief tenants of Gwynedd who could then leave their troops, and also had with us many councillors from the Middle Country and some from the south, for that castle had then become the court of Wales and its parliament. And there Llewelyn laid the archbishop's letters before his full council.

Most neatly and methodically they were laid out, the mark of the man in every line, and the very tone of his voice, voluble, hectoring, kindly-meant, sure of its own God-given rightness. In seventeen numbered articles he had drawn up his message to us, and thus they proceeded, though after so long a time I cannot answer for the exact wording. Yet the gist I remember very well:

1. That for the sake of our temporal and spiritual salvation, always dear to him, he was coming in person into our land.

2. That he came against the will of the king, who was said to be greatly displeased at his intervention.

3. That he begged and entreated us for the blood of Christ to return to our unity with the people of England and the king's peace, to which end he intended to do all that man could do.

4. That we should note that his stay in these parts could not be long.

5. That after his departure we should not find any other advocate to attempt the like for the sake of peace.

6. That if we spurned his overtures he intended to write to pope and curia with the grievous news of our obduracy, on account of the deadly sins that were multiplying every day through this discord.

7. That we should note that unless we accepted peace soon, the war would be waged against us with increased fury, beyond our bearing, since the royal power was every day growing greater.

8. That we should note that the realm of England was under the special protection of the apostolic see, exceeding all other lands.

9. That the Roman curia would in no wise allow the realm of England to be shaken, since that realm was particularly devoted to the faith.

10. That it caused him bitter grief to hear the Welsh described as crueller than the Saracens, since those take Christians prisoner for ransom, but as he had heard, the Welsh cut the throats of their prisoners on the spot, as if they delighted only in the shedding of blood, or, which was even worse, hand over the bodies of the murdered for ransom.

11. That nothing could excuse those who had launched a seditious, homicidal and destructive war at a time peculiarly sacred to the Redeemer.

12. That he begged us to return to true Christian penitence, since we could not long sustain this war we had begun.

13. That he begged us to inform him how we believed the disturbance of the king's peace the public mischief and all other ills attendant, could be amended.

14. That he begged us to inform him how, at this stage, peace could be effectively re-established. Though it seemed vain indeed to believe in the establishment of peace, when it had been so assiduously violated.

15. Since the Welsh claimed that their laws and the terms of their treaty had not been honoured, let them state in detail the particulars complained of.

16. That we should note that even if it were true, as we alleged, though he had no knowledge of it, that the Welsh had been derogated to an inferior status, yet that in no way justified them in being judges of their own cause, that they should thus attack the king's majesty.

17. That unless some method of re-establishing peace were found, we should be proceeded against to the utmost by degree, military, ecclesiastical and parliamentary.

'He has learned nothing, understands nothing, and offers nothing,' said David with scorn, when we had all heard this reading. 'We should have known! He sees but one side throughout. And do you note any word there of a *just* peace?'

'He knows but one side because he has heard but one side,' said the prince. 'At least here he is asking us to put the other, and by my counsel, so we shall, and fully. He asks for our views on how the bitterness can be healed, the peace re-made. He asks us to enumerate our complaints, and say what clauses of the treaty have been broken. Those details we have by heart, for good reason, now let him hear every one, whether he can feel the smart of them as we have felt it, or no. It is our one opportunity.'

There were some among us more ready to be hopeful than he, and some who had less faith in the archbishop's sincerity, yet there was no man present who could afford to say other than yes to the invitation offered us. Late into the night and all the next day we clerks laboured with drafting and copying, answering one by one all the charges made against us, and setting out our own case for taking action in arms when all other redress was denied us, and compiling the huge list of wrongs done to us, and the treaty obligations spurned and broken to our damage since the peace of Aberconway. We had among our complainants the most trusted of Edward's Welsh judges, for Goronwy ap Heilyn, Hopton's colleague on the bench, had cast in his lot in angry despair of justice with David and the men of the Middle Country, and from this on acted as steward to David to the end. For more than four years he had done his best, both as justice and as bailiff of Rhos, to keep the balance between English and Welsh and do right to both, but when the breakage came he could do no other but go with Wales, for it was Wales that suffered wrong without remedy.

Eleven separate schedules of grievances we compiled among us, seven being from individual princes and chiefs, and four presenting the complaints of whole regions. These were from Rhos, Tegaingl, Penllyn and Ystrad Alun. They varied in details as to forests thinned without leave, taxes exacted without right, arbitrary English law imposed where Welsh law applied, meadows misappropriated, vils occupied by force or extorted to add to the holdings of favoured hangers-on, but all cried out in grievous unison that an English tyranny had robbed them not only of their Welsh laws, which had been solemnly guaranteed by treaty, but even of their local customs which harmed none, and further, had proceeded against them with ever-increasing harshness and injustice, in many cases, even by the English law the administrators claimed to uphold. The men of the Middle Country denounced the exactions and cruelties of Reginald de Grey in Chester, those of Ystrad Alun the overbearing rule of Roger Clifford, those of Penllyn burned against the constable of Oswestry. From the prince to the cottager in the remote tref it was the same story, and that story was true.

Those who submitted schedules of their personal wrongs, apart from the prince himself, were David, all three of the nephews from Ystrad Tywi, Rhys Wyndod separately, and Griffith and Llewelyn together, all disinherited of lands rightfully theirs by the crown, the sons of Meredith ap Owen from Cardigan, Goronwy ap Heilyn, and Llewelyn ap Griffith ap Madoc of Maelor. Besides unjust disinheritance and expropriations, all complained of the interference of the king's officials within their lawful Welsh courts, of the arrogance of royal administrators who enforced attendance at their convenience wherever they chose, in defiance of old custom, of the exaction of illegal dues, interference with free movement and trade, and the infliction of English penalties, even to death, where a more humane Welsh law ought to have applied.

I think I myself had not fully realised, until we compounded all this formidable body of evidence in one great accusation, how universal was the attack upon all forms of Welsh life and usage, and how, when seen whole, it could no longer be regarded as the almost accidental product of high-handed and unfeeling officialdom, but emerged as purposeful and deliberate policy, using the resources of Edward's legal mind in pursuit of his ambition. His first object, so it seemed to me, was to extend, by all possible means, the lands on which he could impose English shire systems. His second was to rid all such lands of their Welsh customs and laws, and subject them to English common law and English organisation. His small bailiffs and tax-men were as they were, overbearing and harsh, because they divined, even if they did not fully understand, what was required of them. The shape their actions took, Edward gave them. They may, at times, have gone further than he would have wished them to go, but if so, it was but a difference of judgment due to limited intelligence. He had no quarrel with those excesses that were successful for his policies.

As for the prince, he and I drew up his schedule together, and it went directly to the question of what clauses of the treaty had been dishonoured by the English. Seven separate provisions he cited, in each case quoting the exact words of the treaty, in case the archbishop should need to have his memory of it refreshed, and then giving the instances in which it had been flouted, beginning with the clause under which he had sought to have Welsh law over

Arwystli, and been denied it upon pretext after pretext. Other clauses concerned the promise that all transgressions committed during the war should be remitted from the treaty date, whereas de Grey, for one, had pursued many individuals for previous offences in the Middle Country. Also the article guaranteeing to various princes those lands they held at the time of the treaty, which afterwards were expropriated, and another assuring the tenants of the Middle Country that under the royal rule they should still enjoy all their traditional rights, which thereafter were gradually taken away from them. And sundry specific cases of incursion by royal officials into territory still indubitably Welsh, with the old grievance over Robert of Leicester and the wrongful distraints made in Chester on his behalf.

He added also one small but significant matter which I have not before mentioned, for at the time of his marriage at Worcester the king had presented him a document for agreement and seal, binding the prince not to harbour or maintain in his lands any persons contrary to the king's wish. Which he then sealed, partly unwilling to disturb the time, but also seeing no derogation in it, since the king's harbouring and maintaining the prince's Welsh traitors and assassins had been one of the main causes of the war, and he could not well resent agreement to the consideration he himself had so often urged in vain. But later at least one case arose where he found himself pressed to eject from his lands not an English fugitive or male-factor, but one of his own men, against whom the royal officers alleged some ill-supported offence. He therefore added this also to his list, referring drily to the use of such a clause to strip him of his loyal adherents at the king's will, and deprecated the grant of his seal in the common legal phrase used to object to an agreement obtained by duress or fraud.

'Therefore,' he wrote in concluding the tale of his wrongs, and further, the wrongs done to his people, 'it ought not to cause wonder to any man, if the aforesaid prince gave his assent to those who began the war.' And that was carefully said, for he himself had not begun it, but once begun it was his war whether he would or no, and he could not withhold his countenance from it.

In addition to this detailed schedule, meant to make one among the rest, he wrote also a long covering letter, personally answering the archbishop's seventeen articles.

That letter I remember so well that even now I can set it down, if not word for word, in its full sense and passion, and for the sake of those who will enquire into these things in time to come, when justice lives again, here I give it from beginning to end, that no man may be able to say Llewelyn wrote this, or this, falsely, but what he did indeed write shall endure to be set before the judgment. Thus the letter went:

'To the most reverend father in Christ, the Lord John, by the grace of God archbishop of Canterbury, primate of all England, from his humble and devoted son Llewelyn, prince of Wales, lord of Snowdon, salutation and filial affection, with all manner of reverence, submission and honour.

'For the heavy labours which your fatherly holiness has assumed at this time, out of the love you bear to us and our nation, we render you grateful thanks, all the more since, as you have intimated to us, you come against the king's will. You ask us to come to the king's peace. Your holiness should know that we are ready to do so, provided the lord king will truly observe that same peace as is due to us and ours. We rejoice that this interlude granted to Wales is at your instance, and you will find no impediments placed in the way of peace by us, for we would rather support your efforts than those of any other. We hope, God willing, there need be no occasion for you to write anything to the pope concerning our pertinacity, nor will you find us spurning your fatherly entreaties and strenuous endeavours, indeed we embrace them with all the warmth of our heart. Nor is it necessary for the king to weight his

233

hand yet further against us, since we are fully prepared to render him obedience, always saving our rights and our laws, a reservation legally permitted to us.

'The realm of England may well be the special object of the Roman curia's affection, but the aforesaid curia has yet to learn, and must learn, and the lord pope likewise, what evils have been wrought upon us by the English, how the peace formerly made has been violated in all the clauses of the treaty, how churches have been fired and devastated, and ecclesiastical persons, priests, monks and nuns slaughtered, women slain with their children at the breast, hospitals and other houses of religion burned, Welsh people murdered in cemeteries, churches, yes, at the very altar, with other sacrilegious offences horrible to hear. All which are detailed in these *rotuli* we send in writing for your inspection.

'Now our best hope is that your fatherly piety may incline kindly towards us, and neither the Roman curia nor the realm of England need be shaken for our sake, provided it is understood in advance that the peace we seek be not only made, but observed. Those who do indeed delight in the shedding of blood are identified manifestly by their deeds, and thus far the English, in their usage of us, have spared none, whether for sex, or age, or weakness, nor passed by any church or sacred place. Such outrages the Welsh have not committed.

'It does, however, grieve us very deeply to acknowledge that it is true one ransomed prisoner was killed, but we have neither countenanced nor maintained the murderer, for he was wandering the forests as a freebooter.

'You speak of certain persons beginning the fighting at a holy season. We ourselves knew nothing of this until after the fact, when it was urged in their defence that if they had not struck then, death and rape threatened them, they dared neither dwell in their own houses at peace nor go about except in arms, and it was fear and despair that caused them to act when they did.

'As to the assertion that we are acting against God, and ought to repent as true Christians, seeking God's grace, if the war continues it shall not be set at our door, provided we can be indemnified as is our due. But while we are disinherited and slaughtered, it behoves us to defend ourselves to the utmost. Where any genuine injuries and damages come into consideration upon either side, we are prepared to make amends for those committed by our men, provided the like amends are made for damages inflicted upon us. In the making and preserving of peace we are similarly ready to assist to the limit of what is due from us. But when royal pacts and treaties made with us are of none effect, as thus far they have not been observed, it is impossible to establish peace, nor when new and unprecedented exactions against us and ours are daily being devised. In the accompanying *rotuli* we send to you the catalogue of our wrongs, and of the breaches of that treaty formerly made with us.

'We fight because we are forced to fight, for we, and all Wales, are oppressed, subjugated, despoiled, reduced to servitude by the royal officers and bailiffs, in defiance of the form of the peace and of all justice, more maliciously than if we were Saracens or Jews, so that we feel, and have often so protested to the king, that we are left without any remedy. Always the justiciars and bailiffs grow more savage and cruel, and if these become satiated with their unjust exactions, those in their turn apply themselves to fresh exasperations against the people. To such a pass are we come that they begin to prefer death to life. It is not fitting in such case to threaten greater armies, or move the Church against us. Let us but have peace, and observe it as due, as we have expressed above.

'You should not believe all the words of our enemies, holy father, the very people who by their deeds oppress and ill-use us, and in their words defame us by attributing to us whatever they choose. They are ever present with you, and we absent, they the oppressors, we the oppressed.

235

In accordance with divine faith, instead of quoting their words in all things, you should rather examine their deeds.

'May your holiness long flourish, to the benefit and good order of the Church.'

'Enough!' said Llewelyn in revulsion and weariness, when we had finished. 'There is no more I can do, and no more to be said. I will neither beg nor bend. We have spoken out fully now, and they owe us truce at least until we come to terms, or break off the attempt.'

The next day we delivered all those *rotuli* to Brother John of Wales, and gave him an escort to see him on his way to Rhuddlan.

'Carry also,' said the prince in farewell, 'my thanks and reverences to Archbishop Peckham, for whether he speeds or not, it is great credit to him that he is willing to venture. And if he does not withhold his prayers from us, very surely we will not refuse them.'

'As soon as I can deliver these letters,' said the friar, 'I will beg him to confirm with the king the matter of truce. And I trust to visit you again, if God wills, in pursuit of peace.'

'It may serve,' said David looking after them as they rode down through the fold of the hills until the curve of the track and the deepening of the valley took them from our sight. 'If parliament rebels at extorting still more money for Edward's Gascons, if the king of France refuses them passage, if the clergy grudge him his twentieth, and his Italian usurers begin to bite, if the snow blocks the roads soon enough, and ice closes the port at Rhuddlan, *if* everything in God's earth conspires to hold Edward off from our throats and make him fear for his own, it *may* serve! If not, our swords must. We knew from the first there was no going back.'

Within three days we were reassured that we had truce, for nothing moved, we had gained a watchful quietness which we took care not to break. The weather was growing stormy, with strong winds from the north-east, though as yet the winter cold had not set in. In Anglesey the English garrison sat still, guarding their heaving bridge but not attempting to cross it, and the king, at Rhuddlan, uttered as yet no word, but launched no arrows either. I know that David had it in mind still that Edward was making a tool of the archbishop, however that worthy soul might preen himself on his bravery and initiative, and believe he was leading where in truth he was most subtly led. I cannot say, even now, whether he was right in this. He well may have been. Nevertheless, we began to believe that there was at least a manner of debate going on in the royal camp by the Clwyd.

But when the expected messenger came at last, on the first day of November, under a black and purple sky of towering, scudding cloud, it was not the lean, austere friar for whom we had kept watch. One of the prince's regular patrols escorted into Dolwyddelan, in a driving shower of rain, two horsemen of whom one was plainly groom and servant to the other, and held back obsequiously at his heels. The other sat solidly in the saddle, bedded down like a woolsack, but hopped down energetically enough in the courtyard, shook the rain from his cloak, and putting back the hood showed us the round, self-important, concerned face, not of Brother John of Wales, but of Brother John Peckham, archbishop of Canterbury.

CHAPTER IX

———————

'I am come in person, my lord prince,' said the archbishop, when we had lodged and fed and served him in every point as well as a castle under war conditions could, 'because it seemed to me that those documents you sent me deserve that I should, and need every care I can bring to them. I have obtained his Grace's consent to a state of truce while we confer, and I assure you it will not be broken by his orders. I trust I may rely on you as far.'

'You may, my lord,' said Llewelyn. 'I, too, have given my orders.'

The archbishop stretched out his toes gratefully to the warmth of the brazier in the high chamber, for the nights were growing chill, and he had ridden far, and in very buffeting winds. I doubt if we had then the table to offer him that Edward could have mounted at Rhuddlan, for we went very sparsely fed ourselves, to husband what resources we had for the winter. But give him his due, this priest valued his appetite very little, and the offering of hospitality high, and our ceremonial heated water and towel for his weary feet had perhaps charmed him more than venison and wine. He looked round the private circle of us there, the prince, David, Tudor the high steward of Wales, the chaplain, Llewelyn, the prince's nephew, myself and Goronwy ap Heilyn as David's seneschal. 'I have only good remembrances of the lord prince's hospitality and kindness in Carnarvon, and I grieve all the more at this dissension with which we labour here today, that so severs us.'

'I, too,' said Llewelyn. 'But I do not think it severs us two. For my part, I feel no gulf between. I am too conscious of your former benefits and ever-present goodwill. Such other duties as I bear, however sacred, do not obscure these.'

'You greatly encourage me,' said Peckham. 'And now that we meet again, I beg you'll let me say how much it grieves me that we miss one face that graced our last meeting.' He was hesitant and soft of voice, the only time I ever saw or heard him so. 'I have sorrowed greatly,' he said, 'for your untimely loss in the death of your lady, the princess. God's purposes are sometimes cloudy to us, but doubtless he best knows his own way, and we see but with imperfect vision.'

'Doubtless,' said Llewelyn, courteous and patient as always when any tried to speak to him of her, and he gave thanks, but as always with a closed and forbidding face, so that the archbishop forbore from treading in further, but sighed and shook himself, and turned to business.

'I have studied all those *rotuli* you sent me, and I grant that these are very grave complaints. I brought them to the king's notice, and begged him to give them judicial remedy, and to hold them as sufficient excuse for the faults committed. I fear his Grace did not receive my intercession with any favour, for in his view the offence is inexcusable, since these grievances were not first referred to him as the head and fount of justice. If they had been so referred he would have been ready, as he always is, to give proper remedy where it is due, and no honest suppliant need fear rebuff, or resort to other and lawless means of redress.'

At that his fine delivery, which was by then assured and sonorous, was broken by the stir of indignation that rippled through all of us, and by David's gasp of unbelief.

'He dared say so?' he cried and drew in furious breath, but Llewelyn laid a hand on his arm, and he recoiled into angry silence.

'His Grace's memory,' said the prince hardly, 'is at fault. Every one of those matters of which I, personally, complain has been referred to him for redress time and time again, in his courts, yes, but also directly to his own hand and ear. In letter after letter I have informed him in every detail of my frustration over Arwystli, and let him know that I held it gross injustice, and required a remedy. Every one of those other wrongs I have brought to him, cited the treaty to him, demanded justice, but never obtained it. If now he claims I have passed him by, and makes that his reason for finding this insurrection inexcusable, then I say outright, he says what is not true. And since justice has been refused me at his hands a score of times already, if he expects me to put more trust in it the one-and-twentieth time, he insults both my wit and your credulity. As for my magnates, they will answer for themselves.'

And so they did, David first and most fiercely, recounting almost word for word the letters he had written to Edward, complaining of law that cited him to the Chester shire-court to answer for land purely Welsh. He spoke also for all the men of his two cantrefs, in whose name he had many times raised the issues that troubled them, but always without redress.

'To claim now that these have never been brought to him requires more effrontery than a king should use even towards his brother-kings, let alone those people over whom he has sovereign power, and towards whom he carries a sovereign's responsibility. It is unworthy to resort to lies,' he said in a steady, black blaze of rage, and his voice low, deliberate and sweet, as always when he was most deadly in his anger.

I must say of Peckham that he would listen as well as talk, even when his own indignation was rising. He did not then rebuke David for alleging that the king lied – it may be that his native honesty could not well deny it, and that he had encountered it himself in other connections – but invited those present to testify to the end on this point, and when both Tudor and young Llewelyn had had their say, Goronwy ap Heilyn ended those declarations with a very measured and reasoned recital of his own experiences as a judge of the Hopton bench and bailiff in Rhos. Many times he had witnessed miscarriages of justice and breaches of the rights guaranteed by treaty, and many times, sometimes to the king in person, he had pointed out the unwisdom of official procedures which were driving the Welsh to anger and despair. His moderation was as impressive as David's fury, and did our cause better service, besides sparing us all a long homily.

'This evidence,' said the archbishop earnestly, 'I accept as sincere, but remember that you have spoken of many and diverse incidents and cases, scattered throughout the land and arising at different times. Those of such pleas are remembered which have been unsuccessful, while where redress has been granted the mind keeps no record. To say that his Grace has been informed on so many occasions of so many matters, minor when looked at singly though hurtful when regarded in the sum, is not the same as claiming that he has ever been presented with such a detailed and reasoned schedule of complaints as you have provided now, where the magnitude of the disquiet and grievance is made plain. I think his attitude natural enough, indeed justified, but I understand also the depth of your resentment and distrust. What needs to be done now is not to hurl further charges, but to bring about a reconciliation. I am doing my best to that end.'

'I acknowledge it and am grateful,' said Llewelyn, 'but I cannot relinquish my wrongs on that account. But I think you must have achieved some better hope than this, or you would not be here among us now.'

'I begged the king,' said the archbishop, 'to allow you to have free access to him at Rhuddlan, and freely return so that you could discuss your grievances with him face to face. I will not say that he gave me the answer I hoped for, all he would say was that you could come, and return without hindrance *if you earned that right*. It is not absolute refusal, but for the sake of swift reconciliation I resolved rather to come myself to talk with you, and try to bring you to a degree of reason and goodwill that may admit you again to the king's grace. For I am sure he is not fast shut against you.'

We were less sure, but this ardent busybody had a strong compulsion about him, and as long as he sat here with us arguing and preaching and scolding, there was hope that he would bring forth a minor miracle. So we settled to enjoy, enlighten and convince him, as he strove to comfort, chasten and pluck us from the burning.

Three days the archbishop stayed with us, and during that time had several conferences with Llewelyn, alone and in council, and with David also. And strange it was to see how, as that celibate innocent with his warm, intrusive kindness disarmed David, so did David's insinuating charm melt the archbishop, as it had many another. So that when they parted at the end it was with a wry grace and affection, David pretending a humility he did not feel, Peckham forgetfully blessing the foremost of those he had consigned to outer darkness with his general excommunication, issued from Devizes when the war first began.

At his last full conference with prince and council, the archbishop again exhorted us to humility, and a return to the fealty sworn at Westminster after the previous war, reminding Llewelyn that he had then consented to a form which entailed submitting himself without condition to the king's will – this for the sake of the king's relations with his own barons, which he dared not compromise – but on the tacit understanding that in fact the terms behind the phrase would be honourable and fair. And would he not, he said almost wistfully, again submit himself in the same form.

'The terms behind the phrase then,' said Llewelyn, 'were not merely promised as acceptable, but argued out through a whole month of bargaining, and known and agreed by both sides, so that I knew precisely how that clause of absolute submission was limited and conditioned by all the clauses that followed. So did all those who took part in the negotiations, there could be no withdrawal. I should require as clear an understanding of the limiting clauses this time, before I would consent to the form of unconditional submission. I am the sovereign prince of a free and sovereign state. I am willing to return to the homage and fealty of the treaty of Aberconway, provided its terms are observed, as heretofore they have not been. I am willing to make submission as I did then, the terms of that submission being understood and agreed by us both, and in that case I will keep them, as I kept the others. But always saving my right as prince of Wales, and my responsibility to my people.'

'But you do not refuse,' said Peckham, pleading and urgent, 'the same fealty you pledged before.'

'No, I do not refuse it,' said Llewelyn. 'I incurred it, and I was bound by it. I was not the first to break it then, and if it is renewed in good faith, I shall not be the first to break it now.'

It was not all the archbishop could have wished, but it was enough to encourage him, and send him back to Edward with word that the Welsh were not irreconcilable, if they were offered honourable terms. And he thanked Llewelyn, I am sure sincerely, for his hospitality and patience, and assured us he would return to Rhuddlan to do his best for us.

'I was so unused to these wild lands,' he said, 'and to venturing among men at war, that I thought myself gallant to set out from Rhuddlan, and held my life to be at risk. I even appointed Bishop Burnell, the king's chancellor, to be my vicar in my absence, for fear I might not return. But I find sons here in Snowdon as in Westminster, or

Canterbury, and am confirmed in feeling myself bound to all the sheep of my flock.'

And he took leave of us kindly, and Llewelyn sent a princely escort to see him safely on his way as far as the Clwyd, as much to show his faith in the truce as to honour the archbishop.

David stood at the outer gate and watched them go, down through the furze and heath that skirted the pathway. 'Well, I have bleated my sweetest for him,' he said, mocking himself and Peckham both, but somewhat ruefully. 'Who would have thought that office could truly confer fatherhood upon one so childlike? And he barely my age.'

'He is a good man,' said Llewelyn, but in a manner detached and almost indifferent. 'Honest and kind.'

'By that measured and measuring voice,' said David, 'I read your mind. Honesty and kindness will hardly be enough.'

I do not know, but I think we prayed, all three, from that day, for Peckham's courage, perseverance and eloquence, for the pope's lightnings to strike through his uplifted forefinger, and God's through the pope, loosing angelic justice and truth upon the earth. But we kept all our armouries busy, none the less, fletching arrows and honing steel, hammering blades and repairing mail. And the quiet continued, and the weather wavered between calm and storm, smiling and frowning on our hopes by turns.

'One thing at least he brought us,' said David, 'he and his crusading into savage territory where men eat men, and even priests take their lives in their hands. Not that I underrate his bravery! This is a gallant little innocent as ever was. He told us Burnell is his vicar in his absence. And where the chancellor is – and plainly he's in Rhuddlan now – there Cynan is likely to be, also. We have an ally in the king's camp. We may get useful information yet, if this truce fails.'

244

As it fell out, the first news we got came back to us with the escort, when they returned from seeing the archbishop safely to within a few miles of Rhuddlan. For the captain who had borne him company sought out Llewelyn immediately on his return, to recount what had passed on the way.

'We were well beyond Conway, my lord,' he said, 'when suddenly the archbishop clicks his tongue and snaps his fingers, and says he, he has done ill to let it slip his mind, he should have offered you his sympathies on the death of your cousin Mortimer – '

'Mortimer dead?' said Llewelyn, astonished and dismayed. 'When? This must be new, or word would have reached us somehow.'

'The twenty-sixth of last month, my lord, at Wigmore. Gently in his bed, it seems, after a fever. I made bold to ask further, and he said he knew you two kinsmen had a respect and liking for each other, war or no war, and he was sorry he had failed to speak of it to you. I tried what I could get from the groom, privately, for if Mortimer's gone so unexpectedly there may well be disarray in the middle march. What with the court being at Rhuddlan and the king preoccupied, it seems nobody's paid much attention to young Edmund's claims. Sprenghose, the sheriff of Salop, has all the Mortimer lands in his charge meantime, and the heir can wait for his seisin until Edward pleases to have time for him, and that goes down very ill. You know both the sons better than I, but I know enough of them to know they're like their father, and think a Mortimer equal to a king, any day of the year. They say there was a good deal of sympathy for the Welsh cause round Wigmore and Radnor and Builth already, among the tenants, there may well be a measure of feeling even in the castles now.'

'There well may!' said Llewelyn, remembering his last meeting and compact with his cousin.

'And the groom let out that the king's been none too
245

happy with the way the war was being conducted in those parts, what with the old lord ill, and very little being done to hunt the Welsh out of the hills. I don't say he suspects any man's loyalty, but he has no high opinion of their zeal, that's certain. Yes, and one more thing that will madden the Mortimers above all – Griffith ap Gwenwynwyn is already reviving his old claim to the thirteen vills against the heir, now the old lord's gone, and he thinks better of his chances.'

That was the very cause that Mortimer had successfully defended by Welsh law, when the same was denied to Llewelyn. By Roger's death these townships came formally back into the king's hand, along with all the other Mortimer lands, until seisin was granted to the heir, and doubtless Griffith thought this was his best chance to regain them, seeing they were now at Edward's disposal, at least on parchment. But even Edward would stop to think very carefully before withholding part of his inheritance from a Mortimer, even if he failed to comprehend the degree of offence he could give by delaying the grant of seisin, as though it was of little urgency, and could wait his leisure.

'Yes,' said the prince, pondering, 'there are interesting possibilities there to be exploited, if needs must. While the truce holds and we have hopes of agreement, there's nothing more we can do. But I am sorry,' he said, 'that Roger's gone. He was a rough, fair enemy and a sturdy friend.'

In this great but fragile quietness that had fallen upon us, we needed all the information we could garner, whether or not there was any immediate use we could make of it. If there was disaffection even among the greater tenants round Radnor, and Edward in his single-minded fury against Wales had failed to understand how easily inflamed the Mortimer pride could be, then the central march might be a fruitful field for recruitment if the fighting had to continue, and even the young lords, stung

246

by the king's neglect and delay in establishing the right feudal relationship with them in their father's place, might at least turn a blind eye to what their Welsh tenants did, though it was hard to believe their own loyalty was assailable. But the niceties of feudal usage cut both ways. Until the king gave Edmund seisin of his inheritance, no fealty existed, and no treason was possible and, the boy might well claim, no loyalty either.

'I should be sorry to lure any man away from his faith,' said the prince, 'but what's offered I'll not refuse. Well, let it lie, we are at truce. We may yet have no need of such weapons.' But I knew by his tone, that was steady, equable but joyless, that he had no great faith in Peckham's valiant offices.

Howbeit, we waited, and nursed such resources as we had. And a day or so later one of our patrols brought in a solitary wretch, drenched and shivering, from the bleak hills the further side of Conway, and having heard his account of himself, delivered him to Tudor, who in turn brought him to Llewelyn.

'For he came gladly into their arms instead of running from them,' said Tudor, 'and he has a parchment he says is for the lord prince. We have fed him, for he was famished, he'd been on the run from Rhuddlan for two days, he says, and all but fell into the clutches of a patrol from the outpost at Llangernyw.'

The man was young, no more than thirty, and sturdy, though soiled and unkempt after his solitary travelling. He said he was a borderer from Cynllaith, Welsh by blood, but drafted for the king's work by the constable of Oswestry. He was a carpenter, one of many pressed to serve in the making of the boat-bridge across the strait, and he had left a young wife at home, and sought the first opportunity of getting back to her. Many of the hundreds of carpenters had been discharged now that the bridge was ready, but he as a skilled man had been one of those retained to maintain the work, for the seas were growing rough there, and several times there had been damages to repair. And as he could not swim at all, let alone well enough to risk that passage, he had stowed away on one of the coastal ships returning to Rhuddlan after unloading a cargo of crossbow quarrels. It was going back to the lion's den, but there was no help for it, and he had trusted to his wits and judgment to get clear undiscovered when the ship docked.

'And so I did, my lord,' he said, 'and would have made off upstream to where I could ford the Clwyd, but there was too much bustle about the dock, and I had to lie up among the stores until dark, and there, by what I thought then very ill-luck, I was spied by one of the clerks going back and forth with inventories of the arms and timber being loaded. But it turned out the best of luck for me, for he put a bland face on it, and gave me his scrip and schedules to carry for him, and so hid me until night by not hiding me at all. And by darkness he put me across the river with a bundle of food and this letter to the lord prince, and advised me to cut as briskly into Welsh-held land as I could. Which I have done, and gratefully. And here I deliver his letter, and keep my promise.'

The scroll was but a fragment of a leaf, and the hand not as precise or leisured as usual, but it was still recognisable. Llewelyn smiled as he unrolled it. 'You owe him your liberty, and I owe him many years of staunch service.'

'Did I not say,' said David, also knowing that hand, 'that we should hear from him?' And he leaned at Llewelyn's shoulder to read with him. That was the briefest letter we ever had from Cynan:

'Your advocate here labours hard for you, but against the grain. The truce holds fast, Tany in Anglesey has his orders not to stir unless the king gives the word. But hear what the bearer has to say, and be on guard accordingly. If I can find no further messenger, accept with this my fealty and valediction. God shield you, is the prayer of your servant.'

'What is this?' said David, startled and hushed. 'He is saying goodbye! He is watched! No, or he would not be going freely about Burnell's business checking the loading of ships. If he had lost the chancellor's confidence they would have a man at his heels every moment, he'd have had no chance to help a fugitive out of Rhuddlan.'

'He went about as having authority everywhere,' said the carpenter. 'I could not see that any man questioned it, or looked sidewise at him.'

'He is Welsh,' said Llewelyn dispassionately, 'and feels the day drawing in.' And he looked up calmly at the messenger, and said: 'Tell us what it is you have to tell, concerning Tany and Anglesey. That part of his news he has left to you.'

'My lord,' said the man, 'what the clerk says is true, every man in Anglesey knew that Luke de Tany has his orders not to move until the king bids him cross his bridge. But when the news came that the archbishop had come to Wales, and was going back and forth trying to make peace, Tany flew into a bitter rage, and swore his meddling should not prosper, for he would put an end to it if the king would not. He said the king had set out to annex Wales to his realm, and he should do it, in spite of Peckham and pope and all.'

'Did he so?' said Llewelyn, drawing slow and thoughtful breath. 'You heard this?'

'Not I, but the lads who were working at the end of the bridge, they heard it, for the despatches were carried to him there. My lord, I had friends among them I trust. They have not lied. If I did not hear his ravings, I saw his face not an hour later, and it was still black.'

'He was Edward's seneschal in Gascony,' said David. 'He sees another province within his grasp. I believe it.'

'I, too,' said Llewelyn, and re-rolled Cynan's letter in his hands. 'Take a day and a night of rest here,' he said to the carpenter, 'and then you shall have food and a cloak, and my safe-conduct to pass you south round-about, by the Berwyns, back to your home. You'll be safe enough on the way. But how will you fare in your own village if you're within the English pale?'

The man grinned, stocky and resolute, no way intimidated at the prospect. 'Let me alone, my lord, to take care of that. My village is two men out of three Welsh, and a good reeve to fend for us, and no such tight hold now I judge, as when I was pressed. God grant your Grace as hopeful a way before you.'

'Amen!' said Llewelyn, and smiled and dismissed him.

'Very well,' he said to David, leaning and quivering at his elbow, 'send at once to Bangor, let them know what's said of Tany and his grievance, and have them double the watch on the bridge. But not move until I so bid, or Tany brings it headlong on his own head by treachery. I will not be the one to break this truce. You hear me?'

'Nor I, believe me,' said David. 'I value my life too high to toss away the hope of keeping it. But if he strikes, so may we, and harder. But this half-Gascon courtier will never really venture?' he said, marvelling and rejecting. 'Against Edward's orders?'

'Who can tell,' said Llewelyn, 'what men will dare do? I see no limits to human rashness.' He looked into his brother's face, bent most earnestly, brow and eye, to search his heart and mind. He smiled, bewildered and rueful, as one who stakes nothing of value, and sees others dear to him hurl their souls away. 'I teach where I have learned,' he said. 'Go and set your snare, David, but leave Tany to spring it. Edward will not forgive that, and the guilt will not be yours. We have a mediator, and a truce. It is not time yet to think of how to die.'

Thus we manned our defences above Bangor, and held reserves ready in the hills behind the strait, and made no further move, bound by that autumnal silence that was heavy and still as the lull between storm-winds. While Brother John Peckham argued and sweated both for us

250

and for England, and for his pope and his God, who hated, the one as the other, dissent among believing creatures, and the shedding of Christian blood. I do acquit him whom sometimes I have resented, reviled and damned, of any insincerity. He did as he saw right, he never lied, he never left grieving. It was not his fault if he could not see beyond the end of a very short nose, or stretch his academic mind into the bleak, bare summits of our mountains, and comprehend the love we had for our barren, beautiful land. He came from a softer soil and a narrower learning. He did his best.

In the afternoon of the sixth day of November, in that year twelve hundred and eighty-two, Brother John of Wales rode into our outposts from Rhuddlan, bearing the desperate and devoted fruit of his archbishop's labours on behalf of peace. In camp at Garthcefn, in the highlands of our Snowdon, Llewelyn received Archbishop Peckham's envoy, and the terms of peace he brought us.

Three letters Brother John brought with him on this occasion, and asked at once for private audience with the prince, which was at once granted. Therefore until the council met, which was late in the same afternoon, none but the prince knew what was contained in those two scrolls committed to Llewelyn, or the third, which was for David. After the friar had withdrawn the prince sent for his brother, and those two were closeted together until they came forth into the assembly of the council. Because of the truce we had an unusually full gathering for time of war, as was right and proper when the whole fate of Wales hung upon our proceedings.

When the prince took his place, his countenance was stone-still but calm. The grey that had salted his temples was now a silver dust over the thick autumnal bracken-brown of his whole head, and this gradual frost had overtaken him since Eleanor died. He stood at the threshold of a double winter, of the year and of his own glory, unless

God willed a miracle to Wales. I saw, as suddenly I wa
seeing for the first time clearly all the signs of his advancing
age and mine, that he had lost flesh, and the bones of hi
face stood clear and hard and polished, rather bronze than
stone. The chill winds of war and death had driven him
past the bright summer of his prime. There was no way
now to go but towards old age and the dark. What mat
tered was the manner of the going.

I looked at David, who sat close at his side, very pale
and grim, and noted how from time to time he watched
his brother with strained and passionate attention, a
though he, too, was seeing the threat of ruin as great a
the former glory. But he saw it as in part his own work
and was aghast and stricken mute before that know
ledge.

'By favour of Archbishop Peckham and Brother John
of Wales,' said the prince, 'we have received replies to
those articles we sent in our defence, asking for justice
Before I put them before this council, I must tell you what
Brother John reports of the reception our letters received
in Rhuddlan. The archbishop presented to the king my
reply that I am willing to submit myself to his will, saving
always my sovereign dignity and my duty to my people.
King Edward refuses to allow any conditions. We must
submit to his will absolutely, without reserve. I am grateful
to the archbishop for this, that he understood and said
that unless we were offered honourable terms we would
not surrender, and as Brother John reports, he persisted
until he induced the king to agree that he might consult
the magnates present at Rhuddlan, and with them try to
draw up terms which should be mutually acceptable. For
what the king's own magnates agreed to could hardly be
derogatory to the king's sovereignty and honour. What I
now hold is the fruit of those discussions, and to these
terms the king has given his consent, though I am told not
gladly.' He looked round about at all the intent faces, and
said with slow emphasis: 'I make it clear – if this form is
not accepted, we may very well ask the archbishop to
252

continue his efforts. But whether he will again prevail upon the king to allow another form to be put forward, that I question. It is fair,' he said, 'that you should know what is at stake.'

Out of their great, expectant hush Tudor asked: 'Does Brother John report his archbishop as believing these terms to be fair and just? Does he expect us to find them so?'

'Brother John says it cost his archbishop long and hard labour to get agreement to them, and he is satisfied he could do no better for us. Yes, as I judge, he expects compliance,' said Llewelyn, and briefly and terribly smiled. 'There are three letters. The first and shorter of the two addressed to me I am free to lay before this council, the second is superscribed to be delivered to me in private, and so has been. I make no distinction. My fate and the fate of Wales march together, and Wales must know as fully as I everything that is proposed concerning this war and this peace.'

'Read them,' said Tudor. And David said in a low voice: 'For God's sake, put us all out of our pain! Peace or war I could bear, but this headlong falling in the cleft between the two is too much for me.'

'In the name of God, then,' said Llewelyn, and unrolled the first of the archbishop's two scrolls. 'This contains the open terms.' And he read aloud:

'These to be delivered to the prince in council:

'First: That the lord king will entertain no discussion or dealings concerning the Middle Country, and those lands already granted by him to his magnates, nor concerning the island of Anglesey.

'Item: As to the tenants of the aforesaid cantrefs, if they come to the king's peace they shall be treated as befits and is pleasing to the king's majesty. But we are confident that he will deal with them mercifully if they accept of peace, and with other friends we propose to do our utmost to achieve this end, and are confident of success.

'Item: As to the Lord Llewelyn, we have been able to get

253

no other response but that he must submit simply and absolutely to the lord king's will, and we are convinced that the lord king will deal mercifully with him. To which end we promise to labour with all our might, together with other friends, and we are certain our efforts will be effective.'

'It is no offer of honourable terms at all,' cried young Llewelyn, burning indignantly for his uncle's sake, 'it is an ultimatum, and nothing more!'

'Wait!' said the prince, wryly smiling. 'It is the covering letter of an offer of sorts. The king cannot afford, or thinks he cannot, for the sake of his standing with his own magnates, who may also at some time offend him and be brought to submission – to cede the formula of absolute surrender to his will. The archbishop's intimations about the magnates and their undertakings to obtain mercy for us mean more than they say. He has already extorted King Edward's agreement, however grudging, to what is contained in this second roll – the private provisions which qualify this public declaration.'

He unrolled the second letter, which was but little longer and read in a voice deliberate and firm:

'These to be put to the prince in secret:

'First: This is the form of the royal grace drawn up by the king's magnates: The Lord Llewelyn having submitted himself to the king's will, the king will provide for him honourably, bestowing upon him an estate to the value of a thousand pounds sterling, with the rank of an earl, in some part of England. In accordance with which, the said Llewleyn shall cede to the lord king, absolutely, perpetually and peaceably, his seisin of Snowdonia. And the king himself will provide for the prince's daughter, in accordance with his obligations to his own blood-kin. To this end the magnates are confident of being able to incline the king's mind to tenderness.

254

'Item: Should the said Llewelyn take a second wife, and by her have male issue, the magnates undertake to procure of the lord king that such heirs shall succeed in perpetuity to Llewelyn's inheritance, in his earldom of one thousand pounds' value.

'Item: Concerning those people presently subject to the prince, in Snowdonia or elsewhere, provision shall be made for them as God sanctions, and as is consistent with the safety, honour and wellbeing of such people. To which course the king's mind is already strongly inclined, since he desires to provide for all his people with conciliatory clemency.'

Round that table there were muted cries of disbelief and anger long before he reached the end, but all those who opened their mouths to exclaim aloud held their breath again and heard him out, not because his visage was wrung or his voice torn and jagged, but because his awesome calm rode over them, as a calm at sea takes the air out of a ship's sails, and lays it drifting and helpless.

When he was done he looked up at us all, and in his bleak but serene face his eyes had their old red brilliance, the fire that burned up out of the depths when he was most roused to contempt and disdain. Then indeed they began to cry out, many voices together.

'And we,' cried Tudor, half-choked with his own gall, half so incredulous he could hardly forbear from laughing, 'we are to be handed over with Snowdon, delivered to whatever overlord Edward pleases to set over us, to do homage to a stranger? It is infamous! They have run mad!'

'Say no word yet,' said Llewelyn, loudly and peremptorily. 'We have time for thought, and we have need of thought. After a fashion, make no mistake, this is intended generously by those who send it. We are all offered life – life of a kind, and the means of living. And I require,' he said, his eyes burning into gold flame, 'that no man here shall lightly cast his life away, or prejudice the judgment of another. I require, further, that your answer shall be made

255

only after proper consideration of what you do, for your own future, and without regard to me. In that answer I have nothing to say, it is you who speak for Wales. It would be unworthy to act in haste, for there will be no more such offers.'

'But *your* answer?' cried his nephew, clinging in desperation to the prince's sleeve. 'How can we speak without you?'

'My answer I'll tell you willingly, when you have conferred without me, and not today. Tudor may call you together when he sees fit, and when you need me, send for me. But my answer need not compromise yours. I shall leave you now, and if you will you may continue this council, but I advise that no voice be taken yet, not until tomorrow, or the day after tomorrow. We have a truce. We have time.'

So he said, and in the face of their seething distress, confusion and anger, he rose to put an end to the meeting, but David laid a hand on his arm and checked him.

'Wait! There is one more letter to be made public – mine. I am a Welshman, too, by the prince's grace I am even in fealty, but I hold no lands. I have still a word to say, and I have leave to answer for myself and myself only, having lost already my two cantrefs and all the Welsh who were my charge.'

He stood with the parchment unrolled, in his hands, and there was sweat on his brow and his lips, I saw the torchlight dewed into bright beads there, and saw the anguish of his face, and guessed at the deeper anguish of the mind within.

'Thus Archbishop Peckham writes to me,' he said, high and clear:

'These to be delivered to David:

'First: If, to God's honour and his own, he will take upon him the burden of the Cross, and journey to aid the crusade in the Holy Land, he shall be provided with an establishment suitable to his rank, on condition that he shall never return unless recalled by the king's mercy. We will ask, and we are sure successfully, that the lord king shall provide for his children.

'To all the Welsh, of our own initiative, we add these warnings, that dangers will threaten them ever more gravely as time passes, as we have already admonished them by word of mouth, and written to them most urgently, for it grows infinitely burdensome to continue in arms for a longer time, only in the end to be totally extirpated, for the perils menacing you will every day be aggravated.

'Item: After a longer time it grows ever more difficult to live in a state of war, in anguish of heart and body, for ever among malignant perils, and at last to die in mortal sin and anger.

'Item: Which grieves us sorely, if you do not come to peace to the best you may, we dread the necessity of urging ecclesiastical feeling against you to the last extreme, by reason of your excesses, for which there is no way you can be excused. But in which you shall find mercy, if you come to peace.

'Concerning the above, let me have written answer.'

The beauty of David's voice, whether in mirth, or malice, or ferocious disdain, was equal to the beauty of his face, and even then it kept its piercing sweetness. And most of those who listened, perhaps, heard first how savagely he mimicked Peckham's hectoring and caressing tone in the warning to the people. But I heard the ache of longing and temptation, and was wrung with him. And I saw, as he was seeing, Elizabeth among her darling brood in Dolbadarn, the little, merry brown English mouse bestowed on him in cold largesse by Edward, and charmed alive into limitless excess and delight of love by God's gift and David's, not Edward's, so that she poured out her hidden treasure upon him in lovely, vivid children. And I saw suddenly how little he had believed in deliverance from this, his last act of rebellion, and how immense a gift mere

257

life could be, having his charm and persuasion, and years ahead in which to earn his recall from crusade to wife and children, and a future not all without lustre. He was now wedded to Wales, as Llewelyn was in his widowerhood, he exulted in his children and worshipped his wife, he was by upbringing almost as English as he was Welsh, he had suffered his dual allegiance lifelong, eternally torn, he could as well have chosen England once for all, as twice he had chosen it before, only to be torn anew.

Also, he was afraid of death, as once he had told me, reared up to confront it as he spoke, for fear, though it agonised him, never deflected him. And all this I remembered, watching him shattered and re-created before my eyes, there in the hall of Garthcefn, and loving him, as I did, only a little less than I loved his brother.

'Thus the archbishop writes,' said David, 'to me and to all men of Welsh blood, and now you understand that I had a need to let this council know of this last warning, for it concerns them as well as me.'

He turned his head and stared insatiably upon Llewelyn, as Llewelyn was also earnestly regarding him. Eye to eye they questioned and answered each other in silence, and there were no secrets between them then. The prince lifted a hand, and said quickly: 'Let it rest now! Say no word more till we meet again. This is not the moment.'

But indeed it was the moment, and that was why he spoke. It was the one moment on which David had never counted, the moment when he was offered escape from the consequences of his own act. He had life in his hands again, his submission depended upon no other man, and with compelling eye and compassionate face Llewelyn gave him leave in silence to deliver himself, without blame, fending him off from too impulsive self-committal while his blood was hot, before fear and self-interest had time to work upon him.

'But with your leave I will speak,' said David, deadly quiet, 'for I am the one man concerned, so Edward would say, only with my own personal fortunes, holding no land in Wales, and now none in the Middle Country, which is excluded from the argument. I am the one who has no legal right in the council of Wales, and none to speak for her, and what I say now is no prejudice to any but myself.'

He paused to moisten dry lips, and I saw how Tudor watched him with narrowed eyes, ready to condemn, for Tudor had never loved David or been beguiled by him, and now he thought he caught the drift of this exposition, and knew where it was leading, and where he had expected it to lead. And truly at that moment it could have been what he thought, a cautious withdrawal, the apology for submission.

'I am also,' said David, 'the one who began this war, and whether I owe fealty to the lord prince for lands or not, I have paid it for more than lands, and whether I have rights in Wales or not, I have a great debt to her. And I say now, that no matter what others may answer, my answer to King Edward is no! No, I will never forsake this land in which I hold no seisin. No, I will not be a party to these insulting terms. No, I will not go on crusade at any man's bidding, nor wait on any man's word before I dare enter my own country. I cast my lot here and now, rather for war to the death than for such a peace!'

And having reached this ending, with a loud, clear voice but a white and desperate countenance, he turned and went out from us, a little clumsily, as though he could not see very well before him.

Llewelyn rose in his chair with authority to close that session.

'As for my brother's decision,' he said, 'it cannot be accepted as binding until this council has had time to consider the terms without heat or haste. I will not have the remaining door closed, by my brother's hand or any other, until we have heard all men's voices.'

When I was alone with him in the inner room, he sat

for some moments mute and weary, a heavy sadness upon him, which God knows was no wonder. And when he spoke it was rather to himself than to me, for he said, in a tone of bitter and marvelling derision:

'Who would have believed it? That any man could be so crass and thick of wit!'

I was at a loss, for my mind had been full of David. 'Ah, no, not my brother!' he said, and smiled and took comfort for a moment. 'No, my brother you shall find for me presently. He did not tell me what he meant to do, or I might have contrived to dissuade him, at least for this time. But who knows? He might not have thanked me for it if I had. It is for him to answer as he chooses, and I have no right to ask of him either that he shall go with me or abandon me. I can only ensure that he stays or goes with my blessing. No, all is well between David and me.'

And again he was silent, and shook his head over the all but incredible, and wrung vainly at a stranger grief.

'And I have respected these men!' he said. 'I had an advocate I could almost have loved, for all his faults, to which, God knows, I never was blind. And here he sends me with pride and confidence this contemptible and affronting offer! I thought he had some understanding of me, and he has none. I thought the warmth he had in him could at least feel the reality of another man's warmth, but he is as blockish as a dead tree. And he will be angry and wounded, even amazed, when his service is cast back in his face! Has he no place on earth that means anything to him, that he should truly believe he does me a kindness by uprooting me from Wales, and bidding me strike root in an English shire? He should have known, if he was one-tenth part of the man I thought him, that I would not give Edward one boulder of all the rocks of Snowdon, or one man who was bred among them, for his thousand pounds a year and his earldom. Or is there still hope for Peckham? Did this come solely from Edward, and has Peckham only sent and urged it upon me with shame and reluctance, in despair of better? It does not show in his wording, but then, he might steel himself to banish it, if this was all he could offer. I would I knew! I should have liked to go on thinking well of him!'

I said never a word, for there was no man could ever again give him back the pleasure he had taken in liking and trusting the archbishop. Always he had been too easily given to affection, by nature seeing the best in men, and taking for granted that they would do as much for him. Yet I did remember and recall to him the genuine courage and perseverance with which Peckham had laboured for Amaury's release.

'A Christian obligation,' said Llewelyn, 'and his duty to his church, yes. . . . But was there more heart and wisdom in that than in this blind, arrogant benevolence he now holds out to me? Did he ever feel anything for Amaury, the man and the prisoner? Or only for the papal chaplain over whose detention the pope so bitterly complained? Truly I wonder! Oh, Samson, bear with me,' he said, 'for this is the first pain I have felt since my love died in my arms! For besides this man I took to be my friend, I have lost the one I knew to be my enemy. I respected and esteemed him still! If he had been as large as his body I could well have loved him. And all that liking and emulation I have wasted on the dwarf lurking within the giant. Do you remember, it was she said that of him? He could have crushed me fairly in drawn-out war, and I should not have lost him thus, or felt myself so demeaned by having respected him. He could have stood stark now and refused me any quarter, and that I could have borne ungrudging. But that he should believe of me, or of any decent man, that I would surrender Wales into his hands, and take myself off to some soft English pasture as his broken hound! Sell him my home and my people for a safe earldom! Has he known so little of me, that he could suffer this savage insult to be offered me? Has he no love for his English earth, that he acquits me of love for my Wales?'

'He loves it,' I said, roused and certain of my ground, 'as belonging to him and conferring lustre upon him. He has never loved wife or child in any other way. As for his roots, they are almost all in southern France, where all his forebears on his mother's side come from, and half those on his father's. His roots are everywhere and his heart nowhere. No, he has no understanding of what you feel for this barren, lovely land.'

'Yet he has had pretensions to it from a child,' said Llewelyn, fretting at what was beyond his understanding. 'And he has learned nothing! He understands nothing! He feels nothing! Land is only an enlargement of his own magnificence. And if I can keep Wales from him with my blood and my body and my curse, he shall never have it. And if he wins it, those who come after him shall again lose it, for what he has is still not a right, only a pretension, a greed, a lust. I am delivered from the shadow and the weight of Edward. He is lighter than ash. There is nothing to be done with him but despise him. I never thought to see the day!'

'A good day,' I said, furious that he should so suffer over so unworthy a creature, however gifted of God as he was also maimed of God. 'A good day, when you are freed of the last illusion, and can do your worst against him, and be at peace. You have no obligations to him any longer, none. Even though he may destroy, he cannot match you. He is beneath your feet!'

'More to my purpose,' said Llewelyn grimly, 'that Wales should not end beneath his feet. As for me, I have a life I may throw away as I please, to the best advantage of Wales, and never grieve. Of what other value is it to me? I am a rampart, frail enough, between Edward and Wales. It matters not a whit if I am trampled into the earth, provided Wales outlives me.' He leaned his head into his hands a moment, and drew a great sigh, as though he were indeed lightened of all trivial and unworthy burdens, whether of love or hate. But he was never a hater. He

262

could resent and burn up in flame, but he could not nurse grudges, and when he uncovered falsity and meanness he had no recourse but to heave them from him and draw clear, as swimmers heave off weed and slime to breathe clean air and get back safe to land.

'Well, we go forward,' he said, and shook his shoulders free of Peckham's crass incomprehension and Edward's cold, malignant littleness. 'They'll not deny us the right to a few days of continued truce, and until we have all cooled from our first rage, and considered well what we are doing, I will not let any answer be made.'

'One has already been made,' I said, 'and I do not think it will be changed.'

He gave me a long look, and said: 'Neither do I. He reads me too well, he knows my mind without any word spoken – as Edward should have known it, and should for shame have refrained from so debasing himself and so insulting me. But until John of Wales sets out for Rhuddlan with written answers from us, what has been said can be given back as freely as it was offered. David may save himself if he chooses, with my forbearance and goodwill. I shall never hold it against him. Find him, Samson, and tell him so.'

I did find him, and I did tell him so. He had walked out of camp to the crest of a hill to westward, and was leaning in the shelter of the rocks that cropped out there in the lee of a copse, his shoulders braced in a cleft, and his head tilted back against the slate-blue stone. He was looking across the hills to the west, where level black clouds streaked a sinking sun, though there was yet an hour or two of daylight left. His face was still and calm and awed, as though he had accomplished something that both terrified and assuaged him, and gave him, if not joy, a strenuous satisfaction. When he heard me come, he did not look round.

'And very apt, too,' he said, 'to send me my confessor,

when I have just nailed together my own coffin. And deliberately, mark you! I must be out of my wits.'

'There was no need,' I said, sitting down on a ledge of the rocks beside him, 'to be in such haste about it.' And at that he laughed loud and sweet and still a little short of desperation.

'Oh, yes, there was! For me there was dire need. If I had not done it then I might never have done it at all. You need not tell me, there were some there waiting for me to turn my coat again and buy my life at any cost. Now I am committed. However many times I must repeat it, I can do it, for I dare not for shame go back on it.'

'There's one,' I said, 'won't stand in your way or blame you for it if you do. I think he might even welcome it.'

'I do believe it,' said David, when I had told him what Llewelyn had said. 'But not even for him will I take back what I have sworn. I have pledged it once for all, and I am glad. Not that I look my death in the eyes with any great joy,' he said wryly, 'being flesh, and very self-indulgent flesh at that, and knowing Edward as I know him. Bear with me, Samson, if I preen myself a little on being the first to hurl the glove in Edward's face, who should be the last if I were in my right mind. I, the most hated, the furthest banished from any possibility of forgiveness! The orphan and exile he whines and prays about having taken in and succoured, when he knows, as I know, that what he did was to welcome a useful and unscrupulous traitor, worth an army to him in his war against Llewelyn. I used him openly, and he used me, but in his self-deceiving way, convinced he had bought me and made me his for all time. No, if ever I fall into Edward's hands now it will be my death, and such a death as might well make me turn tail, even now, and rush to embrace his contemptible crusade. But does not!' he said, himself marvelling, and curled a lip in a brief smile, and shook his head helplessly over his own maniac audacity. 'I begin to think well of myself, I am braver than I thought.'

'You go to meet fate too soon,' I said. 'Even if this attempt at mediation fails –'

'It has already failed,' said David. 'You saw Llewelyn's face, you know as well as I he feels nothing but scorn and disgust. I came late to the understanding of his love of Wales, and if I feel it now, I feel it only through him. I could live as merrily in London as here in the mountains, and I daresay I could make pretty good shift at making myself comfortable even in the Holy Land. But not he! We have a few days of truce left out of this great labour, until the replies go back to Peckham. And that is all we have.'

'Yet even so,' I said, 'the war is neither won nor lost, and nobody knows on which side the lot will fall in the end. Wales has fought off all the power of England in the past, and may again. It would be shame to us if we lost the battle before it was even fought.'

'In the past,' said David, 'we had not Edward to deal with, never until the last bout, and then he was but cutting his teeth on us, now he has all his fangs full-grown, and knows how to bite, and for all I will do my utmost, body and soul, against him, I cannot choose but see the scale inclining to his side, and I cannot lie about it to myself, and will not to you. A miracle or two would alter the balance, and prick up my heart very nicely. Do you suppose God is listening?'

He shook himself suddenly out of his mood, and came and flung an arm about my shoulders. 'Come, you've done your errand, and need not fret for me. If ever a man pulled the sky down upon himself, I am that man. And pulled it down upon Llewelyn, too, God forgive me, though I think in the end it would have toppled even without me. There's no way to go but forward! I've committed my life to Llewelyn's cause and the cause of Wales, and there's an end of it. And now, for God's sake, if you can spare an hour before the light goes, come and ride with me, I'm no fit company yet for less tolerant men.'

So I went with him, glad to hear the resolution and gaiety come back into his voice, even if both bore still the edged tone of desperation. We took horses, and rode together over the hill-track to the north-west, and rode further afield than we had intended, for pleasure of leaving thought behind and feeling nothing but the sting of the air and the buffeting of the wind. Earlier in the day great gales had swept the mountains from the north-east, but by that hour in the evening they were no more than boisterous winds, that whipped the blood into David's face and streamed cold and rough through his erected hair.

We had reined in on a crest, and were thinking it time to turn back when we sighted a rider coming towards us at a gallop from the direction of Bangor, and waited for his coming in some curiosity. No one whose business was not urgent would have been riding a hill-track at that speed and in that deepening twilight. He saw us from the distance and spurred to meet us with a shout, and recognising David as he drew nearer, raised a hand in salute, and cried to us that he brought news from Bangor for the prince.

'God make it good,' said David to me, 'for we need it.'

The man heard that as he pulled up glowing beside us, his horse blown and lathered. 'Good enough, my lord! To say all in a breath – a battle and a victory!'

'A breath of life!' said David heartily. 'Draw deep again and tell us more!'

'Why, my lord, at low water this morning de Tany crossed his bridge. A great company, Tany himself and any number of bannerets with him, and some hundreds of men-at-arms.'

David struck his hands together with a shout that made his horse start and sidle. 'Then he dared! He dared break truce, and against even Edward's ban. The fool! Go on, man, what followed? Were they stopped on the shore?'

'We did better than that. The wind was rising, and the sea rough, and our old men foretold north-east gales. You know how they drive in there, and pile the waters as the

266

tide comes in. So we let the English land, all that company, and drew back a mile or so before them as they moved up into the hills, until the gale was at its worst. Then we loosed everything we had down the slopes at them, and drove them back to the strand. It was high water then, and what with the winds driving in, the waves were threshing up among the trees, and sweeping in tall as a man. They ripped the bridge from its moorings on our side, and set it lashing like a cat's tail, and two or three of the boats went plunging away loose down the strait. They had no way of getting back. If they had any eye or nose for weather they'd have known it! We rolled them into the sea, or killed them in the woods if they turned and fought. A slaughter, my lord! A few bold souls fought it out and are prisoners. A few rode their horses into the strait and swam for it, and perhaps one here and there got through, but with their heavy armour I doubt it. Most have drowned. All are dead, or skulking in the woods and being ferreted out now, or prisoner, or gone draggle-tailed back, the very few of them, to tell the tale.'

'And a noble tale!' crowed David, shivering and shaken between laughing and weeping. 'Go on, make this perfect! Tell me de Tany is taken!'

'Not by us,' said the messenger in vengeful glee. 'But taken, surely. The sea has taken him. Myself I saw him go down, his grand Gascon armour dragging him below. He will not again break truce!'

'And all's quiet there now?' pressed David. 'No threat left ashore, and everything in disarray on Anglesey? You do my heart good! Oh, dear heaven,' he said, shuddering, 'I never knew my prayers had such potency. Samson, have you heard? God was listening!'

I took him by the arm, leaning from my broad-beamed mountain pony, for he was shivering and tense like a sick man. I said to the messenger: 'Your horse is tired, friend, and ours are fresh. Let us take the word ahead of you into Garthcefn, and you come after at your own speed, and you shall be not the loser. We will report you faithfully, and have lodging and audience ready for you when you come.'

'With goodwill!' he said heartily, 'and speak me a bed and meat beforehand, and stabling. And this good brute can amble as he pleases now, it's not so far.'

We rode, David and I, at David's pace, that tried the light and the track hard. I kept at his side throughout, watching his face, so long as I could see it still by that failing light, the thrusting profile so beautifully drawn against the sky. He went as one gifted with such perfect assurance that even his mount trod blessedly, wafted on favouring winds into Garthcefn. Only once, short of the maenol, did he rein in, and turn to gaze at me, attentive beside him, and his face was blanched and bright, the last after-light of the sunset gilding it.

'God was listening,' he said. 'We have got our miracle.' And he looked fully at me, and his eyes were wide as moons, and his mouth smiling. 'No, it is not *that* makes me thus drunk,' he said, 'no sense of being spared. I am here to be spent like Edward's minted coin for my brother's dream. No, I am thanking God for something very different, my own honour, my own soul. Now we have a victory in hand that will send the king on the defensive into his castles of Rhuddlan and my Denbigh for five, six weeks, maybe longer. He has lost his bridge and half his Anglesey army. But when I pledged my fealty and spat in Edward's face, we had no such promise. Oh, Samson, this at least I have done in a state of innocence! This at least was pure!'

We brought the news into Garthcefn, and it fell like music on every man's ears, and lifted up every heart, as well it might. We had good reason to rejoice, for we had gained not only the several weeks it must take the king to repair his losses, but also our reputation was enhanced and our position strengthened, for they, not we, had broken truce, and they, not we, had received the sharp reward of treachery. Nor would Llewelyn allow free action against the English forces elsewhere, but maintained truce still upon his part, countenancing only defence against further bad faith, and stressing to Brother John of Wales that he expected the like from the king's side, holding de Tany's treachery to be the crime of one man, and not to be attributed to all his comrades-in-arms. What the friar thought or felt he never gave to view, being well schooled in diplomacy, and less garrulous than his archbishop.

I am certain that this victory, most welcome as it was, had no effect upon Llewelyn's response to the English terms. To him there was only one answer possible to such a suggestion. It did not influence David, either, for his heart was fixed, but it did sweeten the choice for him and fill him with fresh hope. Concerning the men of the council, for individual voices I cannot speak, but I am sure the general voice would have been the same whether or not de Tany had made his fatal onslaught and met his deserved death. Yet it was no wonder if we sat down to the slow and careful work of composing our replies with calmer minds and refreshed courage. There was no question but the situation was greatly changed in our favour, and if fighting must begin again the king would be held in his castles for some time, for want of the very advantage he had planned by the occupation in strength of Anglesey.

So by the eleventh day of November we had ready our letters to Archbishop Peckham, each party replying separately, though all had sat in conference several times together. And that day John of Wales departed for Rhuddlan with these documents, which I give here, David's letter in part, the rest complete.

'This is the reply of David, brother of the prince.
'That when he shall see fit to go to the Holy Land, he will do so of his own free will and in fulfilment of his own vow, for God, not for man. Not at any man's bidding will he go wandering into distant lands, for forced service is known to be displeasing to God. And should he chance indeed to go to the Holy Land of his own free will, out

of devotion, it would hardly be fitting that on that account he and his heirs should incur perpetual disinheritance, on the contrary, they might rather look to be rewarded.

'The war which the prince and his people have waged was not motivated by hatred for any creature, nor by lust of gain or conquest, invading the territories of others, but only by the desire to defend their own rightful heritage, laws and liberties, while the king and his people wage their war out of inveterate hatred, with the aim of conquering our lands. Therefore we believe ours to be the just war, and place our hope and trust in God.'

Then he also repeated the accusations made against the English soldiery concerning their usage of churchmen and sacred places, repudiated utterly the suggestion that any Welsh chief should leave his own lands and go into virtual exile among his enemies, saying that if we could not have peace in the land which was ours by right, how much less could we expect to live at peace in a foreign land. And lastly, he complained of the difference made between himself and other barons holding of the king, who had likewise at times offended against him, and been forced to make reparation, but never by total disinheritance, or perpetual banishment.

And strange indeed did I find it that David should so fight for his own privilege to the last, as the old David, and in the same letter speak out so well for the Wales he had so often deserted, a new David borrowing his love and his light by reflection from Llewelyn, but freer far with words than ever was his brother.

The reply from the council of Wales was drawn up chiefly by Tudor, Master William and Goronwy ap Heilyn, but agreed and approved by all. And thus it ran:

'The reply of the council of Wales.

'Though it may please the king to say that he will allow no discussion concerning the Middle Country, or Anglesey, or the other lands bestowed upon his magnates, neverthe-less the prince's council, if peace is to be made at all, will not countenance any departure from the premise that these cantrefs are a part of the unquestionable holding of the prince, lying within the bounds within which the prince and his predecessors have held right since the time of Camber, son of Brutus. Further, they belong to the principality renewed to the prince by confirmation, at the instance of Ottobuono of blessed memory, legate of the apostolic see in the realm of England, with the consent of the lord king and his magnates, as is manifest in the treaty. Moreover, it is more equitable that the true heirs should hold the said cantrefs, if need be from the lord king for fee and customary service, rather than they should be given over to strangers and newcomers, even though these may have been powerful supporters of the king's cause.

'Further, all the tenants of all the cantrefs of Wales declare with one voice that they dare not come to the king's will, to allow him to dispose of them according to his royal majesty, for these reasons: First, because the lord king has kept neither treaty nor oath nor charter towards their lord prince and themselves from the beginning. Second, because the king's men have used the most cruel tyranny against ecclesiastical establishments and persons. Third, that they cannot be bound by the offered terms, since they are the liege-men of the prince, who is prepared to hold the said lands of the king by customary service.

'As to the demand that the prince shall submit absolutely to the king's will, we reply that since not one man of all the aforesaid cantrefs would dare to submit himself to that will, neither will the community of Wales permit its prince to do so upon such terms.

'As to the king's magnates guaranteeing to procure an earldom for the prince, we say he need not and should not accept any such provision, procured by the very magnates who are striving to have him disinherited, so that they may possess his lands in Wales.

'Item: The prince is no way bound to forgo his heritage

and that of his forebears from the time of Brutus, and again confirmed as his by the papal legate, as is suggested, and accept lands in England, where language, manners, laws and customs are foreign to him, and where, moreover, malicious mischiefs may be perpetrated against him, out of hatred, by English neighbours, from whom that land has been expropriated in perpetuity.

'Item: Since the king is proposing to deprive the prince of his original inheritance, it seems unbelievable that he will allow him to hold land in England, where he is seen to have no legal right. And similarly, if the prince is not to be allowed to hold the sterile and uncultivated land rightfully his by inheritance from old times, here in Wales, it is incredible to us that in England he will be allowed possession of lands cultivated, fertile and abundant.

'Item: That the prince should place the king in seisin of Snowdonia, absolutely, perpetually and peaceably. Since Snowdonia is a part of the principality of Wales, which he and his ancestors have held since the time of Brutus, as we have said, his council will not permit him to renounce the said lands and accept land less rightfully his in England.

'Item: The people of Snowdonia for their part state that even if the prince desired to give the king seisin of them, they themselves would not do homage to any stranger, of whose language, customs and laws they are utterly ignorant. For by so doing they could be brought into perpetual captivity and barbarously treated, as other cantrefs around them have been by the royal bailiffs and officers, more savagely than ever was wreaked upon Saracen enemies, as we have said above, reverend father, in the *rotuli* we sent to you.'

And last, I give my prince's letter, by contrast so brief, courteous, dignified and distant, for he was writing to a man who had been close to being loved, and was now dead to him, and waited only his last retort to be buried.

'To the most reverend father in Christ, the Lord John, by the grace of God archbishop of Canterbury and primate of all England, from his devoted son in Christ, Llewelyn, prince of Wales and lord of Snowdon, greeting, with an earnest prayer for his benevolence towards his son, and all manner of reverences and respects.

'Holy father, as you have counselled, we are ready to come to the king's grace, if it be offered in a form safe and honourable for us. But the form contained in the articles submitted to us is in no particular either safe or honourable, in the judgment of our council and ourselves, indeed, so far from it that all who hear it are astonished, since it tends rather to the destruction and ruin of our people and our person than to our honour and safety. There is no way in which our council could be brought to permit us to agree to it, even should we so wish, for never would our nobles and subjects consent in the inevitable destruction and dissipation which would surely derive from it.

'Wherefore we beg your fatherly holiness, as you are bound to pursue that renewed peace, honourable and secure, for which you have exerted such heroic labours already, to devise some expedient bearing a just relation to those articles we have submitted to you in writing.

'It would surely be more honourable, and more consonant with reason, if we should hold from the king those lands in which we have right, rather than to disinherit us, and hand over our lands and our people to strangers.

'Dated at Garthcefn, on the feast of Saint Martin.'

So read my lord's last letter to Archbishop Peckham.

Archbishop Peckham's last letter to my lord was delivered some days later, combining in one long, voluble diatribe his rage and rejection against all the careful legal points we had urged. Now he had nothing to offer us but damnation, and the prospect of war to the death, and the distant spectacle of his own wounded vanity at having his efforts undervalued, so that all the first part of his letter

273

was an almost incoherent outpouring in his own praise how he had laboured for us, taken compassion on us when none other would, ventured his very life among great perils to rescue his strayed sheep, been the advocate of our necessity – though in the first place he had invited himself into that role – dealt with the majesty and magnates of England, made his frail body a bridge by which we might again cross into grace, all to have the fruit of his labours scorned. It had not fully appeared until then how he rated us as some manner of breed a little below humanity, so that he could not well understand our resentment of subjection, which seemed to him our fitting state, a kindness for which we ought to be grateful.

All the legal points we had made he dismissed as 'pernicious subterfuges', and went on to produce some surprising law of his own. We should not, he said, vaunt ourselves upon being descended from Brutus, fools that we were and worse than fools, since Brutus was one of those Trojans who were dispersed and scattered because they defended the adulterous Paris, and such a descent as we claimed no doubt accounted for our notorious looseness in morals, and the small regard we paid to legitimate marriage, in that we did not bar children born out of wedlock from having a respected place in our kinships, and even inheriting property. He went further, and accused us of encouraging incest, but in the flood of words he could probably barely stop himself by then. And had not the Trojans, our ancestors, he said, invaded these islands and driven out the Scythian giants who then inhabited them?

'Why, therefore, we ask, are the Angles and Saxons of this generation doing you any injury, if in the process of time they are now disturbing your enjoyment of usurped dominions? It is written: Ye who despoil others, shall not you be despoiled? Fools that you are, it is not wise to glory in origins stemming from adultery, idolatry and the plunder of usurpation!'

274

Then he went on to dismiss our indubitable claim that in he treaty made by the papal legate Ottobuono all these Welsh territories had been confirmed to Llewelyn, with King Henry's consent. A frivolous allegation, said Peckham, for certainly Ottobuono had had no intention of hereby weakening the king's law, civil or canon, so as to render it invalid, and for the crime of lese-majeste of which we stood accused, all hereditary rights are forfeit and perish, so that even in Snowdonia, Llewelyn's by rightful inheritance, the prince was now stripped of all power, and we with him, having no rights at all still existent except the right to beg the king's clemency. And to this astonishing proposition he appended his legal references in full, verse and line, of *English law*! English law, to which Snowdon never had been subject, and was not subject now! English law, which with its encroaching claims where it had no right had begun this whole contention!

As to our statement that we could not rely on the king's word, since he had not kept it in the past, Peckham demanded, who says so? Only from us, the Welsh, did this charge stem, and that meant we were presuming to be judges in our own cause. *And he was not?* As for the legal code of Howel Dda, the only authority Howel had had for it had been delegated to him by the devil.

The whole would be wearisome, though I have not forgotten any of it. But thus the gentle prelate, with many threats of excommunication, damnation, and extirpation by total war, ended his favours to us:

'While other men are freely adorned with the gifts of God, in your remote fastnesses these are cast utterly to waste, inasmuch as you give no aid to the Church in contending against its enemies, and confer upon your clergy no wise learning, except in the meanest degree, and the majority of your people wallow in idleness and lechery, so that the world hardly knows that such a people exists, but for the few of you who are seen begging their bread in France.'

275

And with that he consigned us to our fate and turned his back upon Wales.

This letter Llewelyn read with a face of indifferent distaste, and by the end of it his already dead regard for this narrow and unperceptive priest was also buried deep, to be thought of no more. He himself read it to his assembled council, and dusted his hands and left it lying when he had done.

'I had expected to be cursed,' he said, 'but not in the language of the city kennels. Well, that is over. Back to the cleaner business of war!'

CHAPTER X

We held urgent council that same day how to proceed, for the next two or three weeks might be invaluable to us if well used. We knew already that great numbers of carpenters had again been shipped in haste to Anglesey, where the earl of Hereford was now in command, so plainly an attempt was to be made to repair the bridge of boats, but even that enterprise would take some time, and the great loss of men and armour and horses in the strait would not be easily replaced. The king remained at Rhuddlan, and had even withdrawn his advanced outposts, so that now none of his garrisons, apart from that in Anglesey, was further west than the Clwyd valley.

'By the number of foot soldiers he's dismissed,' Tudor said, 'he could be abandoning the fight for this season, but I doubt it. I think he's waiting for his Gascons, and meantime saving money and stores. Feeding such an army as his is no light matter, even with our corn harvest, and when he's ready, and some prospect of the Anglesey division being ready to move with him, he can easily send out fresh writs, and pay whatever numbers he can raise, if he thinks the period of service need not be long.'

Llewelyn heard them all out, and pondered the courses open to him. 'What we must not do,' he said, 'is to be shut up here with no way of linking hands with those allies we have to the south, and no channel by which we can move to help them, or they to help us. David, can you hold everything here for a while, if I go south?'

David grimaced, calculating the possible term of his

security. 'I shall be safe enough for a while, and have nothing to do but keep watch. As long as four weeks surely, perhaps longer. He cannot make good his losses earlier than that.'

The young Llewelyn said, earnestly watching his uncle's face: 'Are you coming to us? My brothers have gone to ground there. If you come, we might do much.'

'I am going into the waist of Wales,' said the prince, 'but you shall come with me, and go home to help your brothers. I shall be holding hands one way with you, and the other here with David, and keeping the ways open. I am going into Maelienydd and Builth, to see what recruiting Edward has done for me there in Mortimer country.'

'Good!' said David. 'It's a right choice. Of all things we need a highway north and south. Go with God, and leave the north to me for four weeks, and if the need arises, I'll send to you.'

So we made ready to march within two days, and the winds that had torn apart Edward's bridge sank submissively into stillness now that Edward was embattled in Rhuddlan with his rage and his hatred and his temporary helplessness. Halfway through November the sun came through, as it does freakishly, gilding all the mountain tops and filling all the valleys with fine blue mist, like a meadow full of harebells. And in this hush we massed and marched.

The parting of those two brothers was as spare and brief that day as their dangers were great, their resolution unbending, and their need extreme. While we were gathering in the bailey they spoke but few words to each other, and those to the point, of arms and supplies, and how the forces each had could best be used. There were clouds massing again to the north, though the rest of the sky was fair, and David said that in two or three days there would be a change, and we might look for snow. And all the while they eyed each other steadily and hard, with great eyes, but never spoke one word from beneath the guarded

278

surface of their minds. But when the prince went to mount, David himself stooped to hold the stirrup for him, and when he was in the saddle, kissed the hand that held the bridle, and Llewelyn leaned down and kissed him brotherly on the cheek. And then we rode, and did not look back.

We made south for Bala, crossing the upper Dee, to keep the great bleak ridge of the Berwyns between us and the forces from Oswestry. Not until we were well south of the river, and I was riding in my own place close at his left side, did Llewelyn say suddenly, as an honourable man grieving over his debts unpaid: 'I have missed telling him so many things! But doubtless he knows.' And no more did he say then of David, but I knew his mind was on the old days before ever discontent and treason came between them, when this youngest was by far the best loved of his brothers, who had after cost him the most loss, danger and grief, and in the end drew close again and made reparation for all, in this final union that not even the fear of death could dissolve. So his evil genius ended loved as he began, and those two were one as never before had they been one.

We kept long, hard marches, and broke into the lands of Griffith ap Gwenwynwyn along with the first snow, about the nineteenth day of November. There we came apparently unheralded, for we were able to help ourselves to the contents of several of Griffith's scattered barns and farms, and drive off a good many head of his cattle, to our great satisfaction, for by then we had cut our rations to the point where most of us were hungry.

Llewelyn had a little castle at Aberedw, south of Builth, that he had used formerly as a hunting lodge, and though it was on the eastern side of Wye, it was still secure, and as an intelligence base for an army, to be used and quitted as best served, it was excellent. There the prince took up his headquarters for a time, while we probed the state of feeling in the country round, and found friends enough, though they went in fear of the king's men, and reported Builth castle as impregnable, a judgment we accepted. When we came there, young Edmund Mortimer had still not received seisin of his father's lands, though it was granted at last about the twenty-fourth of November, and both the young men were said to be much affronted by the delay, and not at all unsympathetic to the Welsh among their tenants, even though they knew these men willed victory to the prince. In some degree, to be a marcher baron was to understand the passion of sovereign lordship in others, and respect it, as kings were unable to do, who lived by overlordship, and desired to suppress that identity with land that such as Mortimer truly felt, and reduce them to mere custodians for the crown.

Roger Lestrange had taken over the command at Montgomery after Mortimer died, and John Giffard had succeeded him in charge of the garrison of Builth, that same Giffard who had so long maintained lawsuit over Llandovery in right of his wife, Dame Maud Clifford. As soon as we were sure that both these crown officers knew we were in their territory, we used Aberedw but sparingly, as a base for receiving news and messages, and moved the army westward into Mynydd Eppynt and the hills beyond, and held aloof from the river valleys except when we had good information as to where the English forces were. It was the one thing we could do far better than they could, against such overwhelming odds, this living wild in the onset of winter, and moving on foot at the speed of horses, and double their agility.

In the last days of November the big snow came, the ally for which we waited. We saw it first glittering on the crests of the distant mountains, and then the heavy clouds came down and dimmed that shining, and all the sky was darkened, and in the night the fall began. It lasted fitfully into the first week of December, drifting strongly in the valleys, swept thin on the ridges, and driving the English back into their castles for shelter. A great snow it was, that

uried unwary travellers and whole flocks of sheep, some
f which we dug out before their shepherds ever got near
hem, and took for our own use. As for us, we were then
ncamped in the forests of the hills north-west of the river
rfon, perhaps three or four miles from the castle of Builth,
lose by which castle the Irfon empties into the Wye.

Those are wild hills with few inhabitants, but we had
ound all those who had their dwellings within that region
vere good friends to us, and would open their huts to us
reely as shelter at need, and for the rest, we were used to
providing our own roofs, and made dug-outs of fir-
oughs and bracken in the drifts, and the forests gave us
oth warmth and covering. All the land on our side the
iver we held, and had a strong party guarding the only
ridge at Orewin, for in these conditions they had little
ope of crossing by any other means to get at us. The
rifted snow made any attempt at fording most dangerous,
very hazard being concealed, and when a partial thaw
et in, about three days into December, the perils were no
vay lessened, for that river drains very mountainous land,
nd in the thaw the waters come down furiously, and
oil out wide over the fields of the lowlands, and where
ormally the stream might be forded with care, then it
uns deep and fast. For that reason we had given the
uard at Orewin bridge more than their fair share of our
est archers, to prevent close approach from the other
ide. And we, from the hills above, raided wherever we
ould sight a party of the English in arms, harried such
f their patrols and ambushed such of their stores as we
ould, and evaded any possibility of being brought to
itched battle in the valley.

Westward we had contact with the sons of Meredith
p Owen in Cardigan, though over some of the bleakest
plands in all Wales, and across the Irfon by night we
ould still get word back and forth to Aberedw. Many of
he local Welshry had risen and joined the prince's banner,
nd there were others who hesitated whether to dare, of

281

whom we had word from time to time, and encouraged
such leanings every way we could, even taking risks in the
matter. So it seemed but one more similar approach, from
Welshmen tempted but afraid to take the plunge, when
a messenger slipped through to us from Aberedw in the
night of the eighth of December, to say that a furtive
stranger had come urgently begging to get word to the
prince of Wales, from some who willed him well but were
close under Lestrange's eye, and must tread softly, and
therefore wanted a secret meeting. Of whom this very
uneasy visitor was only the envoy, and knew little, but
could promise that those who sent him might be of the
greatest help, for they were no common farmers or troopers. So far, apart from this mention of higher personages,
it was much what we had been receiving for ten days or
more, in some cases to good effect. But it took quite a new
turn when our man produced from under his cotte a
written roll, brought and left by the stranger. We had not
expected a letter. Most people were afraid to write even if
they knew how, or could get a clerk to do it for them.

Llewelyn held the roll to the light of our sheltered fire,
but it bore no superscription, and the seal was deliberately
mutilated, which was no wonder. The wonder was that
anyone under Lestrange's eye would dare set quill to
parchment at all. Nor did many of the troopers write, or
have to do with clerks but very rarely.

'And, my lord,' said the messenger, 'this man hid his
face as well as he might, and was in haste to be gone, but
he stayed long enough to say what he'd been told to say,
that here you'll find the time and place where they hope
to come safely to meet with you, and that they entreat you
to come if by any means you can. Also that you will
understand that those matters there mentioned are but
tokens, from which you may guess at truth where others
might miss. Then he went, and was glad to have his errand
done. But I know one thing more that he did not tell. For
he went in a hooded cloak like a countryman, but when

282

he mounted the wind blew the fronts of his cloak apart, and I saw he had a stout leather coat under it, and a badge on the coat. The Mortimer badge!'

'Mortimer!' said Llewelyn, arrested with the seal under his fingers. 'You are sure?'

'Sure, my lord. I know it well. And his horse was no country cob neither.'

'Is it possible?' said Llewelyn in a whisper, more to himself than to any other. And he broke the seal and read the letter, bending close to have the firelight on the leaf, and frowning in doubt and wonder.

'No date or place or salutation. I should expect none. But the rest! The cause of Wales, they tell me, has friends here, where tenant and lord alike may be burdened with fealties that try them hard, and cross the natural bent of their blood and affections, no less than their faith in justice. I am bidden remember a bond of mutual support, never yet called upon but never repudiated, and to think on a double tie through father and mother. And if I trust as they trust me, I am to come two miles north from here, to the track that runs above the bank of the Wye, to a barn at the edge of the forest where three paths meet, as soon as I may after noon on the eleventh day of this month, when by God's grace they will be free of watching eyes, and there wait for me. To come out of mail and plain, like a countryman, as they must, for there are eyes everywhere. And not in force, but alone or with but one companion. And they entreat me, if I am there first, to wait for them in hiding, for they will surely come.'

'It is much to ask,' said Tudor at his elbow, anxious and distrustful.

'It is what they might well be forced to ask, for their own safety,' said Llewelyn, 'if they are what they purport to be. Even a countryman may carry sword or dagger under his cloak, these days, but he would hardly be cased in mail. They ask but reasonably. Modest travellers do not go with armed escorts. And who else claims kinship with me on both sides his parentage? Who else is fast bound under Lestrange's eye on the one side, and Giffard's, according to report, on the other?'

For the Mortimer brothers, who might well recall their father's recent pact of mutual aid with Llewelyn – in peace or war, saving his duty to the king! – had a paternal grandmother who was Llewelyn Fawr's daughter, but also a mother who was sister to the wife of Llewelyn Fawr's son David, from whom my lord inherited. And the elder, Edmund, now newly in seisin of his lands, was attached to Lestrange's force working from Montgomery, and no doubt under close tutelage, since he had made plain his displeasure at the king's neglect of his right. And Roger, the younger, was said to be serving with Giffard from Builth. Moreover, the messenger had certainly worn the Mortimer badge.

Tudor in his turn asked: 'Is this possible?'

Llewelyn thought, and said: 'It is possible. I would not have said it of their father, however warmly he had pledged me support and aid, that he could ever have swerved from his fealty to Edward, for my sake or any other man's. But after Edward has kept this young man landless and owing no fealty and receiving no royal countenance for a month, I would not say but Edmund might consider his faith and service to be slighted and undervalued, and be more inclined to sting in return.'

'Now, when seisin has been granted, and he newly owes his homage for it?' said Tudor.

'But has not yet paid it,' said Llewelyn. And that was true, for homage could not be paid for the lands until Edward and Edmund Mortimer met face to face, and the king was in Rhuddlan, and Edmund here in the middle march.

They discussed it long, not blinking the possible dangers, but the upshot was that he would go. For the promise of reinforcements he thought the risks worth taking, and rated them no higher than many he had taken lightly enough in the past. No man rushes headlong into what may be an ambush, but in this affair he took what precautions were sensible, and then ventured boldly. I myself took the letter by daylight, and scrutinised the defaced seal with care, and I thought that by such traces as were left I was justified in believing it Mortimer's. And whatever we could credit of those two young men, we could not credit that they would lend themselves to personal treachery. A high-spirited young nobleman smarting at neglect and humiliation may take his sword over to the opposing side. We held him less likely to connive at deceit and murder.

'And if I go,' said Llewelyn, 'I go upon the terms held out. I will not put them in peril by any cheat, as I do not believe they would imperil me but in open battle, and fairly. I go alone.'

I said no. And then he looked at me as though he had awakened out of a short and troubled sleep, and stood at gaze. 'Or with one companion,' I said.

'True!' said Llewelyn, and smiled. 'I am allowed to have you with me, now as ever. So be it!'

On the tenth of December there was fresh snow, but moist and fitful, lying wetly over that already fallen, that was dimpling into holes like frayed cloth, and the grudging waters of the slow thaw dribbling down to swell the already swollen river. We rode the hills and surveyed our defences, and made due inspection of the guard at the bridge below, and all was dank and chill and still, not a soul stirring out of Builth. They said that the lady was there, Dame Maud, come hither with her husband when he took over this command, and now held there by the snows from returning to her more congenial Llandovery. A sad lady I think she was, widowed from her first husband, William Longspée, a son of the earl of Salisbury, whom she had loved, and married now to this greedy, ambitious creature whom I fear she loved not at all, and who used her and her royal descent and claims to further his own desires, as often as not against her will. She did not love litigation, and had to suffer his insistent use of her name beside his in case after case, since he had few pretensions but through her. She did not love war, but was trapped within it like so many women before her, her heart-strings drawn out upon both sides.

In the night it froze again, but not hard. We rose to a leaden sky, and made ready.

The prince had with him on this campaign, as always, the full trappings of his chapel, that with us were perhaps more modest than those of the English crown, and could be carried more easily. And let it not be thought that the general excommunication levelled against his person had deprived him of the consolations of his faith. There was never wanting priest or brother to sing his mass. The bishop of St Asaph, cited by Peckham to answer for his failure to issue the letters of excommunication against the prince, had risen in anger to demand the excommunication of the English soldiery who burned his cathedral. And the Cistercians, closest of all brotherhoods to the defiant austerity of Wales, followed, served, harboured him wherever he showed his face, loved him and all his to the last. We had with us then a Cistercian brother who sang mass for the prince that eleventh day of December, in the half-frozen snows in the forest above the Irfon, in the murk of a morning hovering between ice and tears.

Then, when the day was well advanced, with time and to spare for the distance we had to go, he and I rode, dun and plain in homespun cloaks and without armour, but keeping our swords. We had one stream to cross on the way, that drained down into the Wye in the town of Builth, like the Irfon, but here in the uplands it was but a swollen brook, and no stay to us. Some miles to the north there was a bridge over the Wye, too distant to be of value to them in approaching the present position of the prince's army, for we could withdraw long before they got near

286

us, but we guessed that those who planned to meet us at the barn would come by that way, all the more certainly if, as we thought likely, they were coming from Radnor. We made for the track that kept the shoulder of the hills, overhanging the river valley, and rode openly until we judged we must be nearing the place. Woodlands skirted the way on the upland side, and on the river side the slope dipped steeply, and was open grass beneath the snow, but for occasional clumps of trees where the folded ground gave shelter. Here Llewelyn bade me take to the forest and keep pace with him there unseen, while he kept the open track.

'Let me seem to be coming alone, if that is what they want, and still have a friend in reserve to guard my back.'

So I wove my way in the trees, sufficiently withdrawn not to be seen from the road, and at a rise of the track Llewelyn checked, gazing before him, and I guessed that he could see, though without emerging I could not, the spot ahead of us where the three tracks met, and the barn to which we were bound. I drew somewhat nearer, and he turned his head and said clearly: 'It is the place. One track comes up from the Wye, by the valley of some small brook, I judge. There are trees in the cleft. One track moves off to the north-west, into the hills, and the forest swallows it. The barn is there on the edge of the level ground, between those two roads.'

'And no man stirring there?' I said.

'No. We are early. I shall be first at the meeting-place. Stay in cover,' he said, 'but keep close. I doubt if I shall need your help, but I shall be right glad to know it's within call.'

So we held station as before, and went on at this soft pace, and soon I caught between the trees, where they thinned, glimpses of a large timber building, black against the fretted snow. Nothing moved about us as we drew near to it. Llewelyn sat his horse for some minutes, watching, and he and I might have been the only creatures in the world. The great door of the barn hung open, its

287

heavy bar jutting. Within was only a darkness and a silence.

'I am going in,' he said, when he was satisfied. 'Keep within cover and keep watch for me, and do whatever seems best to you.'

I came as close as I could to where the forest path crossed me, and watched him ride up to the open door, and hitch his horse to a solitary sapling that grew from the foot of the wall. A moment he stood in the open doorway, and then, finding the place empty, passed within.

There was a long, judged moment of delay after he vanished, and then suddenly and silently a man broke out of the bushes, above the right-hand path that climbed obliquely from the Wye, and ran to the door and heaved it to, slamming the wooden bar into its socket and shutting the prince within. One man only, for no more followed, and this one was so intent on his task that I was upon him and riding him down before he heard me, and turned with a cry, plucking out a dagger from his belt. A second great shout he uttered, loud and defiant in warning, and flung towards the downhill track, before my sword took him in the hollow of neck and shoulder, and half-shore head from body, and he dropped into the snow, and jerked like a broken spider away from under my horse's hooves, leaving red smears behind him, and after a few crippled writhings, lay still.

I leaped down and dragged back the bar, and Llewelyn burst out into daylight, and grasping the need without words, raced to unhitch his horse, and was in the saddle beside me even before we heard the thudding of hooves and flurry of voices climbing out of the valley.

'He called them,' I said, 'as I struck him . . . God knows how many of them.'

The first rose into view, labouring furiously up the slope from the copse below, where they had lain hidden, and though they were not yet upon us, they were between us and the way by which we had come. Ten of them in view, perhaps even more behind them. There was but one way for us to go, if we were not to fight our way through them, and that was by the forest path and into the hills to westward, and there we headed, crouched low in expectation that they would have archers with them, but there were no shots, only the great shout they launched after us before we vanished into the darkness of the trees.

Llewelyn set the pace, and well for us we had hardly done more than walk our horses on the way, while the company pursuing us may well have ridden further than we, certainly if they came from Radnor. But there was no way of knowing, for they wore no distinguishing livery, and the man I had killed bore no badge. For some time we rode hard and kept to the track to increase our lead, but we knew they were no great way behind, though blessedly out of sight, when Llewelyn struck off to the left, hoping to make a circle in cover and come out upon the road again as soon as we dared. But they had spread out their forces, some to the right of the track, some to the left, the main body keeping to the open where speed was possible. We heard them crashing between the trees at no distance behind, and had the choice of turning again and running ahead of them, or continuing our course at dangerous speed and hoping to cross them undetected and draw clear. Llewelyn chose the former, rightly, for we should surely have run into the arms of the most widely deployed of them. We ran again, weaving, and gained on them, and turned left again, and so gradually bore round across their flank by stages, as the hare runs, until in deep forest we were suddenly aware how the sounds of them were passing us by. Then Llewelyn reined in, and I beside him, and we sat like stone until we were sure. We had drawn clear by so short a distance, their outstretched arms had almost brushed us as they passed. The clash and clamour of the hunt drew away, keeping its forward course. And we turned and bore left again, until we found a foot-track that eased our going, and must lead us back, certainly not to the road above the Wye, but by a much greater circle to reach our camp from the west.

'They meant no killing,' said Llewelyn, now that we could draw breath and talk again, 'or they would have had bowmen and used them. No, I was to be taken alive. Edward would be glad of such a triumph.' And he asked 'Whose men were they? Did you see any trace?'

But they could have been any from among the ranks of our enemies, there was no way of knowing.

'I do not believe,' he said firmly, 'that my young cousins had any hand in this. It is not Mortimer fighting. What if the messenger at Aberedw wore Edmund's badge? It need not have been Edmund who sent him. Far more likely to be Giffard or Lestrange. Both have Mortimer troops with them. Both are in Edward's confidence, and not above using underhand ways to do his will and get his gratitude.'

As to this, I doubt if the truth will ever be known. It was a foul trick, and its dirt has clung to the name of Mortimer in the popular tale, but considering how Edmund showed later, I, too, doubt if the guilt was his. It may not even belong to Lestrange or Giffard or any of the king's captains, but to some ingenious regional officer of his who saw how the Mortimer dudgeon might be exploited to betray the prince and end the war. Of only one thing do I feel certain, that Edward knew of it and had sanctioned it. I do not believe any man of his would have dared without that assurance of approval.

'Well, so may all treacheries fail,' said Llewelyn, and shook the ugliness of it from his shoulders, and pressed ahead, for we had lost the middle part of the day, and had many more miles to go than by the way we had come.

Nevertheless, he thought no further evil, nor did I, until we broke out of the forest into fields we recognised, and were back within a mile or two of our camp. The short day was drawing down into murk and mist an hour or more ahead of twilight, and out of the river valley drifting clouds of vapour coiled. And then, clear of the muffling

290

trees, we heard in the distance the muffled echoes of voices bellowing and horses screaming, and the clash of weapons and stamping of flight and pursuit, fitful and far and terrible, the noises of battle, and battle already as good as lost and won.

He uttered a great cry of grief and understanding and loss, knowing at last for what purpose, besides his own capture, he had been lured away. 'Oh, God!' he said. 'They are here among us! But how have they crossed? They cannot have stormed the bridge. Oh, God, what have I done?' And he set spurs to his horse and rode headlong for those places, invisible in the murk of distance, where the lamentable sounds cried out for him. And I after him as hard as I could go, but even so he drew ahead of me, and for the coils of mist, that shifted and spun, sometimes I saw him clear, and sometimes he showed as a wraith of mist himself, and sometimes was lost.

So we came into those fields below the camp, and in the snow about us there were men lying scattered here and there, huddles of rags hardly swelling the drifts where they lay, and blood spattered along the soiled whiteness, and now and again a horse heaving and crying, or a broken lance. And still before us, but receding, the clamour of fighting, shrill and bitter with despair. Towards that he rode, seeing but twenty yards or so before him clear at any time, wild to get back to his own and live or die with them.

They had come at us two ways, for the sounds encircled the place where the camp had been, closing in both from the river valley and from the heights beyond. And in great force, or so we judged as best we could, for we came too late to serve or save. All we knew was that they had swept all this slope from Orewin bridge clear of life, and only the dead and the wounded and the stragglers remained, scattered round us in the soiled and bloody snow. Even the clash of arms receded before us, mocking his desperate pursuit.

Men, living men, rose out of the mist ahead of us, English lancers prowling the slopes after the main army had passed on, killing and looting. Three of them there were, bent over a tumbled body, when Llewelyn burst upon them hardly even aware when these puny creatures started up between him and his broken army. Two of them sprang clear and ran in terror before the galloping horse. The third, caught on his knees, half-rose too late, and then dropped again, according to his training, and braced his lance in the blood-stained earth, and leaned his body on to it to hold it fast. He closed his eyes and his mind, and made himself all dogged weight, seeing no other escape.

Llewelyn had not even drawn his sword, there was no mail upon him, he was naked to death as men come naked to life. He rode full upon the embedded lance, taking it under the breast-bone. It seemed to me that he sprang erect and stood in his stirrups, tall as the heavens, and the terrified horse raced on from under him, and he was left impaled, upright and motionless in the air a long moment, and then crashed like a great and splendid tree to earth, his fall shaking it so that all that hillside shuddered and shrank at the shock. The lance-head, that had passed clean through him and stood out a foot and more behind his shoulders, snapped off short in flying splinters as he fell. He lay on his back in deep snow, his arms cast wide on either side his body, and the lance shaft erect from under his breast. And the lancer who had pierced him scuttled on all fours away from the impact, and picked himself up and ran headlong after his fellows, seeing me burst out of the murk and bear down upon him.

I over-rode him by some yards before I could draw rein and fall, rather than climb, out of the saddle. I let my bridle go, and dropped into the snow beside Llewelyn. All the sounds of fighting dwindled away and were lost, and that slope from the river was narrowed into a little place of cold and quiet and loss. It was so still I could hear the Irfon bubbling along its bed below us, between the piled stones and under the melting floes.

He lay with his hands braced deep through the snow

beside him, his fingers digging down to clutch at the bereaved and bloodied soil of Wales. Blood welled slowly round the haft of the lance with every breath he drew, and the shaft quivered and leaned to the same measure, counting his remaining moments in labour and pain. His face was like a bronze mask, fixed and motionless, with open, anguished eyes, When I leaned close to be seen, and laid fearful hands upon him, his lips moved, saying: 'Samson? I have spent what you saved for me. . . . I am sorry!' And frantic tears sprang. 'Oh, God, I have failed!' he said in a whisper. 'Now *you* save!'

I felt about his body, and knew, as he knew, that he had his death-wound. Even for the breaking of the lance I thanked God, that he was not impaled in air, in indignity and worse agony, but lay like a king on his death-bed, though his pillows were the drifts of snow, thawed and again frozen into great cushions of white. I shrugged my cloak off me and wrapped it over him as well as I could for the jutting shaft, and all the time I wept like a madman who does not know he weeps. The blood spread gradually like a great, dark rose under him, in no haste, but there was life in him yet, and still he had a voice, soft, feeling and tranquil.

He said: 'Samson . . .' and after a long gathering of his darkened powers: 'I need you! Don't fail me now, you who never failed me.' And then he waited, his eyes fixed upon the sky that leaned in heavy dusk over him. 'A priest,' he said. 'Find me a priest. I have got my death, get me my peace with God.' And again, after long silence, faint as a sigh: 'I cannot go to her in my sins!'

I was loth to go even a pace away from him, all the more with those scavengers already prowling the field and despoiling the dead, but his wish was my law. Priests, like crows, come where battle has been, not to batten on the bodies but to salvage the souls. Where is there greater need of them? All our own people were scattered far, those who still lived, gone to ground in the deep forests until they could gather and form some ordered company once more. But from Builth there was free passage now across the Irfon, and Builth was not far, and here about this desolate hillside there must be English as well as Welsh at the point of most dire need, and they would not be left to die unshriven. Therefore I made a cast down towards the bridge, as close as I could without losing sight of my lord, and saw a small picket of four men keeping the crossing, stamping their chilled feet and pacing to keep their blood moving, and passing in, now and again, a handful of foot soldiers, or a mounted man. And at last what I waited for, a robed priest, distressed and in haste, with a little serving boy at his heels carrying cross and paten.

I let him get some way up the slope, away from the guards, before I stepped in his path and entreated him to come with me, where a man was dying. And he came, unquestioning. A young man he was, earnest and sad, and he said that he was in the service of the Lady Maud, and sent at her instance. When I brought him to the prince he knelt in the snow beside him, and looked long into the upturned face, and marvelled, though he said no word then but to do his office. He stooped low to take confession from Llewelyn's lips, for the prince's voice, though clear, was faint as a breath. I kneeled beside and covered my face. There is no man, not the best, is not better for unburdening his heart even of those matters no other would take for sins. And he was going to another and perpetual bridal, who had been unable to approach the first without first cleansing from his spirit the last shadow and the last bitterness.

But when he had ended and made his act of contrition, and the priest would have pronounced absolution, clearly and loud Llewelyn said: 'No, that you cannot. I do not ask it. I am excommunicate.' And at that the young man started up in wonder and dismay, and drew me a little aside to question.

'This man by his clothing is Welsh. He is unarmed, what

was he doing here in battle without mail, to come by such a death? And excommunicate? All I can do for him I will do, and pray rest to his soul, for with God it makes no difference of what race he comes, or for what cause he fought. But to him it may, and to me, and to others. I must know, who is he?'

And I told him, for soon all men would know it, it would be cried from end to end of England with triumphant joy, and carried throughout Wales in terrible lamentation. 'He is Llewelyn ap Griffith, prince of Wales. Let your lady know of it, for she is his cousin, and give her his thanks for this last grace.'

'God sort all!' said the chaplain, awe-stricken. 'She shall know it, and she shall be the first to know it from me.' And he went back to pray with the prince, and courteously begged his forgiveness that he might not give to him the sacrament he carried to others. Yet he blessed him to God before he left us and went to all those other sad duties that waited for him. And then we two were left alone.

Llewelyn's eyes were closed, and from the effort of speech a few flecks of blood dewed his lips. I watched the great rose of blood, in the heart of which he lay, spread its wine-red petals and melt the snow until the soiled green of grass showed through. I took his hand between mine, that he might be assured, who could, as I thought, no longer see me, that I was still beside him. But at that touch he opened his eyes, and they were bright and fierce, and he gripped my hand hard.

'Samson!' he said, and I leaned down to hear. 'You can do better for me than grieve,' he said, reading my face. 'There is still a prince of Wales. Go to my brother, Samson. Be to him as you have been to me. It is not yet over, because I am out of the fight.'

'As long as you live,' I said, 'I will never leave you.'

'Yes,' he said, 'you will. I bid you, and you cannot refuse me. When did I ever ask anything of you in vain? Now I want three things of you, on your allegiance. No, on your love! The first. . . . Her picture is round my neck. Let me have it in my hand!'

In terror of aggravating his pain, I raised his head enough to lift clear the medallion of the child Eleanor, and laid it in his right hand, closing the fingers over it. In all that bleak expanse of cold and darkness, this one small thing was warm from the great, failing fire of his heart.

'And the second and third are my last commission to you, and then I thank God for you, and take my leave. Pull out the lance – '

I cried aloud that I neither could nor would, for that was his death, and the end of a world for me.

'Dear fool Samson,' he said softly, 'I am a dead man already. I grow weary of this waiting. Pull out the lance, and go to David!'

He was my lord, and I did his bidding. First I kneeled and kissed him on the brow, and then I laid hold on the shaft of the lance, and dragged it out of his body, streaming tears like heavy rain. He was lifted from the ground with it, like a man starting up from sleep, but even then he never uttered cry or moan. Then the shaft came away, and his body fell back and lay still upon crimson, and crimson came boiling out of his riven breast and covered him royally, and still it seemed to me that he smiled.

They say he was still breathing, and lived some few minutes more, when Lestrange's men found him and knew him at last. If so, they must have come very soon after I left him. I let fall the broken shaft out of my hand, and turned and went stumbling and groping up the slope towards the forest, fleeing that field of Orewin bridge as once I fled the field of Evesham, and leaving, as then, a great piece of my own being dead beside the body of a man I loved and revered above all others. And I cried silently to God in the darkness of my spirit and the darkness of the night, as I had cried for Earl Simon, that in this world there was no justice, but the best were calumniated and betrayed and brought to nought, as God himself was when he ventured among the sons of men.

CHAPTER XI

———

Concerning Orewin bridge and what followed, I tell now, to make all plain, those things I learned only long afterwards, by laborious gleaning from many sources, for I could not rest until I knew to the last what had befallen even the poor body of my lord. To this day I do not know who sent the letter that drew him away from his army, but I do know it was written as part of the plan of attack that trapped the Welsh forces into pitched battle at last. For the English had found a local man who knew a secret and safe fording-place upstream from the bridge, and sheltered from view, and on the appointed day, aided by the drifting mist, they put a strong company across the Irfon there and took the outpost at the bridge from the rear, and killed every man. Then they brought all their force across by both routes, and sent one company of cavalry and men-at-arms by a great circuit to the rear of the Welsh position, and only when they had taken station, launched their frontal attack at speed up the slope. They had many archers, who held by the stirrup-leathers of the troopers and ran with them, and as they came within range, dropped aside and began to shoot at will. Without the prince, the Welsh fought savagely and well, but in disorder, being surrounded and greatly outnumbered. In the end they broke, and each man sought his own escape. Had Llewelyn been there, I do not believe it could ever have happened so. He could both plan, and work by instinct when plans fell apart. But he was not there. He came too late to save, only in time to die.

As for the forces that took part in that battle, certainly all Giffard's troops from Bulith were there, and both the Mortimer brothers with their followings, and part of the Montgomery garrison, though I could never hear that Lestrange himself was present. In the evening certain of his men, as he reported to Edward, found and knew the body of the prince, some said they were there before he died. In the pouch he wore inside the belt of his chausses they found the letter that betrayed him, and his privy seal, and in his hand the little enamelled portrait of his wife, the gift of Earl Simon. These Edmund Mortimer took into his keeping. By the very fact that Edmund preserved the letter, and was not ashamed to show it, to notify the archbishop and have it copied for him, I am sure that he was not guilty of uttering it, and of that I am glad. There are also other proofs speaking for him.

It was not to be hoped that those enemies who came upon the prince at his death should respect his body, more than Earl Simon's body was respected after Evesham. Some man of Giffard's or Lestrange's struck off the head, and Lestrange sent it to Edward at Rhuddlan for his comfort and reassurance, and thence it was sent to be displayed at the Tower of London, the brow wreathed in ivy as a mocking crown. For a brow that could no longer bleed or feel pain, ivy served as well as thorns.

And for that dear body, it rests headless, like Earl Simon's body, felon and saint, yet it rests, in the unrelenting memories of men as in the gentle earth. The young chaplain kept his word, and reported faithfully to Dame Maud Giffard the news of her cousin's death, and before worse slight could be put upon his person she sent and had the corpse delivered with all reverence into the care of the Cistercian brothers of Cwm Hir abbey, and forthwith wrote to Archbishop Peckham, requesting absolution for Llewelyn, that he might be buried in consecrated ground. Peckham replied, and dutifully notified Edward that he had so replied, that he could not without sin do as she asked, unless she provided proof that the prince had shown sign of penitence before he died. Whereupon she showed that he had asked for a priest, and that her priest had indeed ministered to him. And further, Edmund Mortimer testified that his servants, present on the field, had also borne witness that the prince had made confession to a priest, while his brother Roger said that a Cistercian had sung mass for the prince the day he died, and the furnishings of his chapel, and the vestments, were in Roger's care, and could be seen.

So they spoke for him, and they prevailed, and he is buried in blessedness at Cwm Hir, in a spot so remote and fair and still, they who are laid there cannot but sleep well.

And for these reasons here set out, I absolve the Mortimers of that cruel treachery that slew Llewelyn and stripped Wales of its shield and sword. And I am glad, as he is glad, where he abides. For they were his kin, and he had a kindness for them.

As for us, the remnant, desolate, broken and bereaved, we crawled westward into the hills and forests as best we could, licking wounds that healed over vainly, since they covered one great wound that would never again be healed, for the heart was riven out of us with his going, however we might still fight for the shell of our hopes. Once we were out of reach of the huntsmen we paused to look for our fellows, and recovered with shame the discipline of an army, gathering in companies, even making war when the chance offered. I found such a party that night, Tudor among them, wounded, shattered and old in a day, and dealt him what I think was his death-blow, for though he lived to reach his northern lands again, he never bore arms more, and his hurts were never cured. The word went forth throughout Wales that the great prince was dead, and the laments the bards made for him cried to heaven that without him we were left orphaned and forsaken, robbed of our only shield and stay. And I could not but think how some of those who thus lamented had turned their coats nimbly enough in the past, and left him naked to the storm, and how, if they had been always as steadfast as he, Wales might have been a nation indeed, and Llewelyn might have lived to see his dream stay with him as the sun rose, instead of vanishing with the dark.

But we are men, faulty and weak and foolish, and we were back in the chaos of the past, and threatened by worse than all the past had ever done to us, and he was dead who was more than my prince to me, my star-brother born in the same night, with whom I should have died also.

So many of the best were dead, or left behind wounded on the field of Orewin bridge, or prisoner to Giffard in Builth, that we were but a remnant, unable to hold the centre of Wales to make a highroad north and south. Rhys Wyndod and his brothers in Ystrad Tywi, Meredith's sons in Cardigan, must fend for themselves. All we could do was withdraw into Gwynedd, for if that heartland was lost, all was lost. So we returned, limping and hungry, to rejoin David in Dolwyddelan, and I, having my lord's charge heavy upon me, took horse and rode ahead at speed, to carry the news to David that he was the heir to his brother's right and his brother's burden.

All was as we had left it when I rode in by the steep track, and climbed to the ward. They had had no fighting beyond occasional brushes between patrols. Edward had kept fast in Rhuddlan, grimly debating whether to force the fight through the winter or lie up and nurse his present gains until the spring. But I think he had made up his mind to press on at all costs, even before he heard of Llewelyn's death. Certainly he felt his load lightened as by a miracle, and his war as good as won, when Lestrange's letter and the envied, respected, hated head reached him together, which may well have been about the time that

300

I went with the same word to David in the armoury of Dolwyddelan.

He was out of mail, for he had his watch well posted, and had not been called to arms since we left him. He was watching the careful tempering of his own sword, and turned from it to stare upon me when I came in. The shadow of my news was in my face, for he said: 'Come within!' and drew me in his arm into the high chamber, and shut us in together. And there I told him all I had to tell.

David sat with white and carven face, and never took his eyes from me. At the end he was silent a long moment, walled within himself, and then he said: 'And this charge he laid on me? Those are his words? There is still a prince in Wales. It is not over yet, because I am out of the fight. That is his message to me?'

I said that it was, word for word.

'God's pity!' said David very softly, as if to himself. And to me: 'What have they done with him?'

I said what I then believed, and after was justified in believing, that the lady in Builth would not suffer him to be misused, and her chaplain had tended him, and sworn to see right done to him.

'God himself has fallen short of that,' said David, 'with less excuse than man, who labours with very faulty tools.' His voice was low, burdened and bitter. 'I speak who know,' he said. 'Who has done more or worse to him? I have been his downfall and his death.'

'You are now,' I said, 'his hope and his heir. The talaith he wore comes down on your brows now. It is no heavier than when he wore it.'

'It has hammered him into the earth,' said David, and laughed, but with so curious and estranged a laughter that it did not jar. 'For God's sake,' he said, 'give me leave to weep a while, you who know me best. I am lost, like you. I loved him out of all measure, and I have been his bane. And he is dead!' But if he wept indeed, it was within. He

301

said aloud: 'Lord, if it be possible, take away this cup from me. Nevertheless, not as I will but as thou wilt!' And he laughed again, very grimly, at his own blasphemy, for he was speaking not to his God, but to his brother.

'Who knows but it may still be possible?' I said. 'The king may be resolved on getting his way, but he may still be glad to get it without further killing or deeper debt. Llewelyn set you free once to buy your life at Edward's price, if you so chose. He would not blame you now. Send and try!'

'You know better than that,' said David. 'I might have been tempted to forsake him, living, to keep my own life. But neither for that nor for any other cause will I forsake him, dead. I am my brother now. I cannot disgrace him.'

So again we addressed ourselves to the war, as the year ended, at great disadvantage but not wholly without hope. Our losses in men and horses were great, and in our food resources still greater, but greater than all was the loss of Llewelyn, who alone could bind the Welsh together, and with whose death the heart was gone out of them. Edward, on the other hand, had had such huge expenses that he was then quite without money, besides owing some near thirty thousand marks to his Italian bankers. But kings have always some way of extorting money. His Gascons were then coming in in considerable numbers, probably as many as two thousand cavalry and foot, including large companies of crossbowmen, and soon we saw only too clearly that he was planning an immediate advance, without waiting for the snows to pass. He had sent his close friend Otto of Granson to reform the disorganised army in Anglesey, and was again amassing great numbers of woodmen and foresters, and putting his Gascons into the field as fast as they came, both in the garrisons of Rhuddlan and other castles, and also in Anglesey. In the first week of January he again moved up a strong force from Rhuddlan to establish an advanced post at Llangernyw, and though we sent out reinforcements for the troops already fighting there, and did our best to prevent, we had not the strength to hold them back for long. They paid heavily in men, but they set up their base. We could do nothing to cut the safe lines of communication they enjoyed with Chester, by which they brought up their newly raised English levies, and thus manned and overmanned, Llangernyw became impregnable. We had expected an advance along the coast towards Aberconway, but he chose instead to cross the uplands to these higher waters.

'He is coming here to uproot us,' said David. 'He wants me out of Dolwyddelan.'

Edward's next move proved him right, for the strike that followed was towards the river at Llanrwst, and thence to secure a closer base at Bettws. David took the field then with all the troopers he could raise, to hold off the enemy from his castle, and there was very bitter fighting and great slaughter all the way, but nevertheless, they advanced. Again great numbers of archers guarded the woodmen as they felled, opening a great road towards Dolwyddelan. Some of the Gascon companies lost as many as half their men, but still they came on, having many more in reserve. We could afford no such losses.

Then also began the inevitable, since all those chiefs cut off from us in the Middle Country, and in Maelor and the south, found themselves facing impossible numbers, and had no choice but to fight to the death or come to the king's peace, and many surrendered on the promise of grace, only to find themselves under grave pressure to change their allegiance and fight for the English. Edward's grace was never freely given.

Worse than these, who were helpless once severed from David's leadership, were those who began, as of old, to calculate where their interests lay, and deliberately change their coats accordingly. Tudor's sickness and melancholy were aggravated when his own son Griffith deserted David, turned to the besiegers, and aided them with his knowledge of the tracks around Dolwyddelan. In acknowledgement of which service he was afterwards made constable of that castle, a traitor in command of the birthplace of Llewelyn Fawr! For before the end of January we could no longer sustain the siege, but were forced to withdraw and hold the mountain ways that protected Dolbadarn. Edward had got his way, and again froze into armed and powerful stillness while he garrisoned and repaired Dolwyddelan to use as a forward base, and waited for the weather to improve. For he now commanded all the left bank of the Conway, and could make his way up and down the valley at leisure.

I think that David had seen the end long before, but he did not waver in his undertaking. When we heard that Granson had crossed from Anglesey to Bangor, and there established a strong bridge-head, David sent to bring the royal child Gwenllian with her attendants to join Elizabeth at Dolbadarn, for once the English were on the northern coast, Aber would not long be safe. All that he could do, to make the best use of such forces as he had left, that he did, always with a calm and resolute face, but by then, God knows, there were some faces among us far from either calm or resolution, for not to put it more gravely, we were exhausted and half-starved, and living wild in the hills, in the wretched end of a cold winter, in continuing frosts. What wonder if a few deserted and made their way to more congenial places?

I shared the shelter of a crevice of rock once with another unfortunate patrolling in a late snow-storm and a howling wind, and found I was sitting beside Godred, my half-brother, shoulder huddled to shoulder for warmth. In the stress of the time I had not thought of him at all, had seen him now and then among the rest and felt nothing, not even a memory of old envies and malices, for we lived only for one thing, life itself, the continuance of a desperate hope and a sacred defiance. And all I felt for him then was startled pity, so wan and thin and soiled he was. So were we all, but I had not realised it until I looked thus closely at him. He knew me, he could not choose but know me, but so little attention had he to spare then from his own miseries that he could not resent me, and had no energy to plague me. He was too empty of food and too full of himself, and even I was an audience.

'We suffer here worse than hunted rats,' he said, shivering. 'Only an army of heroes could survive on meagre pay of a handful of grain and a drop of milk. Can you blame the ones who run? But that they're fools, all the same,' he said bitterly, 'for where is there to run? What use to scurry where there's food enough – and our food, at that! – if you're left no throat for swallowing?'

I had a hunk of bread in my pouch, and broke it with him. He took his share almost greedily, not greatly caring whence it came. I saw as he handled it that he still had the silver ring on his finger, but how it hung slack between his jutting joints, he was so shrunken. I saw in him how we were all grown older, soon to grow old indeed, if we lived on at all. And I was seized with such a grief for us all that it was hardly to be borne. For Godred embittered and disappointed, for Cristin childless and cheated of love, for David driven and trapped in a duty he had never sought, for myself grown old in two loves and fruitful at the end in neither, for Elizabeth who cast all she had without thought into the scale of her loving, and was doomed to be robbed of all, and for Llewelyn and Wales indivisibly, for they were one, harried, cheated, wronged and martyred, the dream and the dreamer hacked down together. I could no longer sit there with my half-brother, my valid image, my bright part grown thus dimmed and withered. For but for his fair colouring and my darkness, his comeliness and my plainness, it was my own face I looked upon. I rose and left him, and rode into the snow.

Yet strangest of all, we still had some who ran to us, and

305

not away, and they were my justification and hope. And the least expected of them was a big, portly, ageing man in a fine, kilted gown and riding a tall, well-fed, stolen horse, who delivered himself into our camp above Llanberis the first day of March, St David's day. He had a sword girt about him, and seemed to know its use, at least enough to be of service, and the horse itself, having sometime been Edward's, was a huge satisfaction to us, for ours were gaunt enough, for want of feed after such a winter. He had a smooth, clerkly face, and the tonsure time had given him, and he spoke very good and forthright Welsh when he was challenged.

'If you want a guarantor for me,' he said, 'bring Master Samson and tell him Cynan is here to fulfil an old prophecy. I tire of the fleshpots. I have come to lay my bones in what is left of Wales.'

He was offhand with me when I questioned him concerning the occasion of his removal to us. He said that he had found himself full of tidings with no way of despatching them, and highly discontented with his isolation, and had worked his way with the commissariat and weaponry to Bettws, as being the nearest base to us, and there simply filched the noble horse he brought with him. To which asset we were welcome, since he had brought whatever he had to add to the common store. Though his wit, he dreaded, was little advantage at this stage, since he had just proved he had none. But even an unpractised hand might be of some worth. And if we were somewhat short of food, he had every hope he might benefit from the restriction, for unlike us, he was too fat for comfort.

I think of Cynan often. I was beside him when he died, he, the arch-clerk, with a sword in his hand. It was in late March, after Edward had moved on to Conway, and there established his new forward base. He had then more than three thousand men in his army, cavalry, foot-men and archers, and Granson had enlarged his bridge-head at Bangor, and pushed westward to Carnarvon, and thence

306

crossed the shoulder of Lleyn and reached as far south as Harlech. The great mass of Snowdon stood encircled from every side, at last reduced to that castle under siege that Edward had desired, and now he had only to close in and strangle it. They had ships at their disposal, and kept touch by sea. We were slowly being walled into our lovely, fated mountains.

If David did not find some means of breaking out of the circle, it was only a matter of time before it closed, and crushed him, and with him his wife and family, for they were still at Dolbadarn, and that fortress in the very womb of Snowdon no longer looked a safe refuge. David had a castle at Bere, in Merioneth, in the equally wild region round Cader Idris, and determined to move his family there and garrison the castle as his main base, and in the middle of March the move was made.

That was a most wearisome journey for the women and children, but they made never a murmur, and never owned to need of rest on the way, and certainly got none until they were well through the cordon, and made welcome at Cymer abbey. To cover their withdrawal, which was made at speed and with a picked escort, the main army following to guard the rear against detection and pursuit, David led a raid in the opposite direction, towards Carnarvon, from which base Dolbadarn was most threatened. He would take with him only volunteers, and Cynan claimed a place.

'You should not, you of all people,' said David, frowning. 'If you ever fall again into Edward's hands, you know what mercy to expect.'

'The better reason,' said Cynan, 'for inviting a different fate. Better a private blade than a public halter. By the same token, you should reason with yourself.'

'I twisted the halters that wait for all of us,' said David with his drear smile, but argued with him no more. So Cynan went with us.

For once we had luck that day, and broke through into

the very outskirts of Carnarvon, and fired the outlying houses and barns. When they massed hastily to beat us off, in greater numbers than we could well stand and fight, David drew us away as though in headlong flight into the hills, and there waited for them in a wooded place, where we might pass for more than we were, and give them the impression that Dolbadarn was still strongly held, and dared take the offensive. The English approached confidently in the open, and we loosed our few archers at them, and then rode their first ranks down between the trees, and did disproportionate slaughter. And while they were in confusion we drew off and rode hard for the castle.

Cynan was beside me for more than half the homeward ride, but before we reached the lake he pitched suddenly sidewise over his horse's shoulder, and crashed to the ground. There was blood upon him, but we had not thought it his, and indeed most of it was not, for he had shown a very apt hand with a sword since he took to it. But when I lighted down to him, and cut away the matted folds of his gown at the left side, I saw that he had taken an arrow close under the heart, and part of the head had broken off in him. I do not believe he had even known, in the heat of fighting, that he was wounded, but the rough ride had shaken the steel into his heart, and he lived but a handful of minutes after. I never knew that man surprised, or at loss for a word. With barely time for a prayer, he said, knowing me and hoisting his brows as I bent over him: 'Write of me that my career in arms was glorious but brief!' And with that he choked on blood and died. And his bones are indeed laid in the land of Wales, as he chose, for we bore him on with us, and buried him at Llanberis. And what few possessions he had brought with him we took to Bere when we abandoned Dolbadarn, and gave to his nephew Morgan, who was among the garrison there.

In Castell-y-Bere we had certainly broken out of the iron ring into more remote mountains, within reach of Cardigan, where Meredith ap Owen's one remaining son at liberty, Griffith, was maintaining his outlaw warfare, but if he was close, he was fully as weak as we, and Valence was almost as close, installed in Llanbadarn castle with formidable forces, and Lestrange at Montgomery had so cleared his own region that he could be spared to come hunting us in the west. Though Bere was withdrawn into a narrow valley, on a shelf from which it covered all the passes, and could be approached in force by only one way, we had not the provisions to stock it for long siege, nor the men to operate at distance from it. There was no escape for us.

Lestrange with his Shropshire men was the first ordered to come and hunt us out, and him we held off successfully for two weeks, but by the middle of April Valence was moving up from the south with fourteen hundred re-inforcements, and David, desperate for his family, resolved to take them with a protective force out of the castle, and maintain a roaming army in the mountains, from which he hoped he might yet help the garrison left in Bere by drawing off the attackers, or at least so hampering their movements that they could not effectively storm the place. David was so far Welsh on this point, at least, that he had a horror of being shut up in castles.

Again we took them secretly, all those beautiful, gallant children, still further into the recesses of Cader Idris, thanking God that at least spring was beginning, and the days not severely cold. Elizabeth never questioned, but what he required of her, that she did, and required as much of others, proud, capable, even-tempered, though God knows her heart was eaten hollow with fear for those chicks of hers, and for David. She rode a mountain pony nursing her youngest daughter in her arms, for the child was not yet a year old. Cristin carried the two-year-old. The rest were shared among us. The elder ones, who understood very well in what straits we laboured, bore themselves like royalty conscious of their rights and their wrongs. The little ones, who understood nothing, looked

309

to their parents and trusted, and took these furtive flights
and wanderings as great adventures, riding them buoy-
antly. I had David's second boy, Llewelyn, on the saddle
before me, six years old, with eyes like the peat-pools of
the mountain bogs in sunlight. He slept confidingly on
my heart when he grew tired, and all my body warmed
from the warmth of his leaning cheek and russet hair,
and for a little while I believed in the future, I believed in
truth again, and justice. David himself carried his heir,
Owen, nearly nine years old, and too proud to ride double
with anyone but his father. Somewhere among the
body-guard, Godred also nursed one of the little girls.
We had contrived but one litter, and that was given to
Gwenllian, born princess of Wales, ten months old and
fast asleep in Alice's arms. What could we do with her
but take her with us wherever we were driven?

Cristin brought her pony close to mine, when we were
clear and covered by twilight, and could speak. The child
rode lightly in her arm, wound securely in her cloak. The
hood had slipped back from her braided black hair, that
showed no thread of grey, and her windflower face, only
clearer and whiter and finer because she had gone so long
hungry, like all of us. In that thin, translucent countenance
her eyes had grown huge and deep. I never glimpsed her
across courtyard or hall, even in these months when we
passed speechlessly because there was all to be done and
nothing to be said, without being enlarged and refreshed
and agonised, never saw her but I saw her for the first
time, young, solitary, voluntarily in peril for her lady and
friend, and pleading for a dying man.

'For God's sake,' she said softly over the nestling child,
'stay close to David. I go in terror for him.'

I understood then that her compassion and her prayers
were still for a dying man. She knew it, and I. And he knew
it also.

'And what's to become of all these?' she said, grieving.

I said all those things that remained to be said by way
310

of reassurance without lying, for it was impossible to lie to Cristin. I said that we were not yet at the end, nor near it, for the most difficult territory in all Wales still lay unconquered, and with the coming of spring and summer, we, light-moving and assured of stubborn support among the people, at least in Gwynedd, would have the advantage over troops hunting us in force. Time and endurance might, after all, fight on our side. And I said that even at the worst, the children were Edward's own kin, and guiltless even by his grim measure, and he did not eat children. But to say truth, I myself saw that this last attempt at comfort wiped out the first, for already I was contemplating the worst as though it had become the inevitable. I said in despair: 'I misuse words, and am of no comfort to you at all!'

'Ah, but you are!' said Cristin, flashing sudden fire from hollow grey eyes. 'It is my comfort that we ride here knee to knee, as we did that first time – do you remember? – on the way from the south to Llewelyn at Bala. That now I see you daily, even if we seldom speak and never touch, and now we shall be close until the end, and nevermore deprived of this unity. I tell you, I would not be anywhere on earth but where I am, with the remnant of Wales, with Elizabeth and these innocents, and with you. I would not change this honourable station for peaceful palaces, nor one stone of Snowdon for all the fat fields of England. So he said, and so I say. But above all, I lean on your nearness to sustain me, for without you even Wales would not be enough to keep up my heart.'

I had no words to answer her that did not sound too poor to be worth offering, so grievously I loved her, and had loved her from our first meeting. My life drew its last courage only from her, since my lord was lost to me. She was the one spring left me when all other wells had run dry. But I said never a word.

In a remote forest holding, difficult of approach, we bestowed the women and children, but such respite as they had there could not last long. The guard left to watch over them could be but small, and had to rely on secrecy rather than strength, but David with all the main part of his forces held ground between them and Castell-y-Bere, covering both as best he could. For ten days more he circled and raided, hindering all attacks upon the castle, picking off any unwary parties that ventured aside from the camps of the besiegers. He had lost none of his fire and audacity, but men he was losing with every exertion, as a wounded man loses blood, while Sprenghose was bringing up new levies to aid Valence, and the English had sufficient numbers to detach one army to link hands with Otto of Granson at Harlech, whence they could provision their camp by sea. There was no way we could get more food into Bere, and we knew they could not last long unless we broke through. On the twenty-fifth of April the starving garrison surrendered. They could do no more. We had left all our sick and wounded there, unable to keep pace of our movements. Only surrender could give them any chance of mercy. So our last castle was gone from us, and we were left a homeless rabble hunted here and there in the mountains. And bitterest of all, the English appointed as constable of Bere the second son of Griffith ap Gwenwynwyn, Llewelyn's enemy, traitor and would-be assassin. Lewis de la Pole this young man called himself, after his family's new English style.

For a whole month following, both Valence and Lestrange remained on guard, repairing the defences of Bere and sending out search parties everywhere to hunt for David. By the end of April it was clear that the English grip on Merioneth was tighter than on Snowdon, and we could not hope to keep a way to the south open against so many. It was better to remove again, while we still had a shrunken but faithful army, into the north, to the heart of our land.

And so we did, bringing off Elizabeth and her household successfully, back to Llanberis, and thence, since the

312

king's companies were everywhere probing cautiously along the valleys, and Dolbadarn, though still not occupied by the English, was too obvious a place of shelter, we took them up into the wilds of the mountains. Even the forests were too accessible. But there was a place we knew of, high in the bleak marshlands on the tree-line, withdrawn into cliffs behind, and covered by a mile of peat-bog in front, through which only those who knew the safe path could hope to pass without the risk of drowning or being sucked under. There were two huts there, where once hermits had chosen to live apart from the world, and one of these was but a wooden cell built directly on to the rock, but with a great and roomy cavern behind. Such places, utterly withdrawn from the world, the old saints of the Celtic church had loved, and now this hermitage made a primitive court for the last prince of Wales. So David had twice styled himself, in letters of credit he issued at Llanberis, though owning his right was irregular.

'It is only a pennant flown against the wind,' he said. 'For Llewelyn's sake I will not let them say there was no claimant after him, nor that he ever ceded what was his.'

Such treasure and valuables as he had he bestowed in hiding in the cave, and we made that and the two cabins habitable for the women and children, and left them a household guard under Godred and two other captains, and posted always a look-out at the outer end of the path, which was not marked out in any way for strangers, but had to be learned by heart. The remnant of the army kept aloof from this place, to avoid drawing attention to it, and was usually on the move, evading notice, striking where it could with secrecy, fighting now for little more than to remain at liberty. For Edward held all Snowdonia in his death-grip, and was piercing it at every point where penetration was possible. Scattered and isolated, Welshmen surrendered in despair everywhere, and the king made their pardon conditional on their joining in the hunt for his arch-enemy.

'He has almost everything he wanted,' said David, lying in the turf with me one night above the head-waters of one of Conway's western tributaries, at the rim of his camp. 'Only one thing he lacks – my heart to eat. He will be hungry until he gets it.'

Could I deny it? More vehemently even than with his soldiery, all the land and the air of Wales was filled and aching with Edward's hatred, all its rivers already poisoned by his venom.

'Oh, I know my fate before,' said David, staring un-blinking upon his downfall and death. 'I knew it when I loosed this war upon Llewelyn, and when I refused the terms Peckham brought me – God knows how he got from Edward any offer that could bear to leave me alive! I cannot complain, I knew what I did. I do not repent! Of many things I repent, but not of this. And of one thing, Samson, I am so glad I thank God every hour. That Llewelyn is dead, safe for ever, cleanly slain with his war still in the balance, neither lost nor won. Edward cannot get at him in the grave. He will never be paraded in chains to satisfy that monstrous malice. As I shall,' he said, in the driest and grimmest of voices.

'It is not yet over,' I said, 'and he has first to get you into his hands.'

'No, not over yet. And we'll make him work for his triumph. But where is there left to run that his shadow does not fall? It is only a matter of time,' he said, 'and time is no longer on our side. I have done what I could, but I am not Llewelyn. To be killed in battle and never surrender is victory. My ending will not be like that.'

I cannot have meant it, but I said what men say to fend off certainty, that nothing is ever quite certain, that Edward had grown up in David's company, and time after time showed him favour. . . .

'As a weapon aimed at Llewelyn,' said David, bitterly grinning.

. . . and that when he had his victory, and had his foe at

314

his mercy, he might be appeased and relent. But there I stopped, for not only was that impossible, but in putting it forward as a thing to be hoped I was affronting David.

'You know better than that,' he said. 'This is a great man certainly – in all but three particulars, without which there can be no greatness. He lacks humility – oh, so do I, I know it! – but he is also insensible, as I am not, of other men except as objects for his own use. And he is utterly without magnanimity.'

He spoke as one having weighed and considered, and sure of his ground. And all his life long, David knew himself and other men through and through, and never blinked what he saw.

It was past the onset of twilight then, the glow of our camp-fires was turfed down to be invisible, but the sky above, a May sky of spring and blossom and promise, was clear and pure and full of soft light, untouched by our trouble. In that light I saw his face clear, honed to a finer edge by abstinence and exhaustion and the unflinching acceptance of the fear of death, his eyes bluer and larger within their fringed black of lashes and hollowed blue of sockets, his cheeks drawn smooth and gaunt beneath the jutting bone. And I ached for him then as I had never thought to ache again for any lord, since my own lord died. The one anguish I knew for an echo and reaffirmation of the other. Surely they were brothers, those two as far apart as the east from the west, and as close as two buds on the same branch.

'I am prepared for Edward,' said David, watching with some wonder the bowl of the sky that poured such distant lustre upon us, and would not darken in spite of the descending darkness. 'As for the children,' he said, feeling his way implacably along a planned course, 'they are his blood, and not through me, and therefore, I trust, sacred. Can Edward's blood err? They never chose their sire. And for Elizabeth, she is his close kin, he'll let her fret a while, and then make use of her, as he does of all who come within his grip. She is royal and valuable. He'll punish her some months, maybe as long as a year, for loving me, and then marry her to some prince or baron he needs for his own purposes, and proposes to buy, and be gracious at her marriage. . . .'

He put up his hands suddenly and clutched his lean cheeks between them, and the wild black hair fell over his eyes, but even so I saw his face shattered as by a mailed blow, fallen apart in terrible grief, that had not quivered for his own doom. He said: 'Lisbet!' through his teeth, in a soft, whining moan, like a wild beast in pain, and then he folded forward into the thick turf, and wept like the breaking of the spring rains after long frost. And I held him, who had nothing else to give, hard on my heart, my head against his head. My mother's nurseling, my charge when he was five years old. God knows what I uttered into his ear. It can have had no mortal sense, I pray God it had some sense beyond mortal. One thing I know I said, like the voice of prophecy, for this I knew to be truth.

'Never fear for Elizabeth! You know her! That lady will never love any man but you to the day she dies, never regret anything done in loyalty to you, or anything suffered for your sake. And to her, if you are gone first out of this world, death will be only a leap into your arms.'

We came into June again, the height of the summer and the beginning of the end.

After many days of absence, David went again, with only myself to bear him company, to visit Elizabeth in her lonely hermitage. The guard in hiding at the outer end of the path passed us through, and returned to his place among the bushes, and we made the winding journey from rushes to heather clump, to the firm rim of a sullen pool, and so by those small marks of nature we had learned by heart, into the rising turf before the huts. The two little boys, brown and half-naked, came rushing out to

316

fling themselves into David's arms, several of the girls like a flurry of butterflies after them, and Godred and his fellows, who had stood to alertly at the first sight of us in mid-passage, went back satisfied to their work. When he came to his family, David took pains to make himself fine and princely still, and wore jewellery, the great gold torque he most prized, and rings in his ears. The rest of his treasury, money, jewellery and plate, was hidden securely in the sand of the floor at the back of the cave.

We slept there the night over, the last night David ever lay with his Elizabeth. By night three guards kept the outer end of the path, ready to give warning at the first approach of any stranger, and all within could sleep in peace. For none but we and half a dozen, perhaps, of the men of those regions knew the place or the way in.

In the darkest of the night, before the dawn hours, we were startled awake by sudden alarms of steel clashing and voices shouting, and sprang up in confusion to reach for our weapons. We in the hut that covered the mouth of the cave were groping to our feet hastily when David burst out upon us from within, sword in hand, and behind him we heard one of the children crying, and the women's voices raised in comfort and reassurance, though God knows they themselves had little enough of either. We gathered to David, and would have fought it out there and then, as he may well have longed to do, but we waited on his order, and he never gave it.

They were there in the hut, blocking out the faint light at the doorway, two braced lances fronting us, and several bared swords, and behind them others, too many by far for us to kill and break loose through their ranks. And the little boys came crowding behind their father, and their sisters peered fearfully, clasped in the women's arms. He could have struck then, and forced them to give him a quick death, but he would not, with those beloved creatures watching. He laid a hand about the head of his heir, who bristled at his hip with his own small dagger in hand,

317

and drew the boy close against his side, and said: 'Hush, now! Put up your bodkin, no need for that.' His voice was soft and even for reassurance.

He regarded the men before him, black against the paler space of sky, mere shapes to him, and said: 'You are looking for me, I think. Have the goodness not to alarm the women within, and my daughters.' And the hand that caressed and gentled his son pointed the exception he made for his menfolk, who were not of a mettle to give way to alarm.

'You are David ap Griffith, the king's rebel and felon?' said the foremost shadow, gravel-voiced.

'I am David ap Griffith, prince of Wales and lord of Snowdon,' said David, and with a deliberate movement, made slowly to be seen and understood as well by us as by them, he reversed the sword in his hand and proffered the hilt in surrender.

They herded us out at lance-point, man, woman and child, to the half-circle of firm grassland, where the men of the body-guard were already overpowered and dis-armed, two of them dead, others dripping blood from gashes got in the sudden onset, Godred among them. There must have been thirty at least of Edward's men in that hunting party, and others stationed at those points across the bog where the path turned, marking the way for the return journey. This was no chance discovery, someone who knew the track had taught them every step of the safe crossing.

They mounted us, the men with hands tied, the women free, of necessity, since they had to carry the babies in arms. Elizabeth, pale as death but mute and proud, never uttered complaint, and her sons did as she did. Some of the English troopers took up the other children to ride with them, and to their greater honour than their master, were gentle and soothing to them, even playful. But David they bound hand and foot with leather thongs, lashing

318

his feet together under the horse's belly. Throughout that journey, Elizabeth never took her eyes from him, pouring towards him the whole force of the pride and courage and love that was in her, when she herself went in such dire need. Thus we set out on our dolorous ride into captivity.

We saw the three men of the outer guard as we passed, tossed bloodily among their hide of bushes, knifed down in the darkness by men who knew where to find them. The traitor had taught these English everything they needed to know. David marked the discarded bodies as he passed, and the frozen stillness of his face shook with grief and anger. And before we had gone far, the first rays of the sun broke clear of the peaks, and levelled like lances across the upland, glittering on David's golden torque, and gilding all the doomed beauty of his countenance, and all those hapless, lovely echoes of his grace that followed him, all those dark girls, fit brides for princes, and the two boys, heirs of the royal line of Gwynedd, themselves princes if there had been any justice left in the world. All of them passing through this mocking radiance of dawn into the darkness of Edward's shadow, and the stony coldness of his prisons.

CHAPTER XII

————

They made a savage show of us in Rhuddlan, parading our chains through the town and into the castle, with the whole garrison, menials, hangers-on and all, crowding to gaze at the arch-enemy in thrall. But there was one who did not come to feast his eyes, whether out of haughtiness or fear and guilt I cannot say, and that was Edward. Surely he savoured his poisoned joy in private, but from first to last he never showed his face.

In the wards of the castle, above the placid tidal waters of the Clwyd, we were torn apart, we men flung into tiny cells below ground, two by two where there was barely room for one, and the devil so contrived that I had Godred for partner. The women were also hustled away into close captivity, but above-ground, with the children to keep them living and believing in goodness, and with their needs supplied. It was but a veil of grace over an implacable purpose, but for all that we were glad of it then.

As for David, he vanished out of our knowledge and out of our sight, loaded down with chains. They say that he urgently prayed the king to give him audience face to face, but if he did, it can only have been for the sake of wife and children. Edward refused him. From the first he was resolved on killing, and memorably, and proceeded accordingly, sending out writs for a parliament to meet in Shrewsbury on the thirtieth day of September, to deal with 'the matter of Wales'. But no writs were sent to the bishops and abbots, for they, as is well-known, have no vote in cases of blood, and 'the matter of Wales' meant, first and last, the destruction of David.

The only one who did find her way into Edward's presence was Elizabeth, for at his peremptory summons she was brought before him in chains. She stood alone and small in face of that giant, and pleaded with dignity for husband and children, though never did she acknowledge, life-long, that David had ever done wrong, since for her he could do no wrong. All the king had to say to her was to upbraid her savagely for her treachery and ingratitude to him, and her guilt in countenancing David's rebellion, and not repudiating the sinner and blasphemer. And she reared her head and looked him in the eyes, that little brown mouse, once so demure and silent with others, and so loud and gay with David, and said in her mild, steely, deliberate voice:

'How have I offended against your Grace? You yourself gave me to my husband, with your own hand, when I was still a child, and taught me that my duty was to love and be serviceable to him all my days, to cleave to him loyally and be obedient to him. And so I have loved, according to your orders, and so will love him while I have breath. It was your gracious bidding I did throughout. How, then, have I been false to you?'

He did not strike her. No, not quite that, but he made her pay for her defiance, and dearest of all for the love she proclaimed and gloried in, even in her anguish. For he took away from her not only the children, but also Cristin and Alice, and every other soul who was familiar and dear to her. David she never saw again in this life. Edward knew how to punish. Her chains, after that public display of her servitude, were removed, but she remained solitary in close confinement.

Two months we lay thus out of the world, knowing nothing of what was happening outside our prison, not even whether David still lived, nor what had become of the children. And Godred and I, perforce, learned to sit side by side and exchange words without sickening or snarling, and I could feel at last nothing but grief and kindness for him, now we were both severed from Cristin and both prisoners. Sometimes he even sounded like the Godred I had first met, sharp-eyed for his own interests, wry in comment.

'God knows,' he said, 'I must have lost my gift for self-preservation, or I should have been off out of this long before it got to this pass. Why did I not take to my heels while the going was good?'

But he had not, and that was commendation enough. Truly I began to feel to him as to a brother, and even that was a possession to be valued, the awareness of another living creature. For there was nothing left after David was taken, nothing to hope for, nothing to fight for. In the south his three nephews, exhausted and forlorn, at last surrendered to the earl of Hereford, and were sent to imprisonment in the Tower of London. Everywhere the cause of Wales was lost, and in the bright summer the winter darkness fell upon us.

There was but one burning, bitter desire left in the heart of every true Welshman, and that was to hunt down the traitor who had betrayed the last prince of Gwynedd, and tear him apart. We even debated in our dungeon, sometimes, who it could have been, and could only suppose that it was some solitary countryman of those parts who had watched us come and go, and thought what he had learned worth a high price. Strange it is that the men of Wales were flighty and changeable, and turned their coats openly for security, or pique, or dudgeon, but never, or almost never, furtively for gain. And for that sin there was no forgiveness.

In early September we were haled forth and allowed to cleanse ourselves of the muck of our fetid cell, and brought out into dazzling light in the castle ward, again chained. And there for the first time we saw Cristin and Alice again, and the girl children, pale, mute and wary, all girded for travelling.

Last they brought out David, for we were bound into England, to Shrewsbury for his trial. He came forth emaciated and pale, but straight and immaculate as of old, with that gift he always had of emerging pure out of any contamination, but now so withdrawn that he seemed already to have abandoned this world. Only so could he pass through it for what was left of his course, unbroken. He wore the same golden jewellery he had on him at his capture, and his wrists were loaded with chains. Sixty archers were his escort through the town of Rhuddlan, no less, so high they prized him, and so greatly they still feared him. All we followed, the children with their nurses, the two knights and five troopers of the bodyguard, and I, his clerk and friend. I saw with my own eyes, and I say this was a more royal progress than many in which Edward played the chief part, and the bearing and grandeur of the prince excelled the mere overbearing bodily menace of the king. But of the ending there could be no question.

We went where we were driven, and we came where we were bound, into Shrewsbury, where all this history concerning Wales and England began. There David, five years old and handsome and clever, first confronted King Henry of England, and charmed him with his wit, and passed into his care, to become the companion and idol of the king's own son, three years younger. In the refectory of Shrewsbury abbey, where that meeting took place, Edward the king caused his sometime darling to be brought to trial of high treason, murder, and sundry other grave charges, before the lords of parliament assembled, and judges duly appointed by the king himself, presiding in his own cause, though in absence. They say he spent those days as guest of his chancellor, Robert Burnell, who had a princely mansion not far from the town. Certain it is that Edward never confronted David after his capture, never once encountered him eye to eye. He hung aloof at Acton Burnell, devouring his own gall and savouring the messages that brought him degree after degree of triumph over his enemy.

Yet what monarch who feels himself triumphant need exact what he exacted? I judge rather that he felt himself eternally bested, by what infernal arts only Llewelyn and David knew. How else to account for his malignant venom?

All we of David's train were shut in close hold within Shrewsbury castle, we saw nothing of that trial. Yet I see him behind my eyelids whenever I remember, still chained, and marked by his chains, still disdainful in his beauty, for what other resource had he but disdain? God knows where Elizabeth was then, not in Shrewsbury, at least he was spared that torture. He stood to be judged, knowing Edward had already decreed what the judgment should be. That he had done homage to Edward, and was in vassalage to him, that he would never be allowed to dispute. That he had revolted against that homage was plain to be seen. He had known, from long before, that he was a dead man. The means he had not known, but I doubt if even they astonished him. There was no barbarism invented by man and speciously justified by legal ingenuity that was enough to satisfy Edward's vengeance. He was forced to find something never before wreaked upon man by the courts of England, and to have his lawyers devise a formula by which it could be sanctioned. Thus for the first time, by awarding a separate part of sentence for every charge they alleged against the prisoner, they fashioned that frightful weapon Edward afterwards used freely against all who offended him, even boys barely grown, a death after his own heart.

And we who had served under David and been true to him were made to witness it. I speak of what I know. They brought us out of the castle prisons in our chains and made us line the open square about the gallows, that was set up at the high cross. The second day of October this befell, and all the town crowded and chattered there where the chief streets met, making a holiday of slaughter. Our part was to be displayed as the object of abhorrence and mockery, and to observe and report to others the reward of the only possible treason, treason against Edward. But I remember rather a great and awful silence when it came to the act, and whispers of pity and horror. The very sight of the tools of slaughter there assembled was terrible enough to sicken the mind, all the more as swordsman, stone slab, knives and burning brazier seemed then inexplicable and monstrous under the shadow of the gallows, itself the instrument of death.

What Edward had lusted after was done in full. They brought David out of his prison, and dragged him behind horses, bound hand and foot upon a hurdle, through the streets and lanes of the town to the high cross. I stood beside Godred, where we were posted, and for truth's sake and love's sake I would neither close my eyes nor turn them away. Everything he endured to suffer I endured to see, and if I still wake sweating and sobbing in the night after dreaming of it, he is at peace long since.

I looked upon him when they unbound and raised him, and for all the dust and dirt of the ways, I swear to you, he still shone, his gift had not left him. It was dry weather. Even for that I was grateful, that he was not utterly soiled and spoiled when he put them off and walked unaided to the foot of the ladder, and there put up his hands, joined by a short chain, and himself unloosed the gold torque from his neck, and handed it like unregarded largesse to the hangman's man who stood at the ladder's foot. He turned back the collar of his cotte and shirt, and looked round him once at earth and sky, and then I saw his face full, an alabaster face from a tomb, and the early autumn sun caught the blue of his eyes still vivid in their bruised hollows, frantic life looking through the submissive stillness of death. He saw neither me nor any other among

325

all those frozen hundreds, his gaze was fixed only on light and air and colour, the brightness of the world. Then he turned and climbed the ladder without faltering, and leaned his head to the noose. He had said truly, he was Llewelyn now, and he did not disgrace him.

When he felt those below lay hand to the ladder to jerk it away, he did not wait to slip tamely into the strangling noose, but suddenly braced himself and sprang strongly out into air, and dropped with a great, shuddering shock that caused all those watching to gasp and groan. I pray, I pray God still, though it is all past, that he did what he willed to do, that he broke his neck in that leap, and all that passed after was contemptible to him and vain. They say it can be done, by a resolute man who has the heart, when he must go, to go quickly. Certainly he never uttered sound after. But I do not know! I do not know! I wish to God I did.

Whether with a living body or a dead, Edward had his way with all that was left of David. They cut him down after barely a minute, they stretched him on the slab, they slit that fine trunk open, tore out heart and bowels and cast them bubbling into the brazier. Godred beside me stood with head bent, barely able to stand at all, he shook and swayed so, and retched and swallowed vomit, his eyes tight shut. I watched to the end. I owed it to David to know and to remember, to remain with him to the last, and if ever vengeance came within my grasp, to avenge. And I owed it to Llewelyn, who had sent me to him with his dying breath, to be to the last brother as I had been all my life through to the second.

When the headsman at last struck off that raven head that had rested so often in half-mocking, half-jealous affection against my shoulder, and I knew that he was free, the rest, though unseemly butcher's work, mattered not at all. That was not David they quartered like meat to display as a dreadful warning in four of the cities of the realm. He heeded it no longer. He was far out of reach.

'You can open your eyes now,' I said to Godred, between comfort and contempt, 'it is all over.'

After that day, King Edward had no further use for the women who had cared for David's children, for good reason. The two boys, Owen and Llewelyn, had already been sent away to close confinement in Bristol castle, and there or in some similar fastness they surely lie to this day, for never, never must that dreaded and hated stock be left free to breed other princes to poison Edward's life. And the girls, it seemed, had also been disposed of in some way, for suddenly I was haled out of my cell and told that since I was but a clerk, and not a soldier, I was to be set free to return to Aber, and escort the royal nurses home to that maenol. The knights and troopers were held several weeks longer, until Edward was more secure in his administration of his newly conquered territories, and even we were required to take an oath of submission before we left. I was glad that Godred did not know why I was removed from him, but it would have been useless trying to win his release in my place, Cristin's husband though he might be, for Edward was very slow to set free any man who had borne arms against him. As I, indeed had, to the best I could, but a clerk should be a clerk, and so I was set down in his lists.

I was given a letter of safe-conduct, permitting me and my companions to travel only to Aber, and reside only in Aber, for he had not as yet extended his administration, and for the time being the Welsh castellans who had submitted continued in office, only the major fortresses were held and garrisoned by English forces. The king wanted a settled people, and where he could compel residence in a fixed place, that he did. It made the task of his bailiffs easier.

Joy we had none then, in any relief or any mitigation, yet there was an aching thankfulness in me when I took my safe-conduct on the appointed day, and waited for

327

Cristin and Alice to come out to join me. And only Cristin came.

She was thin, pale and quiet, with huge, dark-rimmed eyes that devoured half her face, but in their depths there was still the purple flame that kindled when we two came together. We stood a long moment simply looking at each other, after long severance and silence.

'Alice has found a household to take her in,' she said, answering the first unasked question. 'She is English, and some of Hereford's Bohun kinsmen have offered her service. There is no one but me.'

So for us two it was like, and dolorously unlike, that first journey we made together, for we rode, as then, home to Gwynedd, to a royal seat, but now the home was ravaged, the princes dead, the mountains defiled, the land ravished. Yet we two rode together, and there was an anguished, elegiac sweetness in that. I asked her, as we mounted, what she had failed to answer without being questioned: 'What has he done with the children, that he has taken them from you?' And I longed for her to say that Edward had given them back, the girls at least, surely the little ones, to their mother. But Cristin's eyes filled with tears, and she was slow in answering, for the strangling pain that closed her throat.

'He has sent them by some of the queen's women,' she said at last, 'to be brought up in the Sempringham convents. Not even together! They are scattered, they will grow up solitary, not even knowing their sisters. The twins will die of it.'

But David's stock and Elizabeth's did not die easily, they were strong and splendid and sunlit. For such there is no escape into the grave.

'Gwenllian, too?' I asked.

'Gwenllian, too. She is gone to Sempringham in her cradle. They will none of them ever get out,' said Cristin with bitter certainty. 'He will see to it that none of his magnates ever look upon such beauty, to want them in

328

marriage. They will be nuns before they are of age, and no choice offered them. Do you think he will ever let David's daughters, or Llewelyn's, bear children?'

I thought of all those bright beings, so apt for future courtship and love, shut up through long lives of silent rebellion, only to die in captivity at the end of it, and I thought that perhaps after all David had done well to die, even so barbarously. And I was sorriest of all for Elizabeth, who had possessed all possible joy and fulfilment for a time, and been robbed of all, and was barely twenty-six years old, with a life before her totally empty, a life I am sure she did not want. God knows what Edward has done or will do with her. I have not heard of her again. Yet she spoke her mind to her persecutor, and vaunted her love like a blow in his face, and for that I shall always love her, and always be glad.

Having the king's safe-conduct, we made no haste, and had no troubles on the way. Four days we rode leisurely together, my love and I, and there was no third with us, neither friend nor foe, and our tongues were loosened, and talked freely of all that had been, in a strange autumnal world all hush and afterglow, for October was soft, mellow and sad. We spoke also of Godred, a thing we had never done, for he was prisoner still, and we felt for him only pity and sorrow, for he was caught in this immense grief as we were, and with less means of surviving it. I told her how I had left him, not ill but in sorry enough condition. And she told me what David had not known, or he might have told me long before.

'I did not tell you,' she said, 'how I came to lose the child. Nor of the life he led me then, slavering over me, showing me off to the world, he who had never wanted a child for its own sake, but only as a weapon to strike at you and me. If he could have pretended the child was yours, he would have done it, while exulting that it was his. But he could not, it was conceived long after we were in England, and you were left behind in Wales. I suppose he began to value it, after his fashion, but mostly as a blow at you, and time and again he trailed your name before me, this way and that, tormenting me, until I was sick from containing the love I felt for you, and the loathing he gave me for what he had implanted in my womb.'

'That is not true,' I said. 'You could not feel loathing for any hapless child, however conceived. I know you, and I know.'

'That was my penance,' she said, 'if I could not help loving while I loathed. But in the end he went too far in his misuse of you, gloating that you were far away and left like a fool childless for your virtuous pains. And I turned on him, and went down to his level in my rage, and asked him how he knew, in his wisdom, that there were not other men even in England I might prefer to him, and men capable of getting a child. And he struck me,' she said, remembering without hatred or regret, 'a great blow with his fist, here in my breast. I was standing at the head of the steps going down from a gallery, and I fell all that flight, rolling and clutching and missing my hold. They picked me up in labour, and within two hours I miscarried. It was the only time he ever struck me, and he killed his son.'

That was his judgment. And she had told no one how she came to fall, not even Elizabeth.

'Why speak of it?' she said, turning upon me her wan and grieving smile. 'It was done and past. He blamed me, and in some measure I was to blame. He suffered, too. And I was free of him, for he troubled me no more. And now there's nothing left but pity and sorrow, now he is lost in this misery like the rest of us. How can I hate him now? And when he creeps home, how can I desert him if he needs me?'

'No,' I said, resigned, 'I see you cannot. Nor can I do him any injury. He held out to the end with the rest of us, I have shared his prison, and left him still buried alive now I am free. His rights are as safe with you and me as if he rode here between us.'

330

'I shall be still his dutiful wife,' she said implacably, 'if that is what he needs for healing and help. There is nothing else I can do. It does not touch, it never did, it never will, the love I bear to you.'

'So be it,' I said. 'But God has given us this respite in the time of our most need, a harvest to keep us alive through the winter to come, and it would be ungrateful not to use it.'

And use it we did, in such ways as were allowed to us, living out together in shared tenderness and devotion all the love that had no other means of living, like a soul without a body. For those few days, at least, there was no need to contain the words for which we hungered and thirsted. I said to her all the things I had ever wanted to say, I touched her, went hand in hand with her, and at night, where we lodged, I sat with her late over the fire, and kissed her without sin when we parted. And we were middle-aged, stubborn, abstinent in the face of great longing, she forty-seven years old, I well past fifty, and love was as painful and wonderful as ever it had been in youth, more painful, more wonderful, by reason of that long, fasting loyalty, a love more intimate than passion and infinitely larger than lust.

We came to Aber towards the end of October. It was like a household of ghosts, from old habit learned in life still moving about tasks that no longer had meaning, a headless household, bereft of lord, and lady, and family. Cristin was lady-in-waiting to none, nurse to none, and I clerk to none, and bereaved of my friend. All we did was simply wait to know Edward's mind for us, and to receive Edward's seneschal and officers. The very hall rang emptily to our tread. The sea moaned along Lavan sands, and I noticed as never before how the crying of the seagulls over the shallows was more than wild and sad, desperate in defiance, like the shrieking of beings driven mad with grief.

331

Late in November the two knights and five troopers of David's bodyguard came home from their captivity, wretched, gaunt, half-starved, bearing the marks of their chains. Godred wept when he came into Cristin's presence, and went like a heartbroken child into her arms. Over his shoulder I saw her face, blanched and steadfast and without hope, her great eyes clinging to me as he clung to her, just as I had seen it in Dolwyddelan long before, when I brought her lost husband back to her, and watched the light of her face go out as he embraced her. And even as then, I turned and went away blindly, and left them together.

It was the second night after the guards came home that I awoke suddenly after midnight, and she was standing beside my bed, white, mute and strange. I started up and reached to take her hand, in terror that something evil had happened to her, that he, perhaps a little demented from his hardships, had done her some cruel harm. She was cold and stiff, but her hand gripped mine hard, and before I could do more than whisper her name in alarm and dismay, she laid her free palm over my mouth to hush me.

'Let me in to you,' she said, low and fiercely, 'this once let me in! Take me into your bed! No, say no word!' she pleaded, gripping my cheeks with finger-tips icy-cold. 'I entreat you, if you love me, ask me nothing, nothing, only take me in to you at last!'

She shook so, and was so strange, I could not believe she knew what she did, so to tempt me against all that she and I had understood and agreed long since. I held her, and drew her down to sit beside me, and asked her wildly: 'What is it? What has he done to you?'

'Nothing,' she said, and her white face smiled, but terribly, 'to me, nothing! No one has touched or harmed me. I know what I am doing! I am not mad, I forget nothing. Ask no more questions, only trust me and take me into your bed. This once take me!'

I understood nothing, except that she was frantic like a bird trapped in a narrow room, and crying to me for rescue, and even at this pass I could not believe anything she did was without reason and virtue. And I am as much a man as any other man, and what she begged of me was what I most starved for, so that only then did I know fully the magnitude of my hunger. Confounded between anguish and joy, I flung back the covers and drew her in beside me, and at the passion of her embrace I embraced her again with all my heart and soul, and was lost and drowned in agonising bliss. Dismay and wonder I forgot, there was nothing left in the world but the desperation and discovery of our coupling, and the delight of feeling her grow warm and supple and young in my arms, and the mutual, measureless tenderness of her caresses and mine, and our two breaths mingling in silken endearments and fathomless sighs. We loved like frenzied creatures, as though not only for the first, but also the last and only time. And when we were exhausted, we fell asleep in each other's arms.

When I awoke the first light was already turning from grey to pallid gold, and she was gone.

I rose hastily and did on my clothes, for the memory of her passion made me fear for her, and still I did not know what had happened to bring her to my bed. I went to the room where her own bed was, where Godred had joined her on his return, but the door stood half-open, and there was no one within. The brychan was tumbled, as though someone had lain there, and Godred's frayed and tattered leather jerkin lay tossed on the floor beside it. I saw that the stitching of one seam gaped, and a needle with waxed thread was stabbed into it, as though Cristin in resignation and compassion had taken up the coat to mend it, after he was asleep. Godred had drunk deep in his misery, as did so many of us then, and might well have slept while she was still wakeful.

I do not know why this should have disquieted me, but

333

so it did, for surely Cristin had dropped this jerkin where it lay when she came in stark demand and desperate hunger to where I was sleeping. But what there could be in a half-mended coat to turn her away from all former resolves was dark to me, nor could I guess where she was gone now, or Godred either. I went back very uneasily to my own chamber, and looked about for any trace that she had ever been there, and beneath the pillow where her head had lain was a linen wimple which I knew belonged to her, folded small about some coiled object that slid and unfolded heavily within the cloth. I shook it out upon the bed, and stood staring uncomprehendingly at a broad collar of links of gold, twisted and fitted together like leaves, fine work and known to me. There were not two such. I had seen it about David's throat when the English came and seized us all in the cavern beyond the bog. I had seen it last when with his chained hands he unfastened it from about his neck and handed it to the hangman's apprentice at the foot of the ladder.

There was no other hand could have placed this thing under my pillow but Cristin's hand. There was no other place she could have found it, but hidden inside the padding of the leather jacket she had been mending, Godred's jacket. This was what sent her half-mad to my bed, and this she had left for me to decipher after she was gone. Having found it, how could she remain one moment with the man who had provided the goods for which this was payment? But neither could she speak out his eternal shame, only in this way, silently, after she was gone. Who but the betrayer is rewarded with the adornments of the betrayed?

Only for a moment, half-stunned as I was, did I reason stupidly that Godred had been taken with the rest of us, even wounded, though it was but a scratch, that he had rotted in prison beside me, been held like the rest of the troopers when I was released. So he had, and how better bargain to escape all suspicion? His confinement had been no more than tedious, doubtless after I was removed he fared reasonably well, but it was expedient that he should await his dismissal in meek submission like the rest of the household, for his protection. He was sure of his pay. Small chance the executioner's boy had ever had of keeping that princely largesse, it was already promised.

There was no other way this could have been. But now where was Cristin? Where was Godred? She left him sleeping there, snoring, perhaps, but not so drunk but that he awoke after she departed, to find the bed unpressed beside him, no Cristin there. With his conscience, that would fetch him clean out of sleep and out of drink, fumbling for his secret and finding its hiding-place ravished of treasure. If David's torque was gone, Godred's security, Godred's very life, was gone after it. What could he do then but run? He had planned to walk humbly and innocently in Wales like the rest of us, until his advancement in the new administration could pass for acceptable, but now that road was stopped and his gains gone. He would run, yes, knowing his secret would not long be a secret, and only the English could now guarantee his safety. But empty-handed? Perhaps he also had David's ear-rings somewhere in hiding, but they were a small prize compared with this splendid collar from round my breast-brother's mangled throat.

I remembered everything, and understood everything, all his monstrous duplicity, how he had sat beside me in Edward's prison sourly mourning his failure to flee from his allegiance while there was time, and I like a fool had warmed to him for staying at his peril, how he had stood by me sick and shivering at the death, and had not had the hardihood to look on at the abomination he had not scrupled to bring about. I knew why he had chosen this devious way, sharing our captivity and returning with us to Aber, rather than taking service with one of Edward's captains and openly casting in his lot with England. And I knew where he was gone. All we were bereft of our

335

treasure, our princes, our liberty, even our land, what were a few bits of gold and coin abandoned in the sand to us? But his treasure was of this world. He had come back to dig up the balance of his thirty pieces of silver, and he was off in haste now to secure it, before he fled to safety in some English garrison.

I knew then what I had to do. But first I had to find Cristin, and satisfy myself that no harm had come to her, that she would wait here for me and trust me. For I was still confused, and had not yet realised the meaning of her action in full. I understood only after I had hunted through Aber and failed to find her. She came of a long line of bards and warriors, the honour of Wales was her honour. And when I came to belt on sword and dagger, I found I had no dagger, it had been unclasped from the straps sheath and all, and no one but Cristin could have taken it. She had taken upon herself the vengeance of Wales. I had not mistaken that shattering union of ours in the night, it was indeed to be the first, last and only time.

Godred had a good grey horse, and it had been returned to him for the journey home. In trivial matters Edward was honest. There was but one of that colour among us, and it was gone from the stables. The sleepy boy who was just rolling out of the hay of the loft said that he had not heard anyone come or go in the night, but there had been someone saddling up below about an hour before I came. He had not come down to see, but he had looked out at the loft door, and seen a young fellow canter away towards the postern gate, no more than a boy by the cut of him, and his voice below when he gentled the horse was light and young. Then I knew that I was right.

I took the best horse I found, and saddled and rode, inland from the postern gate like Cristin before me, like Godred before Cristin. She had left him sleeping, and come to me to give and receive but once what was her due and mine, and before first light had risen softly from beside me, and taken my dagger, to awake him and do

336

justice upon him face to face, and if need be die in doing it. I knew her. She would never have struck a sleeping man. But he had already fled, and like me, Cristin knew where he would go. She was his wife, a traitor's wife, and there was no way of cleansing herself of his shame but in his blood.

That was no very long ride, but a hard one, by the upland way that she had taken, and it was Cristin I had to overtake, rather than Godred. For I reasoned as I rode that if he reached the cave before full daylight, as he well might, he would lie up there in hiding until the darkness came down again, rather than risk being hunted by day, as he surely would be once the word went out that he was Judas. One more night ride, and he could be safe in Carnarvon, which was strongly garrisoned by the English. They might not countenance Welsh traitors as approvingly as Edward did, but they would not let Edward's lap-dog be handed over to Welsh vengeance. There was time, therefore, for Godred, but little time to forestall Cristin, since she had an hour's start of me. I pressed hard, but saw no horseman ahead. Cristin had been in no less haste.

If she had crossed the bog that protected the hermitage as often as I had, while Elizabeth kept her wild court there, I should never have overtaken her in time. But when I came to the broken tangled copse where our look-outs had been slain, there was a brown horse on a long tether grazing the thinning turf. Godred had crossed mounted. She was wary of attempting that, and had left her mount here and chosen to feel her way along the bog path on foot, to be a lighter burden on the quaking ground, and have a surer sense of the security of her footholds as she went. For a different reason I left my horse beside hers, for a man afoot could go partially screened half the way, but a man on horseback would be seen. I did not want her to hurry, but to go slowly. I knew my way here very well, and hoped to gain on her if she had not already reached firm ground.

337

I saw her when I was close to the halfway mark, slight and dark among the waist-high rushes and the tufted reeds, and blessedly she was so intent on picking her way with care that she never looked back. She had not given a thought to pursuit. I was able to overtake her unheard until I was close, and then the rustle of the reeds alarmed her, and she turned and knew me, and was alarmed no more. I laid my arms round her, and she let her head rest against my shoulder, and neither of us said a word. When I held out my hand for the dagger she turned it and offered me the hilt, surrendering into my hands her quarrel and the quarrel of Wales. And I led her in my arms the rest of the way to safe ground, and we came to the door of the cliff-hut together. There I kissed her and went in, and closed the door after me.

The sun, even on a brighter day, would not have shed much light under these rocks until afternoon, and it was dim and cold in the hut, but the entrance of the cave beyond was shaped in fitful, flickering light. He was there. He had kindled a fire, and lit two torches and wedged them among the rocks to give him light. The brychans that had served David's children for beds were still there, and a stone table, and some other desolate reminders. At the back of the cavern Godred was on his knees, raking with careful hands through the deep sand-pocket where David's valuables were buried, and bringing up coins, one by one, to lay in a pile beside the trinkets he had already raised. Some leathern pouch that had held them had rotted or parted at the neck and spilled the money into the gravel.

I made no sound in the doorway, and the light was before me, I had a long moment to look upon him before he knew I was there. He had lost that curious, furtive look with which he had come home, there was no mask to hide his greed, and rage, and resolution. All his life his first charge had been to take good care of Godred. If he had lost his best piece of gold, he was determined to have all he could get of what was left, and above all his life. And this was my half-brother, my father's son. Gwynedd was beset with brothers, they were the cords of the rack that broke her joint from joint.

I took one step forward into the cave, and he leaped about and stood crouching and staring, the stone table between us. He knew me, and slowly he straightened up, wary and alert, and gradually a small, malicious smile curled his lips.

'You,' he said softly. 'I might have known! Where else would she go but to you? Have you come to make sure of your share even of this, now you've got the other? Oh, but I know my dear brother, my father's bastard, well enough to know he'll have always a noble motive for all he does! You're here to execute the justice of Wales? *You*, the by-blow of a passing guest and a witless maid-servant?'

He was trying to provoke me into some rash onset, but it was strange, I felt no need to speak word to him, and never did so again. I drew my sword, and went in towards him, and he circled and kept the table of stone between us, and still taunted and sweated, watching for a false move.

'You really believe you've followed me here to avenge David? Fool, all you've done is seize on the first, best pretext you ever were offered to be rid of me! What you want is to possess your brother's wife – in purity, oh, in *purity*, naturally! Saint Samson, too chaste to stoop to adultery! Half-man, do you still not know what you are? A whole man would have taken her long ago!'

I was not moved, I came on still, and took care not to veer from between him and the doorway. I levelled the sword before me, and then he raised and showed his empty hands, and I saw by the firelight the sweat glistening on his forehead. Well I knew he must have a sword some-where in that place, but it was not on him, and he did not offer to get it. And I, without a word, flung sword and scabbard from me into the corner where his little hoard

339

lay, sending the coins rolling, and after the sword the dagger. I came on with my bare hands.

I should have known he would always have one more trick in him. He stood up straight and ceased to circle, coming slowly into the open rock floor facing me, his hands at shoulder-level and a little spread, as if to reach for a wrestling hold. But as I flung myself upon him his right hand flashed to the back of his neck where the hood of his capuchon hung in folds, and the blade of a long hunting-knife caught the torch-light and slashed down my sleeve and into my left thigh in a glancing wound. If I had not flinched away from the flash of light, that stroke would have come close to my heart. I had gone for his throat, and forced his head back with my right hand, but I had to use the left to grapple his wrist and hold the knife off from me as best I could. We fell together, the fine sand flying, and hearing the long blade clash flatly on rock I rolled sidewise over it to pin his arm down. He was taller than I, and with a longer reach. It did not matter. It did not matter that he had a weapon and I had none. He never heaved free from my weight to use his knife again, for I got both hands round his throat and clung, he flapping and threshing and choking under me, with his free hand clawing at my wrists. When I felt even the hand on which I lay loose its grip of the knife's haft, forgetting everything but the struggle for breath, I rolled over to the right, dragging him with me, and rolled him beneath me again in the scattered faggots and ashes of his fire. Even with two hands he was past doing more than claw the skin from my wrists and forearms, and when in his throes he again thought of the knife, and groped desperately about the floor for it, it was out of his reach. I think I kept my grip on his throat long after he died. I think I said to him over and over: 'Remember David! In hell remember David!' But by then he may already have been dead.

I got up from him slowly at last, with bloody, aching

hands, and stood back and looked at what I had done. I do not remember any remorse or any exultation. There could have been no other ending. I left him there, sprawled like a trampled spider by his fire, and left the coins and bits of gold finery beside him. Of what value were they now to any man? Wales was avenged on Godred, yes, but not on Edward. Never on Edward! Never until judgment day!

I went out, and Cristin was sitting on the doorstep with her hood drawn over her hair, and her arms round her knees. When she heard me come she rose and lifted her head, and her sad face became glorious. She came and held me in her arms, breast to breast, and I felt great breaths of thankfulness and ease drawn down deep, deep into her body. I came to her red-handed, stepping over her husband's corpse, and she did not turn from me. David had foretold it, long before.

She asked nothing, and I told her nothing then. There would be a time for that. I did not kiss her. The bitterness of rage and hatred was too rank on my mouth. But I led her back over the marsh in my arm, and there we sat by the horses and rested a while, and she bound up the gash in my thigh, and washed the blood from my wrists with water from one of the pools. Only then did I remember Godred's horse, that must be somewhere there about the hermitage. We sent to fetch him later. I could not go back then. I was so full of the deaths of princes and the imperative of vengeance, there was no more action left in me.

After a while a kind of peace came back to us, so strange at such a time that I could not at first account for it, grateful as I was, but then it came to me that it was the removal of Godred that made the world at its darkest endurable. Not only because there was no longer a malignant shadow barring Cristin from me, but because the air we breathed, however chill and sad, was cleansed of the venom that had sought to poison even honour itself, even chastity. In the great darkness there remained this small, clear light, and having lost the land that had been ours, we were given seisin of a free country once again, narrow and profound, the love we bore each other, love justified, married love. We grew aware of it at the same moment. She turned to me, and I to her, and we lay down in the turf together, in that bleak place that so well represented such future as was left to us and to Wales, and loved a second time for affirmation, not wildly as in the night, but with solemn tenderness and tears.

Together, afterwards, we rode home to Aber.

It is not less dark in Wales because we have a private light, a little marsh-light that leads faithfully and does not betray. In the night of Edward's shadow, it is still the gift of God that two may go hand in hand, and not be utterly desolate. If there is another hope, it is that no night, no winter, can last for ever. And when there is promise of another daybreak, there will still be Welshmen to awaken and arise. For I will not believe that my lord has lived and died to no purpose.

Now I have made an end of the chronicle of the Lord Llewelyn, son of Griffith, son of Llewelyn, son of Iorwerth, lord of Gwynedd, the eagle of Snowdon, the shield of Eryri, first and only true Prince of Wales, and of David, his brother. All true men who read, pray for them and for us, that this darkness may pass.